frayed

Willow Springs ~ Book 1

laura pavlov

Frayed

Willow Springs, Book 1

Laura Pavlov

https://www.laurapavlov.com

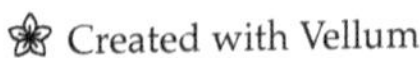

Willow,

You put the Willow in Willow Springs!! LOL!! Thank you for talking through every hurdle and struggle along the way and encouraging me EVERY SINGLE DAY!! I cannot tell you how much I appreciate you reading every word, multiple times, and helping me make this the best that it could be!! Forever thankful for you!! Love you!!

prologue

. . .

Post Bubble Burst

I PULL up the application for Texas University for the millionth time and stare at the essay question. I never thought I'd be sitting here filling out an application to one of the most prestigious schools in the country. I thought I knew where I was going to attend college in the fall. I thought I knew what my future looked like.

For seventeen years this future of mine was engrained in my head.

I stare at the computer screen again.

What is a negative experience you've faced in your life, and how did you overcome it?

I don't have a freaking clue how to answer this question. How sad is that? The reality is that I've existed in a bubble my entire life. A safe little cocoon where everything was decided for me. From the clothes I wear, to the boy I date to the school that I attend.

I've grown up in one of the oldest towns in Texas, Willow Springs, also known as *the heart of Texas*. My father is the mayor of Willow Springs and my mother is what one could only describe as the first lady of Willow Springs, in every sense of the word. They were both born and raised here, and this is most definitely home.

Life in the bubble has been...predictable. Safe. And if it weren't for my life-long friends, I would venture to say it's been a bit boring. Though there have been many happy memories, not many are because I chose to create them. I now realize that my life was mapped out for me long before I even entered the world.

I'm the cheer captain at my high school, just as my mother was. My boyfriend Alec plays football, and anyone who knows Texas, knows that football is the heart of our town. My school, East Texas High (don't get me started on the lack of creativity in Willow Springs). has won the football state meet the last three years, which officially put our town on the map. I am also the editor of our school newspaper, and a straight A student. I've taken every AP course offered at East Texas High, much to the chagrin of my mother. In our home, it goes without saying that if my AP courses or time working on the school newspaper interfere with my role as cheer captain, I will have to walk away from what my mother considers extra curriculars. *I know, I know.* It makes no sense that AP courses and pursuing writing wouldn't trump cheerleading.

Welcome to my life.

I thought this was all normal PBB (pre-bubble-burst). But since my life has been flipped on its side recently, my eyes have been opened. My thinking has shifted. My perspective irrevocably changed. I see things more clearly—and I find myself at a fork in the road for the first time in my life.

Don't get me wrong. I love Willow Springs. I love the people, the lake, my school and my friends. I've grown up with four best friends who are more like sisters to me, and in a way, they've shaped and supported me far more than my family has. My friends may be the only ones who don't want to put me in a box. And when everything changed and I took a step back—I realized that I didn't like the way my life looked anymore. I didn't want to go back to the way things were. I wanted to move forward.

LABB (life-after-bubble-burst) has been eye opening. I've started thinking about my own dreams for the first time ever. I think I've been so busy living the life expected of me, that I forgot to think about the life that I wanted to live. The truth is, I love my family and I've always wanted to please them. I doubt I'm the first person on the planet to face this sort of obstacle in life. It turns out that I have a lot of dreams of my own. And I'm hoping my family will get on board when all is said and done. Because we only get one shot at this life, and I want to live it to the fullest.

Texas University has one of the most competitive journalism programs in the country, and it's something that I'd like to pursue. There is absolutely nothing wrong with being an educator, I have the utmost respect for teachers. It's just not *my* dream. And shouldn't I be allowed to choose my own dream? I have always loved to read and write. I enjoy literature, fiction, anything and everything I can get my hands on. I have a thirst for learning about the world, one that has been stifled my entire life. Snubbed out. Extinguished beyond the existence of Willow Springs. I believe this is why I've always been easily lost in the pages of fiction. But now that a fire has been lit inside me, I don't want to douse the flames burning deep in my soul. Yearning to experience life outside the bubble.

So, as I stare at this question, I realize that I don't have an answer because I've never been allowed to make choices for myself before now. But I am jumping in with both feet, eyes wide open, as I forge ahead toward the fork in the road. I'm not afraid to go right or left. My only fear is remaining stagnant. Spending another seventeen years standing still. Living someone else's life. For the first time, I am not taking the path of least resistance. I am excited about the future, and I want to follow the path that leads me to

Texas University. I want to chase my dreams and see where they take me.

So, do I tell them the truth and risk not getting in? Or tell them what I think they want to hear, like I've done my entire life?

Because I know what I want now.

And I'm ready to spread my wings and fly.

one

. . .

Adelaide

THREE MONTHS Earlier
PRE-BUBBLE-BURST

I grabbed a bag of chips and five bottles of water and made my way down to the basement. My girlfriends were on their way over, and we always met at my house, as we had a finished basement. It meant privacy, aside from my nosy baby sister, Clementine, who wished she were a Magic Willow. We'd made her an honorary Willow, because birthright and all of that good stuff. But our meetings were private, and just for us.

The five of us had grown up together. We met in kindergarten and by fifth grade we were inseparable.

Maura, Adelaide, Gigi, Ivy and Coco.

The first initial of each our names spelled out the word magic—and the magic willows were born. Ivy was our president because the girl took our rituals to a whole new level. She documented everything, as we kept endless notebooks that were bursting at the seams. The cool thing…every memory of our lives thus far was in the pages of these books.

They were like modern day slam books from old 80's movies, aside from the fact that they weren't about other people, they were about us. Photographs, journal entries, stickers and even crazy memorabilia like Coco's training bra because she was thrilled when she needed a real bra, she donated hers to our memory book. My cheer captain letter, Ivy's varsity soccer letter, Gigi's Presidential charity award, and Maura's family's secret barbecue recipe that she stole from her grandmother. They were all glued into the pages of the most recent leather-bound book. We'd have this to pass down some day to who? Our kids maybe? Or maybe we'd just sit around a bonfire when we were old and gray and look back and laugh at all the memories we'd shared. It was all there. From crushes, to first kisses and lost virginities. From fights with our parents, break-ups with our boyfriends and disagreements with one another.

Coco was the first one to slip in through the exterior door down in the basement. Of the five of us, she was the most independent. Blonde hair, blue eyes and a fire that should never be squashed. Much to the disappointment of her parents.

"Before everyone gets here and Ivy insists on documenting what I'm about to tell you, I thought I'd fill you in first. I don't want this in the book, until I have enough evidence to back my claim," Coco said, as she dropped to sit on the turquoise velvet sectional.

Our basement looked like an ad straight out of a Z Gallerie catalogue. It was a bit bougie for a downstairs recreation space. Have I mentioned that my mother is a perfectionist? Our home sat on Willow Lake and had been featured in Texas Home Magazine more than once. My mother's lush pink and red azaleas trailed a path down to the water, and our home was what she liked to call, *Texas Chic.* It was most definitely a magazine worthy abode, much more so than a space where people actually resided. But it was pretty, so I wasn't complaining.

I dropped to sit beside her and handed her a water. "Are we still on the adoption kick?"

Coco had recently come to the conclusion that she was most likely adopted. She didn't look like her parents or her sister, and she certainly didn't act like them. She called them *country club snobs,* and Coco was all about skinny dipping at the lake and shot gunning beers.

"Um, Addy, I need you to really take this shit serious. I went through a box of old photos this morning. There are all these pictures of my mother pregnant with the *princess,* and not one of her pregnant with me. Explain that."

The princess was Whitney Radcliff, Coco's older sister. The girl was a junior at Texas University, one of the most prestigious colleges in our great state, where she studied marketing. But she'd made it very clear that she was striving to be the most successful *influencer* since the Kardashians before she graduated college. She'd done the pageant circuit for as long as I could remember and was a bit of a celebrity in our town. Her parents always doted on her, leaving my best friend to play second fiddle most of her life.

My head tipped back in laughter. "Okay, okay. But that does not mean you were adopted? Maybe she just didn't take as many pictures with her second pregnancy."

She shook her head, tugging at her off the shoulder black tank top with irritation. Of the five of us, Coco was the hipster one in the group. She dressed edgy, rocking her dock martins, and jean cut off shorts which infuriated her mother. It was very un-southern of her, and I loved it. She was gorgeous and unique and sometimes I wondered what it would feel like to break the rules now and again like Coco.

"Think about it. Look at our names for god's sakes. Which one stands out?" She hissed, pushing to her feet and pacing around the room. Her Doc Martin's clunking against the wood floors.

"Your parent's names are Elliott and Cricket. And then there's Whitney. What am I missing?"

"Elliott, Cricket, Whitney and then *Clarice*? What the fuck is up with that? That was the chick's name in that freaking movie, *Silence of the Lambs*. They named me after a girl in a horror film," she shrieked, running a hand through her hair as she walked in little circles in front of me. "Coco only came about because *princess Whitney* couldn't say my serial killer name. She got to pick *my* actual name. She was three years old for god's sakes. They probably would have let her call me *asshole* if she'd wanted to."

I fell back in a fit of giggles. She was being completely irrational, which was not uncommon for Coco. She lived large, had a flare for the dramatics, and never backed down from a fight. Her family was much haughtier than she was, but I knew they loved her, though they had a terrible way of showing her most of the time.

"Coco is very fitting. You're being ridiculous."

The door swung open, and Ivy all but fell inside with Maura and Gigi talking a mile-a-minute on her heels.

"Uh oh. Do we need to clear the air before we start the meeting? You look like an angry elf." Ivy set the enormous leather-bound book on the coffee table and settled her hands on her hips as she stared at Coco. There were newspaper clippings and fabric sticking out of the sides of the book.

Maura and Gigi dropped to sit on the area rug across from us, and Ivy sat beside me on the couch as Coco continued to pace.

"Okay, I'm going to tell you something, but it can't go in the book until I'm certain it's true." She pulled her long hair over one shoulder and everyone stared in silence.

"Well, you best say it now. Everything we talk about in the

meeting goes in the book. It's the rules," Ivy set her pencil down on the table and crossed her arms over her chest.

She and Coco tended to bump heads most often because they were both headstrong.

"The rules? *I just can't with you sometimes, Ivy*. We make the rules. It's our club." Coco dropped back down to sit on the other side of me and rolled her eyes.

"But these rules were put in place for a reason, so we wouldn't be tempted to waver," Ivy said.

Ivy took the Magic Willows serious, and most of the time we all just chuckled about it, but Coco was in no mood.

"Fine. Do not start the meeting until after I say this." She took a deep breath and stared up at the ceiling. "I'm fairly certain I was adopted by the Radcliff's, but until I have proof, I don't want it in the book."

Maura and Gigi burst out in laughter but straightened their faces once they realized she wasn't joking. Ivy tapped her pointer finger against her lips before speaking. "I think you may be on to something. You're nothing like those people."

"*Those people?* The Radcliff's are her family. *You're a Radcliff*," Maura said shaking her head. "This is a stretch, even for you, Co."

"I'm not saying they aren't my family. Obviously, families adopt all the time. I'm saying that I think my entire life is based on a lie. I do not believe I came out of Cricket Radcliff's vagina. There. I said it."

Gigi laughed until tears streamed down her cheeks. "Cricket's vagina would be very bougie."

All five of us fell back in a fit of giggles.

"Can we please not talk about Cricket's vagina. Do you have a plan for how to find out if your theory is correct?" Maura asked.

"I was hoping you could all feel out your parents. I mean, we're the same age. They've all lived in this godforsaken hell of a town forever. So, they would have been pregnant at the same time. We need proof."

Coco was the only one who was dying to get out of Willow Springs. We all loved it here. The other girls all wanted to go away to college, but Maura, Gigi and Ivy all planned to return home after graduation. Coco claimed she was putting this town in her rear view the minute she graduated.

"Fine. Everyone report back with their findings at the next meeting and we'll keep it out of the book for now. Until then, shall we start?" Ivy flipped the book open and reached for her pencil. "Lots to discuss with school starting tomorrow."

"Who'd have ever thought we'd make it to senior year?" Gigi asked, her blonde hair bounced on her shoulders.

"Um. Well, it was sort of inevitable. And it couldn't come soon enough. I'm about to blow up my entire family. I need to get the hell out of dodge." Coco leaned her head on my shoulder, and I patted her cheek and chuckled.

"If you don't want the my-whole-life-is-a-lie-and-I'm-not-a-Radcliff-theory in the book, please don't reference it during the meeting." Ivy raised a brow.

"You know, Ivy, I think you're sexually frustrated and that's why you're so bitchy lately. I think you need to stop being terrified of the penis and just embrace it." Coco leaned over me and shot a glare at Ivy and I put my hand over my mouth to keep from laughing.

Ivy huffed. "For your information, I am actually considering having sex with Ty. I am not terrified of the penis. I don't find it particularly attractive, but I don't fear it either. Are you happy?"

"Well, that's going in the book, girl. You said it at the meeting. You may as well paste your V-card right on those pages now. I just hope Ty doesn't send you any dick-pics, because I do believe those will be public record too," Coco said through her laughter.

Ivy's head fell back with a chuckle.

"He's not pressuring you, is he?" I asked. Ty was a great guy, so I highly doubted this was coming from him.

"No. Of course not. He's just like Alec, he would never pressure me." She shook her head. "I just think at some point, I need to just do it."

Alec and I had been dating forever. Our moms were best friends, we'd grown up together, and our friendship had turned romantic our freshman year of high school. We always joked about the fact that we were told we'd end up together before we ever considered anything different.

"Well, Alec doesn't need to pressure Addy because he made sure *he got some* during that ever so convenient break-up. He's an asshole. And I don't know why he gets to call the shots. Follow Ivy's lead. If you want it, go get it, girl." Coco twisted the cap of her water bottle off and tipped her head back and chugged it.

I rolled my eyes. Coco was not a big fan of Alec these days. She couldn't forgive him for breaking up with me and sleeping with Karina James, who happened to be the co-captain of the cheer team with me this year. *Awkward.* To say we didn't care for one another would be a massive under-statement. Alec and I had broken up the summer before our junior year and apparently, he'd gone off and sowed his wild oats with my nemesis. He claimed he'd just gotten lost for a while and begged my forgiveness. After a few weeks of grov-eling I forgave him eventually. We'd been on a break after all so it's not like he cheated on me. My mom and Alec's mom had been devastated by our break-up, and we'd agreed to keep his fling with Karina a secret, as they were too involved in our relationship as it was. And keeping a secret in Willow Springs was no easy feat. I'd eventually gotten over the whole ordeal, and we'd gotten back together. I'd known him forever. And things had gone back to normal this past year. As if it never happened.

"Alec thinks we should wait. I don't know, I mean, we're obviously going to be together, so there's no rush. But at the same time, I don't want to wait forever. Maybe senior prom? I know it's cliché, but it seems like a good time to do it," I said, and Ivy nodded in agreement.

"Do you hear yourself, Addy? *Alec thinks we should wait.* Sure, he does, because he got his rocks off with some hoe-bag, while you sat home because god forbid you hooked up with someone during your break-up. That asshat would have lost his shit," Coco snarled.

"They only broke up for a few weeks. When was she supposed to hook up with other people? Plus, Alec would have killed anyone who looked at her that way," Maura said with a shrug.

"Listen, I know you all worship Alec, but he's not perfect. He dissed our girl. Have some loyalty people." Coco tore the bag of chips open and reached her hand inside grabbing a fist full of chips.

"He didn't cheat on her. They were on a break. She forgave him. And he owned his shit, and told her what he did," Gigi said, grabbing the bag of chips and setting a pile of Doritos on the table in front of her.

That wasn't completely true. Karina had talked, and word had gotten back to me, and Alec admitted what he'd done when I confronted him. I always wondered if he would have told me if he hadn't been caught.

"Oh my god. I'm having an outer body moment of Ross and Rachel and the whole *we-were-on-a-break* debacle. You all know who I sided with on that one. Girls rule, boys drool. Enough said." Coco shrugged.

"Can we please talk about something else. Alec and I are good. Ivy, have you talked to Ty about, er, having sex?" I asked.

"Yes. I told him I'm thinking about it."

Coco groaned. "You're not supposed to discuss. You don't

need to make a reservation for it, for god's sakes. Maura, you want to pipe in here and tell them it's not that big of a deal. It's just sex."

Coco had lost her virginity to Beau Bannon our sophomore year. He was a senior and she'd crushed hard on him. They'd dated until he left for college and she'd ended it. She didn't like attachments, aside from us. Her four best friends. She'd had a fling with Chuck Woods last year, but as she liked to say, she didn't give him the goods because she wasn't feeling it. He was in college and worked in the valet at the Willow Springs Country Club. But she'd dumped him as well, though not until after she made sure her parents were fuming about her dating a club employee.

"It is a big deal, Co. They shouldn't do it until they're ready," Maura said.

Maura and Kyle just had sex for the first time this summer, and she didn't talk about it much. He'd left for college a few weeks ago, and they'd dated for the last few years, so I think she looked at it as a right of passage. She hadn't been all that impressed by it, which made me wonder what the rush was.

And Gigi didn't have a boyfriend, so she was still in the virgin camp with me and Ivy.

"Okay. So, let's talk about senior year. This needs to be our best year yet. We have to fill the rest of this book with all the crazy things we do. Let's make a list of goals. Tell me what you want for our last year of high school. I'll start. I'd like our soccer team to win state this year. We've been runners-up the last two years, and it would be nice to go out with a win. Not that anyone cares at East Texas High about anything other than football." Ivy was a rock star soccer player, but she was right, football stole all the thunder not only at our school, but in this town.

"That's a good goal. This is your year," Coco said, shoving a handful of chips in her mouth and chewing before she spoke again. "As for me, I'd like to see Shaw Bradley naked this year. There. I said it. I have no shame. Have you seen that boy lately? He was out at the lake yesterday, and I nearly came just looking at him."

We all fell back in a fit of laughter. She was so crude, but I had to give it to her. Shaw was a good-looking kid. If I were looking, which I wasn't.

"That boy is gorgeous," Ivy nodded in agreement. "But have you seen Jett Stone lately? Holy hotness."

"He and Jett are too much. But Jett's just out of everyone's league. I heard he was banging some college chick. You used to be friends with him Addy, maybe you can ask him to snag a dick pic of his bestie in the shower for me. Better yet, ask him to take one of himself too."

Again, laughter filled the space around us.

"Um, that's not happening. And me and Jett are hardly friends. We just have a history." I shook my head. No more of a history than everyone else, really. We'd all gone to elementary school together, but Jett and I had been friends when we were young.

"He calls you by that cute nickname though, and I know it gets under Alec's skin which makes me love it even more," Coco said with one eyebrow raised.

Ace. He called me Ace the rare times we spoke anymore. We were in the same kindergarten class and we had to say our full names. Apparently, he didn't have a middle name which I'd found fascinating at the time. When I'd shared mine, Adelaide Charlotte Edington, he'd used my initials to spell out ACE and had called me it ever since. I guess he was a phonetic whiz because he put that together fairly quick. He and I were friendlier up until high school. Jett and Alec didn't get along very well, so maybe that's why we'd grown apart. Not that we were ever super close. Alec and Jett were on the football team. Jett was the quarterback and Alec played wide receiver. But they didn't care for one another, and it was no secret to everyone at school. They were both popular but in completely different groups and they stayed clear of one another. There were all sorts of rumors that Jett was into underground fighting this summer. Alec thought Jett was a bit of a wild card. They were hoping to win state again this year, and he worried about Jett doing something to mess that up for the team.

"He calls you Ace, right?" Maura asked.

"Yeah. My initials. Very original. He probably does it just to bug Alec."

"Then Alec probably wouldn't approve of you asking for some nudes for me then?" Coco laughed.

"Oh my gosh, what is with you today. You're worse than usual," Gigi said, as she shook her head.

"We're in our prime, girls. This is our year to shake shit up. We're all going different places next year. So, let's make it our best year yet." Coco shoved a handful of chips in her mouth and clapped her hands together, shaking the crumbs all over the table.

A sharp pang settled in my chest at her words. I couldn't imagine not seeing them every single day, as I had for most of my life. I was the only one planning to stay here and attend the state college that was only thirty minutes away. Alec would attend there as well. It had been our plan forever. But my friends were all going to leave Willow Springs for school.

Everything was about to change.

And that terrified me.

two

. . .

Jett

"FIRST GAME TONIGHT, BRO. YOU READY?" Jax asked as we made our way down the hall to our last class of the day.

"Always ready." I smirked before giving him a fist bump as I stopped at the door for AP Calculus.

"That's what I like to hear, my man. Have fun with all the math nerds. I'll be in study hall with a slew of hot cheerleaders."

I flipped him the bird before walking in to see Mrs. Cunningham writing something on the white board. The class was sparse, as not many kids signed on for AP Calculus because for most people it would be a bitch of a class. Numbers were my thing and I wanted to place high on my SAT in math so I could skip basic math courses when I started college next year.

I'd heard from a bunch of coaches about being recruited for football, all promising me the world. I'd wait to see how it all played out after this season. I had my mind set on attending Texas University. It was a damn good school, they had a division 1 football team, and their accounting program was ranked number one in the country. But seeing as I didn't have a pot to piss in money wise, I'd have to go where I got the best offer. My goal was to get a four-year education without incurring a shit ton of debt. But I also needed to be close enough to home to see my Ma and Gram as often as possible, but I couldn't wait to be free of this judgy-ass town that I'd grown up in. I'd been counting down the days for a long time, and shit was about to get real.

Senior year meant that I only had one final season to play for East Texas High before I sailed my ass out of here. Don't get me wrong. I loved coach Stephens, my team—well, most of them. Minus a few rich, preppy assholes that I had to spoon feed the ball to because their wealthy daddy's dangled donations over coach's head like a fucking dog treat. It pissed me off. My two best friends, Jax and Shaw, were hands down the best running back and receiver we had on our team, but I didn't get to call the plays which meant the ball spent a lot of time going to sub-par players.

"First game day, Mr. Stone. Are you ready?" Mrs. Cunningham asked, as I dropped in the desk beside Sherman Saxe. He shoved his bifocal, black rimmed glasses up his nose and I raised my chin in greeting.

"Yep. Ready to kick some ass—er, butt." I laughed, and Mrs. Cunningham rolled her eyes but smiled. Willow Springs lived and breathed football. Hell, since I'd started playing football the people in this town stopped treating me like I was a fucking loser, which only rubbed me wrong. My mother was a single mom, and she worked her ass off at the diner in town to provide for us. Most of the locals loved her, but the haughty assholes who happened to comprise more than half of this town treated her like shit. And they'd treated me no differently—until I became the quarterback freshman year, and our team went on to win state the last two years. Now they acted like my shit didn't stink.

Phony bitches.

"I'm sorry, I'm sorry. We had to get things together for

tonight." Adelaide Edington stormed in the room and nearly knocked her desk over as she took the seat right in front of me. Being two minutes late put the girl on edge. I covered my mouth with my hand to keep from laughing.

I'd known the girl since kindergarten. She gave me half of her PB & J once when I forgot my lunch in third grade. I'd always liked her, but since she started dating her douchebag boyfriend freshman year, I kept my distance. This school was divided by the haves and the have-nots. I was in the latter, minus helping this school bring home a state trophy, I lived on the wrong side of the tracks so to speak.

Adelaide and her friends were part of the haves. Her girlfriends were fairly cool, considering they were all part of the wealthy club in this town. Rich pricks with sticks up their asses. The girls weren't bad. But her dick of a boyfriend and I had never gotten along. He'd tried out for QB freshman year, and they turned him into a running back when they started me in the first game. He never got over it. All his expensive football camps, private coaches and top of the line gear hadn't done shit to seal a fucking high school QB gig.

And that was my fault?

Welcome to the game, asshole. Football was cut-throat and I was more than aware of that the minute I wasn't producing, all those doors that had been opened to me would slam in my fucking face. So, I'd serve my time. Ride this wave and get myself a top-notch education in the process so that Ma and Gram would never have to struggle again.

"You're fine, hon. Pull out your books and get started on lesson seven and I'll walk around so just raise your hand if you need assistance. You can work in small groups or on your own." Mrs. Cunningham was one of the coolest teachers at East Texas, and I'd always liked her.

I pulled my book out and got to work. The smell of oranges and cinnamon flooded my senses, as Adelaide leaned back in her chair. Long, dark waves fell down her back, and she whipped around to face me. I raised a brow. We rarely spoke nor acknowledged one another aside from an occasional nod these days, and after being in this class for two weeks, that's as much as we'd interacted before now.

"Hey Jett," she said, and her tongue dipped out to wet her pouty pink lips.

"Ace." I tipped my chin at her. Been calling her that since kindergarten.

"Are you ready for the game?"

"Always," I said, before glancing down at my book. Pleasantries weren't really my thing.

"Um. Would you want to work together on this? I'm really struggling."

I looked back up to meet her dark gaze. I shrugged. I wouldn't have time to finish this shit later as I had a game tonight and a fight after that, so helping Adelaide was not something I had time for. It meant homework over the weekend which I tried to avoid whenever possible.

But, hell, the girl gave me half her sandwich when I was hungry.

"Fine. But don't ask a shit ton of questions. I'll talk it through while I work," I grumbled, and she quickly turned her desk around, so it was facing mine.

"Uh, is there room for three?" Sherman asked, and turned his desk to face ours before I even answered.

"For fucks sake." I said under my breath. I wasn't a goddamn tutor. Adelaide shot me a look, and I shifted in my seat. "Fine."

I looked up to see Sherman gaping at Adelaide. I'd seen him looking at her all starry eyed every time she walked in the room. I got it. She was hot as hell. Poor bastard would be pining for this girl his whole life while she dated an asshole because her mom was best friends with his mom. What the hell was up with that? Everyone knew their story. This was the twenty first fucking century. Weren't we well past arranged marriages being acceptable? It's like they'd shoved them together since we were kids and I just didn't relate to bullshit like that.

And everyone knew her boyfriend had fucked around on her once, and I suspected more than that. Apparently, they were broken up at the time, but it all played out awfully conveniently for him. He'd banged Karina James who ran in my circle. The chick had hit on me more times than I could count, but I had no interest in going there. I had little time for girls between football practice and the fights I'd picked up on the side for cash. And I had a no strings attached rule. It hadn't slowed things down for me, as I had plenty of girls that were interested in the same thing as I was. Sex. I was as horny as the next guy, and it turned out there were plenty of girls that wanted the same thing.

I spent the next hour teaching Adelaide and Sherman about differentiation and integration. The bell rang and I closed my book thankful to be done. Patience wasn't my strength and the two of them had fired off endless questions which I had no choice but to answer.

"How about we exchange numbers?" Sherman asked, shoving his glasses up his nose again. "You know, so we can text one another if we have questions."

I closed my eyes trying to decide how to tell him I was not going to be texted three thousand fucking questions outside of school. Not to mention the fact that his nasally voice was starting to grate on my nerves. I wanted to hand the dude a tissue and insist he blow. Like I was my fucking Gram. But the dude was chronically congested and now that he'd become painfully chatty, it was impossible to miss. Adelaide grabbed my phone off the desk before I could reach for it and typed her number in, before passing it to Sherman. She smirked at me and handed me her phone. "That's a great idea."

"Thanks, Addy," he said.

Thanks, Addy? Was she going to field his endless fucking questions?

When they were done playing hot potato with my phone, I slipped it in my back pocket. "Don't be blowing up my phone, Sherman."

He nodded. "I'll limit my questions in the after hours."

Adelaide laughed, and I shook my head as we walked toward the door. "See you at the game, Jett."

Her dickhead boyfriend was waiting outside the door for her. Controlling little fucker.

I walked right past him without a second glance.

We were playing the most competitive team in our conference tonight. Talk about coming out the gate hot. It was the first game, and the pressure was on. Everyone in town came out to see us play, and they expected a win. At half time we were down by a touchdown and I was pissed. Coach kept insisting I pass the ball to Charlie or throw it to Alec. He chewed us out in the locker room for getting our asses kicked on our home turf. He was right. We needed to get it in gear.

"We've got to move the ball down the field boys. Come on. Get your heads out of your asses. Jett's putting the ball in your hands, and you're dropping it. We don't win football games that way. You're defending state champs—start acting like it."

We made our way back out to the field and coach called out for me to hang back with him. "Let's give the ball to Shaw and Jax. Change it up."

Fuck yeah.

Time to score some touchdowns.

"You got it, Coach."

The crowd went crazy when we ran back out on the field, and I tuned out all the noise. Just before halftime, Alec's father had been shouting at his son from the sidelines about dropping the ball . I actually felt bad for the asshole. It was easy to stand on the sidelines and berate your kid when you didn't have a dude twice your size trying to take you down. Not that I was making excuses for him dropping the ball. I wasn't. But his father was out of line.

We huddled together, and I called the play.

"Let's get it fucking done," Shaw shouted. The ball was going to him, and I had no doubt he'd make sure he was open when I spiraled it down the field to him. Recruiters would be attending every game this season, and for a lot of us, this was our opportunity to go to college.

Every game mattered.

Every play mattered.

The next two quarters went by in a blur. We'd scored twice, and Shadow Hills had scored once, so the game had been tied for about two minutes. We'd held them off on their last attempt, but they'd just made their way down the field and kicked a field goal, giving them a three-point lead once again. With one-minute left on the clock, I needed to move this ball down the field. We could try to get in field goal range to tie it up or go for the touchdown and win it. I passed the ball to Jax, as the kid was an unstoppable force, as he plowed his way down the field. Shaw finished it up by catching a thirty-yard pass to bring us in striking distance to score.

Coach Stephens called a time out and yelled for me to meet him on the sidelines. Alec's dad was bitching out coach when I jogged over, and I rolled my eyes. The dude had no clue what he was talking about. He'd played for East Texas in High School back in his day and was reliving his glory years through his son.

Coach waved him off and pulled me in. "Let's go for it. Give the ball to Alec."

"Coach. The dude has dropped the ball twice after I put it in his hands. Come on."

He nodded and glanced over his shoulders at a fuming Mr. Taulson. "Call the play to Alec. If he isn't open, get it to Shaw."

"Done."

I jogged out and we huddled up. I called the play and Alec smirked. Cocky bastard. If the dude wasn't open, it wasn't going to him. I shot a look at Shaw, and he nodded. He knew my plan. Alec would get first dibs because he was a punk ass bitch and that's the way things worked around here. But if he wasn't open, the ball wasn't going to him.

We lined up. Adrenaline coursed my veins. The ball landed in my hands and I jogged back and scanned down field. Alec had two dudes all over him and Shaw made it to the end zone wide open. I threw the ball right to his hands, and he spiked it in the endzone as loud music boomed in celebration.

Coach nodded at me as a wide grin spread across his face. Shaw charged me and we jumped up to bump chests. "Fucking badass throw, my brother."

"Nah. That was all you." The dude was fast as hell and managed to shake off the guys that were there to block the play.

We did our traditional high five with the opposing team before heading toward the locker room. I saw Ma and Gram waving frantically at me and I jogged over.

"Hey, thanks for coming." I leaned over and gave them each a hug.

"We'll see you back at home. Are you going out to celebrate tonight?" Ma asked.

"Yeah. I'll see you later."

"Proud of you," she said, and Gram beamed beside her.

I saw Wren out of the corner of my eye not far behind my mom, and he nodded at me. The dude was always around. Over the past few months, I'd found plenty of reasons to hate the man, so I just glared before turning to head back inside.

Someone grabbed the back of my jersey just after I crossed the field and yanked me back, and I came eye to eye with a raging Alec Taulson.

"That was my score you asshole," he seethed. "Coach said to pass it to me."

"Alec," Adelaide shouted as she ran toward us in her cheer outfit and reached for his arm. "What are you doing? Stop."

"Not now, Addy. He fucking took that play from me."

"Dude. You had two guys all over you. There was zero chance of you getting that ball. Hell, you dropped it twice when you were wide open," I said. I didn't want to call the dude out in front of his girl, but if he was going to come at me, I was going to give it to him straight.

His fist came at me before I could stop it and connected with my jaw. I stumbled back before plowing into him. I took him to the ground and got in two hits before a few guys on the team pulled us apart. Adelaide looked stunned as her gaze moved from her boyfriend to me. He pushed to stand and wiped the blood from his mouth before spitting at my feet. I chuckled. He was barking up the wrong damn tree. I fought guys ten times tougher than him to help Ma cover rent. Alec Taulson was fighting because things didn't go the way he wanted. Instead of trying to figure out why he dropped the fucking ball more than once, he wanted to blame me. *Typical.* It's the reason I couldn't stand the kid. He was an entitled prick who thought he deserved the ball because his father donated to the football program. Not because he worked hard. Not because he was a kick ass player or even a team player. He wasn't. He was all about himself, and that shit didn't sit well with me.

He shook our teammates off and stormed toward the locker room. Adelaide stood there with her jaw hanging open as everyone turned to walk away.

"Jett," she said, using her hands to keep her cheer skirt

from flying up in the breeze. Her tanned legs were hard to pull my gaze from. Hell, the girl was gorgeous.

"What?" I scoffed, irritated that I was dealing with her boyfriend's temper tantrums when we'd just won our first game.

"I'm sorry. I don't know what got into him." She glanced around to make sure no one was listening. "His dad is pretty tough on him."

I nodded. Hell, I didn't have a father, so I had nothing to compare it to. "He needs to man up. We won. It's a fucking team sport, it's not a one man show."

"Addy," her best friend Coco called out as she jogged over. "Hey Jett. Great game. What the hell was that with Alec?"

Adelaide shook her head. "He's just upset because his dad was yelling on the sidelines."

Coco rolled her eyes. Coach then shouted for me to get my ass in the locker room. "Good luck with that, Ace. See ya, Coco." I turned away.

"He's so fucking hot," I heard Coco say as I jogged off.

"I heard that." I called out and their laughter surrounded me even after I was several feet away.

I met Coach in the locker room, and saw Alec sitting in his office through the glass window behind him.

"Who threw the first punch?"

"He did," I said honestly. "But I got in a few after."

I wasn't going to deny it. You come after me, and I'm going to fight back. I'd been doing it my whole life.

He nodded. "All right. You and Alec are team captains. You need to figure this shit out. Leave your grievances off the field."

"Got it."

The guys cheered when I moved toward the lockers, and we all high fived. It was a good fucking start to the season. I'd put shit aside with Alec. Nothing was going to derail my last season.

Not even an entitled prick like Alec Taulson.

We headed over to Britney Weber's after we'd showered. It was mostly juniors and seniors there. I bumped into Alec when I walked in the door, and he held his red solo cup in his hand and gave me a shrug.

"Sorry about what happened on the field. It had a lot more to do with my dad than it did with you."

"All right. If you'd have been open, I would have passed you the ball."

Karina was standing behind him, and I glanced around and didn't see his girlfriend anywhere. She rarely attended these parties. Shaw, and Jax kept their eye on me, making sure shit wasn't going down with Taulson again.

"Okay. So, we're cool."

I nodded. "Yeah. We're cool."

I still didn't like the dude. But I'd try to keep that to myself and get through the season.

"Alec, let's go get a drink," Karina said, and I narrowed my gaze at both of them. Alec just tipped his cup up to me, but we both knew what he was doing.

I saw Coco and Maura across the room, so I knew if he was up to anything, they'd be sure to let Adelaide know.

It wasn't my problem.

I didn't do high school drama.

I was too busy surviving and paving a future for myself far away from this place.

Shaw handed me a water bottle. "No sauce for you tonight. My cousin said the dude you're fighting is badass. You need to be on your game."

I nodded. Shaw's cousin, Clyde ran an underground fight club. I'd started fighting for him a few months ago, and I'd been making enough cash to help my mom pay rent as the diner had been slower than usual. She didn't ask questions.

My mother raised me to hustle and do what I needed to survive.

"Good. That means there will be a lot of money in the pot," I nodded, tipping my head back and chugging the water.

"And you need to protect that pretty face of yours," Jax said with a chuckle. "If coach gets wind of this, all of our asses are on the line."

He was right. I was playing with fire. But coach hadn't said anything when I showed up to practice with a fat lip a few weeks ago. We'd also been in preseason, so his radar wasn't up. I'd probably need to cut back on the fights after this one. Mom was short on rent money and I'd told her I'd get it to her. Hopefully, I'd make enough tonight to take a step back until football season was over.

I spent the next hour cruising around the party. I was deep in a make out session with Jessica Hall when Jax gripped my shoulder. "It's time brother. We need to go."

I lifted her off my lap and moved to my feet. "See you later."

She pouted and I chuckled. Hell, it wasn't our first hookup and probably wasn't our last.

"We need to grab Shaw. He's over there hanging all over Coco Radcliff." Jax rolled his eyes.

Shaw looked up and whispered something in her ear and her face lit up. Her gaze locked with mine, and she handed him her phone. He typed something in before making his way over to us.

"What the fuck are you up to?" Jax asked as the three of us headed out to Shaw's beat-up Ford truck.

"Coco's a cool chick. She wants to come check-out the fight."

Jax jumped in the back seat and I slipped into the passenger side up front. "Fuck dude. She's best friends with

Adelaide, and her boyfriend would like nothing more than to get me kicked off the team."

"Dude. She doesn't like Alec. She made that perfectly clear. She said not to worry about it."

I rolled my eyes. The dude acted with his dick not his brain ninety percent of the time. I knew coach would give me a warning before he'd cut me but messing with this shit was risky and I knew it. But I also knew Ma was stressed, and if I could help her without getting into too much trouble, I'd do it all day long.

We pulled up to the warehouse and found an open space near the back door. There were a ton of cars parked in the gravel lot, as the old building was out in the middle of a field far from everything in town.

We made our way inside. The place was packed and reeked of cigarette smoke and stale beer.

"Game time, boys," Shaw said as his cousin Clyde waved us over.

I nodded.

Game time.

three

. . .

Adelaide

I'D BEEN UP in bed for an hour when Coco called. I could hear the desperation in her voice immediately, and I sat up and pressed my back against the headboard.

"Do not say no until you hear me out," she said, her breathing was labored.

"Are you running? Where are you?"

"I'm parked a few houses down from your house. I'm heading toward you on foot."

"What?" I pushed to my feet. "It's eleven thirty. You're coming here? Do you want to sleep over?" I asked. It wasn't completely out of the ordinary. The girls and I spent the night at one another's homes all the time.

"No. Listen to me. Jett is about to fight, and Shaw invited us. I really want to go. And Maura had to leave the party because Kyle just drove home from school and she wanted to go see him. I can't go alone, Addy. *Pleeeeeeeease.*"

"You want me to sneak out now? My parents will kill me if they find out."

"Come on. We made a pact. Senior year would be filled with new adventures. Live a little. Let's go see the guy fight, I can flirt with Shaw, and you'll be tucked back in bed in a few hours. No one will be the wiser," she said. "I'm outside your window."

"Oh my gosh, you're killing me. Let me throw some clothes on. I'll be right down."

It wasn't the first time I'd snuck out of my room. The girls and I had snuck out to toilet paper some of the football players houses a few times during one of our many sleepovers. But it had been a while.

I opened my window and climbed onto the roof. A large oak tree pressed against our house, and the branches scratched my windows any time we had wind. My dad had been threatening to chop it down for years. I held my finger to my lips to remind her to stay quiet before I pulled the window closed and reached for a sturdy branch. I found my footing there. I made my way down easily and jumped to the ground when I was low enough to do it safely. Coco grabbed my hand and we jogged down the street before we both burst out in a fit of nervous giggles.

"I can't believe I'm doing this," I said, trying to catch my breath.

"I can't believe you actually said yes."

She jingled her keys, and I hopped in the passenger seat.

"So where are we going. Don't tell Alec, he'll have a fit that I went because I didn't want to go out tonight."

"I won't say a word. That's part of the deal if I invite you. Shaw said Alec would turn Jett in and he could get kicked off the team if he knew he was fighting. So, let's just leave Alec out of this."

I nodded. "Did you see Alec at the party tonight?"

"Yes. Karina was hanging all over him, but he left with Ty. You should have come."

I rolled my eyes. Karina couldn't stand the fact that Alec and I were back together. "He was in a mood after the game, so I figured he'd want to drink, and I just didn't feel like dealing with it. Plus, I had a ton of AP calc homework."

"Who does AP calc homework on a Friday night?"

"Me and Sherman Saxe." I laughed. Sherman had been texting both Jett and I on a group text, but Jett had yet to respond. I answered Sherman's questions the best I could for someone who wasn't fully grasping the information either.

"Well, that says it all. So, what was Alec's deal tonight. Did you see the way he went after Jett?"

We drove down several back streets, passing the outdoor arena where we'd always attend the country music festivals, and I bounced off the seat a bit when we went over the railroad tracks. The Texas State railroad still ran through Willow Springs just as it had since 1896. It didn't move cargo anymore, but it was a tourist attraction and the girls' and I loved to take a ride through the scenic piney woods of east Texas once a year. She pulled into the old motor warehouse that had been abandoned. There must have been seventy cars parked in the lot.

"Jeez. What the hell is this?" I grumped as we got out of the car. "Oh yeah, about Alec — he was supposed to get that ball, but he had two guys on him, so Jett threw it to Shaw, which pissed Alec off. I think he was just upset about his father, honestly, and he didn't have a great game. He doesn't usually get that angry."

She nodded. "That makes sense, I guess. So, apparently there are fights out here all the time. Jett's only been doing this since summer, according to Shaw. But he's supposed to be really good."

I glanced down at my outfit, suddenly feeling very underdressed as my cowboy booties skittered against the dirt and gravel beneath my feet. How does one dress for a fight? Coco wore a black bodysuit, ripped skinny jeans and booties. I was wearing jeans, a white tank, and my favorite pink cardigan.

"Am I dressed okay?"

"I mean, I doubt anyone here will be sporting a pink cashmere cardi, but somehow that shit works for you."

I laughed. "Thanks."

We entered the warehouse, and Coco shot a text to Shaw to let him know we were here. I pulled my cardigan closed as a few men looked us up and down.

"Well, we're not in Kansas anymore, kid."

"You can say that again. It smells like pee," I whispered.

"Really? It just smells like sexy man to me."

We both laughed as Shaw walked toward us. "Hey. Glad you came. He's up next. Uh, Addy, if you could not mention this to Alec it would be appreciated. Jett's a little pissed at me for inviting you guys."

I nodded. Why the hell were we even here? If Jett could get kicked off the team for being here, could we get in trouble as well?

"No problem. I won't say a word."

A man bumped into me and Coco grabbed my arm to steady me. The crowd was getting rowdy and I suddenly felt an urgency to get out of here.

"Follow me. We can go up front. Jax is saving us a spot." Shaw led the way, and he kept turning back to make sure we were following. Coco held his hand with one of hers and I linked our fingers with the other.

People started chanting the word, "Kong" over and over as we moved to stand beside Jax.

"Hey. Things are about to get crazy if our boy can take this dude down," Jax said, sipping his beer as Shaw had me and Coco slip in between them.

"Who is he fighting?" Coco asked. As if it mattered. We didn't know any of the fighters here.

"Kong. He's supposed to be a badass and he's undefeated. But so is our boy." Shaw searched behind him as if he were looking for someone. "Here they come."

"So, Jett is undefeated too?" I asked Jax and he chuckled.

"Yep. But he's only fought four times. Kong has fought over a hundred times, so he's got experience on him."

Jett and Kong both jogged out and stepped inside the ring or the cage or whatever the hell this contraption was. It wasn't boxing. No one wore gloves nor did they wear fancy boxing shorts. They were dressed in gym shorts, and the crowd was on their feet.

Jett looked over and for a moment his gaze locked with mine, and my stomach dipped. It was hard to believe that this was the five-year-old boy I'd known most of my life. He was all man. Chocolate brown hair. Dark eyes that almost looked black as I took him in. His muscles rippled and his skin was tan. His abs and chest were chiseled, and I found it difficult to look away. There was a tattoo on his right arm, but I couldn't make it out. His jaw ticked, before he jerked his head away.

The fight started and deafening cheers surrounded us. We were close enough to see what was going on and I quickly noted that Jett was faster on his feet, but his opponent looked like he had about fifty pounds on Jett. Kong attempted to take him down a few times, but Jett was able to move away quick enough to avoid it. He was the more precise fighter. I could see the concentration. The first round ended and both men walked to their corner.

"How many rounds are there? Is this like UFC fighting?" I asked, and both of the guys laughed.

"Yeah. Kind of. A little MMA and a little street fighting mixed in. There aren't a ton of rules. May the strongest man survive, basically. And they go three rounds," Shaw said, and he winked at Coco. I could tell my best friend was taken with him, because normally any act of endearment would annoy her, but instead she beamed up at him.

They started the second round and my stomach twisted as I watched them each become more aggressive. Kong kicked Jett in the stomach and Jett gave his opponent several shots to the face. They were down on the ground, but I had no idea how that had happened or who took who down. I hadn't watched anything but Rocky movies before and this was very different. My chest squeezed as they continued to scrap on the ground. Jett was on top of Kong, and had his arm wrapped around the man's neck. Before I knew what was happening, a bell rang, and the crowd went crazy.

"No fucking way," Jax shouted, leaning over me to high five Shaw.

"What's happening?" I asked, my adrenaline pumping as people screamed and cheered even louder.

"Kong tapped out. Our boy did it."

I shook my head with confusion. He'd already played in a lengthy football game tonight. He had to be exhausted. "Why does he do this?"

"To pay the rent, Addy," Shaw said, and the look in his eyes told me he was telling the truth. There was a mixture of empathy and pride in his gaze, and my chest squeezed.

"Come on. Let's meet him at the back door. This crowd is a little crazy. He needs to get his money and get the hell out of here." Jax placed a hand on the small of my back, and I looked back to see Coco right behind me. She nodded to let me know she was fine.

We weaved through the packed warehouse, and Jax continued to push me forward. Once we were in the hallway far from the crowd, we all four walked in a line beside one another. In the dim lighting I saw Kong surrounded by a few men who assisted him out the back door. Jett stepped through a doorway and made his way toward us.

"Dude. That was badass. Did Clyde pay you?" Jax asked.

Jett's eyes settled on me and I didn't miss the discomfort there. He nodded. "Yeah. Let's get out of here."

Once we were outside, I sucked in a long breath, allowing the fresh air to fill my lungs.

"Did you make what you needed?" Shaw asked, as we all fell in stride and moved across the parking lot.

"Yes. And then some. I'll be able to ride it out for a bit. Then I can bank some coin until football season ends. Should be able to help give her a cushion," Jett said, staring straight ahead.

I wondered who he was talking about. Did he have a girlfriend? Or he was giving it all to his mom?

"Okay, well, good job, Jett. Thanks for letting us tag along." Coco stopped beside her car and I did the same.

"Sure. I'll text you this weekend," Shaw said.

"See ya." Jax waved, and Jett's gaze locked with mine once again and he nodded.

We slipped into Coco's car and headed to my house.

"Who do you think he gives the money to?" I asked, as curiosity got the best of me.

"Shaw said it's for his mom and grandmother. I guess the diner has been really slow and his grandma has a bunch of medical bills that they're behind on."

"I can't believe he fights to help his mom. Wow." I shook my head. We were a bunch of spoiled rich kids. I never had to think about money. We'd always had plenty and I'd never wanted for much. I thought it was honorable that Jett would do whatever he could to help his mother, who I happened to like a lot. Jett's mom, Mae, worked at the diner in town, where the girls and I ate every weekend. She was the kindest lady, and we'd always chat about school and life. So even though it was probably wrong to keep secrets from Alec, I didn't feel bad about this one. I knew my boyfriend well enough to know that he'd use it against Jett and that wouldn't be fair.

I waved to Coco and climbed through my window, leaving the lights off in my room. I slipped back into my pajama tank and shorts and climbed into bed. I couldn't stop thinking about that fight. I doubted I'd get much sleep. I reached for my phone beside my bed and pulled up Jett's number. He'd given it to me today, and after Shaw mentioned Jett's concern about me telling Alec, I wanted him to know that he didn't need to worry. It wasn't my secret to tell. I typed out a quick text.

Me ~ Hey. I just wanted to let you know that I won't say a word about tonight to anyone. I didn't want you to worry about it.

I hit send and stared at my phone, chewing on my thumb nail when the three little dots popped up.

Jett ~ Thanks. Why the fuck do I have 23 texts from Sherman?

I covered my mouth with my hand to muffle my laughter.

Me ~ Two of those are my responses so technically he only sent 21 messages. I guess he's a curious guy. LOL.

Jett ~ Jesus. All right. Get some sleep, Ace. This is a late night for you, huh?

Me ~ It's senior year. I'm living on the edge. Good job at the fight. Good night.

The text showed as read, and I dropped my phone on my nightstand and closed my eyes, willing sleep to take me.

"Where you going, Ladybug?" Daddy had called me by the silly name since I was a little girl.

"A group of us are going out to the lake. I'll be home for dinner though."

"I thought you and Mama were going dress shopping?" he asked. Homecoming was in two weeks, and I still hadn't found a dress I liked.

I chuckled. "That's tomorrow. But look at you, daddy. You're all in the know about what's going on." I wrapped one arm around his waist and gave him a half squeeze.

"Hey, I've been told I need to keep up, so this is me keeping up."

"Well, I hope you can keep up with me on our run," Clementine said as she entered the kitchen.

"You still want to do that?" Daddy moaned.

"Daddy-kins. I'm on the cross-country team and our coach

doesn't spend any time training the girls and he barely gives me the time of day because I'm a freshman. I want to stand out."

My father nodded and I laughed. "You're right, Clem. Let's do this."

Mama entered the kitchen looking like a Lily Pulitzer clothing ad. Her dark hair was pulled back in a twist, and she wore a baby blue and pink colorful shift dress and heels. "Alec's on his way to pick you up. Make sure you wear sunscreen. Tan lines will not look good in your homecoming photo's."

I rolled my eyes, once I knew she couldn't see me as she buzzed around the kitchen. "Yes, ma'am."

"Don't get an attitude with me, Adelaide Charlotte. You'll thank me for saving your skin when you're older and for making sure your photos look good." Mama grabbed the orange juice from daddy's hand and reached for a glass. He wiped his mouth to hide the fact that he'd just chugged right from the bottle. She grabbed a glass and poured it for him, tucking the juice back in the fridge and kissing his cheek.

My parents had been together forever. And just like Alec and I, they'd been friends when they were young and then they'd started dating. Mama said it was a fairytale that all girls wished for.

"And when you two get home from your run, you head straight for the showers. It's a humid day out and I won't have my house smelling like sweat." Her gaze bounced between my father and sister.

"Have you ever even broken a sweat?" Clem asked, and daddy laughed which caused my mother to frown at both of them.

"I sweat when I do yoga and when I play tennis. Let me tell you what I don't do. I don't come home and sit on the nice sofa until after I've showered."

The doorbell rang and I was thankful for the reprieve.

"Sunscreen, Addy. And be safe. Keep tomorrow open for dress shopping. We're down to the wire."

"Okay." I jogged to the door and pushed Alec back when he started to step inside. "Trust me. She's on a *sweating is bad and no-tan-lines allowed in your homecoming dress* kick. You do not want to go in there."

Alec chuckled. "Got it."

"How was football practice? Only a few more games, huh? Are you ready to be done?" I asked as we slipped in the car.

"Yeah. I'm tired of my dad riding my ass. He isn't nearly as involved in basketball. And I'll have my girl cheering for me again, so I can't complain." Alec glanced over at me and smiled. He had the most perfect dimple on his right cheek, and his light blue eyes sparkled when they locked with mine.

"I'll always cheer for you. Do you ever think about playing football or basketball in college? I know a lot of the guys on the team are getting recruited. I'm sure you could too, if you wanted to." He pulled up to a stop light and reached over to place a hand on my thigh.

"Nah. My dad says I need to make good grades to prepare for law school, and god knows they aren't good right now so I'll need to up my game for sure. Plus, I want to have some fun in college too." He winked. "I'm glad we'll be going to school together."

"Me too. I just can't decide if I should live in the dorms and have a little bit of the college experience, or live at home which is what Mama thinks I should do." I placed my hand on top of his.

"I cannot live at home for another minute after we graduate. You know I love my family, but dad and I are at each other's throats and I want to have some fun."

"Do you ever think about going anywhere else? Further from home? We could apply other places."

"My father would lose his shit if I didn't go where he

went. You know how he gets. And I don't really have the grades at this point to go anywhere better than state. And we'll be together, so it's a perfect fit. It's a decent school, close to Willow Springs so you can live at home if you don't want to live on campus, and we'll both be there. I heard the teaching program is really good."

I nodded. I don't know who decided I wanted to be a teacher or when that happened, but everyone talked about it like I'd had this lifelong dream of being an educator. I hadn't. My mother suggested it, and everyone just took that as the truth.

"Sometimes I don't know if I want to be a teacher. I mean, I love writing. I wouldn't mind doing something with that." I glanced over and he smiled.

"If you want to write, Addy, you should do it. You don't have to teach if that's not your dream. You know I'll support whatever you want to do."

I nodded. "Yeah. I know you will."

"But teaching would be a great job when we start a family. Although once I'm an attorney, I think I'd prefer you to stay home with the kids anyway, so it doesn't really matter what you decide to do for now. I never went to daycare and I don't think I'd like our kids being raised by strangers."

I nodded. His words rubbed me wrong. I was a seventeen-year old virgin who'd lived in one place her entire life. I wasn't ready to think about daycare. Between Mama and Alec, they had the rest of my life figured out, and it didn't sound all that exciting to me at the moment.

"Are all the girls meeting us at the lake?" he asked.

"Yep. And Hayden and Ty are coming, right?"

"Yeah. I think Hayden's going to throw the after party for homecoming. His parents are going out of town."

Coco had been working on the after party for weeks. It was our senior year, and she did not want us to end up out at a bonfire on the lake in our homecoming gowns the way we had every year before now.

"That sounds good. And Karina can't hang on you if I'm there, right?"

We'd argued over the fact that I'd heard she'd been all over him several weeks ago, and he'd apologized profusely and swore nothing happened. I believed Alec. He wasn't a liar or a cheat. We'd been broken up when he'd been with Karina, and I couldn't fault him that, though I hadn't been happy about the break-up in the first place.

"I've made it very clear to her that you and I are together. You have nothing to worry about there."

I nodded. I wasn't the jealous type, but it bothered me that I had so many insecurities when it came to Alec and Karina. That wasn't me, and I didn't like how it made me feel. Was I just being jealous, or were these warning bells?

"She loves to get under my skin at cheer. She brings your name up at practice in conversation knowing it bothers me. It shouldn't really. What you had with her was nothing. I just hate that she's shared something with you that I haven't."

He parked the car down by the water where we were meeting everyone. I could see a group of people already down there when I glanced through the windshield.

"One time, Addy. That's the only time it ever happened. I regret it so much. I lost my mind when we were apart. And I want our first time to be special, because you deserve that. What Karina and I had, was nothing. Honestly. I try not to think about it. Because I love you. Only you." He leaned forward, pulling me over the console and settling me on his lap, shifting me so one leg fell on each side of him.

He placed a hand on my cheek and he studied me. "You believe me, don't you?"

"Of course. I just think, I don't know. Maybe you strayed because you wanted something that I wasn't giving you. Maybe it's time. I think I'm ready."

He smiled and tangled his hands in my hair. "I don't want you to feel like you have to rush it because of what happened with Karina. I'm not in a hurry, baby. I love you. We have forever together."

I could feel his desire grow beneath me, and I grinded up against him. Alec and I had made out more times than I could count. But we'd never taken things further. I'd never felt the need to rush it. I wondered if something was wrong with me, that I didn't feel that physical need to take the next step.

"I love you."

"Love you more, baby." His mouth crashed into mine and we sat there kissing in the parking lot down by the water for a few minutes before Hayden pounded on the window. I jumped off his lap as heat crept up the back of my neck with embarrassment.

Alec laughed. "Come on. Let's go join the party."

"What were you two doing in there?" Hayden's voice was all tease when we stepped out of the car.

I rolled my eyes and laughed. "Why are you being a creeper?"

His head fell back, and he chuckled. "Oh, I'm a creeper now? I was actually looking for you. What's the deal with Coco and Shaw? Is she going to homecoming with him? I was planning to ask her, but I see she's always hanging out with him at school lately."

My chest squeezed. Coco was definitely into Shaw these days and I knew Hayden liked her as more than friends. Shaw hadn't asked her yet, but she wanted him to.

"I think she is planning to go with him. But don't you worry, I will find you a date," I smiled up at him and Alec squeezed my hand as we made our way down to the water.

"Thanks, Addy," he said with a shrug. Hayden was gorgeous and there was a slew of girls who would die to go to homecoming with him.

Alec wrapped an arm around me and pulled me close. "You're the bomb, Adelaide Edington."

I looked up to see him staring down at me with so much adoration, and I couldn't hide the smile on my face.

It was a perfect day with my perfect guy.

four

. . .

Jett

IT WAS HOMECOMING WEEK, which meant a lot of extra shit to add to the list of things I didn't feel like doing. I sat out on the hammock at my favorite spot on the lake after practice and just chilled. I liked to come out here when I needed to think and clear my head of all the noise. Tomorrow was a big game. We'd be playing our toughest competition in the state for homecoming, and everyone and their mother would be at the game. There were several recruiters coming, and the coach from TU had messaged me to let me know he'd be there.

I'd asked Jessica Hall to homecoming—scratch that, Jessica had asked me about going together three times before Shaw and Jax convinced me to say yes. It wasn't that I didn't like the girl. She was fine. I wasn't looking for a girlfriend, because attachments made you weak. And Jessica was a hook up for me, nothing more. Taking her to a dance made it feel like it was more than it was, and I didn't want to give her the wrong idea. I'd never attended a school dance before now, but my two best friends claimed it was something that we should at least do once in our lives.

My guess was that Shaw just wanted to go with Coco, and

he'd convinced Jax to take some chick he'd been hooking up with since school started, and then he'd gone to work on me.

I moved toward the water, skipping a rock across the lake. The sun was just going down and I took in all the old cypress trees surrounding me. The most vibrant reds and yellows and oranges decorated the trees letting us know that fall was here. It was my favorite time of year. A peacefulness existed out here on the lake, that I'd never found anywhere else. Coach had called practice early so we could rest up for the game and I was grateful to get a few minutes out here alone before it was too dark.

I was ready for tomorrow. Hell, I'd been preparing for this my entire life. This was my ticket out of here, and nothing was going to get in the way of that. I walked back to my bike and drove around the corner to my house. My mom was at the stove cooking and I could see Gram asleep on the couch in the next room. This was a typical night at my house.

"Hey, Ma." I kissed her cheek.

"How was practice?" she asked. "Wash up. Dinner's almost ready."

I stopped at the kitchen sink, my hip bumping hers in the small space. We lived in a little shack just a few blocks from the lake. Our home resided on the side of Willow Springs that was not touristy, which I actually preferred. I had a spot that was just mine, which would never happen on the busy part of the lake where the larger homes in town stood.

My mom and my grandmother did what they could to make this dump presentable. But since Gram had been off work since her breathing issues had worsened these last few years, money was tight. What started as a mild condition had turned into a shitty case of COPD, and Gram had suffered from pneumonia the last two years as well which had put her in the hospital.

We had rent covered for the next two months, so I could

focus on football. After that I'd start picking up a few fights once the season ended.

"It was good. We went over the plan and it sounds like coach is going to let me pass to Jax and Shaw as much as I pass to Alec." I rolled my eyes and filled our glasses with water as mom scooped pasta onto our plates. "Ty has been playing really good too, so we're going to try to pass him the ball tomorrow."

"That sounds good. And Coach Devo from TU will be there, right?" she asked, peeking in the family room to see if Gram was still asleep.

"Yep. So, I need to be on. Should I wake her, or let her sleep?"

"She wasn't feeling well when I got off work, so I think we should let her sleep," Ma said. Dark circles framed her eyes, and a sharp pain settled in my chest. The woman worked on her feet all day. I couldn't wait for the day that I could take care of her. She'd sacrificed her entire life for me, and I'd never forget that.

"Is it the breathing stuff again? If she's not feeling better tomorrow, you stay home with her. You don't need to drag her out in the cold air for the game." I closed my eyes as the red sauce from the pasta flooded my senses. Ma was one hell of a cook. "Damn, this is good."

She chuckled. "You're just a growing boy who likes to eat. And don't you worry about Gram. If she's under the weather, I'll go to the game alone and have her stay home and rest."

I finished chewing. "I see Wren at all the games, and he's always walking out right behind you. What's his deal?"

Wren Staub was the local bad boy in Willow Springs. At least that was the perception. No one messed with the dude and he had his hands in a lot of pots. I'd just found out that he owned the warehouse where my fights took place. Wasn't shocked. The dude was everywhere. And he seemed to take a special interest in my mother, and I didn't like it.

"Nothing. I've known Wren since we were kids. He's a friend and a regular at the diner."

My mom was the queen of secrets, or so I'd recently learned a few months ago when I overheard a conversation between her best friend, Shay. She rarely spoke of my father. She'd only said he'd left her to deal with me on her own, and she didn't know him well. I'd imagined him a million times in my head, and somehow sainted the asshole. I'd always thought maybe he was an undercover CIA agent who couldn't put down roots because he was too busy saving the world. Or maybe he was a Navy Seal, and he was off on a mission working for the government. But after overhearing the conversation that wasn't meant for my ears, I knew why Ma had kept him a secret. And he was no longer a saint in my eyes, but a monster I hoped I'd never meet.

A lot of people in town treated Ma like she was the shit beneath their shoes for getting knocked up as a teenager and raising me alone. It pissed me off. She wasn't the first young girl to get pregnant, but she was the only one I'd ever known to step up to the plate and put her life on hold for her child. Knocked up at sixteen, dropped by all her friends, yet she somehow managed to finish high school and get her GED all while raising a baby. She'd worked at the diner in town for as long as I could remember. She'd given up her dream to go to college because she'd had a baby, and no one had a clue how much she'd gone through. That was some stand up shit in my eyes. A lot of sacrifice for a young girl. And then to have people you'd known your whole life turn on you—it's why I wanted to get the hell out of here.

Since I'd became the quarterback at East Texas High, people definitely treated me and Ma better. But we both saw through it. I could count on one hand how many dates she'd been on since I was born. The woman was selfless. She was the fucking saint in my eyes. And the thought of Wren being the monster that probably haunted her nightmares did not sit well with me. He'd been oddly interested in me most of my life, and I'd always basked in that attention up until a few months ago. But suddenly that attention had me wondering if there was a reason that he had such an interest in Ma and me. Now I cringed at the thought that he could possibly be my father and the man I most despised in the world.

"How often does he come around the diner?"

"Not often, Sweetheart. Good lord, you worry too much." She chuckled. "So, big weekend, huh? You've got the game tomorrow, SAT's on Saturday morning, and then the dance. Do you like Jessica, or are you going as friends?"

I groaned. My least favorite topic. "I definitely do not like her as anything more than a friend, so don't get all worked up."

"I hope that you aren't avoiding having a girlfriend because you've never seen me, you know, in a happy relationship. It doesn't mean you can't have one."

I took a moment as I swallowed a bite of garlic bread. I needed a minute to process her words. Never dawned on me that she'd think it was because of anything she'd done. "Listen, Ma. If I had to choose anyone to look up to in my life, it would be you. I don't date because I've just never liked anyone enough to want to, and the truth is, I can't wait to get out of this shit town. There's no one here for me in Willow Springs."

She shrugged. "Well, you never know. And you may end up missing this town once you leave."

"Nah. If I can get you and Gram out of here, I'd never look back. Shaw and Jax will be leaving for school too, and we all want to put this town behind us. I'm ready to play college ball where the coach doesn't have to call the plays based on how much a players father donates to a program."

"That's not Coach Stephens' fault, Jett. That's just the way life works."

"No, Ma. It's the way Willow Springs works. This town is

judgy as shit." My mom had never talked about the fact that she'd been treated harshly for getting knocked up as a teenager when no one knew the circumstances. They'd just jumped to conclusions like they always did. And she'd refused to leave Gram back then, as she needed her to help with me, so she'd stayed.

Stuck.

I'd never be stuck.

I was born for bigger things than Willow Springs.

I made my way to AP Calc and Mrs. Cunningham started clapping when I walked in the room. Sherman and Adelaide followed along with her, as did the other four nerds in the class. I shook my head and my gaze locked with Adelaide's and her goofy smile made me laugh. She wore her cheer outfit because it was game day. It was a constant struggle not to stare at her tanned, toned legs beneath her short skirt. The girl was small, and toned, and slight curves in just the right places. I shook it off. I was a normal teenage dude with raging hormones. I could appreciate a gorgeous girl—but she was Alec Taulson's girl, and there'd never be a moment where I didn't remember that.

"Game day, Mr. Stone. Are you ready to continue an undefeated season?" Mrs. Cunningham said, sporting her East Texas HS spirit shirt and jeans.

"I'm ready," I said, dropping in my chair behind Adelaide.

"You ready to kick some butt tonight?" she asked, turning around to face me. Her dark hair was pulled back in a long ponytail on top of her head, with a bow that was ridiculously large.

"Do you mean, kick some ass, Ace?" I chuckled.

Sherman coughed beside me and whisper shouted while Mrs. Cunningham turned to write on the board. "They mean the same thing, so why not use the more appropriate language? I'll side with Addy on this one."

Shocker.

Adelaide laughed.

I rolled my eyes. Of course, he thought this was up for discussion. For whatever reason, Sherman had decided the three of us were new found besties. And any time we disagreed on anything, he always followed it up with, *"I'll side with Addy."*

Whatever, dude. I get it. You're pining for a chick you'll never have. I was all about dreaming big, and Sherman was definitely dreaming here.

"Jett might actually be right on this one. It is football after all." She smiled and I opened my book and looked away. Getting lost in Adelaide Edington's deep brown gaze was a waste of time. Sherman was on his own there.

"You going to the game, Sherman?" I asked, because I knew the guy hung on every word we said to him, and well, I wasn't a complete douchebag.

"I am, Jett. I'll be cheering for both of you."

My head tipped back in laughter. I couldn't help it. Why the fuck would he be cheering for Adelaide? *She was a cheerleader.* Last I checked they did the cheering. Damn, the poor bastard had it bad.

"Sounds good, dude."

"You're both still taking your SAT's tomorrow, right? So, we'll all be here at 8AM, I guess?" Adelaide asked.

These two were so deep in my business they gave Ma and Gram a run for their money.

The group texts had become a daily occurrence. I responded to every fifteen texts Sherman sent, and Adelaide responded a little more often than I did. He'd asked for our SAT schedules, and we were all three taking them tomorrow, as were ninety percent of our senior class.

"I'll be here, Addy. Don't forget your pencils. And no cell

phones." Sherman pushed his glasses up his nose and it took everything I had in me not to laugh about the no cell phone rule. There was a text from him every morning when I woke up that was to both me and Adelaide. I was fairly certain he was just using me as a way to talk to her, but I didn't know anymore because he was suddenly very interested in football and where I wanted to go to college. I had to remind myself that I was dealing with the valedictorian and the salutatorian of our class with these two. I knew this because of course Sherman filled me in. He had her edged out by just a hair, and I think he'd give it all up in a heartbeat because he was balls deep in love with the girl. She seemed absolutely fine with being second in line in our senior class, but that didn't surprise me. She was nice to the core, so even if she wanted it, she'd never be a sore sport. She'd been that way since we were kids.

"All right, let's get this done. We've got a busy weekend and I don't have time for homework. You going to the dance, Sherman?" I couldn't fucking believe I was now making small talk with Sherman Saxe. These two had dragged me into their nerdy little world and I had to say—I didn't hate it.

"Yes, I'm going with Sadie Fareweather. *We aren't romantic.* We'll be attending as friends. I feel that being the valedictorian, *Sorry, Addy,*" he said, pulling his goddamned shoulders up to his ears in some sort of apology as his nasally words reached a higher pitch than normal. *What are you sorry for dude?* Being smart as hell? They were both smart as hell. She smiled and waved him off as if it didn't matter to her. Her cheeks pinked but I got the feeling it had more to do with the fact that he kept calling her out about it, and less to do with her being second in our class. "Anyway, I think it's important that I show how well rounded I am."

I'd just taken a sip from my water bottle and I coughed, spewing water across my desk. This guy was as well rounded as a sharp corner. "Sorry. That went down the wrong pipe. Yeah, definitely a good plan."

Adelaide shot me a look and covered her mouth with her hand.

"I saw you both were nominated for homecoming court. Sadie and I were disappointed we weren't selected, but I don't think popularity is my strong suit." He forced a smile and my chest fucking squeezed. What the actual fuck was happening to me? Sherman said he wasn't popular. It was the truth. Why the fuck did I care? I wasn't this dude's babysitter. He was the fucking Valedictorian. That trumps any bullshit popularity game any day of the week.

Jessica and I had been selected for homecoming court which actually made me cringe. I didn't even want to go to this stupid ass dance, and now I had to parade around and get announced at the game tonight. Not my thing. Jessica was really happy about it. Maybe a little too happy about it. She'd been texting me incessantly all week about her dress and making sure I matched. If there was a way out of this at this point, I'd be all about it.

Of course, Adelaide and Alec were selected, as they were the golden poster children for East Texas High. Coco and Shaw were on the court which gave me endless joy, because he was as annoyed as I was. And seeing as he insisted on making me go to this damn dance, it served him right. And the final couple was Ty and Ivy. They'd been dating as long as Adelaide and Alec, so no one was surprised about it.

"Who gives a shit what these people think about you, Sherman. You're a brilliant fucking dude. I'd much rather be the valedictorian than be on the homecoming court." I tipped my chin, and he got all flustered and knocked his water bottle off the desk. He and Adelaide bent down to pick it up at the same time, and he jumped up and slammed his head into his desk, causing his glasses to fall to the fucking floor.

If I'd known a little compliment was going to cause the

train to come off the tracks, I would have kept my damn mouth shut. Adelaide was down on the floor reaching for his glasses and she looked up at me, eyes watery, and face flushed. She shook her head as if she couldn't contain herself another minute. Sherman started hysterically laughing and her head fell back in laughter as tears ran down her face. Jesus. These two were ridiculous. And I fucking joined in. Because seeing Sherman Saxe fumble around was funny as shit.

"Everything okay back there?" Mrs. Cunningham asked. "Calculus isn't supposed to be this fun."

"Sorry, Mrs. C." Adelaide and Sherman returned to their seats.

"I don't know what just happened. I guess I uh, what would you say, Jett? I lost my shits?"

My head tipped back again in laughter. "No need to make it plural, buddy. Just shit."

"Well, thanks for saying that. I've worked hard for my grades. And to be honest, I was happy to see you both on the court. My two best friends."

What the…

Adelaide's plump lips turned up in the corners. "We're an unlikely group, but here we are."

I shook my head. "You're both too smart for your own good. Sherman you text too much. Ace, you have shit taste in dudes. But you're both all right."

She rolled her eyes, and Sherman smiled, his gaze bouncing between she and I.

The bell rang and I high fived Sherman and told Adelaide I'd see her on the field.

It was game time.

Time to focus.

five

. . .

Adelaide

ALEC SCORED a touchdown and relief flooded. He hadn't had his best season this year, and his dad was all over him. He wasn't going to play after high school, and I didn't understand why Boone Taulson felt the need to ride him so hard.

He'd been really stressed out lately and I was happy that he scored because hopefully it would help his mood. He was mad about Coco going to the dance with Shaw, because it meant the two groups would be taking photos together. Alec was not a fan of Jett, and he didn't care for Shaw and Jax. I didn't know why. We'd all grown up together.

His disdain for Jett had only worsened this year, so I kept my new-found friendship with he and Sherman to myself. This morning he'd ranted about Jett driving a motorcycle and how stupid it was. He complained about how Jett didn't throw him the ball enough and ripped my head off when I asked if Jett made that decision or if Coach Stephens did. I understood his frustration, as we were all feeling it with it being senior year when so much change was upon us. It scared me too. But Alec and I would be fine, just like we always were. It was our last year of dances, and seeing the same friends every day, and going to school with the same people. The thought made my stomach turn.

The game was tied, and tensions were high. Karina and I were not seeing eye to eye on what cheers to call, and Coach Hansen told me to call the cheers for the rest of the game. Of course, that pissed Karina off, so she talked over me every time I spoke. I'd never understand what the girl's problem was, but this rift between us had become exhausting. Between cheer practice, and National Charity League which my mother chose to sign me up for every possible volunteer position, and my class load—I was stretched as far as I could go. Catty fights with Karina were not high on my list.

"Hey, I don't want to keep doing this with you. You call the next one. I'm fine with it," I said to her, as the football coach called a time out. This was my olive branch.

"Oh, really? So, you decide who calls the cheers now? I know you think you're the queen of Willow Springs, and the boss of your boyfriend, but you do not call the shots on this team, Addy."

"What? This is me trying to meet you halfway. What is your problem?" I mean, the girl slept with my boyfriend. And she hates me? I was trying to move past it. I didn't blame her for what happened, I'd blamed Alec. But it didn't mean I liked her. She wasn't nice, she talked smack about everyone including her friends, and she was catty as hell. But I didn't want to fight with her all year. We'd be heading into basketball season next and we would have to cheer again together.

"You're my problem, you prima donna, spoiled bitch," she hissed, before flipping her hair over her shoulder and laughing.

Wow. Tell me how you really feel.

"Fine. Let's go with East Texas for the score, next. Everyone line-up. On three," I shouted loud enough that they could all hear me, and we took our positions for the next cheer. The only saving grace was that Karina and I were both flyers, so I didn't have to worry about her intentionally dropping me. Because I wouldn't put her past it.

During half time my mom called me over before we ran out on the field to perform our cheer, and she handed me some lip gloss. "Here, Addy."

Clem ran up and I hugged her. "How did your race go?"

"I won." She beamed, and I pulled her in for another hug. "I'll tell you all the details tonight."

"I'm so proud of you. Can't wait to hear all about it. I'm sorry I couldn't be there." I'd seen Clem race a few times and she was amazing. She squeezed my hand.

"You need a refresher," my mother said, handing me her compact powder with the little mirror inside.

"Oh my god, Mama. You're so shallow. Her gigantic bow won't allow anyone to see her face anyway," Clem said to my mother and my head fell back in laughter.

"She's got a point," I said.

"Clem, someday you will understand how important this is. Your sister is out there supporting our boys and the game is tied."

Clem rubbed her temples. "Mother, please. She's out there dancing in a skirt, shaking her tail. Why is it Addy's job to support the boys? They should be cheering for her."

My mother stilled and turned to face my sister. "I cannot do your whole *feminist thing* right now with a tie game. Go up and sit with Daddy and stop with this nonsense."

Clem went to open her mouth and my mother held her hand up. If Mama were a super-hero she would be The Great Silencer. If she didn't like what you were saying, she ended the conversation. She shut down. It was a brilliant strategy, actually. This is why she always got her way. But I had a feeling Clem was going to challenge her for years to come. My sister stormed off and my mother shook her head.

"I swear that girl will be the death of me. Now go out there and smile pretty, Sweetheart."

I nodded, and as soon as I turned around, I rolled my eyes. I was starting to think Clem might be on to something.

We performed our cheer and my stomach dipped as I sailed through the air circling around in the night sky, before landing in the arms of my teammates. I'd never found it fun to be a flyer, but my mother said it was the best position to be on the cheer team. The wind whistled, and the crowd screamed as I was tossed up one more time. Coco, Ivy, Gigi and Maura shouted for me on the sidelines and I hurried over as the team came back out on the field. They would be announcing homecoming court before the second half of the game started again and I searched the field for Alec.

"I can't believe we have to go out there for this ridiculous ritual. If I wasn't walking with Shaw, I'd refuse to do it. But he's so hot, that I'm willing to go against my moral code and play along with society's ridiculous traditions," Coco said.

Maura came over and fixed my hair, adjusting the oversized bow on top of my head. Gigi made Coco, Ivy and I all get together and she took a picture for our book. Maura and Gigi were relieved they didn't have to partake, but they were excited that the three of us were on court this year.

"You never know, Co, you just might be the queen of East Texas," Gigi said with a laugh. Coco hated this stuff, most especially because her mother was ridiculously happy about Coco being nominated for homecoming queen. She was as excited as my mom, and that made Coco all the more disgusted.

"I'd rather swim in a bath of horse shit than wear a ridiculous crown on my head and watch my mother gush with joy," she hissed.

"Well, I feel confident that Addy and Alec have got this in the bag," Ivy said as she winked at me. "So, no need to swim in horse shit."

Tonight, we'd just be walking out on the field to be

announced, and we wouldn't have to deal with who won until tomorrow. Alec jogged over and reached for my hand.

"Good job out there. You got your touchdown," I said, pushing up to kiss his soft lips.

"I did. And now I get to walk with the prettiest girl out onto the field." He turned, facing the girls and shrugged. "No offense. You're all obviously gorgeous."

"Yeah, yeah, yeah. Sell it to someone who's buying your crap, Taulson." Coco chuckled before jogging over to meet Shaw.

We lined up behind Jett and Jessica, and I studied the little bit of ink poking out of his uniform sleeve on his upper arm. It looked like some sort of roman numerals. That boy and numbers sure were one. He was tall and lean and towered over Jessica and she leaned into him and giggled. A tinge of something ran through me. Jealousy, maybe? Envy? I didn't know but my blood ran hot. What the hell was that about? I glanced up at Alec who was shooting daggers into Jett's back and I tugged at his hand to get his attention. He smiled and shook off whatever demons he'd just been battling. They called each couple one at a time and read a few facts about each one. The other girls all wore pretty dresses, and I wore my cheer outfit. Mama wanted me to try to change into a dress and then change back, but I'd insisted Coach Hansen wouldn't allow it. The truth was, I was fine staying in uniform. Tomorrow night would be all about the dresses and the hair and the make-up. Tonight, I just wanted to focus on the game and cheer on my boyfriend and his team.

Jett and Jessica walked out to the middle of the field to deafening cheers.

"We're next," I said, my fingers interlaced with Alec's. Both of our mothers were screaming over the crowd in the background and we both laughed.

"There's no one else I'd rather be here with, Addy. I love you."

I smiled, just as our names were called through the speakers. "Love you too. Let's do this."

We walked forward as Jett and Jessica made their way back. Jett's gaze locked with mine for just a few brief seconds and my stomach flipped. It had to be nerves being out here in front of everyone. At least that's what I was telling myself.

Coco and Ivy and I all high fived as we passed, and Maura and Gigi shouted from the sidelines. Before I knew it, the ball was back in play and Karina was glaring at me as I called the next cheer. The score was tied, and our team charged down the field. Jett threw a hail mary in the endzone to Shaw, who caught the ball with ease. The crowd was on their feet. I was cannon balled up in the air for a scissor kick as the band played our fight song.

The energy on the field was at an all-time high as our defense held them from coming into field goal range and Jett had the ball again. I studied his arm as he spiraled the ball down the field to Ty, who ran it in the endzone and scored the final touchdown. I looked over to Ivy who was standing with the girls and they were all going wild with excitement.

The game came to an end with East Texas High winning by fourteen points. Alec wanted to go out and celebrate, but that wasn't even an option for me with my SAT's tomorrow. He made a few jokes about me being silly to worry about my score when I could bomb the test and still get into State, and it rubbed me wrong. I wondered why I'd worked so hard all these years only to attend a school that I could get into with no effort at all.

I kissed him goodbye and I slipped in the backseat of Ivy's car. Coco stood near the rear of the pearl white Audi talking to Shaw.

"I have never seen her so into someone before," Gigi said as she scooched over and made room for me. She was sandwiched between me and Maura.

"I know." I chuckled. "She really likes him."

"Well, she's got about two minutes to get this goodbye out of the way, because I need to get home and get my beauty sleep for the dance tomorrow."

"And we need to survive SAT tests first. Whose horrible idea was it to have Homecoming and SAT testing on the same day?" Maura asked with a chuckle.

The car door whipped open and Coco hopped in the front seat. "Man, that boy is so freaking hot, isn't he?"

"No question about it," Gigi said. "And you get to go to homecoming with him, while I go on a pity date with Hayden who's upset that he isn't going with you."

Coco whipped around to face us in the back seat. "Gigi Jacobs, you zip it right now. That boy is lucky to be going with your fine ass. He's only interested in me because I'm not interested in him. And maybe you and Hayden will have a little spark? Crazier things have happened."

"I don't think so. We're just friends. But I'm glad to be going with him because at least there's no pressure and we can just have fun. Remember prom last year?" Gigi groaned. "Patrick was literally hanging on me. I thought the dude would suffocate me. I think he licked my cheek. It was the most miserable night of my life, and then he got super drunk."

"And didn't he end up crying to you?" Maura said as her head fell back in laughter.

"Yep. Because he tried to kiss me, and I said no. He said I ruined his prom experience, and that he could have gone with so many other girls and would probably have gotten laid. He then told me he'd never have asked me if he'd known I was a prude. And then he burst into tears and said he would never forgive me."

"That douche canoe is such a jackass," Coco hissed. "I saw him a few times this summer and gave him my best death glare."

"So, he's probably lying in a puddle of mush right now. I'm totally fine with that," Gigi said and everyone laughed.

"We're all meeting at Addy's tomorrow afternoon, right? We'll take our test, grab some lunch and then head over to her house to get ready." Ivy pulled up in front of my house.

It was a ritual. We'd been getting ready for dances together since our freshman year of high school. The girls always slept over after. The thought that this was our last year of making these memories made my chest ache.

"Yes." Everyone said in unison, and I hopped out of the car.

"Okay, see you in the morning. Get some rest. Love you," I said.

"Get ready to have some fun tomorrow night," Coco wriggled her brow. "Love you, bitch."

"Love you," they all called out as I shut the door.

When I stepped inside, my dad and Clem were sitting at the table with large bowls of vanilla ice cream covered in chocolate sauce.

"Hey, what's going on here?" I said, grabbing a spoon and pulling out my chair to join them. I dipped it in my father's bowl and closed my eyes as the chocolate melted on my tongue.

"Just talking about Clem's big win today," Daddy said, his handsome face beaming with pride.

"Do you want to hear the best part?" My sister could barely contain her excitement. Clem's auburn hair bounced on her shoulders, and the cutest spray of freckles peppered her cheeks standing out against her fair skin. We always joked about the fact that we didn't know if I had freckles because my tanned skin may have hidden them. I had Mama's complexion, and Clem was all daddy. Our dark brown eyes were the only physical characteristic that we shared. And there was nothing that I didn't love about my baby sister.

"What?" I asked, my gaze ping ponging between them.

"My winning time was faster than the boys winning time," she said covering her mouth with her hands to hide her giggle.

"She beat all the boys." Daddy ruffled her hair.

"Damn straight. Why they make us race by sex is beyond me. Put me up against any of those clowns. This is 2020. Women are tired of being held back. It's our year, Addy." My sister fist bumped the sky.

My head fell back in laughter, and daddy laughed.

"Not this again," Mama said as she entered the kitchen shaking her head with disapproval. "Women are doing just fine, Clem."

"Well, I'm proud of you, girl." I smiled at my sister. "I wish I could have been there."

"You should have seen coaches face when he realized my time was faster than the kid from South High that won the boys race. Serves him right for telling me not to have such high expectations this season. *It's a marathon, not a sprint, Clem.*" She imitated him and used two fingers on each hand to make quotation marks. "This one is for all the women who have been told to set their expectations low."

Daddy high fived each of us and Mama rolled her eyes, hands planted on each hip as she stared at my sister. "You're awfully young to be a feminist."

I gawked at my mother's words. That's all she had to say about Clem's accomplishments?

"I was born a feminist, Mama. May I remind you that you should realize how powerful you are, especially after pushing two humans out of your vagina."

Mama gasped. She didn't talk about such things, and my father and I shared a glance, and covered our smiles with a hand.

"Go to bed, Clementine. Addy you have a test in the morning and then I have Lala and her team coming over to do hair and make up for you girls. Let's go to bed, dear."

Mama held her hand out for my father. This chat had clearly pushed her over the edge.

"Good job, Clem. Love you both," Daddy said, pausing to kiss the tops of our heads.

"Love you, daddy-kins, love you mama," my baby sister said as I called out the sentiment with her.

I paused to look at the pretty pink dress that hung on my bathroom door me and mama had found at Lulu's Boutique in town. I ran my hand down the satin fabric, before getting ready for bed. I climbed into bed and wished for a restless night of sleep.

Tomorrow was a big day.

For whatever reason, scoring well on my SAT's was important to me.

six

. . .

Jett

WE TOOK photo's out at the old apple orchard near school. The tall cypress trees were covered in colorful leaves and a light breeze moved around us. Half the senior class was here, as Shaw and Coco deciding to go to a dance together had forced the two groups that normally wouldn't mix—together. I didn't care. I was ready for this night to be over and it had barely started. Jessica was acting like we were a couple, and I'd need to put some distance between us after this dance.

Ma and Gram drove out to take pictures and see everyone all dressed up. I posed for enough photos to last me a lifetime and forced a smile. Jessica wore a tight, short lavender gown, and her blonde hair fell around her shoulders. She was sexy, no question. There just wasn't a spark there, and I certainly wasn't looking to ignite anything.

"Addy?" My mother called out and my gaze followed. "Wow. You look gorgeous honey."

Ma always talked about Adelaide, because she'd been going to the diner every weekend with her friends for years. My mom thought she was sweet and kind, unlike Adelaide's mother who'd treated her as if she no longer existed after she got knocked up with me.

"Hi Mae. Thank you so much." I watched as they embraced, and my eyes scanned Adelaide's body from head to toe. She wore a pink dress, hugging her slight curves and showing off her toned legs. Her dress ended mid-thigh and her tanned skin shimmered in the last of the sunlight remaining overhead. Her dress was longer than the other girls' dresses were, yet she managed to be the sexiest girl here. She didn't have to try. She always stood out. Her dark hair was pulled back in a long ponytail falling down her back and I had a hard time looking away.

"Hellooooo. Earth to Jett," Jessica whined.

I pulled my gaze away and looked down at my date. "Sorry. What's up?"

"Let's take a kissing picture," she said, gripping my jacket and yanking me closer.

Her mother was standing there and the whole scene was awkward. My mom was busy chatting with Adelaide, even she thought we'd taken enough pictures which was saying something.

"No." I said near her ear so only she would hear. I wasn't looking to humiliate the girl, but I wasn't about to kiss her for an audience. "Let's head out."

"We're on court, Jett. We might just win this whole king and queen gig. You're the only one who doesn't seem to know how good we are together." She pouted and her mother finally put her camera away.

"Come on, Jess. Let's just have fun tonight. Stop forcing it." My words came out harsher than I'd meant them to, but this was exactly why I didn't like going to dances.

Shaw and Coco made their way over to us, and thankfully Jessica was easily distracted.

"You guys about ready to go?" Shaw asked.

"Yes, he's definitely done taking pictures," Jessica thrust her thumb at me and rolled her eyes.

"I feel his pain." Shaw shrugged.

Coco laughed, and I followed her gaze over to Adelaide and Alec. He stood behind her now, arms wrapped around her middle, and he buried his face in her neck as they talked to her parents. The dude was a possessive little fucker, no doubt about it.

"What's so funny?" Jessica asked, looking from Coco to Adelaide.

"I can't stop picturing Addy when she first got her hair done today. Her mom hired a team of people to come over. I never let anyone touch my hair or make up, because I prefer to do it myself. Well, Addy's hair was shellacked into a low chignon and she looked like a forty-year-old stepford wife. No way was I letting my girl rock that look."

Shaw's head tipped back, and Jess and I laughed. "How'd she fix it."

"As soon as the hairdresser left, I worked my magic." She smirked. "Fixed my girl right up."

I think Adelaide would probably look good just about any way she wore her hair, but I wasn't about to say that.

"You're a woman of many trades, huh, Radcliff?" Shaw asked.

"You have no idea." She winked at my best friend.

Jax and Siera sauntered over. "Can we please get the hell out of here. All these parents are giving me hives," Jax said.

We laughed.

"Yeah. Let me go say goodbye to my mom." I left Jessica to go speak to her parents and made my way to Ma and Gram.

"You guys getting ready to leave?" my mother asked.

"Yep. Thanks for coming." I leaned over and hugged them both. Gram was a fragile little thing,

"Have fun tonight," Ma called out and I gave her a salute. She knew I hated this shit. But at least my SAT's were behind me, and I felt good about them. Next up was the state meet next week, and then I could focus on where I'd sign to play in college. So, to say I had a lot weighing on my mind was an understatement. I'd go through the motions tonight. Try to have some fun with my friends and let Jessica down easy. I didn't like feeling smothered, and she was definitely coming on too strong. A hookup at a party was a different story—I'd definitely made a mistake agreeing to come with her.

The dance was more fun than I'd expected. Coco and Shaw brought everyone together and we ended up at one table with a bunch of her friends as well as our friends. Turns out we all got along well. Adelaide and I made small talk about Calculus and Sherman came over to say hello. He did not hide his awe of Adelaide as his jaw dropped open as he took her in. My head had fell back in laughter. The only one that had an attitude tonight was Alec. He didn't like his girl talking to any of us, and Coco had snarled at him a few times for being rude. I didn't give a shit. The dude was a dick. Always had been.

"Okay, I need everyone's attention. The votes are tallied for the king and queen of the evening," Mrs. Cunningham said through the microphone. She stood up on stage and raised her hands in the air as if she were trying to hype up the audience. Shaw and I shared a glance, and both cringed before laughing.

Everyone cheered and Jessica leaned in close to me. "Oh my god. What if we win."

If there was a god, I was mentally begging him not to let us win. The girl would think it was a sign that we were meant to be. It would only make the night all the more challenging. I figured Adelaide and Alec would win, as they were the couple that everyone knew and liked. At least Adelaide was. And they'd been together since, I don't know—*birth.* I chuckled to myself. I was ready for the after party and to be done with the formalities of this event.

"Oh, ohhhhh," Mrs. Cunningham purred. "The king, elected by his classmates, is our very own Jett Stone." The table erupted and I closed my eyes with horror for a moment before I gathered myself. Hell, I didn't even want to come to this dance, and now I had to go on stage and put some ridiculous crown on my head.

"Yes," Jessica shouted, and fist bumped the sky as she urged me to my feet.

A few kids chanted my name, and I shook my head and moved toward the stage. If you asked me what my idea of hell was—it would be this moment. I didn't mind people screaming my name when I had a ball in my hands. When I was lost in the game. But this—this was a silly popularity contest that I wanted no part of. I was putting this town in my rear view in just a few months, and that included most of these people.

I stood beside Mrs. Cunningham and she beamed up at me settling a ridiculous black and gold crown on my head. "Would you like to read the name of the homecoming queen, Jett?"

Jessica had clearly dipped into Shaw's flask one too many times because she screamed out, "Say my name, baby."

It was unbelievably awkward. "Nope. You can do the honors," I said.

Everyone laughed, though I wasn't trying to be funny. I wanted off this stage.

Mrs. Cunningham opened the envelope slowly and then clasped it to her chest with a large smile on her face. "Your homecoming queen is Adelaide Edington."

Loud cheers bellowed out, and my gaze landed on the table. Alec's hands were fisted at his sides as he stood and kissed his girlfriend on the cheek. Jessica mouthed the words, *"what the fuck"* to me, and I shrugged. My eyes followed

Adelaide up to the stage. Her cheeks were pink, and her smile forced. This would not go over well with her boyfriend. Coco, Ivy, Maura and Gigi were all on their feet cheering for their girl. I couldn't help but smile. She was the nicest girl in our class, and I was happy for her because I figured this meant something to her. I felt bad for messing up her perfect world by standing up here beside her. Everyone cheered as we both stood there awkwardly waiting for the moment to pass.

"Okay, y'all can go back to dancing and mingling. We're just going to take a few pictures of our king and queen." Mrs. Cunningham placed a crown on Adelaide's head before backing up and telling us to stand together for a few pictures.

"Congrats, Ace," I said, wrapping an arm around her shoulder. The heat that surged through my fingers as I grazed her skin was nothing I'd ever experienced before.

She sucked in a long breath and looked up at me. "You, too."

"Smile," Mrs. Cunningham said.

I leaned down and spoke close to her ear. "I think between Alec and Sherman, I'm getting a shit ton of daggers in the back of my head."

Her head fell back in laughter, while Mrs. Cunningham snapped a few photos.

"Addy. Everyone's ready to go," Alec said from behind us, and I didn't miss the irritation in his tone.

"Oh, yeah, okay." She quickly shifted away from me and smiled. "You going to the after party?"

I glanced over to see Jessica crying at the table and flailing her arms. "I suppose that's up to my date who doesn't look all too happy at the moment."

"See you later, Jett." Adelaide's shoulders were stiff as she walked toward her asshole boyfriend. He glared at me as I moved past him. I made my way to the table and handed the crown to Shaw.

"My man. The king," he said through his laughter.

"Shut the fuck up. What's her deal?" I asked, tipping my head toward my date. A few of her girlfriends were bent down talking to her.

"Apparently, your girl has been dipping into a whole lot of flasks tonight. She's pretty shitfaced," Jax said.

"Great. This night just keeps getting better."

"You two looked good up there." Coco moved beside me and smiled.

"I don't think Taulson would agree with that." I laughed.

"That's because he can't see beyond himself. He's never been great at letting her shine on her own," she said, and Shaw watched her as if he were hanging on her every word. Damn the guy was falling hard. Who'd have thought that would happen? Not me.

"Well, that sucks but it's not all that surprising," Shaw said.

"You guys ready to go?" Jax asked as he came our way.

"Let me check on my date." I made my way over to see if Jessica was okay and she lunged at me, catching me off guard.

What happened to the tears streaming down her face just a minute ago?

"Hey there, King. Let's go to the party. I heard there are rooms we can use. I think it's time you make me your queen," she slurred.

Fuck me.

Could this night get any worse?

"Not tonight. Let me take you home. You've had a lot to drink."

"Fuck you, Jett." She shoved at my chest. What the hell was her deal tonight? She'd never been so hot and cold.

I shook my head. "All right. I'm heading home. I'd like to take you home first."

"Fine. You suck. There are plenty of guys who want to sleep with me," she hissed.

I nodded. "You're probably right. Let's go."

This night couldn't end soon enough.

It was the state meet and we'd traveled to northern Texas to play the only other team that had also gone undefeated all season. Tensions were high, adrenaline pumped, and there was a lot on the line. Texans took their football serious, and the state title was something everyone wanted. Jax was hoping to play for a college not far from here, and the coach had come to see him play. Shaw was pretty set on leaving the state of Texas, and this was his last chance to show off his skills. The stands were packed with college coaches out to see the best high school football players in Texas battle for the state title. I'd already talked to the coach at TU several times this season, and he'd let me know that they wanted me to play for them. But every game, every play mattered now.

Coach Stephens and I had met this morning and he understood how much was on the line. This was about our future now, not just our legacy at East Texas High. And though Alec Taulson's daddy donated the most money to the program, Alec wasn't going to play college ball and coach knew that. He told me to call the plays I thought would be best for the team tonight.

Hell yes.

He wasn't going to force me to throw the ball to Taulson endlessly this game. He trusted me. I'd be fair. I'd do what I thought was in the best interest of this team.

After first quarter no one had scored yet. Their defense was tough, and so was ours. We'd held one another off, and now it was up to our offense to get some points on the board. I passed the ball to Jax who helped us make some big moves down the field. Ty got us close enough to go for a field goal, but I was going to give it to Shaw because I knew he could score. I took a few strides back, finding him wide open in the end zone and sailed the ball in his direction. He made the play, and the crowd went crazy as the first score was on the board. We ran toward one another and jumped up to bump chests. I'd been playing ball with Shaw and Jax since we were in elementary school. My throat caught as I realized that we wouldn't be playing together after today. I was ready to leave Willow Springs. Ready to put this chapter of my life in my rear view. Ready for bigger and better things. But leaving my two best friends was not something I was looking forward to.

I glanced out at the stands just as Adelaide sailed through the sky. I couldn't pull my eyes away. Her small body was controlled as her legs flew up on each side of her. The sky was dark, but the stadium lights shined down on her forming some sort of halo around her, and I smiled.

Our side of the stadium was filled with East Texas High fans, as everyone had traveled from Willow Springs to be here.

Coach called us over to the sidelines and hyped up the defense to hold them off until half time. We weren't so lucky, and they tied the game before the clock ran out and we exited the field for our halftime team meeting.

"So, what, you think you're the king now because you won a dumb fucking popularity contest. You think that gives you the right to stand near my girl and keep the ball from me?" Alec shouted, as he pushed me up against the wall in the locker room.

"You jealous fucking prick. I've passed you the ball exactly three times. The same amount I've given it to Shaw. And guess what. He caught it every time. You dropped it once and missed it twice. What the fuck do you want from me?" I shouted. I wasn't going to be a dick and tell him that I didn't even have to give him the fucking ball. They were pity throws. I knew it was his last fucking time on the field, and I didn't want to take that from him. But he was too entitled to acknowledge when anyone did shit for him, because he was all about what he wasn't getting, and not thankful for the fucking opportunities he had.

He was born into a shit ton of money. He had two parents who attended every game. He dated the girl that everyone wanted. He had the big house. The BMW on his sixteenth birthday. But the little prick always thought he deserved more.

"You make sure that ball lands in Shaw's hands, don't you?" he hissed, and I shoved him back.

"I want to win the game you selfish asshole. I'm throwing you the same ball I'm throwing him. Stop fucking blaming everyone and catch the fucking ball, Taulson." I stormed away from him as coach stepped through the doors. He wouldn't be cool with us almost coming to blows again. Alec was someone I was looking forward to leaving behind. I'd never cared for the kid, but this year he appeared to be unraveling. He was acting more erratic with each game, and I was tired of his stupid ass temper tantrums.

"Everything okay?" Jax whispered as we put our attention on coach.

I nodded. "Same ol' shit with that kid."

"Typical," Shaw said as we all three stared straight ahead.

Coach Stephens reminded us that we were the defending state champs, and this title was ours to take home today. He pulled me on the side and told me to call the plays again the second half.

"I trust you, Jett. You're a natural leader. Now lead this team to victory."

"Yes, sir," I said, a lump forming in my throat.

I jogged back out on the field. The second half was more aggressive than the first half had been. There was a lot at stake, and you could feel the tension in the air. I'd taken a few cheap shots, as had the other players on our team, and I'm sure we'd dished a few out as well. It was part of the game.

We'd each scored again and heading into the final quarter it was a tie game.

A few fights in the stands were broken up, and the energy had shifted as everyone was on edge. When I jogged back out for our final quarter playing for East Texas High, I called the first play. I'd give the ball to Taulson, giving him yet another chance to have his moment.

He ran down the field and I took a few steps back and spiraled the ball right to him. He caught it for the first fucking time tonight, but when he got taken down, the ball slipped from his grasp and it ended up in the wrong fucking hands. The dude on the other team ran it down the field and scored.

What the fuck?

"He cheap shotted me, do your fucking job," Alec screamed at the ref when he got to his feet, and Coach Stephens ran out to get him off the field. He continued his rant, even with Coach pulling at his shoulders to lead him to the sidelines. The ref ejected Alec from the game, and the fans for the opposing team went crazy with excitement. Alec's father was down on the field now, getting in the face of the ref. Who the fuck does that? This had gone from bad to worse in a matter of minutes. Coach ran out once again to try to get things under control, when Alec's father shook the referee by the shoulders and was ejected from the field as well.

Coach shook his head at me with disbelief before shouting at me. "Turn this around, Jett."

I called the play and passed the ball to Ty. No one had been expecting it, and he caught it and tore down the field as the crowd roared in the background. I watched as he spiked the ball in the endzone, and it was a tie game once again.

The next few minutes went by with our defense battling to keep the score tied. Aggressions were rising and a frantic energy surrounded me.

They held us off during the next play. The hits were getting harder. The cheers were getting louder. The refs were throwing flags in response to the attacks going down on the field. I'd taken more hits in this game than I'd taken all season. I stood talking to coach and looked up to meet Adelaide's gaze. She smiled and my fucking stomach did a flip. My tongue slipped out to wet my bottom lip and I nodded. She turned back around and called a cheer just as coach slapped my shoulder.

"You've got one minute to score, or we go into overtime. It's getting cold and our boys are getting tired. Let's win us a ball game."

"Yes, sir," I said, jogging back out on the field.

It was going to come down to one play. One fucking play. I knew where I was throwing it. Into the hands of my best friend. It was his turn to shine and win this game for East Texas. I took a few steps back and everything went silent. A peaceful calm surrounded me. I spiraled the ball into the endzone and right into Shaw's hands.

Fucking, yes.

The band played in the background.

Cheers engulfed the stadium making it difficult to hear anything.

I jogged toward Shaw and Jax met us in the middle. We huddled together as Shaw shouted.

"We did it."

We sure as fuck did.

seven

. . .

Adelaide

I WOKE up Sunday morning to my sister Clem knocking on my bedroom door to tell me the girls were here. I glanced at my phone to see it was only 9AM. I was exhausted. We'd gotten home late on the bus Friday night from the state meet, and I'd spent the day with Alec yesterday watching movies. He was still upset about he and his dad being kicked out of his last game, and I understood how disappointing that would be. He wasn't himself lately. He'd never been so edgy, and I'd tried to talk to him about it, but he just said his dad was riding him really hard and there was so much change coming after this year, he was feeling the pressure.

I understood it. Everyone went to Britney Weber's house for a party last night, but Alec wanted to go home, so I didn't end up going out either. I was supposed to hang out with the girls today, but apparently they were here much earlier than planned.

Coco barreled through the door first with Ivy, Maura and Gigi right behind her. Clem turned to leave and shut the door. I sat up and rubbed my eyes. "What's going on? I haven't even brushed my teeth yet."

"Please. I've slept in this bed and smelled your dragon

breath more times than I can count. Don't go all *Savannah Edington* on us now," Coco said with a laugh. She always made fun of how haughty both of our mothers were.

Gigi sat beside me, and I searched her gaze. She looked upset, and I immediately knew something was wrong. "Oh my gosh. What happened?"

Maura shook her head. "Maybe nothing. We don't know for sure."

"But we knew we needed to come here and tell you right away. We're the magic willows after all." Ivy shoved Coco over on my bed and sat down beside her.

"You guys are scaring me. What happened?" I asked, tucking the hair behind my ears.

They exchanged a look and my stomach dipped. This wasn't good. We never hesitated with conversation unless it was bad.

"Alec was at the party last night and Karina was hanging all over him again," Coco said, and she studied me as she spoke.

I rolled my eyes. "What? He went out? He convinced me to stay home. What's going on with him? And why is she always hanging on him. I'm so over this." I crawled past them and climbed out of bed so I could pace the room.

"That's not it, Addy. He thought we'd left, but I forgot my keys and ran back inside. I saw him go upstairs into a bedroom with Karina and shut the door." Maura pushed to her feet and faced me, placing a hand on each shoulder.

"What? You're kidding me right now." Nausea stirred, and bile rose up in my throat. "Are you sure?"

Now Coco was on her feet. "Maura came out to tell us, so of course, I stormed the freaking castle. I marched upstairs and banged on the door. He never answered and they didn't make a peep. He knows we know."

I shook my head. This was not who Alec was, was it? I couldn't believe that this was even happening. He was thoughtful and kind. He wasn't a liar. Would he really do this to me?

"I need to call him." I reached for my phone on the nightstand.

"Just feel him out. Put him on speaker phone," Ivy insisted.

I was torn about how to handle this, but they'd seen him go into a room with a girl he'd slept with before. The only girl he'd ever slept with. What was I supposed to think? I dropped back on the mattress and dialed his number, pushing the button for speaker phone.

"Hey, baby," he answered on the first ring. His voice was raw and gravelly, making it clear he'd had a lot to drink last night. My stomach churned.

"Hi. Are you up yet?" I tried to act natural, but my heart was racing, and my hands started to sweat. I set the phone on the mattress and rubbed my palms on my things, trying to pull myself together.

"Yeah. Still waking up. How'd you sleep?"

"Fine. Did you go to bed early too?" I asked because I wanted to see if he'd tell me the truth.

"No. I got home after hanging out with you, and Ty came over and insisted I go to that party with him for little bit. He knows I've been down about the last game and I think he wanted to cheer me up."

Ivy shrugged and I pressed further. "Yeah? Did you have fun?"

"It was all right. Nothing special. You're spending the day with the girls today, right?"

"Yep. We're going to the diner for breakfast and then hanging out over here after. Did you see them last night?" I asked. He'd be stupid to lie about it as he knew they'd tell me.

"Yeah. I talked to them for a little bit and then they took off. I ended up helping Karina out with a little family problem. She was upset, so I talked to her for a little bit," his voice got a little higher and I could tell he was nervous.

I licked my lips as my mouth went dry. "You talked to her at the party?"

"Yeah, yeah. We went up and talked in Britney's room for a little bit. Her parents are going through something and she was pretty upset. She needed a friend, and I just listened."

Coco shook her head with disgust, and Maura rolled her eyes. Ivy and Gigi listened intently.

"You were up in a room with her? Really?" Anger coursed my veins, as I pushed to my feet again holding the phone in my hand.

"Come on, Addy. You don't think anything went on, do you? I barely talk to the chick. Her parents might be divorcing, and she needed a friend. That's all it was. I would never cheat on you. You know that." He said adamantly.

Did I know that?

I nodded. "Okay. I don't understand why she's always coming to you. It's hard enough that you two had your little fling, and it bothers me that you hang out with her."

"Okay. You've never told me that before. I knew you didn't care for her, but I didn't know that if she came to me and was crying that you would want me to turn her away. If that's how you feel, I will cut her off completely."

Maura flipped him the bird with both hands, and everyone else shook their heads in disbelief.

"Don't turn this on me, Alec. You wouldn't like it if tables were turned."

"I definitely wouldn't like it, baby. I'm sorry. I'm so fucking hungover right now. My dad has a list of chores for me to do today and I'm just in a bad mood. I'm sorry for talking to her. I won't let it happen again. I love you so much, you know that, right?"

"Sure. Let's talk later. I need to get in the shower." I wanted to end this conversation. Everyone was listening, and he sounded awfully guilty, and I needed to process what was happening.

"Okay. I love you, Addy."

"Yep," I said, before ending the call and dropping back down to sit on the bed.

"That fucker is guilty. Tell me you aren't going to fall for his bullshit," Coco hissed.

"I don't know what to believe. I mean, you didn't actually see anything. How the hell am I supposed to know what's going on. He's acting so off lately. I don't know what the truth is." A tear ran down my cheek and I swiped it away. I'd felt like something was up for a while. Alec had been ice cold after the whole homecoming king/queen debacle. He was pissed about that. Pissed about football. His grades were dropping. And I tried to talk to him so many times, but he always brushed it off.

"It's okay. We'll get to the bottom of it." Maura pushed to her feet and paced the room.

"How are we going to do that?" I asked.

"I have PE last block with Karina." Gigi looked up at the ceiling as if she were deep in thought.

"Okay?"

"You guys meet me in the locker room, and we'll ask her. That girl can't keep a secret, especially if we all question her. If she hooked up with him, she'll be dying to tell us." Gigi was on her feet now.

"And how will we know if she's lying?" I asked.

"Oh, we'll know. Karina James is not clever enough to lie. She's all bark and no bite," Ivy said, crossing her arms over her chest.

"Come on. Jump in the shower. Let's go get breakfast, and then we can bundle up and hang out by the lake today and take your mind off things. Tomorrow we'll know if he's telling the truth." Coco walked to my closet and grabbed my robe and handed it to me. "We'll watch a few episodes of Gossip Girl. You get ready."

I walked in the bathroom and turned on the water, and a sick feeling settled in my stomach. Almost like a warning that the rug was about to be ripped out from beneath my feet.

Monday morning, I drove to school with the girls. For whatever reason, I rarely drove my car, as I usually caught a ride with Alec or Coco. Clem always got dropped off early by my dad because she had cross country practice before school. Today, all five of us piled into Coco's car, and my nerves were frazzled. I managed to avoid Alec most of the day. I told him I was meeting with Mrs. Cunningham during lunch, which was sort of true. She had an open door policy and I asked her if I could sit in her classroom and do some work. I didn't want to see him, because for the first time in my life—I didn't know if I could trust Alec Taulson. The thought made me sick to my stomach. He was my best friend, my boyfriend, a part of my family, really. But my gut told me to talk to Karina. I couldn't stand her, and I knew she would enjoy the doubt and insecurity that I was feeling.

Alec didn't question why I was avoiding him, which made me even more nervous. Like he was aware I was onto him and didn't know how to proceed. I couldn't believe these thoughts were running through my head. I never in a million years thought I would be in this position…doubting the boy I thought I knew better than anyone.

Just before the last bell rang, I asked my Chemistry teacher, Mr. Wyatt if I could leave a few minutes early for an appointment. Obviously, I didn't have one, but he didn't question me. We'd all planned to meet in the locker room before Karina left school for the day. My stomach twisted. I wondered if she would lie. If I would know if she were telling the truth. If all of this could be just a big misunderstanding that I had allowed myself to blow out of proportion.

Ivy and Maura met me in the hallway, and we found Coco outside of the locker room.

"Let's do this," Ivy said, pushing the double doors open as a few girls started to walk out.

The last bell rang just as we stepped inside and found Gigi talking to Karina.

"Oh my god, really Gigi? You're ambushing me?" Karina hissed when she saw us.

"We aren't ambushing you. We just want to talk to you." Gigi placed her hands on her hips and shrugged.

"What is this even about?" Karina tossed her PE clothes in her locker and slammed the metal door closed, and the sound echoed through the large space.

"It's about Alec," I said, hating the way my voice shook when I spoke.

Karina squared her shoulders and faced me. "Just because your daddy is the Mayor and your mama thinks she's the queen of this town does not mean you get to corner me and force me to speak to you. I mean, who the hell do you think you are?"

"We're the magic willows, bitch," Ivy snarled as she stepped in front of me, and we all startled.

Karina took a step back and shook her head before Coco moved in front of Ivy. "Relax, mother of dragons." Coco said, as she often referred to Ivy as Khaleesi whenever she got worked up. "Listen, Karina, Addy needs to know, girl to girl —are you sleeping with her boyfriend? Is something going on? If you are, he's being really unfair to her. We don't blame you—we blame him. But help a girl out."

Ivy huffed behind Coco, probably angry that she was being nice to Karina. But Coco knew how to get what she wanted from people, and you could catch more bees with honey, right?

Karina glanced over her shoulder to see if anyone was around. "Alec and I are friends, obviously."

I moved forward, meeting her gaze. "That's fair. He told me you guys were in the room talking because your parents are going through a tough time. So that was it? You just talked?"

My stomach twisted with guilt. What if Alec had been telling the truth and I'd doubted him?

She gawked at my question. "Is that what he told you? That pisses me off."

"He didn't tell me any details about your parents, just that you needed a friend," I said.

She shook her head. "Wow. He's brilliant. That's not what happened. I don't know why I'm protecting him after all this time."

"What does that mean?" I asked crossing my arms over my chest, desperate to shield myself from what I knew in my gut was coming.

"It means that it isn't *my* parents going through a hard time, it's Alec's parents who are at odds. We weren't talking in that bedroom. Alec and I hooked up *again*. He's going through something and I was there for him. Just like I always am." She shrugged.

My stomach wrenched at her words. What the actual hell was going on?

"Can you be a little more specific?" Coco asked, glancing over at me, and shaking her head.

"We slept together." Karina shrugged.

I took a step back. I thought I was prepared to hear it, but I wasn't. I put a hand over my mouth to keep the sob threatening to escape at bay.

"Is this the first time, since, you know…the other first time," Maura asked. Her voice was calm and cool.

"Umm, no. There were two other times. If it makes you feel better Addy, he told me you two talked about it. But that he didn't think you were ready, and he didn't want to push you," Karina's voice cracked at the end of her statement, as if she felt bad for me.

I hated pity almost as much as I hated liars.

And Alec Taulson was a liar.

I nodded. "So, while you're sleeping with my boyfriend you two discuss me? That's a bit twisted, even for you guys."

"It's not like that. We've been there for one another. He's always been honest that he's going to end up with you long term, you know because of your history. So, this thing with us can't go anywhere. And I'm okay with it."

This was so twisted.

"You're all right with sleeping with someone else's boyfriend?" Ivy hissed.

"I'm all right with sleeping with *Adelaide Edington's* boyfriend—yes. Looks like life isn't so perfect anymore, is it Addy?" Karina's ice blue eyes met mine, and a chill ran down my spine. I knew we weren't friends, but I hadn't realized the depths of her hatred.

"What did I ever do to you?" I asked as a tear ran down my cheek.

"Oh, I don't know. You've got your hooks in the guy I've crushed on since middle school. Your family thinks their shit doesn't stink and your Mama has been a royal bitch to my mom. Coach Hansen has always favored you, hell, every teacher at this school favors you. And you know what? I don't think you're all that great. So yeah, I banged your boyfriend multiple times, and it feels damn good to see you get knocked down a few notches."

Ivy lunged forward and shoved Karina into the lockers.

I reached for her shoulder and tugged her back. "Leave her alone. She isn't worth it."

My friends turned to look at me and I shrugged. "You can have Alec. He's all yours, Karina."

I stormed out of the locker room with the girls in tow.

"Jesus. This is worse than I thought," Coco said when we huddled outside the locker room.

"I'm so sorry, Addy," Maura said.

"I'm totally down to get suspended for a few days just to punch that smug smile off her face," Ivy snarled.

I swiped at my tears. "Don't. She wants us to react. Let's not give it to her. Karina and I have never been friends, so this isn't on her. She's not the bad guy in this scenario. Do I like her? No. I can't stand her. But Alec is the one who betrayed me."

"What are you going to do?" Gigi asked, as she reached in the front pocket of her backpack and handed me a tissue.

"I'm going to confront him. He has basketball practice now. I need to catch him off guard before Karina gives him a heads up. I need to do this on my own, you guys can go. I'll call you after."

"Call me if you need me to come back and give you a ride home," Coco said. "And don't take his shit. The kid is a liar. He's been suspect for a while, and now he's showed his true colors. Believe him, Addy. Don't try to fix this."

I nodded. "I won't. I'll call you if I need a ride. I may want to walk."

I took in their sad faces, and it made my chest squeeze. We'd always had one another's backs. We'd always felt the hurt for the other when one of us was upset. It had been that way for as long as I could remember.

They each hugged me before stepping out the door. I sent a text to Alec.

Me ~ Hey. I'm outside of the locker room. I need to talk to you real quick.

Alec ~ Be right out, baby.

Baby? Had he no shame? He'd been sleeping with someone behind my back and was going to act like we were fine?

"Hey, what are you doing here? I figured you went home

already?" Alec's blond hair was cut close to his head, blue eyes with hints of green landed on mine.

"You want to tell me about Karina? Don't you think I deserve the truth? The truth about your parents and the fact that you've had sex with her three times since we've been back together. The last time being just this past weekend."

His face paled, and I knew in that moment that she'd been telling the truth. He moved toward me, and I stepped back. "Listen, Addy. I've got so much shit going on. I fucked up and I didn't know how to tell you."

I slapped his hand away when he put it on my shoulder. "You fucked up? No Alec, you fucked someone else. There's a difference. Fucking up is forgetting to call or flaking on plans, not putting your dick in someone else."

His jaw dropped at my words. I was done being polite. I'd planned my entire life around him and what he wanted, putting my own wants on the back burner, and I was suddenly raging in a way I'd never experienced. Anger engulfed me and I didn't know how to move past it.

"Addy, please. I love you. I'm an idiot."

His words were empty. I'd gotten what I'd come for. He'd cheated on me. We were done. I turned on my heels and walked out the door.

"Adelaide. Stop." Alec was on my heels and he grabbed my arm. "Baby. Please."

I shook him off and started to run toward the parking lot. I didn't have a ride or a plan. I just wanted to get away from him.

Away from everyone.

eight

. . .

Jett

I'D JUST FINISHED my meeting with Coach Stephens to discuss my college offers and go over the pros and cons of each one. I was definitely leaning toward signing with Texas University as it had always been my number one choice. They'd verbally offered me a four-year, full ride with housing, and I couldn't ask for more than that.

I climbed on my bike, helmet in hand, as I heard shouting and looked up to see Adelaide Edington running toward me with tears streaming down her face. Her dipshit boyfriend was chasing her, and I glanced around to see if anyone else was seeing this. No one was around at the moment, and she called my name.

Fuck.

I didn't want to get involved in their drama.

"Jett. Can you give me a ride? Please." The desperation in her voice cut me deep, and I nodded.

"What the fuck are you doing, Addy?" Alec shouted, still several feet away as she climbed on the back of my bike.

I handed her my helmet and pushed back, turning my head to speak to her. "Hold on."

Her hands wrapped around my middle, and she rested

her face against my back. Alec approached just as I gunned it and pulled out of the parking lot. I saw him in my rear view mirror flailing his arms and shouting.

We were a few blocks away when I stopped at a light and spoke over my shoulder. "Am I taking you home?"

I knew where Adelaide lived. Hell, everyone knew where the Edington's lived. They had the largest house on the lake.

"No, I can't go home. Just go wherever you were going, and I'll figure it out from there."

I pulled away and her little hands fisted my shirt on my stomach and my dick twitched. Damn traitor. Adelaide was not someone I would allow myself to react to. She was as *off limits* as it got. And we were friends again after all these years, and I didn't mind it. Didn't mind anything about her, which was saying a lot because most people bugged the fuck out of me.

Her chest vibrated against my back, and I knew she was crying. I had no idea what was going on, but Taulson was an asshole so I wasn't completely surprised that she'd finally caught on. I pulled down the dirt road toward the spot I'd come to call my own near the water. I'd never brought anyone out here, but for whatever reason, I didn't have the heart to drop her anywhere else when I knew she was upset.

I parked my bike and waited for her to climb off first, before I slipped off and she unbuckled the strap and handed me my helmet.

"What is this place?" she asked, glancing around at the small beach area, the beat-up hammock I'd made out of some rope and some netting hanging between two large trees.

My own little lakeside hideaway. Shaw and Jax knew I came out here to think, but I'd never brought them with me. We'd go to the lake on the weekends all the time in the summer, but never here. This was the one place in Willow Springs that was just mine. Had been for the last four years. I came out here every day when the season was over, and it was probably the one place in this town that I would miss most after I got the hell out of here.

"It's a place I like to come to get away from everyone. Everything." I grumbled, angry with myself for bringing her here. I didn't need her telling her magic musketeers or whatever the hell they called one another about this place.

I tossed my backpack on the cluster of large rocks near the hammock and dropped down to sit in it.

Her eyes were puffy, her nose red, and she glanced around and nodded. "I won't tell anyone about it."

Damn. The girl always seemed to be able to read my mind. "Thanks. I'd appreciate it. No one has ever been out here that I know of, and I'd like to keep it that way."

She dropped to sit next to my backpack on one of the large boulders as she stared out at the water. Her phone kept buzzing and she reached in her backpack and turned off her ringer before staring at her screen.

"God. I'm such a fool."

"I doubt it, Miss Salutatorian," I said, although the fact that she'd tolerated that asshole for so long was definitely her one weakness.

She shook her head. "So, Alec and Karina have apparently been sleeping together and I'm the last to know."

"You're not the last to know. I didn't know. I don't think it's something people were aware of." I don't know why I felt the need to make her feel better, but I did.

Her tongue swiped out to wet her bottom lip. "I can't believe he'd do this to me."

"Are you really shocked?" I asked. I wanted to know.

Her mouth gaped open. "Of course, I am."

"Hadn't they slept together before? That I remember hearing about."

"Yes. But we weren't together then. We'd broken up for a few months."

"How convenient. He's an asshole, you know it, and I

know it. Come on, you're the smartest girl I know, Ace. You're smarter than him. It probably scares the shit out of him."

She shrugged. "He's never been an asshole to me. I mean, sure we broke up last year and I was upset, but at least he didn't cheat on me then."

I shrugged. "The kid is an entitled prick. He thinks he has the right to do whatever the fuck he wants because his parents have money. He was a subpar football player who had a temper tantrum every time he didn't get the ball. His daddy would wave money over Coaches head, and he'd get his way. He wants to sleep with Karina, but he also wants to date the prettiest girl in school at the same time. He's a dick. You're too good for him."

Her lips turned up in the corners and she wiped her nose with the back of her hand. A pink hue spread across her cheeks and I internally cussed myself out for calling her the prettiest girl in school. It didn't mean anything. Everyone gawked over her, and right now, maybe she needed to hear it. "So, let me guess, you don't like him then?"

My head fell back with a chuckle.

"I'm trying to figure out why you ever did?"

"We've just been together for so long, I guess I don't know anything different. And I feel like an idiot because now I wonder if I ever really knew him at all. And he's blowing up my phone right now with apologies, but you know what I think he's most worried about?"

"Not being the center of the universe," I hissed because I couldn't stand the asshole.

"Nope. He's apologizing but he keeps begging me not to tell my parents what happened because his parents will be pissed. This is what he did last time he was with Karina. He begged me not to tell my mom. I think he's more concerned with them finding out what he did than he is with me finding out." Her gaze settled on the water behind me.

"Why would you protect that asshole? Your boyfriend

fucked another girl behind your back. Who gives a fuck if his parents find out? That's on him, not you."

She nodded, as a tear streamed down her cheeks and I glanced behind me to look at the water to give her a minute to swipe it away. I'd never been a fan of seeing women cry. Hell, I'd heard my mom crying behind her bedroom door too many times to count, and it always crushed me. And seeing Adelaide cry did something to me. The girl deserved better. In all the years I'd known her she'd always been humble. And kind.

She nodded, pulling her long dark hair over one shoulder. "I can't even believe I'm sitting here crying like a baby over this. It makes me sick. I'm going to a state school, because it's what he wanted to do. I've planned my entire life around a boy that I don't even think I know anymore. I don't even know if I ever did. Or if I've just been told that we were going to be together for so long that I just believed it." She pushed to her feet and paced in front of me. "I mean, I have no one to blame for any of this but myself. Oh my gosh, why am I rambling about my stupid problems to you? I'm so sorry."

"Stop apologizing." I said, standing up and walking toward the water. I picked up a rock and skipped it across the surface. "I've never understood that whole thing with you and Alec. Your moms are best friends so you two have to be together? That's fucking crazy. And you're one of the smartest kids in our class, and you're going to a state school because that's the only place that your putz of a boyfriend can get in to? Don't you have dreams of your own?"

She picked up a rock and skipped it across the lake and it bounced twice before ricocheting off to the side. "You make it sound like an arranged marriage."

"Well, isn't it?"

"No. I mean, yes, our moms wanted us to date. But it happened naturally, at least it did for me. I love Alec. Maybe it's a different kind of love, like when you have a history with someone." She stared straight ahead, and I studied her profile. High cheek bones, long waves falling down her back and her tan face shimmered under the last of the sunlight shining down on us. Her dark gaze turned and locked with mine, and I cleared my throat.

"Loving someone because you have a history with them sounds like more of an obligation. Like the way you have to love your family because you don't have a choice."

Her head fell back, and she laughed. "Maybe. Everyone in our families sure loved the idea of us being together, and I thought I knew him."

I'd never understood their relationship because Adelaide was liked by everyone, and Alec was such a douchebag. Maybe it was their history, maybe it was something more?

"Hell, I'm not judging you. I've been with girls that I have nothing in common with because we just had good sex," I said, with a laugh.

She coughed twice and shook her head. "Uh, no. That's not it."

She stared straight ahead, and I studied her. "Should have known. I bet he's a selfish lay. Seems like the kind of dude who chases his own pleasure and doesn't give a fuck about anyone but himself."

Her face hardened and she turned to look at me. Her dark brown eyes full of fire as they locked with mine. "I wouldn't know. And I'm guessing you're going to tell me that it's my fault he cheated on me because I didn't sleep with him. Get in line. Karina already slammed me with that theory." She stormed off toward her backpack and turned around again. "No. Apparently Alec felt the need to tell his lover that I'd offered myself up on silver platter, but he didn't think I was ready, so he fucked her instead."

My mouth dropped open. I didn't know many girls that were still virgins, but I'd be lying if I didn't say I was fucking happy she hadn't given her virginity away to a douchebag.

And seeing her all fiery surprised me. Adelaide had always been so even keeled. Never thought I'd hear her drop an f-bomb. I liked it. Seeing her all worked up and pissed off. Hell, I lived in that state most of the time, so it was refreshing to see her lose her shit. She turned on her heels and took off down the dirt path. It would be at least a six or seven mile walk home for her.

I started jogging behind her. "Hey, I'm not the bad guy here. I didn't say it was your fault. I think it's cool that you waited. I wouldn't want you to waste your virginity on an asshole like Taulson. Good for you. It's his fucking loss."

She came to a stop and when she turned around, tears ran down her pretty face. Jesus. I was in the midst of a shit storm that I wasn't even involved in, and the crazy thing—I didn't mind it.

"It is his loss. You're right." She marched back toward me and kept going, heading back to where we'd just been and dropped down to sit on the hammock.

"Make yourself at home," I teased, trying to lighten the mood. Her world had been flipped on its ass and I understood that feeling better than most. I'd experienced the same thing just a few months ago, and I was still dealing with it. I'd spent my life sainting a man who in turn was the devil. And my mother had paid the ultimate price.

"I'm sorry, Jett. You came out here to get away, and I've totally taken over your space. This is so not me. I don't even know what's happening. I feel—I don't even know what I feel?"

I bent down in front of her, meeting her dark gaze. Pops of amber and topaz sparkled as the last of the light shined down on her. I saw the hurt and the disappointment. Hell, I recognized those feelings every time I looked in the mirror and saw my own reflection. But there was something else there that I couldn't put my finger on.

"Obviously you're feeling betrayed. That's fair. And it's okay to feel that."

She nodded. "Why are you being so nice to me?"

I laughed. "Am I not normally nice to you?"

"Well, honestly, before taking AP Calc together, you barely acknowledged me." She tucked her hair behind her ears as she spoke. She wore a white sweater, faded jeans and some sort of ankle high cowboy boots that I'd seen her in most days.

"It's no secret. I don't like your boyfriend."

She nodded. "So that means you and I can't be friends?"

"Seeing as you aren't together anymore, sure." I raised a brow.

"Can I tell you something, and you swear you won't tell anyone." Her voice was just above a whisper.

I rolled my eyes. "If you haven't noticed, I'm not big on high school gossip."

"As much as I feel completely betrayed by Alec, I don't know—a part of me feels," she paused and bit down on her plump bottom lip glancing back at the water.

"What?" I asked, now she had me curious with how anxious she was to say it.

"*Hopeful.* It sounds terrible, but the truth is, my mom and Mama T, that's Alec's mom. They've had this plan for us for so long and I just went along with it. Alec drove the train and I was the passenger. And now, I don't have to feel guilty about choosing a different path. One that I'm actually excited about."

Hell, she was speaking my language. "I get that. What does that look like?"

She cocked her head to the side. "I don't know for certain, but I kind of like that. I don't see myself being a school teacher if I'm being honest. I see myself being a writer. That's my passion, not that anyone really knows that."

I nodded. "You are the editor of the school paper, so it

shouldn't be a huge surprise to people that that's what you want to do. And you could do that anywhere. You don't need to stay in this shit town your whole life just because you were born here. Spread your wings, Ace. See where they take you."

She smiled, and I swear to fucking god my chest tightened. What the hell was up with that? Maybe we had more in common than I'd ever realized. Maybe talking to her was easier than talking to anyone else.

"I just might do that. Why do you hate this town so much?"

"I wouldn't say that I hate it, per se. I'd say that I resent it." I chuckled and she laughed, shaking her head at my ridiculous choice of words. "The people here are small minded. They judge you by what you have, not who you are. Well, that is until you become the quarterback of East Texas High, and then you walk on water. But before that, the way a lot of people in this town treated my mom…treated me, I don't like it."

"That's terrible. I'm sorry you and your mom have had to go through that. I feel like in a way this town shaped me for the good, but a lot of things have just been expected of me, you know? Being Ellis and Savannah Edington's daughter comes with a lot of perks, but it also comes with a lifetime of expectations. Some that I'm not interested in fulfilling or even passionate about."

"So, you're not passionate about cheerleading?" I chuckled, pushing up to stand and crossing my arms over my chest.

"Not even a little bit."

"Why do you do it then?" I asked because I was surprised to hear that she didn't like it.

"Haven't you ever done something you didn't want to do because someone expected you to?" Her eyes searched mine.

"No. Never. My mom raised me to choose my path, and I've done exactly that. Down to the sport I played, the school I choose to attend. It's all on my terms."

She frowned. "Wow. I can't say the same. I cheer because my mom told me I would cheer for East Texas since I was old enough to walk."

"Maybe it's time you start making your own decisions about who you date, what you do with your time and where you go to school."

"Maybe it is." She wrapped her arms around her shoulders, just as the sun dipped behind the clouds.

"Come on. I better get you home. I can drop you a block from your house if you want."

"Why would you do that?" she asked, pushing to her feet and pulling her backpack over her shoulder.

"Because your mother will probably lose her shit if she sees you on the back of my bike. She doesn't like me. That's no secret."

Adelaide studied me, her tongue peeking out to wet her lips. "She doesn't know you."

We walked toward my bike and she hopped on the back and I settled between her legs. My dick on high alert once again, sitting this close to her. Breathing in all that goodness.

"Jett," she said, as I started the engine.

"Yeah?" I glanced over my shoulder and waited for her to speak.

"Drop me off in front of my house, please."

I nodded and my lips turned up in the corners for reasons I couldn't begin to understand.

This day had not gone as planned.

And I didn't mind it one bit.

nine

. . .

Adelaide

POST BUBBLE BURST

When I walked through the front door the smell of barbeque and corn bread filled my senses. Mama was a fabulous cook. I could hear her talking on the phone, as she usually did when she made dinner. I glanced down at my cell to see a group text from the girls.

Coco ~ We need an update. Quick meeting at Addy's. Be there in ten minutes.

She'd sent the message two minutes ago and everyone had responded to say they were on their way.

I peeked my head in and waved, motioning down to the basement to let her know the girls were coming over.

She covered the phone with her hand. "Dinner's in thirty minutes, Adelaide. Don't be late."

"I won't." I waved over my shoulder and hurried downstairs.

Ivy was the first to arrive, and then Maura, Gigi and Coco followed in shortly behind her. Ivy set the large notebook down and looked at me for a long moment before speaking. "How are you?"

"I'm okay, actually." I shrugged. My world may have been turned upside down, but my heart was surprisingly in one piece.

"What did he say? We're dying here," Coco asked.

I shook my head with disbelief. "He admitted it. He said he messed up."

"He messed up? What the hell?" Maura hissed, falling back against the couch.

"Wow. I thought he'd deny it," Gigi said.

"Nope. And he's been blowing up my phone and begging me not to tell my parents what he did because he doesn't want his parents to know." I rolled my eyes. "He's more concerned about them finding out then me finding out."

"You need to tell your parents what an asshole he is. Your mom thinks he's so perfect. She needs to know what she's pushing on you." Coco stood and paced in front of us.

"That's what Jett said."

The room fell completely silent and Coco stopped walking. "Jett Stone?"

I bit down on my lip and tried to stop myself from smiling. He'd made a horrible day kind of fun. "Yeah. Alec and I fought, and he chased me out to the parking lot and Jett was there. I asked him for a ride. We just talked for a bit."

"Talk about life giving you lemons and making lemonade." Ivy burst out in laughter.

"He is one fine ass boy. That must have pissed off Alec that you left with him," Maura said.

"Yeah. He wasn't happy about it. But he doesn't get to tell me what to do."

"Damn straight. Thank god you didn't give that asshat your V-card. And you rode on the back of Jett Stone's bike. Jesus. So sexy." Coco dropped back down to sit beside me.

We all laughed and talked about all the reasons Alec

needed to be out of my life. I didn't know if that would ever really be possible. He was a part of my life no matter how I dissected it. But he didn't need to be my boyfriend.

Been there.

Done that.

And I wasn't interested in going back.

Maura's parents were texting her to get home, and my mom shouted downstairs that dinner was in five.

"Quick dance party?" Coco asked, before grabbing her phone and hooking her Bluetooth to the speaker sitting on our media center.

This was her solution to everything that ever went wrong. Coco Radcliff believed dance parties fixed all of life's problems.

"Up," she said to each of us.

House of Pain belted out the lyrics to Jump Around, and we shook our asses and danced until we fell back on the couch in a fit of laughter.

It worked every time.

I mean…my boyfriend still cheated on me. My future was in a complete shambles. Everything I thought I knew was turned upside down. It was all still there. But laughing with my girls helped ease the sadness that sat heavy on my chest.

And the lingering feeling of hope still resided there.

Stronger than ever.

We said our goodbyes and I made my way upstairs. Daddy and Clem were already seated at the large farmhouse table in our kitchen. I stopped at the sink to wash my hands and dropped to sit beside my father. Mama carried over the basket of cornbread and set it beside the coleslaw.

"So, I just got off the phone with Lila." Lila, a.k.a. Mama T, was my mother's best friend. They'd been joined at the hip for as long as I'd been alive, and apparently since they were little girls. *Here we go.* Nothing got past Mama T. "She tells me you broke up with Alec?"

I dropped my napkin in my lap. That sure didn't take long. I hadn't even had a bite of food yet, and here we were talking about it.

"Did something happen?" Daddy asked, and I looked up to see his sympathetic gaze. Mama showed no signs of empathy, in fact, she appeared angry.

"Yeah. Um," I thought about Alec's request. But I was done catering to him. If he was going to run home and tell his mom I broke up with him, he'd have to deal with me sharing the reason it happened. "Alec cheated on me with Karina James of all people."

I forked a bite of barbecue chicken and took my time chewing it. Waiting for the uproar to start.

"I'm not surprised. Men have been putting themselves first for years. No offense daddy-kins, not you." Clem spoke first.

"None taken, Clemmy. And I'm sorry to hear that," Daddy said. "I'm sure it hurts."

I nodded. "It definitely makes me question everything."

"Pfft," Mama rolled her eyes. "Please. Let's not over dramatize this. He's an eighteen-year-old boy. It's a phase. Don't make it a thing."

My jaw dropped and I stared at her with disbelief. She was actually defending him after what I'd just shared?

"Mama, you're actually a big part of the problem. Do not tolerate unacceptable behavior from *the man.* It's our time to say no more. To stand together. March together." Clem was on her feet, fist bumping the sky, lost in a cause that far exceeded Alec Taulson. And I loved her for it. Loved her for always having my back.

"Clementine, sit down and eat your dinner. No one is marching. Teenage boys have been straying since the beginning of time. Alec and Addy will get through this. I understand why you're angry, but it will pass. You'll be back together by the end of the week, and I'm sure he'll clean up his act." She reached for her glass of wine and took a sip, before winking at me.

Winking at me.

As if Alec had just toilet papered my house or played a prank on me.

"Mama. Alec fucked another girl while he was dating me. Is that not registering with you?" My body startled as the words left my mouth. I'd never cursed in front of my mother, and I was certain I would pay a hefty price for doing so, but damn if it didn't feel good.

"Yes," Clem shouted. "This is the year of the woman. Amen, sister. He doesn't get to get away with this. It is time for men to sit back and listen to our voices. No means no. Enough means enough. Suck it, Alec Taulson."

My sister sat back in her seat and took an oversized bite of corn bread as the table sat in complete shock over both of our outbursts.

"Everyone needs to settle down," Daddy said, looking between Clem and I.

"Settle down? I will not allow that language at my table. Adelaide, clear your place and excuse yourself. You may spend the rest of the night in your room." Mama's hard stare landed on me. Normally I'd be in tears to see her this disappointed in me. But I wasn't. I was still trying to tamper down my anger that she was siding with Alec after what he'd done.

"Don't threaten me with a good time, Mama. I'm done here." I carried my plate to the sink and stormed out of the room.

I heard Clementine chanting in the background. "It is time. You go girl. We are done being silenced."

I tried not to laugh. Such a strange mix of emotion. I was so angry I could spit nails and I fought back the desire to break out in a fit of giggles at the same time.

I heard my mother scold Clementine and send her to her

room as well and I slammed my door before dropping down on my bed.

The door flew open. "Proud of you, sister. I always wondered what you were doing with that tool. I know he's mama T's son, but I was sick of everything always having to be his way. It's your time to shine now. And your light is so bright, Addy."

"I love you, Clem," I said, swiping at the tear that ran down my cheek.

"Love you more. I better go before the warden comes up and finds us conspiring." She closed my door and I laughed.

I thought about her words. Did everything always have to be Alec's way? Maybe. But I was at fault too, if that were true. I had a voice. And it was damn well time I started using it.

I moved to my desk and opened my computer. I searched for information about the journalism program at Texas University. It was only a few hours away from Willow Springs and it was one of the most prestigious colleges in the country. I probably wouldn't get in, but there was no harm in trying.

I was done being told what I should do.

It was time to start doing what I wanted.

And I wanted to be a journalist. I wanted to write. I wanted to learn.

I wanted to attend a university that would challenge me.

I pulled up the application and got to work.

The next morning was very chilly in our house. Not because the heat wasn't on or because it was a crisp fall morning in Texas. The iciness came from Mama, who barely acknowledged mine or Clem's presence. Daddy rubbed her back when he entered the kitchen. He gave us each a half smile.

The poor man was between a rock and a hard place. He

adored my mother, and he loved his daughters. So, keeping the peace was his only hope of survival.

"Are you not speaking to us, Mama?" Clem asked. I had to give it to her. The girl had balls larger than life.

Mama dropped to sit at the table as we each took a slice of French Toast off the platter and started eating. "I'm just trying to cool down, Clem."

"I don't understand why you're angry. I get it, Addy dropped the infamous f-bomb, but you were angry before that. If daddy cheated on you, would you be okay with it?" she asked.

My father coughed and spewed his orange juice across the table, and I covered my smile with my hand. Mama reached over and rubbed his back before facing my sister again, while Daddy used his napkin to clean up his mess. "Don't be silly. We're married. Addy and Alec are kids. Kids do dumb things sometimes. It doesn't make Alec a bad person."

"No. But it does make him a bad boyfriend. I'm sorry that you and Mama T are so determined for us to be together that you're overlooking my happiness. It's sad, really." I pushed my food around my plate as I had no appetite.

My mother's face paled and she glanced at my father who looked away. He knew it was true. This obsession they had with us being together. I understood my mother's loyalty to Mama T. They'd been best friends since they were in preschool. More like sisters really. Mama's parents struggled financially, they worked a lot and were never around. She'd spent a lot of time over at Mama T's house. She'd told me many times that their family had stepped up when no one else did, even helping her apply to college where she'd met my father. Mama always said she'd still be living in a trailer if it weren't for Mama T and her family. And they'd decided a long time ago that their kids would get married someday and make them family for real. It had started out as more of a joke, but somewhere along the way, it had become serious.

Something they'd decided and weren't willing to consider any other possibility.

And stepping back and looking at the situation, I realize that what Alec and I shared was just a comfort level. A history. The thought of he and Karina being together didn't make me sick to my stomach the way it should. It made me sad that he'd lied to me and didn't have the respect to tell me that maybe we'd outgrown one another. We didn't have the passion that a young couple should have for one another. And it hurt. I'd lost my best friend. But I knew in my gut that I hadn't lost the love of my life—because I hadn't found him yet. And shame on my mother for not expecting me to be treated with more respect and love.

"Adelaide Charlotte," Mama said, pushing to her feet and coming over to reach for my hand. "Your happiness means everything to me. I thought Alec made you happy."

"Maybe he did for a while. But clearly, we had issues, or this wouldn't have happened. And I'm not devastated or broken. I'm—"

"*Angry? Appalled? Disgusted*?" Clem asked from across the table and my father covered his mouth with his hand to keep his laughter at bay.

"Sure. But mostly, I'm hopeful. Maybe even a little relieved. That's not how I should feel after my boyfriend of over three years cheated on me, right?"

My mother nodded. "You may be feeling some of those things as a coping mechanism. I believe you and Alec really love one another. You're just young," she said, pushing my long hair back from my face.

"And you're blinded by this weird obsession." I shrugged.

"Let's see how things play out. You have every right to be upset with him right now."

She didn't get it. She wasn't listening.

She never listened.

"What are you doing here this morning?" I asked,

suddenly wondering why my sister wasn't at practice. And this conversation with my mother was pointless and I was done engaging her about it.

"The state meet is Saturday. No more double practices. And our run after school will be short this week." She picked up her plate and set it in the sink. "I'm riding with you today."

"Perfect." I pushed to my feet, dropped my plate in the sink and grabbed my jean jacket and my keys, before slipping on my booties. "Let's go."

My stomach wrenched and twisted. I didn't know how it was going to be at school today. Clem and I pulled out of the driveway and she reached for my hand. "Don't be nervous. You didn't do anything wrong. Alec should be nervous. And don't worry about Mama. She'll figure it out."

"Thanks for always having my back, Clem. I'm excited to see you race this weekend."

"I'm actually nervous. I'm a freshman. I'm just lucky to be there," she said. Clem never got nervous. That's how I knew she cared. She wanted to do well. This was her passion. I thought about starting the basketball cheer season after Thanksgiving and I cringed. The idea of standing up there with Karina, of cheering for Alec. It made me nauseous.

"You're going to kill it."

"I'll try. I wonder if Mama will come?" Clem asked, as we pulled into the school parking lot.

"Daddy and I will be there for sure. And I'll talk to her and try to get her to come."

"She never misses your games when you cheer. But she's only gone to one of my races. Isn't that weird?"

My chest tightened. I never realized how much our mother favored my activities. But that was only because I always did what she wanted. "That's because Mama T is there, and they both cheered for East Texas High. I don't even like cheering. And the thought of seeing Alec at the games, and Karina at practice. I don't even want to do it anymore."

We sat in silence and I turned the car off. "Then don't. You're about to graduate high school, Addy. It's time to start doing what you want."

I nodded. "How did you get so wise?"

We stepped out of the car, and she laughed. "I was born this way."

The sound of a motorcycle rumbled beside us as. Jett pulled in the spot next to my white Volkswagen convertible bug and Clem and I stood there staring in silence.

He pulled off his helmet and his dark hair was tousled on his head. He wore faded jeans, a white T-shirt and a black worn leather jacket.

Oh my god.

I couldn't look away.

"Hey Ace. What's up Clem?" he asked, before he winked at us and walked right by.

"Now that's a boy I'd bend all the rules for," Clem whispered.

My head fell back in laughter. "Stop it. Let's go to class. No more staring."

"Uh, you were staring too. And don't look now, but Alec is heading our way."

"Hey, Addy, can we talk?" he asked. He had dark circles under his eyes, and he looked sad. I hated seeing him this way, but there really wasn't anything to discuss.

Clem growled and I couldn't help but laugh. "Okay, my little wolf. Go to class. I've got this."

"Love you," my sister said before shooting a glare at Alec and walking away.

"Jesus. I guess you told her what I did."

"They all know, Alec. You told your mom I broke up with you. My mother wanted to know why. I wasn't going to cover for you after you threw me under the bus. Besides…it happened. We all need to move on." I was surprised he didn't know already. Surprised that Mama hadn't called his mom and told her what happened. This was a first. Maybe our fight had actually made her think about things.

"Fuck. I can't believe you told them." He ran a hand through his hair.

"And I can't believe you fucked Karina James," I said, before turning on my heels and walking away, leaving him standing there with his mouth gaping open.

And it felt…good.

The days of me being polite were long over.

I was ready to figure out who I was, and there'd be some people who wouldn't like it.

And I was okay with that.

ten

. . .

Jett

I STAYED after school to meet with Coach Stephens as we had a conference call with Coach Devo from Texas University. We went over the verbal agreement once again, which was everything I'd hoped for. A four-year full ride, but I wouldn't sign my letter of intent until February per NCAA policy.

"You sure you want to stay in Texas?" Coach Stephens asked, as he clapped me on the shoulder on my way out of his office.

"Yeah. I don't want to be far from Ma and Gram." They'd both sacrificed everything for me, and I needed to stay close. And TU offered everything academically that I wanted, and it got me out of Willow Springs.

"Well, it's a top-notch education, and a damn strong football program. Coach Devo has helped a lot of kids continue on to the pro's out of his program." I nodded. I would be happy to be playing for a Division 1 football program under one of the best college coaches out there. But I had a long-term goal, and I certainly wasn't basing it around a pipe dream. Very few college quarterbacks went on to play in the NFL, so I was covering my bases. If it happened, it would be an unexpected surprise. Hell, the fact that football was going to pay for a college education I otherwise wouldn't have been able to afford—it had already far exceeded my expectations. But I was going to ride this wave, get my degree, which would allow me to call the shots about where I lived and how I lived my life.

"That sounds good, Coach. Thanks for your help."

"Players like you come around once in a lifetime for high school coaches like myself, Jett. It's truly been an honor to watch you grow into the player you are, as well as a fine young man to boot. You were just named one of the top three high school quarterbacks, not just in Texas, but in the country. So, prepare for a battle. Several schools are going to try to sway your decision but stay true to yourself and what you want for your future. I'm here if you need me."

"Thanks, Coach. I appreciate everything you've done for me."

"It's been my pleasure. Come back and see me next week and let me know if anyone gets aggressive. I'm guessing you're going to have a lot of persistent coaches trying to sway you."

"I'll keep you posted. See you next week." I made my way out of the locker room and saw Jax and Shaw at the drinking fountain in the gym. They both played basketball for East Texas, and I paused to give them a high five, bro hug.

"Dude, remind me why I thought I should play two sports this year? I'm tired as shit from football season, and Coach Peters is riding my ass already," Shaw said.

"You gettin' old, brother?" Jax burst out in laughter and slapped him on the back.

"If getting old means I'd rather be hanging with Coco than run up and down the court with your stank ass, then yes. I'm getting old."

"Stop whining you pussy whipped, mother fucker." Jax fell back in hysterical laughter and I shook my head and tried to hide my smile.

"All right call me later. I'm out of here," I said.

As soon as I turned, I saw Alec fucking Taulson heading my way with a scowl on his face. "Stay the fuck away from Addy, do you hear me?"

"Of course, I hear you. Everyone within a hundred feet can hear you, Dickhead."

His gaze narrowed and he pointed his finger in my face. "Stay away from her. She's off limits."

Was this guy for fucking real?

"Shut the fuck up and get your fucking finger out of my face, Taulson."

"You've been warned." He stormed away.

"That fucking kid is such an asshole," Shaw said shaking his head. "What's he talking about? Are you hanging out with Addy?"

"No. She was fighting with him yesterday and she asked for a ride. He's just a jealous little bitch." I rolled my eyes, shoving my hands in my pockets.

"She's so hot, dude." Jax looked off into space as if he were day dreaming about the girl.

"There's nothing going on. I'll see you later," I said, as Coach Peter's shouted for them to get a move on.

Things were falling into place for me and it was a lot to digest. I'd always worried something would get in the way of me getting a football scholarship, and I'd be stuck in this shit town forever. But I'd done it. I'd made it four years without any serious injuries, and not only had my first-choice school made me an offer, but I would most likely have options. I'd never had options in my life, and for the first time, I felt a shift. I drove out to the lake because that's where I always did my best thinking. When I pulled down the dirt path, I stiffened when I saw the white convertible VW bug parked off to the side.

What the fuck?

No one knew about this place before yesterday.

I parked my bike and walked toward the hammock to find Adelaide sprawled out with her eyes closed and headsets in her ears. I touched her foot, and she screamed out a high-pitched noise that could shatter glass before flipping out of the hammock and falling to the ground.

Jesus.

"Oh my god, what are you doing?" She asked, pushing to her feet and yanking the ear buds out of her ears. Her jeans were covered in dirt now, and she brushed it away, before tucking her hair behind her ear.

"That's what I was going to ask you." I crossed my arms over my chest.

"Oh, right. This is your spot. Sorry, you just startled me." She shook her head and chuckled. "Um, well, Jett, here's the thing. I needed somewhere to get away where no one would find me. Aside from you, of course."

"Why is that?"

"I quit cheer. My mother is going to be very angry about it. But I've never felt better about a decision in my life."

I narrowed my gaze. "Well, aren't you the little rebel."

"Never have been, but it feels good. Why would I want to stand next to Karina and cheer for a boy who cheated on me? I don't even like cheer. I don't know why I've done it for so long." She huffed, sitting back down on the hammock.

"Well, good for you then." I dropped to sit beside her, and my weight caused her to slide closer to me. Oranges and cinnamon engulfed my senses, and I didn't mind it at all.

"Yep. Good for me is right. And I did something else. Something crazy," she said, just above a whisper, placing her hand between us to keep from tipping into me. Her fingers grazed my thigh, and desire coursed my veins.

What the fuck was that about?

"What did you do? Leave class five minutes early? Break curfew?" I teased, because I knew the girl had never done anything bad in her life and I doubted this would be any different.

"I started the application process for my dream school last night."

"Why is that a bad thing?" I asked.

"Because Mama expects me to go to State. Hell, everyone expects me to go to State. I'm supposed to be a teacher not a journalist. I'm also supposed to be a cheerleader for the next couple months, so, I'm on a real roll. Trust me, Savannah Edington is not going to be happy about this at all. So, I'm going to keep this one to myself for now until she digests the fact that I just quit cheer."

"That's crazy. It's almost like you have no say in what you do." I couldn't relate to that shit. I'd been planning my future for as long as I could remember. My mom was just always proud of me for it. She never forced anything on me. I couldn't imagine living my life that way.

"Well, when I say it out loud it does sound a little crazy. And then I got stuck on the essay question, so I came out here to think about it."

"What's the question?"

"They want to know about an experience that was negative and how I worked through it. And I realized that I don't even know what negative experiences I've had because I've always done what I'm told to do. Obviously I could tell them that my boyfriend cheated on me. That he went behind my back and made me look like a fool. But in the end, I realized I wasn't even happy with him. I probably sound crazy."

"You don't sound crazy. It's all you know, so all you can do is try to take control of your life moving forward. And it sounds like that's what you're doing." I glanced over as she tucked the hair behind her ear and smiled.

"Yep. I could make something better up, you know? I doubt a college application wants to hear about a teenage break up. But they don't know how twisted the whole thing is. How involved our parents are. I could just make something up, tell them what they want to hear, but I'm just so tired of playing by the rules. And it seems disingenuous to write an essay about something that isn't true."

"Then tell the truth. Tell them what you just told me. Hell, I doubt many kids tell the truth on those fucking essays. They'd probably find it refreshing." I laughed. "Maybe you could explain why your cowboy boots end at your ankles? What's the story with those?"

Her head tipped back in laughter, and she kicked up her feet. "Their shooties. You know…shoes and boots mixed together. Cowboy boots make my legs hot. So, these are my favorite."

"Never heard of shooties before. See, I learn something new every day."

"Stick with me kid, I'll teach you all the things. I call them booties because it's easier." She smiled. "So, what are you doing out here, Jett Stone. Do you train for your fights?"

I pushed to my feet. I was fine talking about her, but I wasn't in the mood to start sharing my shit. "Nah. I just come out here to think."

"I like it out here. I've never been anywhere on the lake where it was actually quiet. How'd you find this place anyway?" she asked.

"I live right up the street. No one comes out to this side of the lake because it's a bit overgrown, but I found this little patch a few years ago and I've never seen anyone out here—*until now.*" I raised a brow and crossed my arms over my chest.

She chuckled. "Sorry about that. I just needed to figure out how I'm going to tell Mama about cheer. I knew no one would find me out here."

"It's fine. It's not like I own the place." I walked toward the water and picked up a few rocks to skip across the water. She came down and stood beside me.

"Well, thanks."

I squinted my eyes when I turned to look at her, as the sun blazed from above. "What did your mom have to say about Alec fucking around on you?"

I didn't know why I asked. Why I cared.

But I did.

"Pfft." She threw her arms up in the air and shook her head. "Go figure. She didn't think it was that big of a deal. But me dropping an F-bomb at the dinner table—that was a big freaking deal."

I laughed. "Was your F-bomb freaking or fucking?"

"The latter."

"You can't say it again, can you?"

"Well, you heard it yesterday. And I certainly did the honors last night," she said. "And she sent me to my room for it. She said that boys will be boys, and that we'd work through it."

"That's interesting. I would have guessed your mom would be pissed. She strikes me as the judgy type."

"Why do you say that?" She placed her hands on her hips and faced me.

"Because she sure as shit judged my mom back in the day. Seems like she'd do the same to defend her own daughter."

Adelaide's head cocked to the side. "How'd she judge Mae? I didn't even know they really knew one another."

I rolled my eyes and shook my head. "Fucking figures."

"What is that supposed to mean?" she huffed.

"It means that your mom lived down the street from mine. They've known one another their whole lives. Your mom used to babysit my mom when they were young because she was a couple years older. And then my mom got pregnant with me, and your mom never spoke to her again. Hell, most of the rich assholes in this town did the same thing. Like I said. Your mom strikes me as someone who might get a little pissed about a dude who fucks around on her daughter."

Adelaide's mouth dropped open, and she clamped it shut and turned to look back out at the water. We stood there in silence for a while before she finally spoke again. "I didn't know they knew one another. I like your mom a lot. She's a really nice lady. I see her every Saturday when the girls and I meet at the diner."

I chucked a rock across the water and it bounced and glided across the lake. "Yep."

"You don't have to get all quiet on me now. Seems like you might be a little judgy too," she said, turning to face me and raising her brow.

I chucked another rock, but this time it didn't make it very far.

"How do you figure?" I didn't hide my annoyance.

"Well, first you barely talked to me for years because you didn't like my boyfriend. And now you're being a little icy because you don't like my mom. Just because Mama and Alec are assholes, does not mean I'm one."

My head fell back in laughter. "Touche, Adelaide Edington. You're a lot of things, but I agree—you're not an asshole. You just seem to know quite a few."

"Agreed. And my dad and my sister aren't assholes."

Now we both laughed at her words. This is not how I saw the day going, but I wasn't complaining. Hanging out with Adelaide Edington did not suck.

"That's good to know. Then there's hope for you."

"Gee, thanks."

"I heard that Clem made it to state as a freshman. That's impressive. What does your mom think of her being a runner instead of a cheerleader?" I asked.

She sighed. "Of course, she hates it. She'll make up some excuse as to why she can't go to her race this weekend. But my dad and I will be there cheering her on."

I nodded. "That's good you're going."

"Yeah. I need to be there. I see your mom and Gram at all your games."

"Yep. Ma's never missed one in all my years playing," I said.

Adelaide dropped to sit on a large rock next to where we stood. "How old was she when she had you?"

I didn't answer at first. It wasn't something I talked about often. But I knew she liked my mom, and she wasn't coming from a judgmental place.

"She got pregnant at sixteen and had me at seventeen."

She nodded. "Your dad didn't stick around to help her?"

"Nope." I chucked another rock across the lake and it glided along the water with ease.

"That had to be hard on her. Hard on you."

"It was definitely hard on her. Doesn't matter much to me."

"Why's that?" she asked, pushing to her feet, just as the sun started disappearing behind the clouds.

"Because I didn't know any different. You can't miss what you never had, right?"

"I don't know. I think it's normal to wonder about things that you've never had. I know I do lately."

"Are you wondering what it's like not to date a douchebag?" I asked, and we both laughed.

"Something like that."

My phone buzzed in my back pocket. I glanced down to see a text from Clyde letting me know there was a fight tonight, which meant it was an opportunity for me to make some cash.

"Come on. It's getting dark. You need to go face your mother and stop hiding."

She rolled her eyes, but I didn't miss the smile. "Fine. Thanks for letting me hang out here today."

"I'll tell you what. You get Sherman to stop texting me eight hundred times a night and throw in a decongestant for his nasally ass, and you can come out here whenever you want."

Her head fell back in laughter, as she continued to walk beside me.

"You're an ass, Jett Stone. But I'll answer his texts if you don't mind me napping on your hammock every now and then."

"Deal," I said, pausing at my bike and waiting for her to get in her car.

"Are you afraid I'm going to stay out here when you aren't here?" she teased, as she opened the door to her car.

"It's getting dark. You shouldn't be out here alone."

She cocked her head to the side and smiled. "Who knew you were such a gentleman?"

"No one. Let's keep it that way. Get going." I slipped my helmet on as she climbed in her car.

I motioned for her to pull away, as I waited.

"So bossy," she shouted out her window through her laughter, before pulling down the dirt road.

I followed her until she turned right, and I turned left.

It didn't matter that we lived on different sides of town.

Turns out shit happened no matter where you lived.

eleven

. . .

Adelaide

THERE WAS a knock on my bedroom door after I'd showered and dropped down at my desk to stare at the essay question again. I closed my laptop.

"Come in," I said. My mother had house rules. You never walked in a room without being invited in. She said it was all about being proper. Coco made fun of the silly rule and was convinced my mother was some sort of haughty vampire which always made me laugh. The Edington's respected privacy and it was one rule I didn't mind.

"Hey," Mama said, standing in my doorway before she walked in and dropped to sit on my bed. She smoothed my comforter with her hands because she couldn't help herself. The woman was always tidying up and making everything look perfect.

"Hi." My stomach twisted. Had Coach Hansen called her? Did she already know I quit cheer? Either way, I'd need to tell her myself.

"So, I wanted you to know that I spoke to Mama T, and we are both very disappointed in Alec's behavior." She crossed her arms over her chest and her mouth remained in a straight line. Like the fact that she didn't approve of my boyfriend sleeping with another girl was something I should be impressed by. Seriously?

"Okaaayyy. Good to know." I pulled my knees up on my desk chair and wrapped my arms around them.

She nodded. "I do understand why you're angry. It's good to make him suffer for a while."

I closed my eyes and sucked in a long, slow breath. "Suffer for a while? Mama. It's over. I don't want to be with Alec anymore. Why is that so hard for you to grasp?"

"Don't be silly. It's a bump in the road, Sweetheart. You are both going through a lot of change. Getting ready to start college, leaving your high school and your friends. But you and Alec will be together. You'll support one another like you always have."

I fought back the lump in my throat. She didn't get it. "Why don't you want more for me?"

She gasped and her hand flew to her chest. "What? Why would you ask me that? I want everything for you."

"Mama, I don't want to be with a boy who cheats on me. And honestly, I'm not that sad about our break up, which makes me wonder if I was with him for the right reasons in the first place. Maybe I was with him because you told me to be with him. Because it was expected of me. I don't even know if Alec and I really even know one another. We've just been together for so long—and we're changing. And that's okay. But I want more. I want someone who only wants me. And I want things for myself that I never stopped to think about before."

She pushed to her feet and ran a hand over her perfect dark chignon. Not a hair was out of place. "Tell me what you want, Adelaide."

"I don't know exactly, but maybe I want to go to a different school. Major in journalism or creative writing."

She rolled her eyes so dramatically I thought they might stay stuck up on the ceiling. "Oh, please. You're clearly just having an outburst because Alec made a mistake. Life is messy, my dear. Things happen."

I covered my face with both hands in frustration. Had she always been this close minded? Just then my father stood in the doorway and of course he knocked even though the door was open.

"What's happening in here?" His smile instantly relaxed me. My anger almost dissipated. He had a way of doing that. Daddy was kind and fair. Honest and loyal.

"Well, our daughter is deciding to throw everything she's worked for away. All because of Alec's little indiscretion. Now she doesn't know what she wants to be or where she wants to go to school. You can't jump ship every time things don't go your way, Addy."

I stared at my mother like she had three heads. Was she actually saying this?

"I think Ladybug is seventeen years old and she's still figuring out life, and that's okay," my father said.

"Thanks, Daddy." I nodded.

"No, Ellis. We are not doing good cop, bad cop. That's not fair to me. We had a four-year college plan for Addy, and we aren't throwing it all away because she and Alec hit a bump in the road."

"Mama. Are you actually hearing what you're saying? That's not what this is. I'm not even that upset that Alec cheated on me, because in hindsight, I don't think we were all that happy. And he didn't cheat on me once, he cheated on me multiple times. *We* never had a plan. You had a plan for me. And maybe it's not one that I actually want. That should matter right? What I want should matter? This is my life. I should be able to choose where I go to school and who I date and what I want to be when I grow up."

My father nodded, before Mama turned to glare at him.

"Where is this even coming from? You never had a problem with any of this before." She paced in little circles in front of me. "I've already got Clem fighting me every step of the way. Can't one of you just go with the flow."

I pushed to my feet and reached for her hands. She loved me. I knew she did. But it was her way, or the highway and I'd always gone along with that. But I didn't want to do it anymore.

"I love you, Mama. I own my part in this. I should have spoken up sooner. I need to tell you something."

Her dark eyes searched mine. "What is it?"

"I quit cheer today. I don't want to cheer with Karina. I don't want to cheer for Alec. I honestly don't like being thrown up in the air anymore. I haven't liked it for a long time."

She let my hands go, and she moved to sit on the bed, shaking her head with disbelief. "It's a little early for a midlife crisis, Adelaide. I don't know what is going on with you. What did Coach Hansen say? Can this be undone, or did you burn that bridge."

"Savannah," my father said, his voice harsher than I'd ever heard it. "She doesn't want to cheer. She shouldn't be forced to do something she doesn't like."

"You have both lost your damn minds. Edington's don't make commitments and then break them."

"I've never broken a commitment in my life before now. Maybe sometimes it's okay. Just like you think Alec breaking his commitment to me is okay." I crossed my arms over my chest and faced her. "You know what Coach Hansen said?"

"What?" she huffed.

"She said she was proud of me."

"Proud of you? For being a quitter?" she hissed, pushing to her feet and moving to the door.

"Yes. She tried to talk me out of it at first because she

thought it was just about Alec and Karina. But after we talked, and I told her that I haven't liked cheer for a long time. That I did it because *you* wanted me to. She said that life was short and that she was proud of me for finally doing what I wanted. Do you hear that, Mama? My cheer coach is proud of me for finally finding my voice. Why can't you be?"

A tear ran down my mother's cheek, and a part of me wanted to tell her I would make things right with cheer. I would fix things with Alec. I would stick with her plan. Because I couldn't stand the idea of breaking her heart. But I didn't. I couldn't do that anymore.

"All right. I think we're all tired, and we need to put this conversation on the back burner. Let's talk again when we've all calmed down." My mother huffed and stormed out of my room.

Daddy winced before walking over to me and kissing the top of my head. "Good night, Ladybug."

"Goodnight," I whispered.

I went to close the door right as Clem came flying around the corner and whisper shouted. "I told you. We are woman. Hear us roar."

She ran back to her room and I heard her giggling through the walls.

I dropped back down at my desk and stared at the essay question. Well, I'd just had a very negative experience with my mom. But I hadn't a clue how to turn it around.

I decided to climb in bed and call it a night.

I group messaged the magic willows and called for an emergency meeting tomorrow after school. They all agreed to meet. And then I scanned my phone to read the texts from Sherman asking us if we'd finished our homework.

Asking if we wanted to start a weekly study group.

He wanted to know how many colleges we were applying to, as he had narrowed his list to seventeen.

Seventeen.

And I'd applied to one so far.

I responded and said that I was still deciding on schools. Because I was. I had plenty of time to change the course of my future. And I intended to do it.

A text popped up from Jett and my stomach flipped.

Jett ~ Seriously? Seventeen schools? Any luck with that essay, Ace?

Me ~ Working on it. Just told my mom about cheer and she's not happy.

Jett ~ One rebellious thing at a time. Ease her into it.

Me ~ What are you doing? It's late.

Jett ~ Just getting home.

Me ~ Hot date with Jessica.

I couldn't believe I wrote it, but I wanted to know. I didn't think they were together, but I couldn't stop myself from asking.

Jett ~ Nope. I had a fight.

Me ~ Did you win?

Jett ~ Yep.

Me ~ Good job, I guess? But you could get hurt. I don't know if fighting is the answer.

Jett ~ Not for you, Ace. You're too good for that shit. Night.

Butterflies swarmed my belly for some reason.

Me ~ Good night. See you tomorrow in class.

He didn't respond. But I climbed into bed with a big smile on my face. Because I liked my new friendship with Jett. He was smart and funny. Obviously, he was painfully good looking. And he understood me in a way that most people didn't. And I liked it.

"Okay, there's a lot to go over today," Ivy said, flipping the notebook open and holding her pencil up as if she were ready to start documenting our every word. She was still on a high about the East Texas girls winning the state soccer meet. We'd all been out there cheering her on as she'd scored her final goal in her high school career.

"So many rules with you lately," Coco hissed, sitting forward on the couch and resting her elbows on her knees.

"I call it as I see it. So, let's start with what we found out from our mother's about Mrs. Radcliff being pregnant."

Maura reached in her pocket and tossed a photo on the table. "I found this late last night. My mom attended your mom's baby shower, Co. And she looks hella preggers here."

We all leaned forward and studied the photo. Mrs. Radcliff looked huge.

"Jesus. It looks like she's carrying a full grown body builder in there," Gigi said through her hysterical laughter.

"Preeclampsia," Maura said. "I asked my mom about it and she said your mom had a really tough pregnancy with you. She was puffy and miserable."

Coco threw her hands in the air. "Of course. And she holds it against me to this day. It all makes sense now. I'm not adopted. I'm responsible for nine months of her looking like shit for the first time in her perfect little life."

"At least you know you're a Radcliff," I said.

"Or so we believe. Maybe I was artificially inseminated with someone else's egg and sperm. I just can't believe I come from those people." Coco huffed.

We all fell back in laughter.

"There is no way Cricket Radcliff would allow a foreigner to come out of her vagina. It just wouldn't happen. She's far too haughty for that shit," Ivy insisted, and we all laughed some more.

"Okay. Mystery solved for now. But I'm going to watch them closely over the next few months. There's something off, and I will get to the bottom of it. But let's hear what's happening with you," Coco said, turning to face me.

"Well. I quit cheer." I sucked in a long breath after I said it.

"You did?" Maura asked. "Finally. You hated it for so long. It's about time."

"Hell, Alec cheating on you might be the best thing that's ever happened to you," Gigi said.

"What did your mom say?" Coco asked, and the concern in her eyes made me laugh. Turns out, everyone feared my mother.

I loved that my best friends weren't surprised that I'd quit cheer. They were aware that I hadn't been happy doing it for a while.

Because they listened.

Because they knew me.

"She's currently not speaking to me. And my dad and I leave this weekend for Clem's race up north. Of course, Mama claims she has a board meeting for NCL or something. It's the state meet. Clementine made it as a freshman. I can't believe she's missing it."

"Clem is going to take over the world before she graduates from high school," Ivy said as she continued to write in the book. "What about Alec? Have you talked to him again?"

"He's coming over in a half hour. He wants to talk. And I do too. I need him to know that I don't hate him, but I also don't want to get back together. Ever."

"Fucking finally," Coco fist pumped the sky. "You've outgrown that kid. He was never good enough for you."

"Ty said he's pretty broken up about it," Ivy said. "But I don't think you should get back with him either."

I nodded. We continued talking and laughing until the doorbell rang, and they all hopped up to leave. I made my way upstairs and slipped on my jacket. I didn't want to talk to Alec in the house where Mama could eavesdrop. I stepped outside, and we dropped to sit on our porch swing.

"Hey," he said, turning to face me. "I haven't seen you much at school. I'd almost think you're avoiding me."

"I kind of am. It's a little awkward, right?"

"It doesn't have to be, Addy. We can get past this. It'll just take some time." He pulled his hoody up over his head as the wind bustled around us.

"That's the thing. I don't want to get past it, Alec. I'm not even that mad at you anymore. I think our mom's sort of forced this whole thing on us. We just didn't know anything different. But I think maybe you have something with Karina and you should give that a try. You keep going back to her, so there must be a reason."

"What? I don't want to be with Karina. I want to be with you. What are you saying? You don't want to get back together? *Ever?* You can't mean that." He grabbed my hands and held them in his.

I nodded. "That's exactly what I'm saying. I think this has run its course. I want to move on, and I think you should do the same. We're not going to be best friends at first, because there's obviously some hurt there. But eventually, I think we'll get past it. We have a history."

"You're not making any sense, Addy. My mom told me you quit cheer. This is all because you're upset with me. And I get it. I fucked up. I should have told you that my parents were fighting. I've heard my mom threaten to file for divorce a few times. I don't know what's up with them. But I lost myself for a bit. I know I screwed up. You have to forgive me."

"That's the thing. I do forgive you. This isn't about me being mad at you. It's about me figuring out what I want for the first time in my life."

"Oh, so now you're quitting cheer and you're quitting me?" He pulled his hands away in a huff.

"You don't get to be the victim in this, Alec. *You* quit us long before I did."

"I never quit us. I just messed up. I thought with my dick

and not my head. That's what guys do sometimes." He crossed his arms over his chest.

Oh my gosh, he was taking a page out of the Savannah Edington handbook. Justifying his actions. I thought about what Jett had said, and he was right. Alec never took responsibility for his actions.

He was an entitled little prick.

"Well, not the guys that I want to date. Listen, I don't want to fight with you, I really don't. But I'm done, Alec. I'm moving on. And you should do the same." I pushed to my feet and he reached for my hand.

And I felt absolutely nothing for him.

"Addy, please. We're going to State together next year. You know we're going to end up together, so why torture us during our senior year. I love you. This is our time."

Our time? Didn't he just have sex with Karina a week ago.

Was it not *our time* then?

I pulled my hand away. "I don't know how to make this more clear for you? We're done. I'm done. Maybe we'll find our new normal as friends down the road, but for now, I think it's best that we both do our own thing."

He pushed to his feet. "So, you don't care if I fuck Karina a hundred more times, huh?"

I yanked my hand away. "There's no need to be cruel. But honestly, no. You can fuck whoever you want, Alec. And I can do the same."

"You dated me for four years, and never put out. And now, what? You're going to fuck around on me?" Alec said, reaching for my hand again.

The door flew open and my father stood there staring at us. "It's time for dinner, Ladybug. It's time to say goodbye, Alec." His tone was stern, and his eyes were hard as he stared at my ex-boyfriend.

Oh my god.

Had my father overheard our conversation?

So much for making peace with Alec. We had a long way to go before we'd find a friendship, and at the moment I couldn't imagine things ever being normal with Alec Taulson again.

I was claiming my life back.

And it felt damn good.

twelve

. . .

Jett

MY MOTORCYCLE RUMBLED down the dirt road, and I passed the white VW bug before pulling over and parking my bike. It had been almost a month since the first time I'd brought Adelaide out here, and the girl had come every day since. I gave her a hard time about it, but honestly, I didn't mind at all. We mostly talked about school, and life, and sometimes we both just did our own thing and didn't say much. She was working on her damn college essay for TU and still hadn't made a dent in it. I knew she was going through a lot, but she claimed she'd never felt better.

I didn't have a lot of time today because I had a fight tonight, but I felt like coming out and sitting by the lake for a bit. Jax and Shaw were at basketball practice, and they had no idea I spent so much time with the girl outside of school. It didn't mean anything. We were both going through some shit with her trying to figure out where to go to school without pissing off her mom, and me trying to make sure I made the right decision about which school to sign with. The offers were coming in and I had a few impressive schools that I hadn't expected to recruit me. The whole experience was humbling.

"Hey. What's up?" I said, as I walked down to the water and watched Adelaide trying to skip a rock for the millionth time. I couldn't take it any longer. The girl had clearly never been taught how to skip a rock properly.

"I'm practicing my rock throwing skills," she said.

I came up behind her and reached for her hand. I'll be damned if my dick didn't jump to attention at the mere contact. I'd never cared much for oranges and cinnamon, but now it was the scent that I craved. This is why I didn't do attachments. The last thing I needed was to be craving anything about Adelaide Edington. I wrapped my large hand around her small one, forcing her to grip the rock between her fingers.

"You don't fucking chuck it. It's not a baseball." I pulled her arm back, and her head settled against my chest. "Slowly and with purpose, let it go with enough finesse to skim along the top of the water."

She let me move her hand forward before she released it and it was far from my best work, but it was a hell of a lot better than anything she'd done to date. It bounced a few times before sinking out in the distance. We stood there watching it before I realized her hand was still in mine and I jerked it away and moved to sit on the large rock beside her.

"Wow. That wasn't bad, right?" she asked, clearing her throat.

"It wasn't terrible."

She laughed. "I didn't think you'd come out today. I thought you had a fight?"

Was she keeping tabs on me now? I guess when you hung out with someone every day, this is what happens. It wasn't my thing normally, but for whatever reason, I didn't mind telling her what I was doing.

"I had some time to kill. I got a verbal offer from UCLA today, so I met with Coach Stephens after school to talk about it."

"Wow, Jett, that's amazing. What do you think you'll do?"

I shook my head. "My gut still tells me to go with Coach Devo at TU. I verbally committed, and my word means something, at least to me it does. And I wouldn't be able to afford to fly home to see my mom and Gram if I were in Los Angeles. If I'm in Austin, I can hop on my bike and come home whenever they need me. And they can come see my games if I'm close too." I knew that was important to my mom.

"I think you have your answer. But it's got to feel good to know that you have options." She dropped beside me on the rock, pressing her hip up against mine as there wasn't enough space for two people here. Didn't stop her from crowding my space though.

"How about you? How's that essay coming?"

"Well, Alec has texted me forty-two times today, and he made a scene when I left school because I didn't want to talk to him. That was a fairly negative experience." Her head fell back in laughter. "But I think the admissions committee might be looking for something deeper?"

I rolled my eyes. "What the hell is that dude's deal?"

That dickhead, Taulson, had no problem cheating on her, but now that they were broken up, he suddenly couldn't live without her.

"I don't know. He wants everyone to feel bad for him, but according to Ty, he and Karina are still hooking up, so I have no idea why he's hell bent on getting back together? I don't know why he doesn't just date Karina? I'm actually disgusted that I dated him for so long. I don't think I ever really knew him. And there's this weird awkwardness with Mama T. Almost like she blames me for our break-up."

What were we, girlfriends now? Why was she telling me all this stuff?

This was a shit ton more information than I normally wanted—but I liked Adelaide and I didn't even mind hearing about this stupid shit. Although it aggravated the hell out of me how Taulson's mom treated her. Hell, I hated the way her own mother treated her.

"She's an asshole just like her kid, if you ask me. He fucks around on you, and she blames *you* for ending it. That's why that kid thinks he can do whatever he wants and not be held responsible. I'm so happy Clementine put her in her place a few weeks back."

Her head fell back in laughter at the memory. She'd barely been able to get the words out at the time because she couldn't stop laughing.

"The girl gets ninth place in the Texas state cross country meet as a freshman and comes home to find our mom and Mama T talking about me and Alec. They never even asked Clem how she did. So, yeah, she gave it to them. She reminded Mama T that Alec was the one who went poking around with Karina James. *No pun intended,* she'd said. I thought Mama would faint at her words."

"Maybe next time you should stand up to her too. Don't let her intimidate you." I pushed to my feet because I needed some fucking space from the girl. She was all consuming in the most unexpected way. And oddly, I only wanted more which scared the shit out of me.

"I might have to take a tip from the Clementine Edington handbook." She chuckled. "So, you've got the fight tonight. Are you nervous?"

"Nah. I'll go out and do what I need to do." I kicked at the dirt beneath my feet.

"And Kylie's coming in town this weekend, right? Are you excited to see her?" she asked, and her gaze locked with mine.

Fuck. I wasn't much for lying. She'd inquired about Jessica, my homecoming date, and I'd told her we were just friends. And then she'd asked about Kylie because apparently Adelaide Edington had done her research and knew a bit about the college girl I'd had a brief fling with this past summer. I'd let her believe there was something more between Kylie and me than there actually was. Hell, it wasn't a complete lie. Kylie wanted more. I didn't. We had good sexual chemistry, and I didn't mind hooking up with her when she was in town. But she'd been calling and texting a lot more than normal, and I'd cut ties when she left for school a few months ago. I wasn't looking for anything deep. She asked if we could meet this weekend when she was home to talk about why I'd ghosted her. I'd let Adelaide believe there was something more there for reasons I couldn't even begin to explain. Adelaide and I were friends. I didn't need a goddamn safety net from this girl. But for whatever reason, I needed to make sure this friendship never crossed the line. I'd never hung out with a chick this much before, and it made me —uncomfortable.

Chronically fucking uncomfortable.

My dick didn't know what to do with her nearness, and neither did I.

But I couldn't seem to stay away.

So, if letting her believe I had a college girlfriend helped set some boundaries, so be it.

But I was irritable about the whole situation. About how hanging out with Adelaide made me feel. Made me want things I had no business wanting. Yet, I couldn't seem to stay away from her.

"Yeah. She'll be here tomorrow."

She nodded. "That's cool. Are you guys going to do anything fun?

I rolled my eyes. "We aren't like you and Taulson, Ace. We won't be singing Christmas carols to the neighbors and talking about our fake future. *We fuck*. That's about it."

Where the fuck did that come from?

She raised a brow and studied me before pushing to her feet. "Good luck at your fight, Jett."

And she stormed to her car without looking back.

Well, that was one way to keep her at arms-length.

But I regretted being an asshole to her.

She didn't deserve that.

Hell, Adelaide Edington deserved everything.

Three fucking brutal rounds later, I wiped my face off with a dirty fucking T-shirt and chugged my water. I'd won the fight in the last round, but I was feeling it. The dude had landed some serious hits to my ribs, and I took a good shot to the cheek. It didn't help that I'd looked up to see Adelaide sitting with Jax, Shaw and Coco up front. I didn't know why the fuck she was there. Coco had come to three of my fights over the last few weeks because she and Shaw were inseparable these days. But Adelaide didn't belong here. And she was a huge fucking distraction. I didn't have time to worry about her, but I didn't know how to not worry about her at the same time. Thankfully, my opponent, Joey T, had tapped out in the end.

Gram had been given a new prescription that was supposed to help with her breathing issues, but it wasn't covered by insurance. The diner was always slow between Thanksgiving and Christmas, and Ma needed help covering all these bills. Clyde handed me a healthy cut of the earnings and I thanked him.

"I got a few fights for you next week if you want in. People are starting to ask about you now that you've got ten wins under your belt. But er, we've got a little situation," Clyde said, rubbing the back of his neck in discomfort.

"What's that?" I asked.

"Wren wants me to keep your fights to a minimum." He shrugged. Shaw's cousin Clyde was a cool dude, but I knew he wouldn't go against Wren. Hell, Wren owned the place, so he called the shots.

"What the fuck is his problem?"

"No idea. But he's always asking who you're fighting, and to keep the fights to a minimum."

"I'll talk to him. Plan on putting me on as many as you can, and I'll let you know what he says."

It pissed me off that I'd have to deal with the guy. Wren had always been around, and I used to be a lot friendlier to him. Hell, I actually liked the guy before. Looked up to him, even. That was before I realized that he might be my father. He might be the man that wrecked my mom's life. And that was unforgiveable. But if I had to play nice to get a few fights in order to help Ma, I would do it. A few more months and I'd be free of this god forsaken town.

"You got it, Jett. Great fight tonight. See you next week."

I turned to walk toward my friends at the end of the hallway. My gaze landed on Adelaide's fine ass, and it took all I had to pull my eyes away. We hadn't ended things in the best way when she left the lake today, so I didn't know how to even act at the moment.

"Hey," I said, giving Shaw and Jax a hard look. They knew I was pissed they'd brought her here by my chilly greeting.

"Great fight, dude. Ten and O. You're making a name for yourself," Shaw said, clapping me on the back.

"Yeah, I'm even starting to learn some of the moves. That takedown was badass." Coco smiled proudly. Shaw put an arm around her shoulder and kissed the top of her head. Jesus. These two were starting to look like an actual couple.

"Thanks. He was the toughest guy I've fought yet." My gaze locked with Adelaide's and she looked away. "Hey, Ace."

"Hi. Good fight." She refused to meet my gaze and her smile was forced. Clearly, I'd hurt her feelings and I was surprised that I felt like shit about it.

I nodded. "Thanks."

"So, we were thinking, maybe we'd go sit out at the lake

for a while. Maybe start a bonfire so we don't freeze our balls off. Are you up for it?" Jax asked.

"Sure," I said, unable to stop staring at Adelaide.

"All right, let's do it," Shaw said.

Coco and Adelaide agreed to meet us there, and Shaw and Jax walked beside me.

"Dude, you swear there's nothing going on with you and Addy?" Jax asked.

"We're friends. Why?"

"Well, if you're not into her, I'm thinking of asking her out. She's fucking hot and she's sweet too. I know that shit-head Taulson is threatening everyone that they aren't allowed to ask her out, like he fucking owns her. But I don't answer to him. Just want to make sure you aren't into her."

My hands fisted at my side. "No. You can't ask her out."

Jax and Shaw's heads fell back in laughter and Shaw pulled out a ten-dollar bill and placed it in Jax's hand. "That was far too easy."

"Fuck off. What are you talking about? We're friends. But she's not going out with your ass. That's all I'm saying." I huffed as I walked toward my bike.

"Sure, you are. You just showed your cards, asshole," Jax said through his laughter.

I flipped him the bird and followed them down to the water. There were spots where everyone liked to hang out, and we parked near the south end of the lake. There was a group of kids down on the beach, and two spots with fires burning already. The girls stepped out of their car and we walked beside them down toward the water.

"Jax," Lydia yelled out and he jogged over to talk to her. She was a cool girl that went to school with us. I still wasn't sure if he was into Adelaide or just giving me shit, but either way, I didn't like it. And that made no sense. She wasn't mine. Not by a long shot. Who was I to act like a possessive shit like Taulson? I wasn't about that.

But something about Adelaide made me feel protective of her. And I had no idea why.

Shaw put an arm around Coco and whispered something in her ear and she laughed. I moved closer to Adelaide so only she could hear me. "Sorry about being an asshole earlier."

"That's big of you." She stared straight ahead.

"Are you seriously pissed at me?" I mean the girl was as tolerant as you got. Her dickhead boyfriend had fucked around on her and she didn't hate the dude. I made one asshole comment, and now she wouldn't talk to me?

She came to a stop. "Well, why were you so rude?"

I shook my head. "I don't know. Sometimes I'm rude."

"That's a lame answer, Jett. I tell you everything about my life, so I didn't think asking about Kylie would make you mad." She dropped to sit on a log that had been there for as long as I'd been coming out to this side of the lake. Shaw and Coco said they were going to gather wood to start our own fire, and Jax was still off with Lydia doing god knows what.

"I wasn't mad. I just don't have much to say about it. It's not all that deep." I looked up and she finally met my gaze. She wrapped her arms around her shoulders to keep warm while we waited for the fire.

"Okay." She looked away and gazed out at the water.

I unzipped my hoody and handed it to her. "Peace offering."

She smiled now, and it was goddamn worth freezing my balls off for. "No way. You'll freeze."

"Trust me, I'm fine. Take it."

She pulled it over her shoulders, and the navy fabric hung around her small frame like a blanket. Her hands were buried inside the sleeves somewhere and she pulled the hood up over her head.

Fucking adorable.

Jesus, dude. Pull your shit together. Adelaide Edington was not someone I could mess around with. We were friends.

Nothing more.

"Thank you. Are you hurting from the fight? It looked like he got in a couple good kicks to your ribs."

"Look at you…paying attention to my fights, huh?"

"Something like that," she said, as she stared out at the water again.

"You shouldn't be hanging out there, Ace."

She rolled her eyes. "I like watching you fight. And Coco invited me, so I went. I'm a big girl. I can take care of myself. I'm surprised Kylie wasn't there to cheer you on."

What was her deal with Kylie? Jesus.

I didn't want to dig myself into a bigger hole.

"Kylie and I aren't really a thing anymore. I ended it a while back."

She turned to look at me. Studying me as if she were trying to figure me out. "I thought you were seeing her this weekend?"

"I am. She wants to talk about why I ghosted her." I shrugged.

"Why did you ghost her?"

"Hell, if I know. Just not feeling it," I said because it was the truth.

"Why didn't you just tell me that?"

Now it was my turn to look out at the water. "I don't know, Ace."

There was a group of kids walking down by the water and laughter pulled my gaze off to a patch of oversized cypress trees to the right. Adelaide and I both stared as Alec and Karina walked out of the trees and down by the water. It was obvious they'd hooked up by the way she was hanging on him. He had a beer can dangling from one hand, and he was stumbling around like an idiot.

"I wish he'd just date her," she whispered.

"Do you? It wouldn't bother you?"

She laughed. "I know. It makes no sense. It should bother me, but it would almost be a relief. He's acting like he wants to get back together which complicates things for me with our families. If he'd move on, I think it would make things easier on both of us."

"You dated the dude for years. I'm surprised it doesn't hurt you to see them together."

"It's been very eye opening for me too." She shrugged. "Because it honestly doesn't hurt me even a little. I don't think we really knew each other at all. I realize now that we never really talked about me. It was always him telling me what our future would look like. What he wanted. We'd never talk about anything meaningful or real, you know? I just thought that's the way it was supposed to be. But stepping away from him has showed me just how broken our relationship was. And I don't miss it."

"That doesn't surprise me. He's a selfish asshole."

She laughed. "He's not a bad guy, Jett. He's a little selfish and entitled, but that's not totally his fault. He'll find his way, at least I hope he will."

"Why are you so fucking nice to him?"

"Because he's family. Because his mom has been like a second mother to me. Because I've known him a long time and I want him to be happy," she said, turning her gaze away from them and out to the water.

"What about you? What do you want?" I asked.

"I want to go away to school. I want to study journalism. I want my family to support my dreams. Hell, I'm still figuring it out. But I know I want—*more*."

"Good for you. You deserve all those things. And you aren't going to find them in Willow fucking Springs," I rubbed my hands together to create some heat, scooching closer to her because I needed to.

Like my life depended on it.

"Why do you hate this town so much?"

"I don't know. For a lot of reasons. Why do you love it so much?" I asked because I really wanted to know. Adelaide was smart and witty, so it surprised me that she had such blind faith in this place.

"What time are you meeting Kylie tomorrow?" she asked, her head cocked to the side.

"Tomorrow night. Why are you avoiding the question?"

"I'm not. Good. We had to move our magic willow breakfast to Sunday because Ivy's grandparents are in town. Meet me at the diner at ten tomorrow morning. We'll have breakfast and then I'll show you why I love this town so much, and I'll bet you ten bucks you'll love it by the end of the day too. And you'll be done with plenty of time to meet the girl you keep ghosting." She laughed.

I rolled my eyes. "Fine. But I've been everywhere in this shit town already, so keep your expectations low."

"We'll see about that." She laughed, as Coco and Shaw finally showed up and dropped some wood down in front of us. He bent down and started the fire, and Jax and Lydia walked over with a few other kids.

I didn't know if I was suddenly warm because of the fire burning in front of us, or because I was spending the day with Adelaide Edington tomorrow.

Either way…I was warming up in ways I couldn't explain.

thirteen

. . .

Adelaide

"HEY THERE, sweetheart. Where are the girls?" Mae Stone asked me as she dropped a menu off in front of me.

"Hi. I'll be here with the girls tomorrow. I'm actually meeting Jett here for breakfast today."

Her entire face lit up. "Really? He didn't mention it. But I was asleep when he got in last night, and of course I left long before he rolled out of bed this morning. I swear that boy could sleep all day."

The Rusty Pelican was the oldest diner in Willow Springs. There were views of the water out the back wall of windows. It always smelled like blueberry muffins and maple syrup. Mae looked a lot like her son, with chocolate brown hair and dark eyes and a strikingly gorgeous face. Although she was petite in size, but I knew she was a strong woman. She worked long days and had raised her son by herself. I respected her and she'd always been so nice to me.

"I'm taking him on an old-fashioned tour of Willow Springs. He can't seem to get out of this town fast enough, so I'm going to show him why I love it here so much." I chuckled dropping the menu beside me because I had the whole thing memorized.

"I think that's a great idea. Good luck with that. I swear that boy has been planning his escape for years," she said, just as Jett came up behind her and wrapped his arms around her shoulders and kissed her cheek. He towered over her, and I found myself short of breath as I took him in. Thick brown hair tousled on his head, a sharp jaw and a perfectly angular nose. Jett Stone was carved to perfection in every way. His tall, lean frame was surrounded by strong arms, and cut muscles. I'd found myself entranced during his fight last night. I'd told my own little white lie, as Coco hadn't even invited me to go see his fight. I'd invited myself because I'd hated the way we'd left things at the lake yesterday, and I wanted to make sure his fight went okay.

We were spending an awful lot of time together. More than I'd ever spent with Alec. Oddly, I spent more time talking with Jett than I'd ever spent talking with Alec over all the years I'd known him.

He'd become a friend.

A good friend.

"Hi, Mama." He moved to sit in the booth across from me.

"I hear you're getting the full tour from Addy today," Mae said, brushing down the front of her apron, pressing out the small wrinkles.

"Whatever. She's got zero chance of changing the way I feel about this place, but I'm down to let her try."

"She? Her? You do know I'm sitting right here?" I said, raising my brow in challenge.

"So easy to infuriate. Can't say I don't enjoy it sometimes. And yes, I see you sitting there with a shit eating grin like you think you're going to change the world today. Just don't want you to be disappointed, Ace."

Mae rumpled his hair. "Watch that mouth, Jett. So, do you know what you want?"

"I'll take the special." I handed her the menu and Jett said he'd have the same thing as me.

His mother left us alone and I turned to face him. "Don't you worry about me being disappointed."

"Whatever you say. So where are we going?"

"Leave that to me."

We made small talk and he told me he was dreading his meeting with Kylie tonight. We talked about Sherman and his dozens of text messages from the night before. We laughed about the fact that Sherman had apologized to me about my break-up with Alec, because he and Sadie Fareweather were actually dating now and he felt badly that I was single.

Mae set our food down and we both dug in.

"That dude is madly in love with you, you know that, right?" Jett said over a mouthful of pancake.

"He is not. He and Sadie are super cute together."

"So how many times did dickhead blow up your phone after you got home. I thought he'd piss himself when he realized you were out there last night. And sitting by me of all people. *The horror,*" he said dramatically through his laughter.

Jett was funny.

And charming.

And warm.

And trustworthy.

He'd become an important person in my life over the last few weeks.

"He called a few times and I sent him to voicemail and then he started texting. I texted him back and said I wasn't upset with him at all and was totally fine with him and Karina doing their thing. That led to, I don't know, another fifty texts. I'd turned my phone off and gone to bed, but I found all the messages this morning. How did I not see how out of control he can be?"

"Because you always did what he wanted before. Now that he's not getting what he wants from you, you get to see the real Taulson. That's the guy I've known for years." He pulled out a wad of cash and dropped a twenty-dollar bill on the table.

"No. It's on me." I insisted, pulling my wallet from my purse. "I invited you."

"Do not offend me, Ace. My mom won't let us pay for breakfast, and I'm leaving the tip," he said, moving to his feet.

He was also a gentleman which surprised me for a boy his age. Alec was totally fine with going dutch or taking turns paying. Which I'd never minded, but it was nice that Jett wanted to cover the tip for his mom.

"Thank you. I appreciate it. I feel like I owe you because you've let me take over your whole man cave lake area." I followed him out and he paused to hug his mother. I waved goodbye and pulled my coat closed. It was a chilly December morning, and I tugged my hat over my head once we stepped outside.

Jett wore a hoody under his black leather coat and slipped on a pair of gloves. "My man cave is your man cave, Ace. So where are you taking me?"

"First stop, Violet's floral shop." Violet was one of my favorite people in Willow Springs. She owned the local floral boutique and I always loved visiting her there. It smelled like pine and cinnamon when we walked in.

"Addy Edington, say it isn't so." The older woman had to be pushing eighty years old, but she didn't act like it. Her gray hair was slicked back in a tight bun, she wore a red sweater with brown reindeers on the front and sparkly pom poms were sewn on to give it some pizazz. "And is that Jett Stone? Well, I'll be damned. What did I do to deserve being graced by two amazing youngsters?"

Jett laughed and I beamed up at him before he rolled his eyes at my excitement. "I'm taking Jett to all my favorite places in town today. Mama asked me to stop by and pay for an order she placed with you yesterday."

Violet smiled and I handed her a credit card. "I told her

there was no rush. Wait until you see the arrangements that she ordered for your holiday party. Mmmmm Mmmmm. They are gonna be something."

"You always have the prettiest flowers in town." I tugged at Jett's arm and led him toward the large glass case holding endless blooms. "Are you telling me these don't put you in a good mood?"

He laughed. "I'm not big on flowers. But sure, Violet's nice. I've always liked her."

"She's easy to love. And this place always puts me in a good mood for some reason." I pointed to the peonies. "Peonies aren't in season often, but they are my absolute favorite. Look at those colors."

"Nice. You might be the only girl in Texas who doesn't favor the Azalea," he said, staring at the peonies as if he were trying to memorize them. I was surprised he knew about the famed Texas azaleas.

"How do you know about azaleas?" I asked.

"They're Grams favorite. Mom and I get her a bouquet every year on her birthday."

He continued to study the flowers just as Violet came around the counter and handed me my credit card back. "All set. You two have a nice afternoon. I'm honored that you stopped here first. Where are you off to next?"

"The Chocolate Fountain for the world's best hot cocoa." I tucked the credit card in my purse and gave Violet a hug goodbye.

She reached for Jett and pulled him in for a hug. "Tell your mama I said hello. I need to head over to the diner for that sweet potato soup I love. I swear she adds a little extra cinnamon for me."

"Will do, Violet," Jett said as he patted her on the shoulder.

Once we were outside, I peeked up at him. "Not a terrible start, right?"

"You get props for starting with Violet. But if you think that old grumpy ass named Ballsack is going to win you any points you are dearly mistaken. I don't like that dude."

My head fell back in laughter. Lenny Balsalcki was famously grumpy, but tender-hearted underneath all that hostility.

"Do you know that Lenny's wife ran off with his brother twenty some years ago. And then Kyle Peters opened his donut shop right next door, which cost Lenny a lot of business. You can't really blame the guy for being bitter." I shrugged as I pulled the door open and the bells chimed.

Lenny looked up to see Jett and I walking in, just as he set down a cup of coffee for Old Lady Winters. I'm not making up her name. She actually introduced herself as Old Lady Winters and that's what everyone in town called her. In her defense, the woman had to be in her nineties, and she'd been old since the day I was born.

"Adelaide Edington. Who'd you drag in today?" Lenny squinted at Jett. "Ah, the quarterback. Don't be thinking I'm going to tolerate a bunch of rowdy football players in here now, kid."

"I wouldn't dream of it," Jett seethed sarcasm as he lifted a brow when he looked down at me.

On the surface, it would appear that coming here was a mistake. But he had no idea how awesome this was going to be. Lenny Balsalcki was one of my favorite people in Willow Springs.

"We'll take two specials, extra sprinkles," I said proudly, slapping Jett's hand away when he reached for his money. "It's my turn. Don't even try it."

"I wouldn't even take your money, son. I don't need your pity. Addy here is a loyal customer, so if she wants to pay, she gets to pay."

Jett shook his head with disbelief. "Seems like a tough business plan, but okay. No sprinkles on mine."

"Did he really say no sprinkles?" Lenny barked out, slapping his hand down hard on the counter.

I covered my mouth with my hand. "Saying you don't like sprinkles is a real slap in the face to Lenny. No one in town adds those sprinkles. It makes him one of a kind."

"So does the fact that he's rude as hell," Jett whispered in my ear and his warm breath tickled my cheek. Goosebumps covered my arms, and it wasn't because there was chill in the air today.

"He'll take the sprinkles," I said before leaning in close to him and whispering right back. "I'll eat them you big baby."

I paused to greet Old Lady Winters who had her nose in the newspaper, on our way to a table. "Good morning."

"Good morning, young lady. And who do we have here? Ah...the football player. I've seen a few of your games and you've got a nice arm."

Jett laughed now. "Uh, thanks. I appreciate it."

"And you have a nice Mama. She's good people. Now skedaddle and let me read my paper in peace. I could die at any moment, and I'd like to know what's happening in Willow Springs if that happens."

We both chuckled before dropping to sit at a table in the back, and seeing as the place only had four tables, it wasn't a far walk. "That woman creeps me out. You know there's rumors that she murdered her husband."

"Well, he apparently robbed the post office when he was young, so I think he had a lot of enemies," I said trying to cover my smile.

"Why the hell are we here?"

"Just wait. I drag the girls here every once in a while, but I come here alone most Saturdays when we finish eating at the diner. I find Lenny to be one of the most interesting characters in town. It's part of the tour. Quit complaining and embrace it."

He rolled his eyes for the millionth time today and pulled

off his leather coat, placing it on the back of his chair. Lenny walked over and set down two hot chocolates covered in sprinkles.

My favorite.

Jett scrunched his nose and stared at the sweet monstrosity.

"Don't make faces at it, boy. Eat it," Lenny grumbled before pulling up an empty chair and joining us. Jett's eyes widened and I shoved a spoonful of whipped cream in my mouth to keep from laughing.

"So, what's been happening, Lenny?" I asked. He always sat with me when I visited his shop. I'd learned to love our lengthy conversations, even if they were a bit torturous at times.

"Well. For starters, that bastard, Kyle Peters is now serving dogs at his so-called *donut shop.* Did you hear me? Four legged creatures are now customers of that fool. The damn scoundrel doesn't know how to run a business."

Jett cocked his head to the side, looking out the window to see the line forming next door. Kyle Peters' donuts were famous in Willow Springs. Not that I'd ever tried one out of loyalty to Lenny. He'd never forgive me.

"I've had his donuts and they're damn good." Jett scraped some of the whipped cream off the top of his cocoa and dropped it on the little plate that held his mug, and Lenny gasped.

"You eat his donuts, and you scrape off my whipped cream? Let me tell you what I think, Mr. hot shot quarterback. That bastard doesn't make his own donuts. He sources them out and then he resells them to humans and *dogs.* He's got long hippie hair and no manners. I can't believe he gets returning business with the way he's running things."

Jett stared at Lenny with surprise as the older man proceeded to tell him his life story. About how his wife ran off with his brother. How his dog got hit by a car fifteen years ago and he'd never gotten over it. He told Jett about Flutterbug, his cat who has peed all over his carpet and brought down the equity in his home. His car didn't start this morning, and he wasn't about to take it to Wrens Mechanic shop, because one of the guys that works for Wren stole his lunch box when they were kids. So now he'd have to walk the whole block home.

"Wow. That's—a lot." Jett drank the last of his cocoa and I didn't miss the empathy I saw when he looked at Lenny. Alec found Lenny to be annoying and wouldn't sit through a conversation with the older man, so I never brought him back after the first time he'd come here with me.

"Thank you. And did I tell you most of my friends are all dead? Yep. And they all had open caskets at their funerals, which wasn't a good thing. Can't get that image out of my head now. Not that it'll matter much in the future with my cataracts. Won't be seeing much by next year this time anyway, and god knows my teeth are no good. Hell, these top ones I've got here," he held up his gums to show Jett his unusually white top set of teeth. "These aren't even mine."

"You don't say," Jett said, with a smirk.

"I do say. I swear that scoundrel dentist of mine gave me my dead friend Peters teeth and called them veneers. He thinks he can just paint dead men's teeth white and sell them for new. He's nothing but a crook that Dr. Jason. And who uses a first name after doctor. A thief I tell you."

Jett chuckled as he leaned back in his chair. "You want me to borrow my friend Shaw's truck and come jump your car later today?"

Lenny looked from me to Jett and smiled. The man actually smiled. Those ungodly white teeth nearly blinded me, and I used my hand to cover my mouth. "Well, look at you Mr. hot shot quarterback. That would save me from going to that scoundrel for a jump."

"Consider it done. I'll stop by tonight."

Lenny pushed to his feet when the door flew open and Mr. and Mrs. Goldsmith walked in.

"You know a lot of people say those two might be swingers. Do you know what that is?" Lenny whisper shouted so anyone within ear shot could hear him.

Jett's head fell back in laughter. "Yeah, I know what that is."

"I think she's been hitting on me for years. You know. Trying to recruit me as some sort of sex slave."

"We can hear you, you crazy old bastard. We're barely gettin' it on ourselves these days, what with my sciatica and her bad hip. No one's recruiting you for anything more than some goddamn hot chocolate. So, get your ass over here and make us two specials, you grumpy old fart."

"How'd he hear me?" Lenny asked as he walked toward the counter.

"I heard you loud and clear and I'm older than dirt," Old Lady Winters said.

"Shall we?" I asked Jett, holding back my laughter.

"See you later, Lenny," Jett called out as we made our way outside and he slipped his jacket back in place.

"Holy shit, Ace. That was fucking amazing." His dark eyes danced with mischief and I couldn't help but smile.

"Stick with me, Kid. I'll show you all the magic that is Willlow Springs. How am I doing so far?"

"I've got to say, you're two for two. That Dude is one crazy, grumpy old fucker, and I kind of love him."

"Right? He's one of my favorites."

"And for your information, I've heard the same rumor about the Goldsmith's." Jett winked and my stomach did some kind of flip.

I didn't analyze it or wonder what it meant.

I was just enjoying myself.

We walked through town and I pointed out Lulu's boutique where I always found my dresses for dances. and the old-fashioned candy store that I'd been going to since I was a kid. We paused at the fountain in the courtyard and I handed him a penny and we both made a wish. I reminded him that come spring the azaleas would be in bloom and the sidewalks were lined with pink and red flowers.

"Have you ever taken a ride on the Texas State Railroad?" I asked, as we approached the small train station.

"Nope. Shaw told me and Jax it was haunted when we were kids, and I've stayed the hell away." He laughed.

My head fell back in laughter. "Buckle up, Stone. Prepare for the beauty of east Texas' piney woods. Hopefully, we don't see any ghosts." I teased, bumping his shoulder with mine.

"I don't fuck with ghosts, Ace." He shoved his hands in his pockets and the corners of his mouth turned up.

As we boarded the train, I realized this wasn't only a tour for Jett.

This was the most fun I'd had in Willow Springs in a long time.

And I was in no hurry for this day to end.

fourteen

. . .

Jett

"WHAT CAN I do for you, Jett?" Wren asked, as he pushed to his feet. I'd heard he spent his days at the auto shop that he owned, and I knew Clyde wasn't going to give me those fights without Wren's approval. His office was fairly spacious, and he came around his desk, so we were standing eye to eye.

"Well, it seems that I can't get my name down for any fights because you aren't allowing it." I crossed my arms over my chest and my worn leather jacket stretched with the movement.

"I don't think your mom would be all too happy if you got hurt when you're just a few months away from leaving for school."

Who the fuck did he think he was?

Even if Wren was my sperm donor, he hadn't been in my life the way a father should be, so he had no right to tell me how to live.

Not to mention the fact that if he were my father, it meant that he'd violated my mother in ways I couldn't allow myself to comprehend. Because that would mean that I'd have to hurt him. Make him pay for what he'd done.

"I don't think that's any of your business." I squared my

shoulders. He was about my size in both height and weight, but I figured I had youth on the old bastard, although he struck me as a bit of a badass.

"It's my club, so it's my business."

"So, do you tell other guys how often they can fight? Or you're just singling me out for some fucking unknown reason."

"No. You're the only one. Your mom is a friend of mine. She's a good lady. I know she loves you so I'm just trying to keep you safe."

"Why is that Wren? Is it guilt?"

"Guilt? No, kid. I don't do guilt. Like I said, your mom is a friend of mine," he said, keeping his voice even and his eyes never wavered from mine. I'd heard Wren could be an asshole and people in this town feared him, but I'd never seen that side of him.

"Well, she's not making enough money at the diner to keep up with Grams medical bills. I need these fights so I can help her out." I hated the desperation in my voice, but I knew I needed him if I wanted to make this happen.

"You're giving the money to your Mom?"

"Yeah. Why wouldn't I?" I hissed with irritation. I hated kissing his ass. But until I knew for sure if he'd hurt my mom, I'd keep my thoughts to myself. Ma did not appear frightened by him, but then again, she was a tough lady who never showed fear, so how would I know?

"All right. I want Clyde to run the fighters by me, and I choose the refs for your fights. Fair?"

I searched his gaze, trying to find an ulterior motive. I came up empty.

"Fair. Thank you."

I backed away and walked toward the door.

"Hey, Jett," he called out.

"Yeah?" I turned to look at him.

"I'm not the enemy."

I nodded.

But I didn't know if that were true or not.

"Why are you being so stubborn? Shaw and Jax agreed to come. You're being such a baby." Adelaide huffed, as she skimmed a rock across the lake with absolute precision. Damn. I'd taught the girl well.

We weren't even hiding how much we hung out these days. She'd become part of my daily life at this point. We even found reasons to spend time together on the weekends. I knew her mom wasn't a fan of mine, and I'd yet to hang out at her house. But we spent a lot of time out at the lake and a lot of time hanging out with our friends, now that the two groups had sort of come together.

"Did you seriously just call me a baby? Listen, I know your mom doesn't like me, and it's her party."

"My mom doesn't know you, Jett. And it's not her party, it's our party. There will be a ton of people there and you don't even have to see her if you don't want to. But she's not a mean person. She'll be perfectly nice to you, because that's who she is. She'd never let you know if she didn't like you, at least not in public." She laughed.

I didn't laugh.

Those were the kind of people I avoided.

Fake people who didn't let you know whether or not they liked you. This town was filled with them.

Yes, Adelaide had shown me a side to Willow Springs that I didn't even realize I actually liked, and I'd be lying if I said I hadn't had fun the day she took me around to show me her favorite places.

But the Edington home was not somewhere I was dying to visit; however, it had become impossible to stay away from this girl, and I was learning quickly that I didn't like saying no to her. Hell, I'd never been someone who struggled with doing what I wanted. But when it came to Adelaide, I found myself in a gray area.

All the fucking time.

"Good to know. Fine. I'll come." I rolled my eyes, because I knew I was playing with fire letting her get this close.

But I didn't know how to stop.

"Yay," she squealed, and I couldn't help but laugh because she was ridiculous. "So, I finished my essay last night and submitted it."

I tugged on the rope that held the hammock between two trees to secure it, before she dropped to sit down on it.

"Yeah? How'd it come out? Did you think of a negative experience to write about or did you sell out and tell them what they wanted to hear?" I asked, picking up a piece of rope that was lying on the ground before sitting down beside her. She always tipped into me because I weighed a lot more than her and I didn't mind it one bit.

"Nope. I didn't sell out. But I probably won't get in because I was honest." She shrugged.

"What did you write about?"

"My whole life. How I lived in a bubble up until a few weeks ago, and now I'm just…I don't know, discovering who I really am? I don't know how to put it into words." She looked at me and smiled, and my fucking chest squeezed.

What the fuck was up with that?

I'd never had a best friend who was a girl, but somehow, she'd managed to become that for me.

I looked down at the rope between my fingers. One side was sealed, and the other had started to fray. "You're kind of like this rope, right? Your whole life you've been like this," I handed her the sealed edge, and she ran her fingers over it. "But eventually all ropes fray if they aren't lying dormant. You're just fraying a little later than the rest of us. But it means you're living."

She took the rope from my hands and her fingers grazed mine, sending a zip of electricity coursing through me. She held the frayed edge in her hand. "You're exactly right. And once they start fraying, there's no stopping them."

"There's no stopping you, Ace."

She nodded and bit down on her bottom lip. I shifted away a bit because I had an overwhelming urge to taste her sweet mouth. To pull her on my lap and feel all her soft curves against me. To tangle my hands in her thick, dark, silky hair.

I pushed to my feet abruptly and she fell over on the hammock.

What the fuck was this girl doing to me?

She burst out in laughter as she pushed herself to sit up. "A little warning next time would be nice. But thanks for the pep talk. Can I keep this?"

"Of course. It's a scrap of rope." I rolled my eyes.

"Not to me. It's so much more. I think I'll put it in the Magic Willow book as a symbol of what's to come for me."

My head tipped back. Her little girls club was important to her, and as ridiculous as I thought it was—I was happy she had friends who seemed to genuinely support her.

"Lenny and Violet will be at the party. He thinks you're his new best friend so I'm sure he'll be thrilled to see you," she said, pushing to her feet and smirking at me.

"Damn. I jumped his car *once* and the dude texts me daily to let me know all the shit that's wrong in his world now."

A wide grin spread across her face. "He likes you."

"Come on. The suns going down. We need to head out." I started walking toward my bike and she followed.

"This is my favorite part of my day, you know? Hanging out here," she said.

I glanced over and she didn't look at me. I noticed a pink hue climbing up her delicate neck and covering her cheeks as the last bit of sun shined down on her. Hell, I understood it. It was the best part of my day when I was with her too.

"Yeah? Well don't get too attached to this place. We're both off to bigger and better things in a few months." My words came out harsher than I'd meant them to, and they had a hell of a lot more meaning behind them. It wasn't just this place that we'd grown attached to. It was one another. And we needed to proceed with fucking caution.

"You're going to miss it here more than you think you will," she said, turning to face me when she stopped beside her car.

"No time to miss things, Ace."

She nodded. "Well, I'm glad you're coming to the party tomorrow even if you refuse to admit that you're actually excited."

"Excited is a strong word." I chuckled. "Your mom will probably be shooting daggers at me, and Lenny will complain about the color of the sky, and I'm guessing all the magic musketeers will be there documenting my every move, and god knows what your dad thinks of me."

Her head cocked to the side and she smiled, raising one brow like a smart ass. "Trust me…the magic *willows* were documenting your every move long before now. My mom shoots daggers at everyone that isn't in her inner circle, so don't take it personal. My dad is not who you think he is. He's goofy and funny and he followed your every stat in football, so he might go all 'fan-girl' over you. And Lenny will just be Lenny, which I think you actually like deep down."

I couldn't help but laugh. Damn, I'd never been one for laughter, but this girl had me feeling all sorts of things I'd never felt before. Which was exactly why I shouldn't be going to this party. Hell, the smart thing to do would be to find a new place to hang out. She was invading my world—and it was all consuming.

"It's getting dark. I'll see you tomorrow."

She hopped in her car and waved as she drove past me. I didn't know if Adelaide felt the pull between us like I did. Hell, I was a teenage boy with raging hormones. I'm sure this was one sided. I hoped it was. Because I wasn't about to act on it. I knew better. I just hoped she did too.

Shaw insisted on picking me and Jax up so we could all drive to the Edington's together. He knew me well. Knew I'd try to get out of it. These type of social gatherings were not my scene. Not by a long shot.

"I think it's nice that you're going to the Edington's party. I've heard their house is stunning and they go all out on these things," Ma said, as I chugged some orange juice right from the container and set it back in the refrigerator, just as she swatted me with a dish towel. "Jesus, Jett. Use a glass."

"Sorry, Ma." I kissed her cheek.

"Your grandfather always did that too. Not the worst thing in the world. Is that what you're wearing to the Christmas party?" Gram asked, shaking her head as she looked me up and down.

"Yeah. What's wrong with it?" I glanced down at my dark jeans with a few tears in the knees, black hoody and leather jacket. Hell, this was as dressy as I got.

"In my day, a gentleman wore a suit to a fancy party." Gram ran her hands down my jacket as if she were trying to press out the wrinkles. Leather didn't wrinkle as far as I knew.

"Who said I was a gentleman?" I winked and wrapped my arms around her.

"You may pretend to be a...what do they call that these days? *A bad-boy.* With your leather coat and your motorcycle. But I know who you are, Jett Stone. You've always been soft on the inside," Gram said reaching up to pat her bony hand against my cheek.

"That's our secret." I teased, as I heard the honk coming from out front. "All right. That's Jax and Shaw. I'll see you later."

"Don't forget the apple pie. Gram made it special for you to bring," Ma said handing me the box Gram had packaged the pastry in, and I cringed. I wasn't about to offend Gram, but this wasn't a date. It was friends hanging out. Shaw and Jax were going to have a fucking field day when they saw me carrying a pie.

"Thanks, Gram. Love you." I kissed them both on the top of their heads and jogged out the door with the box in hand.

Shaw whistled when I jumped in the passenger side. "I see we're wearing our best jeans. And please tell me you brought cookies."

"Are we trying to impress the Edington's for some reason?" Jax asked, pushing his head between us from the back seat and poking at the box.

I flipped them both the bird. "Gram just chewed my ass out for wearing these jeans. Definitely not trying to impress anyone."

Except for Adelaide, maybe.

"And the reason for the baked goods?" Shaw smirked.

"Gram baked them a pie. What the fuck am I supposed to do? Break her heart?"

"Nah. I'd do just about anything Gram asked. But you and Addy sure do hang out a lot these days. Coco told me she goes out to the lake with you every day after school. You sure there isn't something going on there?" Shaw asked, glancing over at me with a dumbass smile on his face.

"I'm sure. We're friends. We're both leaving for school soon. I'm not about to get into something when I'm leaving." I looked out the window as we pulled up in front of their house. The house was lit up on the outside like something you'd see in a magazine. A huge display of nine reindeer and a sleigh holding Santa sat on their roof. White lights covered the outline of their home. And light up candy canes lined the walkway.

Jesus. I was so out of my element here.

"Don't overthink it, Dude. I'm seeing Coco, and we're both leaving at the end of summer. So what? Why not enjoy the time you've got?" Shaw asked, parking a few houses down from Adelaide's house.

"I agree. Lydia and I are having a damn good time lately. It's just something for right now. Doesn't have to be forever." Jax unbuckled and hopped out of the car.

Adelaide was not a right-now kind of girl. I'd had a bunch of those over the years. She was definitely a forever type a girl. And that wasn't an option for me. Nor should it be for her. Hell, she just got out of a lifetime of misery with Taulson. This was her time to figure out who she was and what she wanted.

"Thank you for your input, *Ladies*. But I know what I'm doing. You two dickheads don't think before you act," I said, taking in the endless poinsettia potted plants on our way up to her front porch.

"Maybe you should stop thinking so damn much. Dumb it down a little," Jax said over his laughter.

"Dumb it down? That's your brilliant advice?" I rolled my eyes as a woman pulled the door open and stood in the doorway staring at us.

Mrs. Edington. Everyone knew her. She's what you'd call Willow Springs royalty. She was pretty, in that rich, stuck-up way. Her dark eyes landed on me and her gaze moved from my feet up to my face. I suddenly felt very underdressed. Adelaide said casual, and this was my idea of casual. Her mom wore a red dress that looked like something a first lady would wear to an acceptance speech. Clearly the jeans weren't working for her and I wished she'd move her gaze to my two asshole best friends who were dressed worse than me, but instead it settled on the pie.

"Hello, Jett. Addy said you were coming. You must be Shaw and Jax?" She said, moving her icy gaze off of me and onto the two dudes beside me. *Thank Christ.*

I wasn't sure why she was giving us so much attention, as she clearly had a houseful of people behind her. The place looked packed from where I was standing, which was still out on her front porch.

"Boys, boys, come on in," Mayor Edington said, holding a glass of something that made him appear much jollier than the ice queen. "My god, dear. You've got them standing out in the cold. And is that a pie?"

Mrs. Edington rolled her eyes and then smiled at her husband before taking the pie from my hands. "Take it easy on the eggnog, handsome. Thanks for the pie, Jett." Her tone was much softer when she spoke to him.

"Sure. My grandmother made it for you, and she sends her best." I wouldn't remind her that they'd known one another their whole lives, as she used to babysit my mom.

"Well, please thank her for me and send her my best." She turned to face Mr. Edington and he told her he'd join her shortly.

He invited us inside. "You had quite a season. Are you all planning to continue playing ball in college?"

"Yep," we all said in unison as we stood awkwardly in the fancy entry way.

"Jett, I hear you have a few offers you're entertaining?" he asked, putting all his attention on me as Coco came up and wrapped her arms around Shaw and winked at Jax and I.

"Yeah, we'll see what happens. I've verbally committed to TU and that's my top choice."

"Good for you. That's where I went," he said. "They have a lot to offer on top of having a fantastic football program."

"Oh my god, Daddy. Please, stop. Are you grilling them?" Adelaide walked up behind her father and the air left my lungs. She wore fitted skinny jeans and some kind of wrap around black sweater that hugged her curves in all the right places. Of course, she had on her favorite booties or shooties or whatever the hell she called those things. Her dark hair was in a ponytail with soft waves tumbling down her back. She looked sexy as hell and she made it look effortless. Her little sister walked up behind her and made googly eyes at me, and I used my hand to cover my smile because I didn't want her to think I was laughing at her. But she was ogling all three of us and she made no effort to hide the fact that she liked the way we looked.

"I'm not grilling anyone, Ladybug. Just making small talk."

"Okay, Ellis. Let the kids go to the basement. Clementine, stop staring at them like that. It's not ladylike. Adelaide, you must have some heels you could put on with that outfit instead of those worn boots. And Coco, borrow some pants from Addy. I fear your legs are going to get a bit cold in that *short skirt.*" Mrs. Edington said when she walked over and tugged at her husband's arm.

"The definition of ladylike is a matter of opinion, Mama. A woman can appreciate a fine looking man if she wants to." Clem winked at me, and I no longer hid my laughter. The kid was hilarious. Adelaide talked about her often but seeing her in action was even better.

Their mother rolled her eyes and pulled her husband into the group of people beside us. Adelaide shook her head and her gaze locked with mine. "Sorry about that. Let's go downstairs."

"Um, are we going to talk about the fact that your Mama just slut shamed me?" Coco said over a fit of laughter. "Jesus. I don't know how you two live under that judgy gaze of hers."

"Preach," Clem said in an awkwardly high tone and fist bumped the sky.

When we got down to the basement a few of their friends were already there. Gigi came over and greeted us and Ivy and Ty were sitting on the couch. I liked him a lot more when his asshole friend wasn't around. Adelaide had told me that the Taulson's had left for Florida today as we were officially on winter break. I was relieved I wouldn't have to deal with him tonight. Maura sat beside them on the couch and waved us over.

"Hey," Adelaide said, walking close enough that her hand grazed mine as we made our way across the oversized basement that looked more like something you'd see in a magazine.

"Hey. You look nice." Jesus. Who was I? I sounded like an asshat. But I couldn't stop myself from telling her. She looked fucking gorgeous just like she always did.

"Thanks. You, too. Sorry about my parents. I hope they weren't too nosy."

"Nah. They were good. Your dad said you told him about my offers. You been talking me up, Ace?"

Her cheeks pinked and my head fell back with a chuckle. I couldn't help it. She was so damn cute.

She smiled and covered her eyes with her hand, as if I couldn't see her standing right there in front of me. "I may have bragged on you a little. But I didn't ogle you the way Clementine did."

Now we both laughed.

"Did I hear my name?" her little sister moved beside me and wrapped her arm through mine. "Nice to see you, Jett Stone. You're looking mighty fine tonight, if I don't say so myself."

"Um, I believe you've made that very clear already." Adelaide's eyes were wide when she looked at her sister.

"Someone's a bit jealous I think?" Clementine taunted.

"Um, hate to interrupt this awkward family moment, but my mother just texted me and told me that your mother said I could borrow some pants. What is her deal?" Coco looked down at her short, tight black leather mini skirt. "They're legs, not boobs. You show more in your cheer skirt. Why is your mother stirring the pot?"

"Our mother was born stirring the pot," the two sisters said at the same time.

"Ignore her. You look amazing," Adelaide followed up.

"Oh, I'm ignoring her. No offense. I'm not taking fashion tips from Savannah Edington or Cricket Radcliff. The day I dress like them, I'd like you to strip me naked and force me out in the cold." She looked over her shoulder and winked at Shaw and we all laughed.

I moved to sit beside Adelaide on the couch, and we all sat around shooting the shit and laughing. Clementine did a brief speech about women no longer being repressed and told us she planned to take over the world someday. Maura told us about how her parents had gone off on the drive over here tonight because they ran into the Carlisle's at the liquor store when they stopped to grab some wine for the party.

"I mean, this war between the two families is so ridiculous I don't even think they know what they're fighting about," Maura said with a shrug.

"Isn't it all over the land? Didn't their family steal land from your family?" Gigi asked, reaching over and snagging a cookie.

The coffee table was loaded with sweets, and a buffet table ran along the back wall with nachos and meatballs and all kinds of finger foods.

"I guess so. It's been going on since before my father was born. You should have seen the way my dad hissed at Mr. Carlisle."

"I've heard tales that it all started over a woman. That the older Mr. Carlisle was in love with your great grandma," Ivy said, raising a brow at Maura.

"I don't even know. I'm too afraid to ask because my dad gets so worked up at the mention of their family. He claims they robbed us blind back in the day."

I wanted to laugh. Mauras' family, the Benson's, were loaded. One of the wealthiest families in Willow Springs, as were the Carlisle's. So, why'd they care if they all ended up with a shit ton of money?

"We need to get to the bottom of that," Coco said.

"Not tonight." Ivy brushed her hands together as if she were off the clock.

It was impossible to miss how close the five of them were. And, surprisingly, I didn't mind being here at all.

At this point, it appeared I'd find just about any reason to spend more time with Adelaide.

fifteen

. . .

Adelaide

THE PARTY WAS WINDING DOWN. At least for us basement dwellers. Gigi was heading home with her parents to go see her brother who was due home from college in an hour. Maura wanted to go hang out with Kyle who'd also just gotten home from school. Coco, Shaw, Ivy, Ty and Jax were going down to the lake to meet some other kids at a bonfire. Willow Springs never had a dull moment. I wondered if Jett would leave with them, but he hadn't said anything yet.

It had been a fun night. We'd eaten too much, shared stories and laughed our butts off. I was happy that we'd spent some time tonight with both of our friends, as I wanted my girls to know him the way I did. I could tell they all liked Jett a lot, which made me happy. I didn't know what we were, but I liked being around him and I wanted my friends to know him better. Alec always complained when we spent time with my friends, and it had always bothered me, but I'd assumed that it was just a guy thing.

Turns out it was an Alec thing.

"Stone, are you coming or staying?" Shaw asked.

Jett cocked his head to the side and studied me and I

couldn't help but smile, which must have meant I wanted him to stay because that was all he needed.

"I'll stay and help her clean up a bit. I'll call you tomorrow."

"Good. Coco's driving so I can have a few beers at the bonfire. Take my truck home and you can come get me in the morning." Shaw tossed his keys to Jett, and he caught them and dropped them in his pocket.

We said our goodbyes and moved to sit on the sofa again. "You want to watch a movie?"

"Sure," he said, and I reached for the remote.

"Oooh, Elf is on. That's my favorite Christmas movie. Do you like it?"

"Never seen it," Jett leaned back against the couch. "Let's watch."

For the first time since we'd been hanging out, I was nervous. It felt more like a date. And I didn't mind it at all. Every time I said goodbye to him, I missed him. It was strange. I'd never experienced that feeling before, and I'd had a boyfriend for years.

I missed Jett Stone when I wasn't with him.

The feeling was foreign to me. And it didn't scare me. Now that I was discovering who I was, and what I wanted—I was learning to trust my instincts for the first time in my life.

And I wanted Jett.

I didn't know what that meant. But I knew a few things.

I trusted him in a way I'd never trusted anyone outside of my girlfriends. I could tell him anything and he'd listen to what I had to say, and he would protect it at all cost.

I desperately wanted to kiss him. I wanted to feel his lips against mine. I thought about it whenever we were together. And whenever we were apart. I'd never really craved anything physical before. Alec and I had obviously made out more times than I could count, but it never left me wanting more, aside from feeling some sort of obligation to eventually do more. Like a right-of-passage. But what I felt, sitting here next to this boy, was different.

So incredibly different.

It took everything I had in me not to move closer. To reach for his hand. Press my lips to his.

Who even was I?

I'd never had these kind of thoughts before, well, not since I'd started hanging out with Jett. I didn't know if he felt the same way about me. He'd never acted like he wanted anything more than friendship. But this pull I felt toward him had been consuming me more than ever the last few days.

I sat rim-rod straight on the couch throughout the entire movie. Clem came back down to check on us and said she was going up to bed because the parents were acting "loopy and embarrassing."

The movie ended and Jett pushed to his feet. "I should probably get going, Ace."

"Yeah, it's late. Sorry for keeping you so long."

I grabbed my coat and followed him out the back door. We walked a few houses down toward Shaw's truck. I didn't know why I was walking with him all the way to the truck. Maybe to make the night last a little longer.

"Well, now I need to walk you home." He chuckled as he fiddled with the keys and stood beside the truck.

"Don't be silly. I'm fine." I shifted from foot to foot trying to think of something to say to make it last longer. Music trickled out from my house as the party was still going strong.

"They're going to keep it going, huh?" he asked, reaching forward to tuck a piece of hair that had slipped from my ponytail behind my ear.

I reached for his hand and held it there. My heart was beating so hard and fast that I was certain he could hear it. I closed my eyes for a minute, holding his big hand in my small one.

"Do you ever think about kissing?" I opened my eyes and was horrified that I'd said those words aloud. What was I thinking?

"About kissing? Kissing who? Random people?" he smirked.

My cheeks heated with embarrassment and I pulled my hand away. "Ignore me. I don't know what I'm talking about."

I turned on my heels and started to walk away, because I wanted to go bury my head under my pillow and die a slow death of humiliation.

"Ace," he called out and I turned around to face him. "Don't leave like that. Come here."

I slowly made my way back to him but kept some distance between us this time. "What's up?"

He chuckled. "I was just messing with you."

"About?"

He cocked his head to the side and reached for my hand. "I think about kissing you, too."

My heart raced faster, and butterflies swarmed my belly. I wiped the palms of my hands on my jeans because even though it was cold out, I was suddenly sweating. "You do?"

"All the fucking time." He smiled.

What was the problem then? I'd just given him the green light.

I stepped closer. "Okaaaayy…"

"Listen. Just because we want to, does not mean that we should."

I let out a long breath I hadn't even realized I'd been holding. "Why?"

"Because I'm not that guy. There are things you don't know about me—about my family. And I'm leaving for school in a few months, so I couldn't give you what you deserve." His gaze locked with mine under the moonlight, and I swore in that instant Jett Stone was the most beautiful boy I'd ever seen in my life.

"I'm not asking for forever, I'm asking for a kiss." I crossed my arms over my chest because I was determined to make this happen. Just this once. I wanted to feel his mouth on mine. Run my hands through his hair, and feel his hard body pressed against mine. Hell, I'd been dreaming about it for weeks, and now that we were here. This close.

He studied me and reached for my hand. "That's not who you are. We both know that."

"I have kissed one boy in my life, and he promised me this grand future that I didn't even want. One that he clearly didn't want either. I'm tired of planning for tomorrow. Maybe I just want to kiss you today—and not have a plan. What are you so afraid of?" I saw the panic in his dark gaze, and I wanted to know. I needed to know.

"I'm afraid that once I start kissing you, I won't want to stop." He tugged me closer, wrapping a hand around my waist. My sweater creeped up a bit and his fingers grazed my skin.

"That doesn't sound so terrible," I whispered, and it came out all shaky and laced with need. My breaths were coming hard and fast and he hadn't even kissed me. My mouth went completely dry as he held me against him, staring down at me with his dark, beautiful gaze. I felt just how much he wanted me as his desire pressed against my belly.

"Maybe we just take it one day at a time." His fingers moved beneath my chin and tipped it up until my eyes locked with his.

"I'm fine with that. And if you want to kiss me tomorrow, I'm sure that would be fine too." I laughed and shook my head because I couldn't believe what a dork I was.

"Oh, you're already wanting more when I haven't even tasted that sweet mouth yet?"

Oh my god.

Jett Stone had a way with words, and I was all about it.

"You can kiss me whenever you want as long as you aren't kissing anyone else at the same time, because ewwwww… that's gross. Have you been kissing anyone else?" I asked, because I needed to know.

"Not since you came to the lake and took over my quiet place," he smirked.

Interesting. I'd been going there for almost two months.

"Okay, then. My sweet mouth is all yours," I teased, but I could barely feel my legs anymore because I was so nervous.

"You haven't been kissing anyone else, have you, Ace? No bootie calls from Taulson?" His mouth was so close I could feel his warm breath tickle my cheek.

"I haven't talked to him in a few weeks, and I have no desire to kiss anyone but you."

"Yeah?" His lips grazed mine and my eyes fluttered shut. His hand hooked around my waist, and I was pretty sure he was fully supporting my weight because I'd lost all feeling in my legs.

"Kiss me, already," I whispered.

His mouth crashed into mine, and he spun me around, pressing my back against the truck. He lifted my feet off the ground and my legs wrapped around his waist, keeping us at the same level and making it easier to take the kiss deeper.

My fingers tangled in his hair like they'd been itching to do, and one of his hands was pressed to my bottom holding me in place, while the other cupped the side of my face so gently it sent chills down my spine. He took his time, and tilted my head to the side as his tongue slipped in.

He tasted like peppermint and I laughed against his mouth as I thought about how he'd tortured me sucking on that candy cane during the movie.

He pulled his mouth away, and I yanked at his hair to keep him in place.

"Are you laughing?" He chuckled against my mouth.

"No. You taste like a candy cane and I kept thinking about kissing you the whole time you were eating that thing during the movie."

He rubbed his nose against mine. "Oh yeah?"

"Yeah," I whispered.

I pulled him closer and took control of our kiss. My hips were grinding against all his hardness, and…Oh. My. God.

Nothing had ever felt so good. I could kiss this boy forever and it still wouldn't be long enough.

He groaned into my mouth before pulling away.

"Okay, I'd say this was a damn good first kiss," he said, his lips still teasing mine.

Now that I'd had a taste of Jett Stone, I never wanted to stop. "Why are you stopping then?"

"Trust me, it's not because I want to." He started walking toward my house, still carrying me with my legs wrapped around his waist. My head fell back in laughter.

"Oh my gosh, what are you doing?" I nipped at his ear with my teeth and he yelped.

"I'm walking you home after the hottest fucking kiss of my life." His gaze locked with mine and he didn't laugh.

"That was something. Maybe it's because we've both been thinking about it for a while?" I covered my eyes with my hand when I realized what I said. "I mean, I've been thinking about it for a while."

He stopped at my back door leading to the basement and set me on my feet.

"I've been thinking about kissing you since you gave me half of your peanut butter and jelly sandwich in third grade." A wide grin spread across his handsome face.

"You lie. You weren't thinking about kissing me back then." My fingers gripped a fistful of his hoody beneath his leather coat. The fabric kept me from exploring him the way I wanted to.

"I don't know, Ace. That was a damn good sandwich."

I smiled. "Are you going to let me kiss you tomorrow?"

"Already thinking about tomorrow, huh." He pulled me into a hug and wrapped his strong arms around me. I buried my face in his neck and breathed him in. He smelled like pine and fresh water, if that's even a thing. It was my new favorite scent.

"One day at a time."

He pulled back and opened the door. "Go. I'll call you tomorrow."

I pressed up on my tiptoes and kissed him one more time, needing to feel his lips on mine just to make sure I hadn't dreamed this whole thing up.

"Good night, Jett Stone."

He walked backwards, watching me like he was trying to memorize every curve of my face.

"Night, Ace."

And then the darkness swallowed him whole and I walked inside. I made my way upstairs to the main level, and laughter and loud chatter surrounded me. It was nearly midnight and this party was still going strong.

I climbed the next set of stairs and saw the light on in Clem's room, so I peeked inside. "You still up?"

"What happened? Did he kiss you? Man, oh man, you two were putting off some serious heat!"

My head fell back in laughter. "I did kiss him. Go to bed."

"Addy," she called out as I started to close her door.

"Yeah?"

"You never looked this happy when you were with Alec. It's nice to see you doing what you want these days. You were so much more boring when you were living in mom's shadow."

I smiled. Because she was right. At least about the part that I was happier now than I'd ever been. And it felt damn good.

"Thanks. I'll see you in the morning. Love you," I said.

"Love you, too."

I pulled the door closed and made my way to my bedroom. I washed my face and slipped on my pajamas before reaching for my phone to send a group message to the girls.

Me ~ Emergency meeting in the morning. Donuts at my house. I have news.

Coco ~ It's about time. We all bailed on the party so you two could stop pretending to be besties, and admit you like each other.

Gigi ~ I cannot wait for the deets.

Maura ~ Dying.

Ivy ~ Morning can't come soon enough. I'll bring the notebook. It's senior year girls. Looks like we are filling this book already.

Me ~ See you in the morning. Love you.

They all responded with an *I love you text,* and my phone vibrated as I set it on my nightstand.

Jett ~ Is it tomorrow yet?

My stomach dipped and I bit down on my bottom lip as I tried to think about how to respond.

Me ~ Tomorrow can't come soon enough. You want to meet at the lake in the afternoon?

I stared at the three little dots as they moved across my screen.

Jett ~ How about I pick you up at noon and we go to the diner for lunch? I want to feed you first.

Me ~ First? What happens after?

Jett ~ I kiss you until your lips are swollen and aching.

Me ~ Yes, please.

Jett ~ One day at a time, Ace.

Me ~ As long as I get to kiss you again, I don't care what day it is.

Jett ~ Sweet dreams.

I fell back on my bed and touched my lips with the tips of my fingers. They were still tingling from where he'd kissed me.

Left his forever mark.

Me ~ *They're already sweet… and I haven't even fallen asleep yet.*

I wasn't normally so gushy. But Jett Stone brought something out of me. He'd awakened parts of me that I didn't even know existed.

And I only wanted more.

sixteen

. . .

Jett

I PULLED up in front of the Edington's home and parked my bike. I walked to her door which again made it feel more like a date, which was not something I'd ever really done before. I wasn't normally one for picking a girl up, but Adelaide was different. Everything about her was different.

Including kissing her.

I'd never kissed a girl and felt like she'd marked me.

Adelaide Edington had marked me.

In the best fucking way.

I'd had sex with girls and walked away without a second thought. But just kissing this girl had made me want things I had no business wanting. Hell, I'd barely slept as the thought of her soft lips made it tough to sleep. My dick was still having a temper tantrum even after I'd given him sufficient attention. So, I wasn't going to overthink it. I liked hanging out with her, and I was not going to fight it.

Was I playing with fire even letting things get this far?

Sure.

But for the first time in my life, I wanted something that didn't involve getting the hell out of this shit town, and I was going to let myself enjoy it. There were very few things in

Willow Springs that I enjoyed outside of the few people I was close to and football—but Adelaide Edington was a blind spot that I hadn't seen coming.

I knocked on the door and let out a long breath hoping that her mom wouldn't open the door.

"Hello, hot stuff," Clementine said, pursing her lips and batting her eyelashes.

I couldn't help but laugh, just as her father stepped up behind her and rolled his eyes at his youngest daughter.

"Jett, hello. Come in. Ladybug will be right down. Her girlfriends just left." I assumed this was a nickname he had for Adelaide as I'd heard him call her that last night.

Shit. I wasn't planning to go inside.

Family small talk was not my thing.

"Hey, sure. Thanks." I shoved my hands in my pockets and followed him inside. Clementine winked at me, and I winked right back. The girl was a character for sure.

"Agree with everything my mother says and you'll be fine," she said under her breath when she leaned close to me. "And if not, I've got your back."

I nodded and fought back the urge to laugh because she was funny as hell the way she conspired against her mother.

"Sweetheart, you remember Jett. He was here last night for the party. He and Addy are going to grab lunch at the diner," her father said. He appeared to be a nice dude. No airs about him.

Her mother was a different story.

"Ah, yes. The football player, right?"

"Sure," I said, trying to hide my irritation. I was more than a football player, but I wasn't about to debate that with Adelaide's mom.

"Your mom is a waitress at the diner I believe?" she asked. She knew my mom worked at The Rusty Pelican. This town was small, and Ma had worked there for as long as I'd been alive.

"Mother. She is a food server, not a waitress. Jeez. That's so 1990's of you," Clementine hissed, and I wanted to high five her for sticking it to the ice queen.

I cleared my throat. "Yeah. She's worked there for years. Pretty sure you two know one another. She said you used to babysit for her when she was young." Before you fucking dropped her and judged her for bringing a child into the world on her own.

"Yes, I knew Mae before—you know, before we both had families of our own." She crossed her arms over her chest as if she were preparing for battle.

"I love Mae. She's the reason I even go to the diner. No offense. The foods just okay. But your mom is super cool," Clementine said. "I didn't know you knew Mae when you were young, Mama. You never said anything."

Damn straight. I wanted to hug Adelaide's little sister for calling her out.

"There she is," Ellis Edington said as his oldest daughter entered the room and I finally took a full breath. She had a way of calming me. Just her presence. It did something to me.

Her gaze ping ponged between her mother and me, and I didn't miss the concern. "When did you get here? Why didn't anyone tell me he was here. You didn't have to come in."

She reached for my hand and led me out of the kitchen.

"Will you be gone long?" her mother asked, as they all followed us to the door. Jesus. They were so involved. I wasn't used to that. Sure, Ma and Gram were in my business, but not to this extent. Not even close. I wondered if she did this when that asshole Taulson was around.

"I don't know. I'll call you. Love you." Adelaide led me out the door and they followed. Her fingers intertwined with mine.

"Nice to see you," I said, waving with my free hand and winking once more at her little sister.

"Wait. Are you driving on that monstrosity?" Her mother hissed as we made our way to my bike.

"Mom. I'll wear a helmet. We're taking side streets and only going two miles away. Relax."

"They'll be fine," her father said, waving at us as she slipped on my bike. It was awkward as fuck having them stare at us as I fastened the helmet beneath her chin.

"I'm down for a ride anytime you want to take me around the block, Jett Stone," Clementine shouted, before her mother pulled her in the door and closed it behind them.

Thank, Christ.

"Sorry," Adelaide said, searching my gaze.

"Don't be."

I climbed on, and her arms wrapped around me. Her hands slipped beneath my leather coat and fisted my hoody, while her head rested against my back. I took off for the diner, pushing away all the negative thoughts I had about her mother. About the way she looked at me when she spoke of my mom. A reminder of why I wanted out of this place. The irony was not lost on me.

People like Savannah Edington were the reason I hated this town. But her daughter had quickly become one of my favorite things about Willow Springs.

I pulled in front of the diner and climbed off my bike, before leaning down to help her remove the helmet. Her dark eyes locked with mine and she didn't move from the seat.

"Did my mom say something?" she asked, reaching for my hand.

"No. What little she said your sister put her in her place for."

She smiled. "I'm sorry. I don't know why she's like that."

"Don't apologize for your mother, Ace."

She pushed to her feet and we made our way inside the diner. My mom hugged us before leading us to my favorite booth in the back. "So, this is a nice surprise. I didn't see you last night. You got in late. How was the party?"

"It was great," I said and turned to see Adelaide's cheeks all flushed.

"It was fun. Nothing out of the ordinary happened. It was all—ordinary. Very normal," she said, and my mom and I gaped at her.

I doubt my mother suspected anything was going on before now, but it was impossible to miss how nervous Adelaide was at the moment.

My mom's head fell back with a chuckle. "Good to know it was all very normal. I love a normal party."

"Oh my gosh," Adelaide whispered and shook her head. "I mean, it was good. *Really good.*"

Her gaze locked with mine and I couldn't help but laugh along with my mother. She'd managed to make things worse. Her cheeks were bright red, and her tongue dipped out to wet her bottom lip.

"Okay. Let's do two burgers and two chocolate shakes," I said, trying to rescue her from herself and end this conversation. She'd already told me that's what she always ordered when she came here for lunch. And I was a damn good listener when it came to Adelaide Edington's likes and dislikes.

"Two very normal burgers and shakes coming up." My mom winked at Adelaide before walking away.

"Oh my god. I don't know why I said that?" she whispered, shaking her head and laughing.

"Don't sweat it. It's an acceptable reaction after kissing me."

Her cheeks flamed even brighter, and my head fell back in laughter.

"Whatever. I barely remember," she said, smiling up at my mom as she set down two chocolate shakes with whipped cream and sprinkles.

"Hey, I have an idea. I mean, you had Jett over last night. Why don't you come by for dinner with Gram and I tonight? I know she'd love to see you." Ma stood there with a big smile on her face and I rolled my eyes. Normally I'd be pissed if she pulled a stunt like this, but I didn't mind if Adelaide came over for dinner tonight or any night honestly.

"I'd love to. Thank you."

Once the devious little matchmaker walked away, I chuckled. "So, you barely remember huh? Shall I refresh your memory after lunch?"

A wide grin spread across her face and she shrugged. "Sure. You can give it a shot."

"Check please," I threw my hand in the air and teased—but I was dead fucking serious. I couldn't wait to have my mouth on hers again.

We both laughed and my mom studied me as she set the two burgers down in front of us.

"Everything okay?" she asked.

"Yep. I forgot we were meeting some friends down at the lake, so we're in a bit of a hurry."

"All right. Well, eat up and get a move on, then. I'll see you both tonight for dinner." She shook her head with a chuckle and walked off.

"You in hurry?" Adelaide took a bite of her burger and tried to hide her smile.

"Hell, yeah I'm in a hurry." I wolfed down my burger and stared at her as she took one bite at a time.

Her head fell back in laughter and my phone buzzed on the table just as hers did the same.

"It's Shaw. He and Jax are heading down to the lake with Coco, Ivy, Ty, Maura, Kyle, Lydia and Gigi." I laughed. Such an unlikely group, but we'd all been hanging out a lot lately.

"Yep. I got the same text. Do you want to go meet them?" She studied me before biting down on her plump bottom lip.

I gripped the table to stop myself from leaning over and taking her sweet mouth right there.

"No. Do you?"

"No," she laughed. "Maybe we can all hang out tonight."

"That sounds good. You ready?" I asked, anxious to get the hell out of there.

"Yep." She sent a quick text, and we made our way out to my bike. I drove to our favorite spot on the lake, and the wind whipped around, as her hand fisted the hoody against my stomach.

And I fucking loved being with her.

When she got off the bike she started running. "I call dibs on the hammock."

I rolled my eyes. "It's my spot. You can't call dibs." I dropped down to sit beside her, and my mouth was on hers before I could even think about it.

This girl had become my drug of choice. I craved her. Thought about her when we weren't together. Like some sort of fucking junkie.

Her fingers were in my hair, and a little moan escaped her mouth, as my tongue dipped in tasting and exploring. She fell back on the hammock, pulling me along with her. Her hips grinding against mine, and I nearly came undone right there. I kissed her until my lips ached. Until I was so hard my dick was ready to explode. I pulled back, pushing the hair out of her pretty face. Her dark eyes were wild and needy. Her lips swollen and red. Her chest rising and falling, and I just stared down at her. Needing to take her in.

What the hell was happening to me? I was not the poetic, romantic type. But Adelaide brought something out in me that I hadn't even known was there. And all I saw was beauty and goodness when I looked at her. I wanted more, but I knew better. We needed to slow down. One day at a time.

"Why'd you stop?" Her words came out all breathy and needy, and I adjusted myself as casually as I could seeing as though I was propped on one arm, trying to keep us from tipping out of the hammock.

I slid beside her, and carefully shifted her so we were lying side by side facing one another. "There's no rush, Ace."

She nodded. Her cheeks pinked. "Okay. Is this normal for you?"

I laughed. "Is what normal?"

"I don't know. The way you kiss me. The way we are together." Her gaze searched mine. Pops of amber and gold sparkling as the sun shined down on her. She looked like some sort of angel lying there acting like I held the answer to all life's questions.

"There's nothing normal about the way I kiss you. The way you kiss me. The way we are together."

She nodded. "Okay, good. Because this is…very different from anything I've ever felt."

I smiled, couldn't fucking help myself. "Yeah? I think it's called desire," I teased.

"I think you're right."

My phone buzzed, and I reached for it in my back pocket. I read the text from Clyde and rolled my eyes. "Jesus."

"What's wrong?" Her fingers stroked my hair and I wanted to close my eyes and get lost in all things Adelaide Edington. Her touch could heal the fucking dead.

"Goddamn, Wren. I have a fight tomorrow night, and he's holding it up because he doesn't like the guy I'm fighting. I don't know what the dude's problem is."

"Wren? Why does he care?"

"He owns the fight club. He's always in my business and it pisses me off. He said he wouldn't stop me from fighting, but here we are."

"Why does he care who you fight?" Her gaze locked with mine and I could see that she genuinely wanted to know.

I scrubbed a hand down my face, trying to decide how

much to share. Hell, I never talked about this shit with anyone. Not even Shaw and Jax.

"If I tell you something, you have to promise me you won't tell a soul. Not even the Magic Musketeers."

She pushed up on one arm, so she was propped above me. "*Magic Willows.* And I promise. Your secrets are safe with me, Jett Stone."

"I think Wren might be my dad. I mean, I don't know. He's just always hanging around and I don't know why he gives a fuck what I do, but he's always there."

Her jaw dropped open before she clamped it shut, and it was adorable how she tried to pull herself together and compose her reaction. "Has he always been there? Or is this new?"

"No. He's always been around but I never used to mind it. I mean, the fighting is new, so I'm definitely feeling him hovering around me much more now."

"Why do you mind it now?" she asked. So, fucking perceptive. A reminder that I wasn't used to hanging around people that asked questions. People that cared about what I did and how I felt.

"I have my reasons." My words came out harsher than I meant them too. That shit was not something I was ready to share. Not now. Maybe not ever.

She didn't back down. She nodded and cocked her head to the side. "Why don't you just ask him? Or better yet, ask your mom."

"I can't ask my mom." I shook my head. "It's a sensitive subject for her."

"Then ask him."

I nodded. I honestly never thought about asking him. Would he tell me the truth? Probably not. How do you own up to that shit?

"Maybe. Enough about me. What do you want to do? If I keep kissing you, I think we'll both end up naked in this hammock and you aren't ready for that." I teased. "So, tell me Adelaide Edington. What do you do for fun?"

She giggled and my fucking chest nearly exploded. Jesus. This girl was turning me into some sort of sappy asshole.

"I just finished reading Hunger Games and was going to start Twilight. Have you read it or seen the movies?"

Now it was my turn to laugh. "Have I read Twilight? No."

"It's supposed to be amazing. Let's read it together. I have the kindle app on my phone." She reached in her back pocket and I shifted to keep us balanced. "I'll read the first chapter aloud and you can take the second."

I rolled my eyes. "As long as I get to kiss you between chapters, I'm game."

And we spent the next several hours lying in hammock next to the water, all bundled up and huddled together to keep warm reading about Edward Cullen and Bella swan and the whole vampire, human romance.. We made out a couple dozen times and took turns reading.

And I'll be damned if it wasn't the best day of my life.

Better than winning football games.

Better than winning fights.

Better than breathing.

seventeen

. . .

Adelaide

CHRISTMAS BREAK WAS OVER, and I was not looking forward to getting back on my routine. I'd spent every single day of break with Jett. I'd never craved another person the way I craved him. Like I couldn't breathe when he wasn't there. Nothing felt right when he wasn't there.

We'd hung out with our friends almost every night and had a big New Year's bonfire out by the lake. It had been an amazing couple of weeks. He'd given me the sweetest Christmas gift which I hadn't expected at all. He made us each a rope bracelet that he'd burned to seal the edges. He said it was a reminder that it was okay to fray, and part of finding my way. I decided that the being sealed part was how I felt when we were together. Like everything made sense. He listened to me. Cared about my hopes and dreams. We'd talk until our mouths hurt, and then we'd kiss until our lips ached. He'd never tried to take things further, but truth be told—I'd never wanted to take things further more than I did now. He'd awakened something in me that had been lying dormant before now. I'd never wanted anyone the way I wanted him, and that terrified me.

I wondered how our first day back at school would be. I

hadn't seen or talked to Alec in weeks. My mom kept me updated on him, as she talked to Mama T every single day. Usually more than once. I heard them conspiring a few times and rolled my eyes. My mother told Mama T that I was spending a lot of time with Jett. I'd had dinner at his house a few times now with his mom and Gram and I loved every minute I spent with them. His house was full of love and acceptance. You could feel it when you stepped inside. He'd yet to come have dinner at my house, and I was ready to rectify that. My mom made him uncomfortable and I understood it. She made me uncomfortable most of the time too.

I drove Clem and I to school in the bug and we'd picked up Gigi on the way. We stepped out of the car and Alec was standing there as if he were waiting for us.

"I guess King douchebag is back," Clem whispered and we all three chuckled.

I stepped out of the car and he moved toward me. Clem and Gigi waved, and kept walking. "Hey, Addy. Good to see you."

"Yeah. You, too. Did you have a nice time in Florida?"

"Sure. I missed you though. Ty told me he hung out with you a few times. Said you and Jett are together now? Is that true?" He shoved his hands in his pockets and his blue eyes searched mine.

I knew Ty was in an awkward position. We'd all hung out a lot over break and Alec was his best friend. He wouldn't like Ty being friendly with Jett and I'm sure he would punish him for it. Alec had a vindictive side to him that I hadn't seen often, but I'd seen it enough times to know it existed. I'd always thought it was something he'd outgrow with maturity but looking back I think I made excuses for the things that I didn't like about him. I just accepted them because I thought I was supposed to.

"Yeah. It's true." I crossed my arms over my chest and squared my shoulders. I didn't owe Alec an explanation nor did I need his approval. But it would sure make life easier if he didn't make this into a big deal.

"Interesting. How long has this been going on? Did it start when we were still together?"

I rolled my eyes and shook my head. "You're unbelievable. You cheated on me, Alec . This is new, and I owe you nothing. So, you don't get to ask me questions about my relationship."

"Your *relationship*? Give me a break. That dude doesn't date. He'll just try to fuck you and then leave you for someone new."

"No, I'm pretty sure that's your MO," I hissed, aggravated that I was even having this conversation.

"If you fuck him, I swear to god, Addy, I won't forgive you."

I fell forward in laughter. "*You won't forgive me*? Are you kidding me with this? You cheated on me. Multiple times. We're done. I am dating someone and I'm actually happy for the first time in—" I paused because I didn't want to be cruel. But I was happy for the first in forever. Everything felt right. Not forced. Not convenient. Not comfortable. Not arranged. What I had with Jett was exciting and passionate and real.

I looked up to see Jett standing with Shaw and Coco thirty feet away watching me. He wasn't storming over in a jealous rage, but he was making sure that I was okay. He tipped his chin up. Letting me know he'd jump in if I needed him to. My stomach fluttered just like it always did when I was around him.

"I'm not fucking around, Addy. I made a mistake. You need to get over it."

"No. You need to get over it. Move on, because I have." I turned and walked away. I was done with this conversation. There was nothing left to say. My hope was that we could find a way to be friends once all of this settled.

"You okay?" Jett asked, lacing his fingers with mine like it was totally normal. When this school year started, I'd never have thought in a million years I'd be here. Holding hands with Jett Stone just a few months later. But just the simple act of reaching for my hand…it settled me. He had a way of doing that without even trying.

"Yeah. I'm good."

"I'd like to smack that kid upside the head," Coco hissed. "How did you date him for so long?"

I shrugged. "I honestly don't know."

And that was the truth.

The four of us caught up to Ivy and Ty who appeared very uncomfortable about walking with us. Alec wasn't going to make this easy on anyone. But it didn't matter. Because his opinion was no longer a factor in my life.

The next few weeks went by in a blur. I'd applied to a few more schools because I'd come to the conclusion that I didn't want to go to Texas State. I didn't know if I had a chance of getting into TU as I'd gone rogue on my essay, so I was going to have a back-up plan.

"You have a birthday coming up." Jett and I were sprawled out in the hammock facing one another and he played with the rope bracelet around my wrist. My mother hated it. I think the twine represented the new me in a way, and she wanted nothing to do with it. She continued to go to all of Alec's basketball games with Mama T, and I found it disheartening. She'd barely attended her own daughter's cross-country races, but she'd support Alec to the ends of the earth. My father didn't go with her anymore, and I'd heard them arguing about it several times. It was hard for me to wrap my head around the fact that my parents were basically fighting because I'd ended my relationship with Alec. Jett was right—her obsession with it was not normal.

"Good memory." I smiled up at him.

"You brought heart cookies and cupcakes every year to school for as long as I could remember. Of course, your birthday is on Valentine's day. It's very—"

"Very what?" I asked, and my tongue dipped out to wet my bottom lip.

"It's very Adelaide Edington of you." He laughed.

"I have to say, I don't mind having a birthday on Valentine's day. I wish we'd been together on your birthday though." Jett's birthday was in September. I'd always remembered it because he had always been the first birthday in elementary school when we were growing up. His Gram was a great baker and she'd always make delicious treats for the class. Jett was the first in our class to get his driver's license.

He was born to lead.

"Oh yeah? What would you have done if we were together?" His fingers moved to my hair, brushing it out of my face. My heart raced at his touch. It always did.

"I'd have kissed you every time I saw you," I chuckled. But I meant it.

His mouth came over mine, and I tangled my fingers in his hair. I couldn't get enough of this boy. His hand glided up my side, grazing my breast and I arched into him. I wanted more. But he was insistent on taking it slow. Everyone that looked at Jett saw this rugged football player, a fighter, a bad boy on a motorcycle…but I saw him for who he was.

Gentle and kind.

Patient and honest.

I loved everything about him. How he made me feel.

Safe and wanted.

Cherished and loved.

He tipped me back as he hovered above me, taking our kiss deeper. His hand slipped beneath my cardigan and tank top and his fingers traced the hard peaks over my lace bra. He cupped my breast and squeezed as he moaned into my mouth. I grinded up against him, and I could feel how much he wanted me, because I wanted him just as badly.

His hand moved behind me and unclasped my bra. His fingers took turns teasing each of my breasts and my breathing was out of control. I grinded up against him as the most sensational feeling took over my body. An unbelievable need burned inside me. His hand moved down to the waist band of my jeans pausing at the button.

"Is this okay?" He whispered between labored breaths.

"Please," I whispered.

He continued to kiss me as he slipped his hand down, teasing my most sensitive area over my lace panties. My hips bucked and moved of their own volition. Grinding up against his hand.

"Let yourself go, Ace." He covered my mouth with his after he spoke.

I gasped as the most intense orgasm ripped through my body. I'd never known I could feel that good from just kissing. And touching. But here I was, writhing beneath all his hardness as I rode out every last wave of euphoria.

"Oh my god," I whispered, covering my eyes with my hand.

This was embarrassing, right?

We hadn't even had sex, and here I was crying out my release like a fool.

He pulled my hand away from my face. "Don't cover yourself from me, ever. That was fucking beautiful. I'll be rubbing it out to visions of you coming apart just grinding up against my hand for years to come. No pun intended."

We both laughed and I shook my head. "That's never happened before. I mean, with another person."

Oh my god. Stop talking. Shoot me now.

"That's because you dated a selfish prick—so, of course you had to touch yourself because he was too lazy to do it for you. I love giving you pleasure, seeing you come apart like that."

"One day at a time," I whispered, wrapping my arms around him and settling my head on his chest as he adjusted my jeans and rolled me on top of him.

"So, what do you want for your birthday."

"I have everything I want," I said, staring down into his gorgeous dark eyes. It was the truth. Jett and I were together. I had amazing best friends. I was figuring out what I wanted in the future and making it happen. Aside from the distance I felt from my mother, I'd never been happier. I wished she could be happy for me.

His hands reached behind my back, beneath my top, and I shivered. "Just fastening your bra." He chuckled at my reaction.

"You were pretty smooth the way you unlatched it so quickly," I said, trying to hide my smile.

His gaze studied mine. "Was it okay that I did that? I mean, I know it felt good, but I don't want to push you, Ace."

"You're the one holding back, not me. I'm ready for more. I'm ready for everything." I raised a brow, demanding him to tell me differently.

"Not holding back. Trust me, I've never wanted anyone the way I want you. But I want to do it right, you know? You deserve that. You deserve everything."

He stole the air from my lungs with his words. He had a way of doing that to me.

"You know what I want for my birthday?"

"What?" He smiled up at me and my stomach dipped.

"I want you to come to my family birthday dinner. Mama always makes my favorite, and I want you to be there."

He nodded. "Done."

"Thank you. She's really not that bad, I promise." His body tensed beneath mine, and I ran my fingers over his arm to help him relax. My mother had been pretty awful to him every time he'd come over to pick me up and the few times he'd come to hang out in the basement and watch a movie. I went to Jett's house much more often. It was small and cozy, but most importantly, I was welcome there. I felt it every time I walked through the door. I hated that my mother didn't treat him the same way. My father and Clem loved Jett.

I wanted to tell him that I loved him, but I was afraid to say it first. I didn't know if he felt the same way. He treated me like he loved me. I now knew the difference. Alec never loved me like this. He loved me like I was his possession. Something that belonged to him. Not something he cherished.

With Jett everything was different.

"There's nothing I wouldn't do for you. Doesn't really matter if your mom likes me. It only matters if you do." He stroked my hair, and I closed my eyes.

"I do. I like you a lot," I said. Wanting to say everything. Tell him how much I loved him.

"I like you a lot too, Ace."

He pulled out his phone and he read me another chapter from Twilight. We were on the third book, and it had sucked us both in, even if he wouldn't admit that he liked it. We'd watched the first movie together as well.

I settled against his chest, listening to the steady beat of his heart as he read the most romantic book of all time to me.

And I wished I could freeze this moment in time because I never wanted it to end.

The girls and I were meeting downstairs for our usual catch up. I waved to my mom who was on the phone with Mama T, per usual when I walked in. I pointed to the basement to let her know the girls were meeting me downstairs.

"Thirty minutes, Adelaide," Mama said as she covered the phone with her hand.

I nodded and jogged downstairs just as Gigi and Maura came in. Coco and Ivy were right behind them and we all settled in our usual spots.

Ivy dropped the enormous book on the table and laughed. "We may need two books for senior year."

"Good. Then we're doing what we're supposed to be doing," Coco said, leaning back on the couch and propping her feet on the table.

"Okay, who wants to start?" Ivy asked.

"Kyle and I are calling it quits." Maura shrugged and Ivy paused before writing it down.

"What?" I asked. "You guys seemed so happy over break."

"We were. But he's staying at school this summer for an internship and I'm leaving for school in the fall. We're still going to talk all the time, I'm sure. And I'll see him when he's home. But it's too much pressure trying to keep a relationship going when I have no intention of going to TU. I didn't even apply there, not that I'd get in. So, it's just not realistic."

"Are you okay with it?" Gigi asked.

"I am. He said he'd still come take me to prom if I wanted him to, but I don't know if that's the best idea. I think we both need to put a little distance there, you know?"

"Okay. Maura is on the market," Ivy said, scribbling into the book as she wriggled her brows.

Maura's head fell back in laughter. "I'm hardly on the market. I think I just want to enjoy these last few months together and head off to college with no attachments, you know?"

"Good. We can be the only single ones together," Gigi said, wrapping an arm around her shoulder.

"Well, I guess I should say it. Ty and I had sex. The deed is done. The canary has landed. Yadda yadda. Boom." Ivy folded her arms over her chest and stared at us as if she'd just told us the weather.

Coco squealed and jumped to her feet. "I'm shocked. You were hanging on to that V card like Addy's mom is holding on to hope that she and Alec will get back together." She bellowed out a laugh at her own joke. "Tell us everything. How was it?"

"I'm not a girl who kisses and tells, but I will say this…it was so much better than everyone said it would be. Ty is, well, he's amazing. And he wrote me a song, you guys." She paused and placed a hand on her chest. Ty was a budding country singer. It started with him singing in church when we were growing up, but a music producer had discovered him last year and he'd started performing at a few country music festivals over the last few months. His voice was amazing. "It was worth the wait for sure. But I don't want to talk about it anymore, because I think it should be something that is just for Ty and me."

"Damn. You're all so virtuous. Paste that V card right in there and date it," Coco said, before falling back on the couch. "Well, I'm thinking of taking the plunge with Shaw. He is just so…I don't know. Hootttt."

I laughed. "You really like him, huh?"

"It's not like you and Jett. But it's pretty damn awesome," she said.

"What do you mean?"

"I mean that you two are just oddly connected. I never saw that with you and Alec. You never seemed like you fit to me. It always seemed so forced. It looked good on paper, but there was nothing really there. You never laughed together or seemed like you had deep conversation. But you and Jett…"

"I have to agree, Addy. I need a cold shower whenever I'm around you two. The way he looks at you—it's…something to see." Ivy fanned her face with her hand.

I couldn't hide my smile. Because that's how I felt. "I really think I love him, you guys. I've never felt anything like this before. I may have said the words to Alec, but this is the first time I've actually felt it. It's that can't live without you kind of love, which is scary because we're taking it one day at a time." I shrugged. I loved that I could say anything to them and never had to worry about being judged.

"You could both end up at the same school," Gigi whispered, because she knew my parents didn't know yet that I'd applied to several schools. Mama had refused to discuss it, and we weren't speaking much about anything lately.

"Maybe. He's signing his letter of intent at TU this week, and that's a long shot for me."

"What does Jett say?"

"He says I should go wherever I want to go and shouldn't consider anyone else when making my decision. He encouraged me to apply to more schools and have options. But we don't talk about the future. We made a deal at the start of this, that we would take it one day at a time. I never had that with Alec. It was always expected that I'd go along with his plan. He wanted me to go to the school that he wanted to go to. He never considered what was best for me. Jett is so different. He wants the best for me."

"That's how it should be," Coco said. "And he's not even trying to get in your pants. Damn that boy is something."

I shook my head and felt my cheeks heat. "Well, it's become challenging for me not to beg for more. The way he makes me feel…" I said, shaking my head and trying to tamper down my thoughts.

"I'm happy for you. You deserve this," Maura said, leaning over and squeezing my hand. "How about your mom? Is she still being a royal bitch to him?"

"He's coming over for taco's tomorrow night for my birthday. His mom has me over all the time, and he's never come to dinner with my family. My dad and Clem love him, but my mom is still desperate for me and Alec to get back together. I wouldn't get back together with Alec even if Jett weren't in the picture. There's nothing there. I just had to step away to realize that. I wish she'd just be happy for me."

"That woman has such a stick up her ass, she wouldn't know happiness if it slapped her in her botoxed face." Coco huffed.

"I'm putting that in the book," Ivy said through her laughter.

"What's happening with you?" I asked Gigi. "Is Hayden still trying to get you to go out with him?"

"I guess. But I think we're just friends. He came over to watch a movie, and oh my gosh, I wanted to kill Cade and Gray. They came in and grilled him. And then that stupid ass, Gray, plopped down right in between us and reached for the popcorn. Cade went off to bed, and Gray just sat there like the bastard that he is, for the entire movie." Gigi huffed. Her older brother Cade's best friend, Gray Baldwin, was a thorn in her side. We all thought he was charming and funny. Gigi not so much. She despised him.

Coco's head fell back in laughter. "Gray totally cock blocked you."

"Oh my gosh, you are so crude. There was nothing to block. Hayden's kissed me once, and there was nothing there. But that doesn't mean Gray needs to involve himself. Ugh. I can't stand that kid."

"He is hot though," Maura said. "And if you get into TU, you'll have to deal with him."

"Don't remind me. It's been my dream school forever, but I don't know if I have the grades to get in. And the only negative thing about going to TU is that freaking Gray is there. I don't know how that dipshit got in there, anyway." She closed her eyes and clenched her jaw. "It would be so cool if you and me went there together, Addy."

My stomach dipped. We both definitely had the grades. Gigi was fifth in our class, so we were fairly similar on GPA's and we'd both killed it on our SAT's, but I was worried about my essay. I should have just answered it the way I knew they wanted me too. Instead, I'd decided to be totally honest, and that just might be the nail in the coffin that kept me from going there.

"It would be amazing. We could room together. But I don't want to get my hopes up." I shrugged.

"I'm pretty set on Dallas. They have an amazing fashion design program. I can't wait to see where we all end up going."

Ivy shut the book and glanced up at us, eyes watery. "I can't believe we're down to these last few months together."

We all leaned forward and grasped hands, as my mother shouted down the stairs that it was time for dinner.

"The warden beckons. Love you guys," Coco said as we all pushed to our feet.

"Love you," we called out, before they walked out the door.

I took a minute to gather myself. I needed to tell my parents that I had applied to several schools and I had no intention of going to state. My mother thought I was bluffing when I'd mentioned the idea of going elsewhere.

But I was dead serious.

I just had to find the right time to tell her.

eighteen

. . .

Jett

I'D TOLD Adelaide to meet me out at our spot on the lake after school. We didn't have AP Calc today, and I'd had my mom call me out of English a few minutes early so I could come out here first. I wanted to surprise her for her birthday, so I grabbed the flowers from Violet's floral shop on my way over. When she found out they were for Adelaide, she added a few more of her favorite flowers to the bouquet. I'd never bought a girl flowers before aside from Ma and Gram.

I'd also bought her a bracelet which even surprised the shit out of me that I'd thought of it. Shaw and Jax had gone with me and helped me pick out the charms, razzing me the whole time about it. I wasn't sure if it was a stupid idea because we were supposed to be taking this one day at a time, but that shit had gone out the window a few weeks ago. I was all in on this girl. I'd never felt anything close to this and I didn't know what to do with all these feelings. But just like I knew to look out for Ma and Gram as early as I can remember or the way I knew what to do the first time a football was placed in my hands—I knew in my gut that this was right. This thing with me and her was the first thing that felt right in my life in a long time. And it made no sense.

Adelaide and I being together made no sense.

We came from different worlds.

But right now, I wasn't going to question it. I was just living in the moment. And she made me feel like a fucking king. Being with her ignited things in me I'd never experienced, and I didn't mind it at all. Feeling thankful, feeling joy, those weren't part of my usual demeanor. But fuck it. I was going to feel all of it for as long as I could.

"Jett?" she called out, and I pushed to my feet, shifting around like some sort of dorky, romantic, shithead.

"Hey, I'm down here." My gaze locked with hers and she started running my way. She wore a white dress that hit her mid-thigh, a jean jacket and her favorite cowboy booties. And she looked fucking gorgeous.

She whooshed into my chest, and I caught her. "Why'd you leave school early? I got your note to meet you out here."

I laughed and set her down on her feet. "I wanted to give you your birthday present."

If anyone had told me six months ago that I'd be picking up a certain type of flower and personalizing a bracelet and going to all this trouble to make it special for a girl—I'd have called them crazy. But here I was. Doing all the things I thought would make her smile. Hell, I hadn't even slept with her, and I wanted to give her everything.

She worked hard at everything she did, and she listened better than anyone I'd ever known. She hung out with people like Lenny and Violet just because she knew they needed a friend. She was good to her very core. And I fucking love that about her.

I'd told her things I'd never shared with anyone. Not everything, obviously, or she'd be running for the hills. But I shared parts of myself I'd never thought I'd be comfortable sharing.

So yeah, I was going to make an effort to make her birthday special. That included having dinner at her home and kissing her mother's ass because I knew it was important to Adelaide. Never thought I'd go that far for a girl. But I was just getting started.

Her gaze moved from me to the hammock where a bouquet of flowers sat surrounded by some sort of tan paper with a ribbon around it.

"Oh my god. You got me peonies?"

I shrugged. "They're your favorite, right?"

"Yeah. I can't believe you remembered." She moved over and picked them up, pulling them to her nose and breathing them in. Long dark waves tumbled over her shoulders.

"I love them. Thank you so much. That was so thoughtful. You aren't trying to get out of dinner, are you?" She chuckled.

Hell, I wish I could. I wasn't looking forward to it.

"Nope. I wanted to give you your gift before we were at dinner. I'm not big on doing things with an audience." I reached in my pocket and handed her the little box from Saxe Jewelry Store.

Her jaw dropped. "There's more?"

I chuckled. *This girl.* She'd be happy with me just coming to dinner. Giving her a bracelet made of twine. I didn't come from money, obviously, but I'd covered rent for mom this month and I'd pulled in an extra fight this past week to pay for the bracelet. I was happy to spend it on her. And I had a fight tomorrow, so I'd have more money coming in soon.

She opened the box and tears sprung from her eyes as she took in each of the charms hanging from the delicate gold bracelet. There was a book charm because I knew she loved to read, a little laptop charm because her passion was writing, a willow tree charm because she loved this godforsaken town, and my jackass friends convinced me to add the little gold jet charm as a reminder that it was from me.

"Jett," she croaked. "This is…it's gorgeous. I love it so much. Thank you."

A tear ran down her cheek and my fucking chest

squeezed. I wasn't a sappy asshole, but something about this girl had a way of bringing me to my knees with no warning.

"Happy birthday, Ace."

I helped her clasp the bracelet around her slender wrist, and it sat next to the tattered rope bracelet that I'd made her for Christmas, and she'd never taken off. I'm sure her mother was having a field day with that monstrosity.

"I," she paused, and looked up at me with so much adoration it nearly took my breath away. Dark eyes watery and full of emotion. "I love you, Jett Stone. I really love you."

My tongue dipped out to wet my bottom lip. Hell, I hadn't expected that. Not because I didn't feel it. I did. But love was a dangerous emotion. One that could cripple you if you allowed yourself to feel it too much. Too intensely. But I couldn't stop myself from saying it, because I'd be a liar if I didn't admit I felt the same way. And I was a lot of things, but a liar wasn't one of them.

"I love you, Ace. Happy birthday."

I went home to change because I knew her mother would have me under a magnifying glass, so I may as well not give her more ammunition to work with than necessary.

When I held my hand up to knock at the Edington's door, it whipped open before I even made contact.

"Hey there, Handsome. Are you ready for the shit show?" Clementine said, before her head fell back in laughter.

Damn, she definitely was the rebel of the family.

I fucking loved it. Every family needed one.

"I'm ready." I smirked.

"Jett, happy you could join us for Ladybugs special day." Mayor Edington was a genuine guy who adored his family. It was impossible to miss.

"Thanks for having me." I shoved my hands in my pockets and looked up to see Adelaide's mom staring at me.

"Come. Sit." Savannah Edington said, leading us into the dining room before shouting up the stairs for Adelaide to come to dinner. I didn't miss the edge in her voice and alarm bells were going off. She was up to something and her husband seemed completely unaware, but Clementine locked eyes with me as if she were thinking the same thing.

"Hey," my girl said, coming over and wrapping her arms around my middle. "Thanks for coming. Here, you can sit next to me."

We dropped down to sit. Her father sat at the head of the table and her mother and sister sat across from us.

"Forgive us, Jett. My daughter requested her favorite, chicken tacos, not the most elegant meal. But it's her day." Her mother shrugged, and I gazed around at the platters of rice, beans, chicken, chips, tortillas, cheese, guacamole and salsa. The woman didn't do anything half ass, that's for sure.

"No problem. I love tacos."

"So, I hear you're signing your letter of intent with Texas University this week?" Her father asked.

"Yep. It feels good to know where I'm going," I said, and Adelaide beamed up at me.

"Ah…I understand that. I thought Addy knew where she was going as well, but she mentioned now that she doesn't know if she wants to go there. After all our years of planning." Her mother's tone was hard, and her cold stare landed on me.

My hand found Adelaide's thigh beneath the table. She placed her hand on top of mine to let me know she was okay.

Classical music played lightly through the surround sound in the dining room, and the elegant setting didn't match the casual dinner on the table nor the tension that stirred in the air.

"You're bringing this up now?"

"Well, it seems Jett has something to do with this new found interest in spreading your wings. You're going back on everything we planned, Addy." Her mother turned her attention to Adelaide and I shifted in my chair with discomfort. If looks could kill, I'd be diving in front of my girl to take this bullet for her.

"It was never my plan. It was just something you said for as long as I can remember, and I never said anything different. But there's nothing wrong with changing the plan, Mama. I'm young. You should be encouraging me to chase my dreams." Adelaide dropped her fork on her plate and the loud clank startled everyone.

"*Chase your dreams?* Don't be so dramatic. Let me ask you, Jett. Is this your doing? Are you a dream chaser?" Her tone was laced with sarcasm.

"Oh my god," Adelaide shouted, and tossed her napkin on the table. "Of course, you think it's his fault. I've been trying to talk to you, Mama, but you don't listen. I don't want to go to the state school. I've told you that, but you end the conversation and walk away."

"You never had a problem with it before you broke up with Alec," her mother hissed.

"Mother, do you hear yourself? This isn't about Alec. Nor is it about Jett. This is about *me*. I'm really happy because I'm finally finding my way. Why can't you embrace that?" A tear ran down Adelaide's cheek, and I squeezed her thigh, wanting to pull her onto my lap, but afraid that would put her mother over the edge. I scooched my chair closer, our legs touching, and wrapped an arm around her shoulder to comfort her. I couldn't help myself.

"Listen. It's Ladybug's birthday dinner. We have a guest. This is something that can wait until later, yes?" Her father spoke, and apprehensively looked up at his wife.

"I think it's fairly simple," Clementine spoke up. "Addy is tired of being told what she wants, and she's finally making choices for herself. And it's about time. Women have been repressed long enough, am I right?"

"Oh Clem, please. I am in no mood for one of your ridiculous speeches. Can you save it for later?"

"Mama, if everyone stayed silent and waited for a convenient time, there would never be change." Clementine rolled her eyes before winking at me.

"You okay?" I asked, looking at Adelaide who sat completely still in her seat. She nodded.

"She's fine. What's that on your wrist, next to the dirty rope?" Her mother asked, staring at her daughter.

Adelaide stiffened, and looked up to meet her mother's gaze. "It's a charm bracelet from Jett. Isn't it beautiful?"

"Ah, so nice. Very thoughtful." Her father nodded. But it was obvious that everyone was on edge.

"What are the charms?" Clementine asked, cocking her head to the side, and smiling.

"There's a Willow tree, a little jet," Adelaide said, turning to look at me. I pulled my arm back and started eating again as everyone at the table had gotten back down to business as if they hadn't just had a huge argument. "A book because I love to read and a laptop because I want to be a writer."

Clank.

Now it was her mother's turn to drop her fork on her plate and cross her arms over her chest. Her face flushed red, but she didn't speak. She looked like she might explode, and her husband put his hand on her shoulder.

What the fuck was her deal? This was all because she wanted to be a writer? Why the fuck did that piss her off? Mrs. Edington was three shades of southern crazy. I wanted to tell her that arranging a marriage for your child and deciding how their life would play out before they were even born was an ass backwards way of thinking. But it wasn't my place, so I fought the urge to call her out.

"You're a great writer, Addy. You could lead the charge for all women," Clementine said, over a mouth full of chicken.

"Manners, dear," her mother hissed. She didn't eat again and stayed quiet the rest of dinner, as she continued to sip her wine.

Adelaide's father asked me some more about my plans with school and football, and my girl relaxed a bit beside me.

We all cleared our plates, and Savannah Edington brought out a chocolate cake with sprinkles all over it. "Happy Birthday and happy Valentine's day, Adelaide. I love you."

"I love you too, Mama," she said, and I saw the sadness in her eyes.

There were a whole lot of head games going on at this table, and I knew that her mother was not done with the conversation, but she'd wait until I was gone.

We ate cake and Clementine told us all about her argument with Principal Walker and how he declined her offer to host a women's rights protest on campus. My head fell back in laughter as she called him a pretentious, stubborn, jackass.

"I've had enough, Clem. Help clear the table and head up to take your shower please. It's been a long day." Adelaide's mother pushed to her feet and started clearing the table.

We all stood, and I helped clear my plate, but Mrs. Edington shooed me off and told me she had it covered. I definitely got the vibe she wanted me to leave.

"Addy, you need to get your homework done and get showered as well. It's getting late."

Adelaide rolled her eyes and pushed up to kiss my cheek. "Let me run to the bathroom and grab my coat, and I'll walk you out."

I made my way toward the front door, ready to get the hell out of this house.

"Thanks for having me," I said to her parents and her sister, as Adelaide ran up the stairs and I grabbed my leather coat.

"Thanks for coming, Jett. Please come by more often." Her father said.

Clementine hugged me and her cheeks pinked. I ruffled the top of her head because the kid was fucking adorable. A little hellion, but charming as hell.

"I'll walk you out, I'd like to speak to you," Adelaide's mother said, reaching for her jacket. Wow. She wasn't waiting for her daughter to return, she wanted me out of the house now.

We stepped out on the front porch, and she crossed her arms over her chest. "Listen, I don't know what game you're playing with my daughter, but it's run its course."

Her hard stare had me squaring my shoulders. This wasn't a goodbye-thanks-for-coming-to-dinner, this was a goodbye-get-the-hell-out-of-my-daughter's-life. Jesus, this woman could give Wren a run for his money when it came to intimidation. Lucky for me, I didn't intimidate easily.

"Not playing any games, Mrs. Edington."

She nodded. "All right. You want to do this. Let's do it. Addy tells me you're a smart kid. You and I both know you're not good enough for my daughter. Your mother got knocked up as a teenager, and you don't even know who your damn father is. Sorry, but family matters to me. And I want a hell of a lot more for my daughter."

Holy shit.

The woman doesn't mince words.

And my mother was off limits.

"You know nothing about me. Nothing about my family."

"That's where you're wrong, Jett. I know exactly who you are. And you may have dazzled my daughter because she's a little lost right now, but your shtick doesn't work on me. You're only going to college because you can throw a ball. And I'm sure you'll manage to screw that up too and follow in your mother's footsteps with a dead-end job. There's nothing more I need to know. The apple never falls far from the tree." She shrugged.

My hands fisted at my sides. "Thankfully the apple falls far from the tree in *your* home. Your daughters are nothing like you, and you can't stand that she has a mind of her own. Tell Adelaide I had to go. I'm done with this conversation."

"You best be done with a lot more than the conversation, Jett. Stay away from my daughter, or I promise to make your life a living hell."

I jogged down the steps and didn't stop until I got to my bike. I was still in shock. Savannah Edington had never been kind to me, but this attack was a stretch even for her.

I started up my bike and saw Adelaide running toward me with confusion. "Hey, my mom said you had to run. But I wanted to say goodbye to you."

I didn't meet her gaze. "Grams not feeling well. I need to get going."

She reached for my hand and intertwined her fingers and moved her head in front of mine to meet my gaze. "Okay. Text me and let me know she's okay. I love you."

"Will do." I pulled my hand away and revved my engine before taking off and leaving her standing there. I should never have told her I loved her.

I should have never started this with her.

Because now it would hurt like hell to walk away.

But her mother was right. I wasn't good enough for Adelaide. That's the one thing we could agree on.

I sent a text to Shaw and Jax when I got home, and they were both at my house within ten minutes. We climbed out on my roof, just like we always did, and Shaw pulled a beer out of his coat and handed it to me.

"How did dinner with the in laws go?" he asked over a chuckle.

"Not fucking well. Her mother is a psychopath. She went all gangster on me and told me to stay away from her daughter. I should never have started this shit up with Adelaide. We don't fit. I fucking knew better." I tipped my head back and slammed the beer. The cool liquid hit my system and I relaxed a bit.

"Fuck that," Jax said. "Are you kidding me right now? Everyone knows Addy's mom is a haughty bitch. She doesn't know what she's talking about. Tune that shit out."

But there were things even Jax and Shaw didn't know about me. Things I didn't want anyone to know. Especially Savannah Edington because then the whole damn town would find out. That wouldn't be fair to Ma. Hell, she didn't even know that I knew her secret.

"Come on, brother. You've never let anyone tell you who you are. Addy is crazy about you. And keep in mind her mother wanted her to date that piece of shit, Taulson. She's clearly a poor judge of character."

"We don't fit. She's right about that much." I shook my head, tipping back the last of the beer in the can. "Why the fuck do I have to love the one girl that I shouldn't?"

Jax's eyes doubled in size. "Holy shit. I didn't know you loved her. I never thought I'd see the day. That icy heart of yours finally softened."

I flipped him the bird.

"Listen, Jett. People in this town can be judgmental little shits, and Addy's mom is the leader of the pack. But anyone who knows you—they know you're a winner. Why else did thirty-two schools try to recruit you, huh?"

"Because I can throw a fucking football." I rolled my eyes, wishing he had another beer tucked in his coat pocket.

"Bullshit. You're fucking brilliant, and you know it's true because I would never compliment you unless it were absolutely necessary," Shaw said through his laughter.

"What are you going to do?" Jax asked, and I saw the empathy when I met his gaze.

"I'm going to take a step back and try to figure this shit

out. We're both leaving for school soon, and I'm guessing she'll be staying here and going to state if her Mom has anything to do with it."

"Dude, you know we always have your back, but I think you're making a mistake on this one." Shaw tipped his head back and looked up at the stars in the dark sky. Crickets chirped in the background, but it was otherwise a peaceful night.

"You're right about that. I've made a mistake by letting it get this far. All right, thanks for coming over. I'm going to sleep on it and try to figure this shit out."

"You want me to stay and hang out?" Jax offered, but I insisted I was fine.

I wasn't.

But I'd figure this shit out on my own.

Just like I always did.

nineteen

. . .

Adelaide

I'D CALLED Jett several times last night after he'd left, and he hadn't answered. Clem told me she heard our mother out on the front porch talking with him, but when I'd grilled Mama, she'd claimed they had a pleasant conversation and she'd inquired about his mother and grandmother.

But when he didn't show up to school or respond to any of my texts, I knew something was up. I'd pestered Jax and Shaw all day, and they wouldn't say anything, but I didn't miss the way they kept looking back and forth between one another.

So, here I was. Driving to his fight with Coco, who'd just picked me up and I'd snuck out my bedroom window. It was a school night. Edington's didn't go out on school nights, and certainly didn't attend illegal fights. But I was quickly learning that I was a lot more than just an Edington. And Jett Stone was a part of me. He owned my heart. And I was determined to figure out what happened.

I jumped in the passenger seat of the car and Coco turned to face me. "Okay. I'm going to tell you something. It took a lot to get Shaw to crack, but I think I know what happened."

"What?" I asked, my gaze searching hers for answers.

"Freaking Savannah Edington went all mobster and told him to stay away from you. She said he wasn't good enough, which is ironic, considering she thinks Alec is good enough, and we all know what a douchebag he is."

I shook my head. This was a stretch even for my mother. She wasn't a monster. Sure, she was set in her ways, but to pull him aside and tell him he wasn't good enough. My hands fisted at my sides and I tried to calm my breathing. "What is wrong with her, Co?"

"I think she lets Mama T get to her, and she's probably been chirping in her ear every day about you moving on from Alec. Who knows? But you need to put her in her place, Addy. This is like a bad B movie where the Mama goes all crazy and kills everyone in town because her daughter didn't win the beauty pageant." She pulled away from the curb and laughed.

I rolled my eyes. "You have a twisted imagination. But I need to fix things with Jett first. Mama and I are due for a conversation, but I don't even know if I can talk to her right now. I can't believe she would invite him to dinner and then behave like that. I knew my mom could be snobby, but I never thought she was mean spirited. My father will not be okay with this either."

"First things first. Get your boy back, and then we'll figure out how to deal with your momager."

I laughed now, but a sick feeling settled in my stomach. People like my mother gave Willow Springs a bad name. And Jett might not want to deal with this kind of drama. He might not think I'm worth it. But I was damn well going to make sure that he knew I loved him, and if he was going to walk away, he wasn't going to do it easily because I was going to fight for this.

For him.

For us.

We pulled up at the warehouse and Shaw met us at the

door. "Jesus, Co. You know he's going to be pissed that you brought her here. Sorry, Addy. No offense to you."

"Listen, you're hot as hell, Shaw. And if you're lucky, this thing between us can keep going until we both leave for school. But make no mistake, it's always going to be *Sisters before Misters* with me. *Chicks before dicks. Ho's before bro's*. You get it? This is my girl. She deserves to have a say before he kicks her to the curb."

"Okay, then. You had me at sisters before misters. No need to bring my dick into it." Shaw crossed his arms over his chest.

"Nor did you need to call me a ho." I grumped, searching the space for Jett.

"Addy was coming whether she came with me or not. I wasn't about to let her come alone. So, let's do this."

We followed Shaw up near the front with a good view of the cage. Jax looked at each of us and raised a brow at Shaw. "He's going to kill you. You know that, right?"

"Unless you want a lengthy explanation about sisters and chicks and dicks and ho's, I suggest you drop it. She wants to talk to him." Shaw motioned for me to slip in first and take the seat next to Jax. Coco sat beside me, and Shaw took the end seat.

"Hey, Jax," I said, looking behind me to see if I could find Jett. "Shaw didn't invite me here. I came on my own. Don't be mad at him."

"I'm not mad, Addy. I'm actually glad you're here. He's in a mood tonight and I'm guessing it has a lot to do with what's going on between you two. But he's definitely going to be pissed you came. That's just Jett. He'll get over it."

"I don't really know what's going on between us because he won't tell me. He's ghosted me since dinner last night. But apparently my mother tried to run him off. I'm just surprised he didn't tell me."

"Maybe he didn't tell you because he doesn't want to hurt you," Jax said with a shrug.

"Well, ignoring me hurts a lot more than telling me the truth about my mom."

The crowd moved to their feet as Jett and the other fighter were announced. They made their way out to the cage and my stomach turned as the first round started. Jett was quick on his feet as his opponent went for a leg sweep and missed. They both got in a few hits and kicks, but Jett was definitely dominating the fight. He hadn't looked our way yet and I was grateful. I didn't want to distract him, but I was damn well going to talk to him after. He made some sort of move with his leg and dropped the other guy to the mat. I screamed louder than I meant to, and his head turned in slow motion and he found me. All the air left my lungs when his dark brown gaze locked with mine.

His opponent used the moment of weakness to his favor and flipped Jett on his back, taking control. My heart nearly jumped out of my chest. Jett took a hit to the face and scrambled to get back to his feet.

"Shit," Shaw whispered under his breath and I bit down on my bottom lip. "That was close."

Jett didn't look back over again, as they went into the third round. He came out with a force, dropping the other guy to the mat and using a choke hold. Just beneath his right eye had started to swell and sweat dripped from his forehead. And he looked sexy as hell. I made a mental note that if he ever let met touch him again, I would definitely be inquiring about that tattoo on his left arm.

Jett's opponent tapped out and the fight came to an end, as the crowd went absolutely crazy. Jett was making a name for himself in the underground fighting world, and people came out to see him fight now. I didn't like when he fought, but I found it admirable that he did it to help his mom.

"Holy shit, Addy. He lost his focus when he saw you,"

Coco said, coming up beside me as we made our way down the long hallway to meet him.

"I know. I feel bad. He took a hard hit."

"Maybe it'll knock some sense into him," Shaw grumbled. "Don't back down when he pushes you away. He'll try, trust me. Be persistent. It's the only way you'll get through to him." Shaw wrapped an arm around my best friend, and I nodded.

"He's really just a soft pussy under that badass exterior," Jax said, and I appreciated Jett's friends trying to help me with the situation.

They could have judged me for how my mother had behaved, but they didn't.

But apparently, Jett did.

"Okay," I said.

Jett stormed out of the locker room and pointed his finger at his two best friends. "You fucking brought her here?"

"Her? You can't speak to me now?" I said, moving in front of them to get in his face.

"You shouldn't be here." He crossed his arms over his chest.

"They didn't bring me here. I came on my own because you're being a stubborn ass and you won't take my calls," I hissed, assessing the damage beneath his eye as I spoke.

"Did you ever think that I didn't take your calls because I don't want to talk to you?" he asked, squaring his shoulders and showing no emotion.

Shaw, Jax and Coco turned on their feet and pushed through the doors to the parking lot, giving us a minute alone. The cool air whooshed in, and I poked him hard in the chest with my finger.

"No. I didn't think that. Because typically you don't tell someone that you love them, and then ghost them right after. I know my mom said something to you, and instead of talking to me, you shut me out. You don't like being judged by everyone in this town, yet that's exactly what you're doing to me. *I'm not my mother.* You're a coward, Jett Stone. You walked away the first time things got tough." I stormed out of the warehouse a few steps behind our friends.

He didn't say anything.

He was going to let me go.

When I got to Coco's car, I turned around to see him standing at his bike, running a hand down his face.

"Ace," he called out.

"What?" I shouted, anger still coursing my veins.

"Take a ride with me?"

"Atta girl. You made your point. Give him a chance now," Jax said under his breath, as he stood beside me, his back to Jett.

"Go. Text me no matter how late to let me know you're home," Coco said, shoving at my shoulder.

"I think we found Jett's weakness." Shaw's words were barely audible, but I heard him. I nodded at Coco before walking toward his motorcycle.

"Where?" I asked, standing with my hands crossed over my chest.

"Get on."

I rolled my eyes, but I took the helmet from his hands and placed it on my head, before jumping on the back of his bike.

We took off, and I had no idea where we were going, and I didn't care. I just wanted to be with him. I slipped my hands beneath his hoody and leather coat, feeling his warm skin against mine and I tucked my head behind him as the wind whipped around us. I was thankful that I'd chosen a heavy sweater tonight.

We drove for what felt like hours, but in reality was probably only thirty minutes as we made our way around the opposite side of the lake from where we usually hung out. He pulled over down by the water, less than a block from my house. His motorcycle wasn't quiet, so I was grateful that he'd thought of that. The last thing I wanted to do was wake my parents before we got to speak. He got off his bike and undid my helmet and reached for my hand.

"Let's go sit," he said.

I took his hand and followed him. We dropped to sit on the small beach area. It was dark, with just a little bit of light coming from the stars above. Water lapped against the shore, and I stared out at the darkness.

"I'm sorry for ghosting you."

"Okay. Let's talk about it." I turned to face him and reached for his hand.

"Listen, Ace, I don't want to talk shit about your mom. Hell, there was some truth to her words. She doesn't think I'm good enough for you, and she's right. There are things that you don't know about me. Things that would change the way you looked at me."

I pushed up to sit on my knees and used my thumb to stroke over the area swelling beneath his eye. "There is nothing you could tell me that would change the way I feel about you. My mother is dead wrong. Keep in mind she thinks Alec, who has lied and cheated on me multiple times, is good enough for me. So, we aren't dealing with someone rational. She doesn't know what she's talking about. I love you. That's what's important. Not my mother's opinion. You can't shut me out like that."

He covered his hand over mine, and his gaze studied me so intently, I lost my breath.

"What is it?" I whispered.

He removed his hand from mine and looked out at the water. "I overheard my mom talking to her best friend, Shay, a few months ago. She didn't know I was home. I always thought my father just abandoned us."

He paused and his tongue came out and swiped his bottom lip. The water lapping against the shore didn't sooth me enough to stop my heart from racing.

"What did she say?"

"She was raped, Ace. My father was a monster." His words were so soft, so full of pain, and every part of me ached to comfort him.

I moved forward, wrapping my arms around him, and holding him as close as physically possible. Wanting to make him feel loved. Because he was.

"I'm so sorry, Jett."

He shifted away a little, and pulled me onto his lap, wrapping his arms around me. Tears streamed down my cheeks, and I felt wetness where he'd buried his face in my neck and I knew he was overcome with emotion too.

"I've never told anyone what I heard. Promise me you will keep this between us." He looked up to meet my gaze.

"I would never tell a soul. But maybe you should talk to your mom about it? It might be good for both of you."

"No. She obviously doesn't want me to know what a monster my father was. She prefers that I just think he left on some adventure. This is her secret to tell me when she's ready." He let out a long breath.

"You can talk to me any time you need to about it. I'll always be here for you, okay? And I'm really, really sorry that my mother treated you badly, Jett. She doesn't know what she's talking about. She treats everyone poorly, if I'm being honest. But I'm not her. I think you are—" I paused as tears ran down my cheeks and I clasped a hand to each side of his face. "You're so brilliant, and talented, and beautiful to me."

A wide grin spread across his handsome face, and I saw the wetness in his eyes in the glow from the moon. "Brilliant, talented and beautiful might be a stretch, Ace."

I put a hand on my chest. "Not a stretch. Not by a long shot. You are one of the smartest people I know. Look at Sherman and I…we can't function in AP Calc without you. You were offered a four-year full ride from more than thirty amazing universities to play football. You willingly get in the cage with badass fighters to help your mom pay the bills, and, come on, look at you." I bit down on my bottom lip to keep from laughing at how sappy I sounded. But it was all true. Jett Stone was the whole package and then some.

"I'm sorry for shutting you out," he whispered, grazing my bottom lip with the pad of his thumb. Chill bumps spread down my arms.

"We need to stick together, okay? Have one another's backs. If my mom says something to you, you have to tell me and let me handle it. Deal?"

"Deal."

"And thanks for telling me about what happened to your mom. But Jett, that has nothing to do with you or who you are," I said, running my fingers through his wild, disheveled hair.

"Doesn't it? What do you think your mother would say if she knew the truth? She basically called my mother trash and said the apple doesn't fall far from the tree. What would she think if she knew about my father?"

Rage engulfed me at his words. That my mother would say such disgusting, hurtful things to him. It stung and it angered me, and I didn't know how I would be able to look at her with anything other than disdain for a long time.

"He was a sperm donor, nothing more. And the fact that your mother faced all that judgment after going through so much trauma, is horrific. My heart hurts for her. Does your grandmother know?"

"I don't know. This is the first I've ever heard of it. That's why I'm struggling with Wren. He's always hanging around, looking after her. Keeping an eye on me. For a lot of years, I wished Wren were my father. But after I overheard this conversation, I hated him. Because who else could it be?"

"It doesn't make sense that he'd be violent and then be watching out for both of you, though, right? Maybe you should just ask him?"

"How do I ask him if he raped my mother?" He asked, his fingers tracing the side of my face as my head rested on his chest.

"You don't. He doesn't know you know. Nobody knows you know besides me, right?"

"Right. So, what do I ask him?" he asked, and I swiped at the last of my tears that had run down my face. Sadness had swallowed me whole, and I was still processing all that he'd shared.

I sat up, meeting his gaze. "You ask him if he's your father. Or you could ask your mother if Wren is your father."

"I'll think about it. It would suck if I'd been hating him these last few months for no reason. But if he did it, then what? I can't let him get away with that. Maybe it's better if I don't know."

"Maybe. But the truth usually comes out. Whatever you want to do, I'll support you."

His face was so close I could feel his warm breath on my cheek, as his eyes searched mine. "I fucking love you, Ace."

"I love you more. We're in this together, okay?"

"Okay."

"That means if you're sad, you talk to me about it, Jett. It's normal to feel all sorts of things about this. I know you're hurting for your mom. I can't imagine how that feels, but I'm here. I'm here, okay?"

He wrapped his arms around me and pulled me close. His heart pounded against my chest. I'd never felt closer to another person than I did in this moment. Not my family. Not the Magic Willows. He'd trusted me with his deepest secret, and I wanted to be there for him. I wanted to fix it, but I knew I couldn't. But I could love him with everything I had. And that's exactly what I intended to do.

It was nearly two o'clock in the morning when we walked to my house. He didn't want to risk waking my family by driving his bike, so he walked with me to the tree, and his eyes bulged out of his head.

"You're climbing a tree?"

I chuckled and covered my mouth to keep quiet. "This is how I sneak in and out."

I kissed him one last time. "I love you, Jett Stone. Thanks for telling me what was bothering you."

"Thanks for listening to my shit. I love you."

I turned and started to climb, and he followed.

"What are you doing?" I whisper-shouted.

"I'm making sure you don't fall."

I made my way up and leaned over to push my window open. I climbed inside and turned around to face him as he balanced between two branches and I blew him a kiss and watched as he made his way back down.

I washed my face, got on my pajamas and slipped into bed. The tears started to fall again, and I covered my mouth to muffle the sobs. My heart hurt for Mae Stone. The thought of her being raped, and then finding out she was pregnant. And raising that baby all on her own with all of Willow Springs judging her.

I stopped and said a prayer of thanks that out of all that darkness came this beautiful boy.

I thought about how my mother had treated him. The things she had said to him.

I wondered if I would ever be able to forgive her.

But right now, that wasn't my priority. I didn't have time to focus on how small minded my mother was.

Because all I cared about was making sure Jett was okay.

And I'd be there for him no matter what.

Because I'd never loved anyone the way I loved him.

twenty

. . .

Jett

THE NEXT FEW weeks went by in a blur and things had shifted for Adelaide and me, and the whole drama with her mother had only brought us closer in the end. It felt good to tell her what I'd overheard about my mother and my monster of a sperm donor. The crazy thing—I trusted her completely.

She had my back and I had hers.

She and her mother had not discussed what happened, and they were barely speaking. I encouraged her to let it go, because truth be told, Savannah Edington didn't need to like me. I didn't give a shit. All that mattered was that her daughter did. But Adelaide had a lot of pent-up anger toward her mother and I didn't want to be the reason they grew apart.

Did I think her mother was batshit crazy? *Hell yes.*

But I wanted my girlfriend to see that all on her own. I didn't want to come between them. Hell, my mother was the center of my universe, so I knew they'd need to work this shit out or it would just weigh my girl down.

Adelaide, Ma, Gram Jax and Shaw had all been by my side when I signed my letter of intent with Texas University. It was a big day and the most important people in my life were there. Shaw had signed with a big football program out in California, and Jax would be playing ball in Colorado. Everything was falling into place.

We were meeting friends at the lake. Adelaide's arms were wrapped around my middle as she held on for dear life as she sat on the back of my bike. She always slipped her hands beneath my shirt to feel my warmth. I fucking loved it. We parked down by the water of a popular area everyone liked to hang out. She climbed off my bike, and I reached for her hand. I swung a leg over so that I was still sitting, and she moved to stand between my legs, looking down at me and searching my gaze.

"You need to talk to your mom, Ace. It's eating you up."

She smiled and pushed the hair out of my face. "How do you know me so well?"

"It's a gift," I chuckled. "I think I've always known you."

She nodded. "How about you then? I'll make you a deal. You talk to Wren and at least find out if he's your father or not, and I'll talk to my mom."

I let out a long breath. "All right. I'll do it."

I needed to fucking know if he'd been the man who violated my mother. Took away her ability to trust and love another man again.

"Good. I'll go with you if you want me to." She wrapped her arms around my neck and rubbed her little nose against mine.

So, fucking adorable.

Yes, I had a wicked case of blue balls, but I didn't even fucking care. That's how much I loved this girl. We made out until my balls threatened to explode every day. We explored and touched and brought each other over the edge every time we were together. But we hadn't had sex and I sure as shit wasn't going to pressure her into it. Hell, I knew she was it for me. Didn't matter when it happened, because I knew it would. And Adelaide Edington was more than worth the wait. I'd wait for her forever if she needed me to.

"You going to be my backup?" My hands slipped beneath the cardigan and T-shirt she wore and moved up her back feeling her soft skin against my fingertips. She moved closer, and my dick strained against my zipper.

"Always."

"I think I've got this one. You want me to be there when you talk to your mom?" I settled my hands on her slim waist.

"Nope. If you're there, I'll probably end up tackling her if she looks at you wrong."

My head fell back in laughter.

"I love you," I whispered against her lips.

"Love you more." She giggled.

"Um, somebody call the fire department, because you two are on freaking fire," Coco's voice pulled me from my haze.

Adelaide's head whipped around to see her best friend and Shaw standing there laughing.

"Damn. Where did they come from?" she said, stepping back and straightening herself.

I pushed to my feet and grabbed her hand, intertwining our fingers.

"What's up?" I said. Ivy, Ty, Maura, Gigi, Jax and Lydia waited for us a few feet away. We'd all been hanging out a lot and Ty and I had become damn good friends despite the fact that his best friend gave him endless shit about it. We just never talked about the elephant in the room, but Adelaide told me Ty was taking a lot of heat for hanging out with me.

"I'm guessing, your dick," Shaw said with a raised brow.

I shook my head and laughed because he was an asshat, but he wasn't wrong.

Adelaide and her friends were laughing about something that happened at school before she glanced back up to look at me.

"Are you going to jump off Key point?" she asked.

We always came out here this time of year and jumping off Key point was a rite-of-passage when you lived in Willow Springs. It was the highest point on the lake and taking the plunge when the water was still freezing had become a local challenge. I'd done it a couple hundred times, so it didn't faze me. It wasn't actually all that high, it had just been built up by the locals for as long as I could remember.

"Sure, do you want to?"

"Um, no. I mean, yes. Someday. It's a bucket list. But I've never done it. I'm afraid of heights." She paused and shook her head. "I swear that's actually Alec's fault. I was going to jump two years ago, and he pretended he was going to push me, and I lost my footing and slipped. Cut my shin pretty bad, and almost fell in."

"Are you talking about when that douchebag pretended to throw you off a cliff and you nearly fell in?" Coco hissed.

Adelaide's cheeks were flush, and her eyes welled with emotion. That piece of shit had only made her fears worse. It pissed me off.

"Yep. I haven't even climbed up there since then," she said.

"In his defense, he thought it would be funny. He didn't mean for you to fall. He just took it too far, and it backfired majorly," Ty piped in.

What the hell was fucking funny about threatening to push someone off a cliff who was already afraid of jumping?

"He's an asshole, Ty. I don't know why you defend him," Coco said.

"Tell us how you really feel, Co." Ivy looked up at Ty and winked. I understood it. Ty was loyal to his best friend. Saw beyond his flaws. The dude obviously had some good qualities or Adelaide and Ty wouldn't have been as close to him as they were. I'd just never seen those parts of Taulson. He'd reserved all his douchebag qualities for me.

"Oh, I will. Trust me."

"Are you going to jump this year, Addy?" Gigi asked, as she Maura walked beside us.

"I want to do it before we graduate. I hate being the only one who hasn't done it."

"Well, it's not the only thing you haven't done." Coco winked at Adelaide. "Although when we pulled up, I thought you two just might do it right here in the parking lot," she said, before whistling and causing everyone to break out in laughter.

I squeezed my girl's hand. There was no shame in saving herself for someone special. And I knew her best friend's teasing was in good fun.

"Why are you so crude?" Gigi said through her laughter. "Don't feel pressure to jump, girl. You'll do it when you're ready."

"That water is also cold as hell. I don't know if I want to do it today. Maybe we should wait until it's warmer out," Maura added.

"Do you want to do it?" I whispered to Adelaide, so only she could hear.

"Yeah. Someday."

"I'll do it with you if you want. We can jump together." I shrugged. I'd do it all day long with her. Because I'd already jumped off a cliff with this girl in my mind. Taken the plunge and let someone in in a way I'd never done before. Doing it in the literal sense would be a cake walk.

She nodded. "Really?"

I laughed. "Really, Acc. I got you."

"I didn't bring my swimsuit because it's so cold."

"I don't think anyone brought swimsuits," I chuckled. Everyone jumped in their underwear, it was just what we did. And then we'd huddle up with blankets around a bonfire to get warm.

She bit down on her bottom lip and stared straight ahead. "Let's do it."

She wasn't afraid of heights—she was afraid of falling. And I'd never let her fall.

"I'm jumping today," Adelaide announced when we dropped all our shit on the beach. Her friends all turned to look at her.

"All right. If she jumps, we all jump," Maura said.

Jax agreed to collect all the clothing and bring it back down to the beach, as he had a cold and he'd jumped more times than he could count. He was happy to sit this one out.

"You really doing this?" Coco asked, as we hiked our way up to the top.

"I think so."

Her hand trembled in mine and I squeezed it. "There's no pressure. Get to the top and see how you feel."

She smiled. "Good plan."

We made it there quickly and a cool breeze bustled around us, and I wrapped both arms around my girl. I rubbed my hands up and down her arms to warm her up. The water would be cold as hell, but your body adjusted quickly, and the fire would warm us up within a few minutes.

"Okay, I'm getting it over with," Gigi said, and she dropped her clothing, down to her panties and bra and didn't hesitate. We all leaned over to watch as she hit the water, and then screamed out in laughter. "It's cold as hell."

"Oh my god," Adelaide whispered. "I don't know if I can do it."

"Then don't do it. We can do it another day," I whispered against her ear.

She nodded as Ivy and Ty took the plunge next, screaming all the way down like fools. We all laughed, and Adelaide squeezed my hand harder.

"I'm going first Shaw. You best meet me down there," Coco said, sauntering to the edge. She glanced over her shoulder to look at her best friend. "You've got this, Addy. Love you, girl."

Shaw jumped next, completely unfazed, and he howled when he came up for air.

"Don't feel pressure," Maura said squeezing Adelaide's hand. "You don't have to do it, okay?"

She nodded. "Okay. Be careful. See you down there."

It was just me, Adelaide and Jax now. She looked down at her friends who were still in the water but had swam out of the way. They didn't yell for her to jump, because they knew she was nervous. But they waited, just in case she got the nerve to do it. I realized in that moment what a supportive friendship they all had. They were always there for one another, and that was what friendship was all about. Hell, Shaw and Jax were always there for me, and I knew Adelaide had my back too. I guess I had a little more in Willow Springs than I'd ever given it credit for.

"What do you want to do, Ace?" I asked as Jax gathered all the clothes in a pile.

"I want to do it. I just don't know if I can." Her gaze bounced around, landing everywhere but on mine.

"Of course, you can do it. If this is something you want, I promise I'll help you do it."

She nodded. "Okay. Let's go." She yanked her sweater and tank over her head and unbuttoned her jeans. I'd never seen Adelaide beneath her clothing. Sure, I'd felt her. Felt every inch of her. But seeing her…Jesus. She was fucking perfect.

"Turn the fuck around," I snarled at Jax, and he bellowed out in laughter.

It was just known that you didn't stare or gawk when people stripped down to take the plunge. I'd always looked away when the girls walked to the edge. But Adelaide was different. I couldn't look away if I tried. And I sure as fuck didn't want Jax staring at her. Adelaide didn't seem to notice. Her mind was on jumping and nervous energy radiated from her hot little body.

The sun shined down on her, and her tan skin glistened. She wore light pink panties and a matching sports bra. Her nipples poked against the fabric, as it was cold as hell. My dick had no shame. He was standing on end at the sight of her.

I dropped my jeans and yanked my shirt over my head, chucking it at my best friend as he smirked.

Asshole.

"Let's do this." I held her hand in mine as we walked to the edge. "Do you trust me?"

"Completely."

"I won't let anything happen to you. We're going to count to three, and jump. If I lose your hand in the air, I promised I'll find you in the water, okay?"

She nodded "One. Two. Three..."

We flew down, and I gripped her hand in mine. Never losing contact. Everything went silent around me, as I focused all my energy on her. My feet hit the water first, and we went under. It was shockingly cold, but I'd expected that. My hands found her hips beneath the water and I pushed her up toward the surface.

"Oh my god," she shouted. "I did it."

Everyone screamed and cheered from a few feet away, and I swore I heard Coco yell out something about *bitches taking over the world*. I laughed.

"You did it, Ace."

"We did it. Thank you," she said, through her gasps. Her breaths came hard and fast, and I pulled her toward the shore where I could at least stand. I settled my feet on the ground and pulled her against me. Her legs came around my waist and I held her close.

"I'll always catch you," I said. And I fucking meant it.

"I know you will. And I'll always catch you."

Her fingers traced my tattoo, and she studied as if she were trying to figure out the meaning.

"What are these dates?" she asked.

"My mom and Gram's birthday's in roman numerals."

"Just a boy and his numbers," she said smiling up at me and pushing the hair out of her face.

I laughed because I couldn't fucking help it. Her friends swam over and congratulated her. I looked out at the beach and Jax had a fire going and he'd brought the blankets we'd always kept in Shaw's truck over as well.

I looked at my girl. Eyes dancing with excitement. Pops of amber and gold sparkling in the bit of light from above. I made a mental note to memorize every curve of her face. Her perfect nose and pouty lips. She was fucking beautiful.

And I don't know how it happened. But she was mine.

And nothing had ever felt more right.

After I dropped Adelaide off at home, my phone buzzed. It was a text from Wren telling me he needed to talk to me before my fight tonight. Fuck me. It was like the universe was trying to force me to have this conversation. I didn't respond. Instead, I drove to the mechanic shop where I knew he'd be. Because when I finally asked him the question that I'd been avoiding asking for months, I needed to look him in the eye and see if he was telling me the truth.

I parked my bike and walked in. My clothes had finally dried, but I could still feel Adelaide's soft skin on my fingers. Still feel all her sweetness around me.

"Wren here?" I asked Joey Pucci who worked for Wren. I'd known the dude most of my life and he hung out at the fights.

"Hey Jett. I heard you're fighting Donny West from Summerhaven tonight." The guy was a big deal one town over, and I'd agreed to fight him.

"Yep. We'll see how that goes," I shrugged, because I was

fighting tougher opponents lately, and I didn't have a clue if I was getting in over my head.

"You'll get him. I have zero doubts. Wren's in back."

I nodded. "Thanks. See you tonight."

I knocked on his office door, and I saw Wren sitting there through the glass window. He waved me inside and motioned me to take the seat across from his desk as he finished up a phone call. When he set his phone down, his gaze narrowed as he studied me. "Didn't expect you to come here. Just meant for you to call me."

"Well, I'm here." I looked anywhere but at him, as I tried to decide how to do this. How I'd ask him if he was my father. Which was basically asking him if he'd raped my mother. And how I'd deal with it if he was. How would I let the man walk out of here?

"All right. Well, I wanted to discuss the fight tonight and some things that I'm hearing."

"Which is?" I crossed my arms over my chest and studied his features. We looked nothing alike. He had light hair and blue eyes. But I'd always resembled my mother, so that didn't mean anything.

"Well, Jett, you're winning a lot of fights and not everyone is happy about it. There's a group of guys that bet a lot of money on their fighters, and you've thrown a bit of a wrench in that."

"Tough shit. Then they need to find better fighters," I said, leaning forward to rest my elbows on my knees.

He bellowed out in laughter. "Just be aware. There are guys that don't want you there. This Donny you're fighting tonight, works for a bad dude. Get in and get out. Don't stick around after, especially if you beat him. And don't have your girl there. Not with this guy."

I nodded. "All right. I can do that."

"I've got a few of my guys watching out for you, so it should be fine. Just wanted to give you a heads up."

I wanted to thank him, but I couldn't be nice to him. Not until I knew the truth.

"I need to ask you something." I looked up and met his gaze. He didn't look away.

"Go ahead."

"Fuck," I mumbled. "This is awkward as hell, but I need to know." I thought about Adelaide, and we'd both agreed to get this shit off our chests. She'd jumped off a fucking cliff because she trusted me. This shit was holding me back. I needed to know.

"What?" He appeared confused as fuck.

I let out a long breath. "Are you my father?"

He pushed back in his chair. "Wow. I did not see that coming. Uh, no Jett. I am most definitely not your father."

I watched his movements, his reaction—he didn't seem to be lying. But how would I know?

"You sure about that?" I folded my hands, intertwining my fingers and rested my chin there.

He chuckled. "Pretty fucking sure. I'm fairly certain you need to have sex with someone to make a baby. And as much as I've tried to win your mother over, that's never happened. Is that why you've hated me these last couple of months? You decided I was the one who'd knocked your mother up and left her?"

I rolled my eyes and my hands fisted at my sides. "He did a lot more than just knock her up. He fucking raped her."

For some reason I didn't feel like I was betraying Ma by talking to Wren about it. And looking him in the eyes as he said the words, made it clear that he wasn't my father. There was no doubt he cared about her. Always had.

His face hardened and he leaned forward. "You know about that?"

"She doesn't know I know, but yes. How the fuck do you know about it?"

"Your mom and I have been friends since we were kids.

I'd heard what happened to her back in the day, and she admitted it to me. Asked me to keep it a secret because she never reported it. And I'm pretty fucking sure she never wanted you to find out about it."

I scrubbed a hand over my face. "Fuck. I overheard her talking to Shay a few months ago. I want to fucking hurt him."

"Get in line." He chuckled. "Been there, done that. You don't need to worry about it. He was dealt with and he won't be coming back. Not ever."

A chill ran down my spine. "You killed him?"

He rolled his eyes. "I'm not in the business of murdering people, Jett. Let's just say that a friend of mine made sure he'd never hurt her again. No more questions. You got it?"

What the fuck?

"Yeah. I got it. Thanks for looking out for her." I pushed to my feet, still in disbelief over the conversation.

"Always. I'd never hurt your mother. She's the best woman I know," he said, as he stood and clapped me on the shoulder.

Holy shit. The dude was in love with her. He'd spent his whole life pining for a woman who'd been too wounded to see it.

"She sure is. Hey Wren," I said, before turning to face him as I stood in the doorway.

"Yeah?"

"Thanks for looking out for my mom, and I guess for looking out for me, too. Sorry for being a dick to you these last few months."

"Well, I'd always hoped to end up with your mom, if I'm being honest. So, I guess in a way you're kind of like the son I never had."

I nodded. Jesus. The dude had been at every football game I'd ever played. I'd never thought it was to personally see *me* play. But things were starting to make sense. And he wasn't being a dick by monitoring my fights, he actually had my back because he cared about what happened to me.

"I appreciate that. I'll see you tonight at the fight."

"I'll be there. Watch your back, Jett."

I sat on my bike processing all that had happened. Wren had been in love with my mom for as long as I'd been alive, and he'd made sure the man who'd hurt her was handled.

Whatever the hell that meant. Had he had him killed? Scared him off? I didn't have a clue. But I saw the look in his eyes, and I knew in my gut that he'd never be back.

I sent a text to Adelaide.

Me ~ took care of things on my end. I'll fill you in tomorrow. Talk to your mom, Ace. Stay home tonight. Wren said there's some heat at the fights and I don't want you there. I'll call you after. Love you.

I slipped my phone in my back pocket before heading to Shaw's to fill he and Jax in about the fight. And make sure that Shaw didn't invite Coco to come. The last thing I wanted was for Adelaide to be there if anything was going to go down.

twenty-one

. . .

Adelaide

I MET the girls down in the basement. We were meeting quick to catch up on a few things and Mama had already called down twice to tell me to come to dinner.

"So, are you going to finally tell her why you've been so mad at her?" Maura asked.

"I guess we need to talk about it at some point." My mother and I had been on edge for almost two months. I'd never been this angry before, but we needed to get past it. And Jett had talked to Wren. I couldn't wait to find out what he said. This was the one topic that was off limits with my friends. It was Jett's secret, and not mine to tell.

"I have something to tell you guys, but I just, I don't know…" Gigi trailed off, and she fidgeted with her hands.

"What is it? You can talk to us," I said, reaching for her hand because I could see she was struggling to tell us.

She stared at me, with as much empathy as I'd ever seen before. "I, um, Addy, I got into TU."

I squealed and jumped to my feet, urging her to hers before wrapping my arms around her. "Gigi, what? Oh my gosh. Why would you not be screaming from the rooftop? I'm so happy for you."

"I don't know. I mean, you're a better student than me, and you haven't heard back yet, so I feel bad about it. I was hoping you'd hear today, and we could both share our news."

"Don't be ridiculous. I told you I bombed the essay. I'm okay with it, I promise. And I'm so proud of you. You deserve this," I said.

She looked down at the ground, and I hated that she was allowing my not getting in to cloud her achievement. What she was afraid to say was that TU was a top tier university, and it would be unlikely for two of us from the same small high school to both get in. And honestly, if I had to pick, I'd want her to go there. She'd wanted it for as long as I could remember. She deserved this.

"Congrats, Gigi. At least you know Addy will visit a lot because her and her hot boyfriend can't stay away from one another." Coco pushed to her feet when my mother shouted for me down the stairs. Again.

Jett and I hadn't discussed what would happen after this year. He never pushed me to choose where I'd go based on him. He just encouraged me to chase my dreams, and I loved him even more for it. It didn't matter where we went. My heart belonged to him. It was that simple.

"Damn, the warden is on one tonight. Can you please have it out with her so we can be here without her yelling at you every five minutes," Coco hissed, as she made her way to the door.

"Hey, I got a weird text from Jett telling me not to come to his fight tonight. Do you know what that's about?"

Coco shifted on her feet. "Shaw said there's people that aren't happy with how well Jett is doing, and he needs to watch his back. He told me not to come tonight either."

"Looks like we're all going then. Can you sneak out?" Ivy asked me, as she hugged me goodbye.

"Yep. I'll text you. The fight isn't until eleven tonight. Are you sure you all want to go?" None of the girls had been out to the warehouse aside from me and Coco.

"Sounds like we need a united front. And it's senior year. I'm in." Gigi hugged me goodbye as she spoke.

"Co, are you driving? Just pull around the corner so my parents don't hear your car," Maura said, and Ivy chimed in with the same sentiment.

We said our goodbyes and I made my way upstairs.

"Mama's been acting super weird since she got the mail today. Something's up," Clem whispered, as we both stopped in the bathroom to wash up before heading to the dining room.

"She got the mail today?"

"She's been beating me out there every day this week." My sister took her seat at the table. Clem or I always got the mail.

I held my phone in my lap and quickly logged into my TU account. I figured the status would be updated on-line since I hadn't received a letter.

ACCEPTED.

The word stunned me, and I scrolled down to see that my acceptance letter had been sent a week ago. What the actual hell.

"Tell me about your day, girls." Daddy dropped to sit at the head of the table.

"Um, actually, I have a question," I said, passing the salad to my sister after I scooped some onto my plate and my gaze landed on Mama.

"Oh, you're speaking to me now?" My mother said, dropping her napkin in her lap.

"I am. And my question is for you, Mama. Did you receive some mail for me this week?"

Her cheeks flushed and my stomach dropped. Would she really go this far? Did she honestly believe that keeping the letter from me would deter me?

"Savannah," Daddy said. "Are you feeling all right?" He leaned over and used the back of his hand to feel her forehead.

"I'm fine. Yes. You've received some mail, but as your parent, I don't feel that these letters are of any relevance to your life. You know where you're going to school, and this is just you having a little temper tantrum because Alec messed up." She pursed her lips before pushing the salad around on her plate.

"You took her mail?" Clem gasped. "Did you open it?"

"Of course, I did. I'm her mother."

My father set his fork down on his plate and stared at her. "You opened Ladybug's mail and didn't share it with her? Why?"

"I believe one is an acceptance letter to TU. She doesn't want me to go there, so she hid it from me. I'm guessing the others are acceptance letters as well." Tears ran down my face.

"Mama, that's actually against the law. Did she get into TU?" My sister asked.

My father pushed his chair back and the legs made a screeching sound against the floor. "Where are the letters?"

I'd never seen him so angry. Mama pushed to her feet and moved to the drawer in the dining hutch and tossed three letters on the table. The letter from TU was on top. I already knew what it said.

"Did you really think you could keep these from me? I have an account, Mama. I would have found out."

She shrugged. "I'm doing what I believe is best for you."

I rolled my eyes, as a sob escaped my throat and tears made it impossible to see. "You're doing what's best for *you*. You've got a lot of secrets, don't you? On top of hiding my mail, you also said horrible things to Jett which is why he's never come back here."

"What did you say to Jett?" My father was still standing, his face in complete disbelief.

"I told him the truth."

"No. You told him *your* truth. That his mother is trash, and he isn't good enough for me. That he's only going to college because he can throw a ball. He's a straight A student mother. A hell of a lot better student than Alec Taulson. He's brilliant. And talented. But you are too blind to see that." My voice quaked as I tried to get the words out. I pushed to my feet and swiped at the tears streaming down my face. "You're a judgmental woman. You know nothing about Jett or his mother. You babysat Mae Stone when she was young, but you turned your back on her when she got pregnant. When she needed her friends most. Because you make up the rules as you go, and you treat people horribly. I'm disgusted by you." I didn't even recognize my own voice as I shouted ugly words at her, and my family watched me in silence.

I ran up the stairs and slammed my bedroom door. My mother was not who I thought she was. She'd hidden acceptance letters from me, she'd said horrible things to Jett. She'd turned her back on a friend. I dropped on my bed and sobbed, as my door flew open.

"Ladybug." Daddy's voice startled me. He dropped down on my bed, scrubbing a hand over his face, and I pushed up to sit. He held three letters in his hands. "What your mother did is inexcusable. But right now, I'd like to look at these letters with you. Getting into TU is a huge accomplishment, and I will not have it overshadowed by your mothers need to control your life. I won't do it."

I reached for a tissue on my nightstand and blew my nose. I pulled the first paper from the already opened envelope from Texas Central University and dad and I read the acceptance letter together. I did the same with the letter from the University of South Texas, and I smiled past all my sadness, because I'd gotten in to that one also. I pulled the final letter from TU out of the envelope and read my acceptance aloud, as tears blurred my vision once again. Because it stung that my mother had done this. And the combination of sadness and betrayal mixed with pride and excitement were overwhelming.

My father wrapped an arm around me and pulled me against his chest. "Proud of you, Ladybug."

"Thanks, Daddy."

"Mama will come around. She's struggling with all the change that's coming and this desperate need to hold on to you. To say she's handled this poorly is an understatement, but I know that she loves you."

I nodded. What more could I do?

"Okay," I whispered.

"And what she said to Jett." He paused to shake his head with disbelief. "Well, he's a fine young man. I'll make things right with him."

I pushed to my feet and set the letters in the top drawer of my desk. "Thank you."

Dad moved to his feet and kissed the top of my head before leaving. Closing the door behind him. I texted the girls and let them know what had happened. The response was a mix of horror and excitement that I'd gotten in to three great schools. But the sadness over my mother had definitely cast a shadow over my joy. Things with her had gone from bad to worse.

I reread the text from Jett. I didn't want to tell him what happened with my mother before his fight. He needed to focus. He didn't want me there, but I was going. I'd have the girls with me, so nothing was going to happen. Because nothing could keep me away. I needed to be there for him.

A few hours later, I'd flipped my lights off, pretending to be asleep and listened to my parents arguing for the next hour. Doors slammed. Feet stomped down the stairs, as obviously my father had decided to move to the couch. My stomach wrenched with anxiety. My family had always been solid. The four of us were a unit. Or at least I'd thought we were. Right now, there was such a separation, and I felt it in the depths of my soul.

And it hurt.

Mama T had barely spoken to me since Alec and I had broken up. She avoided my gaze when she came over and had made it apparent that she wasn't happy with me. My own mother had taken sides with the boy who'd cheated on me, so why would his mother be any different.

I sent Clem a text. She always had my back and I'd always have hers.

Me ~ Hey. Jett has a fight so I'm sneaking out. Let me know if Mama and Daddy wake up, okay? Sorry about all the fighting tonight.

Clem ~ Proud of you, Sissy. You're finally standing up to her. It's about time. I've got your back. Text me when you get home, so I know you made it back. Love you.

Me ~ <crying emoji> <blowing kisses emoji>

Coco texted that they were down the street and I climbed out my window and onto the tree. I made my way down to the ground and jogged to the corner where Coco sat in the drivers' seat. Ivy was beside her, and Maura and Gigi were in the back. I slipped in next to Gigi and let out a long breath I hadn't even realized I'd been holding. The night sky was lit up by more stars than usual.

"Hey, girl. How are you holding up? Mommy dearest really threw you a curve ball tonight." Coco whipped around to look at me.

"Well, forget about her. I can't believe we both got into TU," Gigi said, wrapping her arms around me as she squeezed me tight.

"I know. I'm so happy."

"Did you hit accept?" Maura asked.

"No, because with all the turmoil at home, I haven't even

had time to process it. And then Jett sent me that cryptic text about not coming tonight, so I know something is up. I haven't even told him that I got in yet."

"Oh my god. You, me and Jett will all be together. That makes this so much better. And we can be roomies," Gigi squealed.

That felt so far ahead of where I was with all of this. I wasn't speaking to my mother. Our family was in disarray. I hoped that she would support me, but I really didn't know. And I didn't know how to feel about making a choice that would distance me from my mother even further.

"Hey, you okay?" Ivy asked, as we waited at the stop light.

"Yeah. Of course. It's just a lot right now. Mama admitted what she said to Jett. She wasn't even sorry about it. My parents had a brutal fight. They never fight. Dad's sleeping on the couch. I mean, all of this is over me not wanting to be with Alec when you get through all the layers of crazy. And I just don't understand it. Why can't she be happy for me? TU is a top tier university. There is no comparison to the education that I'll get there versus state."

"I think you hit the nail on the head. She doesn't care about your education or your happiness. She and Mama T want you and Alec together because it makes *them* happy. It's ridiculous. And twisted. And I believe she broke a federal law opening your mail and hiding it from you. You could press charges," Coco huffed.

"This is it?" Ivy asked when we pulled in the dirt parking lot in front of the warehouse.

"It's a little sketchy, huh?" Gigi asked, twisting her head to take in our whereabouts.

"Yes. But it's filled with sexy fighters," Coco said. "So, how are we going to play this. Shaw told me not to come, and Jett told you not to come. And here we are."

I glanced down at my phone as we sat in the dark car.

"His fight starts in twenty minutes. We can wait to go inside and then hide in the back. I just want to make sure he's okay."

"That sounds like a good plan," Maura said.

"What is that?" Ivy asked and we all turned in the direction she was pointing.

There were about four men, yanking someone by the arm through the parking lot near the side of the building. My stomach dipped and my heart raced.

It was Jett.

What the hell was this?

Instinct kicked in and I whipped the door open.

"You guys go inside and find Shaw and Jax. Tell them to get Wren. Hurry," I shouted, before I jumped out of the car and sprinted toward the back of the building where they'd taken him.

Adrenaline pumped, and my breaths were labored, but I felt nothing. Just a need to get there.

To him.

"Hey," I shouted when I came around the corner. Two men held Jett's arms back as one punched him in the stomach.

They all paused and stared.

"Get the fuck out of here, Ace," Jett shouted.

"Who the fuck is this?" One of the men asked, moving toward me and I didn't back away.

"I'll tell you who the fuck I am," I hissed, seeing blood drip down Jett's cheek. "I'm Mayor Edington's daughter. If you touch him again, you'll have to go through me. Do you really want to bring that wrath on?"

I moved toward Jett, and he squeezed his eyes shut as if he was trying to come up with a plan. I wrapped my arms around his middle as tears streamed down my face.

"Jesus Christ. I thought you said this would be easy. No complications. The fucking mayor's daughter is a complication." The man holding back Jett's right arm said, before he dropped it and threw his hands in the air. Jett's arm was wrapped around me in an instant.

"She doesn't have to be. We could send a message to the mayor while we're at it that his piece of shit town has nothing on us."

"Not a battle I'm interested in," the man who'd dropped Jett's arm crossed his own over his chest and stared at the others.

The most ear-piercing sound cut through the air, like a missile heading for destruction. Everyone's hands moved on instinct to their ears, as Ivy came around the corner with her rape whistle in her mouth and I stared at her with my jaw on the ground.

"Yeah. I have my father on speed dial. He happens to be the chief of police, so you've just opened a can of worms, *bitches."* She blew the whistle one more time before holding up her car keys and setting off her car alarm. The man holding Jett's other arm let go and backed away. They all stood there staring at one another.

"Not worth it. For fifty fucking bucks. I'm out." The first guy took off jogging as the other three looked at one another.

"It wasn't personal man. Just business," an oversized man said to Jett before walking off. He chuckled as he passed me and Ivy.

"Jesus. What the fuck are you two thinking?" Jett asked, wrapping his arms around me as Shaw, Jax, Coco, Gigi and Maura came around the corner with Wren in tow.

"Can we turn off the car alarm now," Wren asked, his voice calm and steady, but his gaze searched Jett to make sure he was okay.

Ivy hit her key fob and the horrific noise stopped. My ears were still ringing but a calm settled over all of us when the loud noise came to an end.

I glanced up at Jett and wiped away the blood on his cheek with my fingers. He looked down at me and swiped away the falling tears that I hadn't even realized were still streaming down my face.

"All right, let's all get the hell out of here. Just got a tip that the cops were called. We're getting raided in less than an hour." Wren never took his eyes from Jett as he spoke.

"Fights cancelled?" Jett asked.

Wren laughed. "We're getting raided. Fights definitely cancelled. And I warned you these guys weren't happy with you. Probably predicted you were going to kick their guys ass tonight, and thought they'd rough you up first. We can talk about it later. You all need to get the hell out of here."

"I'll call you in a little bit," Jett leaned down and kissed me.

"No way. I'm leaving with you." I hugged my girlfriends, and we all shook our heads with disbelief over what had just happened.

"Well, we're definitely filling the book with adventures. I nearly peed my pants when I came around that corner," Ivy said.

She wasn't the only one.

We were definitely going out in a blast for our senior year. More had happened to me over the last few months than had happened in my entire lifetime.

And I was okay with all of it.

Because it had led me to Jett.

twenty-two

. . .

Jett

JAX AND SHAW gave me those half bro hugs and apologized another dozen times' before heading out. Hell, they couldn't have predicted I'd be jumped when I came out of the locker room. And I'd been outnumbered. For the first time in my life, I'd had no exit strategy, so I'd prepared for the beating.

What I hadn't prepared for was Adelaide coming to my rescue, jumping right into the fire and putting herself in harm's way. *For me.* What the fuck was that about?

And then Ivy jumped in, as all the magic musketeers had gone balls to the walls to try to stop what was going down. If I hadn't been so terrified at the time that they'd be hurt, it would have been laughable. My girl was small, but she was fierce. She showed no fear which shocked the shit out of me.

"Jett, you got a minute?" Wren asked, after everyone walked away and it was just me and Adelaide standing there still processing the shitshow that had just gone down.

"Yeah. She can stay. You can trust her."

"Looks like the mayor's daughter is a bit of a badass," Wren said, with a brow raised when he smiled at her.

She laughed. "Not normally. But I knew I needed to do something. Thank you for coming so quickly."

He nodded. "All right, so what I'm going to tell you goes no further than right here. Got it? People's jobs are on the line."

"No problem."

"I have someone on the inside. The call I got about the raid, it's personal. You were specifically named," Wren said.

I sucked in a long breath. Could this day get any worse? "What the fuck? Why?"

"My guy told me that Alec Taulson placed the call. Apparently, he has a personal beef with you. Said you'd be fighting and that your girlfriend was to be left out of it. He wants to see you go down, Jett."

"That mother fucker." I shook my head and my hands fisted at my side. Adelaide reached for my hand and mouthed the words 'I'm sorry' to me.

"Don't retaliate. Listen, you're so close to leaving for school. Get the hell out of here and make something of yourself. Don't let this punk take you down. He's got a rich daddy to cover his ass. You don't. We're going to shut things down here for a few weeks anyway. If you want to make some cash, you can work for me down at the auto shop. It's decent money and I'll work around your schedule."

People were hustling to their cars in the parking lot, as Clyde and his men were emptying the warehouse before the cops arrived. And this was all on me.

"Yeah, thanks. I'm sorry for the mess I've caused. I'm sure you'll lose a shit ton of money."

"Nah. Just glad you didn't go down in the mess. We've been taking some heat because we've grown so fast because everyone in this shit town is looking for something to do. People are talking about the fights. I'll have to look into a new location down the road. Now get your badass girl home and get out of here. Stop by tomorrow and see me, and we'll figure out the job."

I nodded and shook his hand as he pulled me in for a shoulder bump. He turned toward Adelaide. "Go home. No more ass kicking tonight, girl."

She chuckled. But I saw all the worry on her face. This had taken a toll on her, which is exactly why I'd told her to stay away. But I was learning pretty quickly that she rarely listened to me. And she had my back at all cost. Aside from Jax and Shaw, I wasn't used to that kind of loyalty. That kind of trust.

Definitely not that kind of love.

But here we were.

"Scouts honor," she said, holding up two fingers.

He rumpled her hair and laughed. "Get out of here, you two."

I led her over to my bike and handed her the helmet. We didn't speak. I knew something was up, because I could see it in her eyes. Feel it as I dropped down to sit in front of her. She was off. She'd just had a glimpse into my world, and it had sent her sideways.

"You okay?" I asked, turning my head to speak over my shoulder before I fired up my bike.

"Yeah. Are you?" Her words wobbled, and I knew I needed to get her the hell out of here. Get her somewhere we could talk.

"Hold on, Ace."

I fired up my bike and her hands slipped beneath my hoody and my skin heated instantly. My cheek stung from the shot I'd taken while my arms were held down. They'd told me to throw the fight. Why the fuck would you come out to fight knowing that the other guy was going to throw it? Maybe the dude should spend his energy training instead of giving his opponent an unfair beat down before the match. A calm came over me as she hugged me tight and rested her cheek against my back.

I pulled down the dirt road by the lake and rolled to a stop. We didn't get off the bike. I swung my leg over and pulled her onto my lap. I couldn't get close enough to this girl. I unbuckled her helmet and dropped it to the ground.

Orange and citrus overwhelmed my senses.

"I'm sorry I dragged you into my shit," I said, and her hands settled on each of my cheeks. She studied my wound like she was a medical doctor. Turning my face side to side before letting out a breath.

"You didn't drag me into your shit. I charged right in. I saw them pulling you around the corner, and I knew I had to do something." She covered her mouth with her hand again, as a sob left her sweet lips.

"You know I would have been all right if you'd just gone inside to get Wren. Next time don't put yourself in danger. I can take a beating, trust me." I pulled her hand away and grazed my lips against hers to comfort her. "You're all right, Ace."

She pulled back, her dark eyes blending with the night sky. The street light a few feet away casting enough light to make out her features. "So, Wren isn't your dad, huh? You two seem to be getting along now?"

"No. But he knew about what happened to my mom. I'm pretty sure he's been in love with her his whole fucking life."

I wouldn't tell her that Wren made sure my father went away. It might scare her. Hell, it shocked the shit out of me. But I knew in my gut that Wren would never do anything to hurt mom now, and that's what I cared about.

"See. This is an example of why talking about what's on your mind can be helpful." She laughed.

"What else is going on? Something's off. Did you talk to your mom?"

She closed her eyes and shook her head, as tears ran down her cheeks again.

"I did." She wiped her nose with the back of her hand and opened her eyes. Her gaze locking with mine. "She admitted to saying what she did to you. She makes no apologies. I also found out that I'd received three acceptance letters which she'd opened and hidden from me. Who does that?"

Savannah fucking Edington.

"Someone who's scared. Terrified of losing you. Losing control."

"I guess. Her and daddy had an awful fight, and our house is just broken right now." She fell forward, burying her face in my neck.

"They'll figure out." I pulled her back to look at her. "What schools did you get in to?"

"Texas Central, University of south Texas, and…TU," she said, and a wide grin spread across her face.

"No fucking way. Congratulations. You fucking did it." I wrapped her back up and held her close.

She laughed and looked up at me. "Where do *you* think I should go?"

"I'm not going to be another person in your life who tells you what to do. Tells you what I want. I want you to do what's best for you."

Her gaze narrowed. She looked wounded. "You don't want me to go with you to TU?"

"Fuck yeah. If it's what you want. But I'd never pressure you to go where I'm going. You've already got my heart, Ace. And you can take it with you wherever you go. I'm yours. Where you go to school doesn't change that."

Hell, I wanted to tell her right there to go to TU. I wanted to be together. But I wasn't about to make that decision for her. She'd had people doing that for her her entire life.

She nodded. "I love you."

"I love you. But don't ever bring your little musketeers to a street fight again. Deal?"

Her head fell back, and I fucking loved the sound of her laugh as it filled the space around us. "The magic willows, not the little musketeers."

"Same difference. But I'm glad they always have your back."

"And I'll always have yours."

"Same. All right, I better get you home. The last thing I need is your mother thinking I'm breaking you out of your house now and getting you in back alley fights."

She leaned forward and kissed me. Her lips meeting mine, and I swore to fucking Christ this girl owned me in every way. Her fingers tangled in my hair, and I shifted her on my lap, so she was straddling me. Grinding up against me. I nearly came undone right there on the seat of my bike. I wanted to carry her over to the hammock, drop her down and strip her bare. Show her how good I could make her feel. But I knew she'd been through a lot tonight, and it wasn't the right time. My hands slipped beneath her sweater and I fucking loved the feel of her soft skin against my fingers. I teased her hard peaks through the lace of her bra with my thumbs and she gasped. Her head fell back, as little pants escaped.

"Jett, I want you."

My lips moved to her neck, kissing my way back up to her face. I kissed her cheeks, her nose, her eye lids, and stopped at her sweet mouth.

"You already have me."

"You know what I mean," she said, her voice raspy and full of need.

"Not tonight. Not after what you've been through. When I have you it won't be after pulling you into the middle of a shit show, or after you went at it with your mom. But I will have you, Adelaide Edington. And I promise to rock your fucking world."

She laughed and ran her fingers through my hair. "Oh, I have no doubt."

"There's no rush."

She nodded. "Okay. I'm going to hold you to it."

"I'm a man of my word." I placed a chaste kiss on her lips before lifting her up and dropping her back down on the seat. I grabbed her helmet and placed it on her head, buckling it beneath her chin. Her dark eyes never leaving mine.

"I know you are."

I climbed on in front of her, and my dick raged against my zipper just like it always did. I laughed. Chivalry had never been something I'd thought about. But when it came to this girl—I wanted to do everything right.

The next day at school Alec Taulson looked surprised to see me when I passed him in the hall. Walking hand and hand with my girl.

"Didn't expect to see you here, Jett," he said, as he stood with Hayden and Karina. I noticed he and Ty weren't hanging out much these days, and I wondered if his best friend had finally figured out what an asshole he was.

"Yeah. You took your shot, and you missed. That's kind of your thing, right?" I smirked. He'd had a shit basketball season, and I normally wouldn't stoop that low. But fuck this kid made it difficult to be decent.

"I can't even believe you'd do that," Adelaide said, shaking her head.

"Well, remember, you don't really know me anymore, right Addy?"

She rolled her eyes. "It sure doesn't seem like it."

"Don't worry about it. I've always known who Alec is," Karina said.

He shrugged her off when she placed a hand on his shoulder. "Would have sucked for you to get busted and lose your scholarship. Hope you don't do anything to fuck that up."

I flipped him the bird. He wasn't worth my time. Adelaide and I walked away. He was one person I couldn't wait to put in my rear view.

"I can't believe how low he's stooping these days. I don't know what happened to him," she said. I glanced down, and I saw the pain on her face. Like it or not, she considered the kid to be family. They'd grown up together, and she tried to find the good in him. I couldn't fault her, I loved that about her. She didn't see the worst in people the way I tended to do. I admired it.

"I think people show you who they are, Ace. At some point you've got to believe them."

She nodded. "I get that. But Alec isn't all bad. He's a good son and a good brother and he can be a good friend. He just seems to be teetering toward the bad lately." She chuckled.

"I love that you see the good in people." I pressed her up against the wall next to the library and kissed her. Hard. Because I fucking loved her.

When I pulled away, her cheeks were flush, and she was breathless. My dick strained. He was getting angrier with each passing day, though I took care of business in the shower this morning. I adjusted myself as conspicuously as I could, and she laughed.

"A little uncomfortable?" she teased. "Come on. Let's get to class before we get carried away."

"I've been carried away since the first time I tasted that sweet mouth of yours."

She tugged at my hand to lead me down the hall. She left

for her class and I met Shaw outside of Creative Writing and we walked in the classroom and dropped in our seats.

"Dude, have you thought about how you're going to ask Addy to prom? Coco expects some fucking creativity. But I don't have a clue on how to ask her."

I'd been planning it for a while, but I wouldn't tell him that.

"Yeah, I have an idea on what I'll do. What does Coco like?"

"Coco likes me and her friends." He looked up at the ceiling as if deep in thought. "She likes shopping and Starbucks and cupcakes and going to the lake."

"Okay." I laughed. "How can you tie it all in?"

"I don't have a fucking clue. Maybe a scavenger hunt?"

"That's an idea. You willing to put in all that work?" I raised a brow.

"Fuck yeah. I think she'll string me up by my balls if I don't make her senior prom ask a good one."

My head fell back in laughter. "Spoken like a pussy whipped mother fucker."

"Takes one to know one."

I shrugged and laughed. Because he was fucking right.

I told Adelaide I had some shit to do for Gram and I couldn't hang out after school. I was going to ask her to prom tomorrow, and I needed to get everything together. I got home and placed the flowers in water and went in the room to check on my grandmother. She was sleeping. She was doing a lot of that lately. Ma was at the diner and I flipped on the TV.

There was a knock at the door and my jaw dropped when I saw Mayor Edington standing on the other side.

"Hey," I said, unsure of what to say. "Uh, do you want to come in?"

"Sure. Thank you."

He stepped inside and I offered him a bottle of water, and we both dropped to sit at the kitchen table. He didn't look around my house like he was surprised at the size or appalled by anything about it.

"So, I was hoping we could chat. Ladybug came home today, so I figured you weren't with her. Hard to find a time when I can catch you alone these days." He leaned back in his seat and smiled to let me know he was just giving me shit.

I nodded. "Sure. What's up?"

"Well, I've wanted to come by and tell you that what my wife said to you a while ago, is not how our family feels about you. Hell, I don't even think Savannah feels that way. She's just finding it difficult to see Adelaide make choices for herself. But she'll figure it out."

"Okay. Glad to hear you don't all feel that way."

"Listen, Jett. My wife isn't a monster. She loves our girls. She gets a little lost sometimes, stuck in her ways. Caught up with her best friend in ways that bring out the worst in both of them. We've been talking about it a lot and I think she realizes that she's actually pushing our girl away by behaving like this."

"I don't think she's a monster. Hell, I get it. On paper I probably don't look like the best option for your daughter. But I can promise you this…I love her. And I'm determined to get a good education and make something of myself." I hated the way my voice shook. I hated the way I felt like I had to prove myself to some of the people in this town.

"You've already made something of yourself, Son. You don't owe us an explanation about who you are. My daughter loves you and that's enough for me. I don't know if you know this, but I was raised by a single mother. My father left when I was young. I didn't grow up with much, but there was always love. And I worked hard to *make something of myself.* So, I understand what you're saying, but trust me when I tell you a lot of that comes from your own need to do so. Not others." He paused to take a sip of water and took his time screwing the lid back on as he appeared to be deep in thought. "What I've learned is that none of that matters. What matters is the people in your life. Family. That's what it comes down to. And from where I'm sitting, you have all of that. And I feel quite proud that my daughter is dating such a fine young man. Before you, Ladybug never talked about her own dreams. About this desire to be a journalist and attend a more challenging college. You've helped Adelaide figure out who she is, and what she wants. And I'm thankful for that."

My stomach dipped and my chest tightened at his words. Jesus. Is this what it felt like to get a father's approval? And damn if it didn't feel good.

I cleared my throat. "Thank you, Sir. That means a lot to me."

"We'd like to have you to dinner tonight, if you're free. Maybe give us a second chance? I know you two spend a lot of time together, and it's about damn time we got to know you better too."

I leaned back in my chair. "Is your wife okay with that?"

"It was her idea. She didn't feel like you'd receive it as well if she came with me today, but she's the one who asked me to extend the invitation. She's desperate to patch things up with our daughter, and she knows getting to know you is a part of that."

I crossed my arms over my chest. It wasn't the most genuine of reasons to get to know me, but for Adelaide I'd do it. Because she needed to patch things up with her mother.

"Okay. I'll be there."

He smiled. "Great. So now that that's behind us, tell me about the football program at TU. I can't wait to see you play for them."

I spent the next hour and a half chatting with Ellis Edington about football, and school, and his time growing up in Willow Springs and becoming the mayor. Turns out his journey wasn't all that different from mine. He didn't come from much, but he went after what he wanted.

And I'd go to dinner tonight because I loved my girl, adored her crazy baby sister, and admired the hell out of her father. Was I guarded when it came to her mother? Sure. But I was all about putting this shit behind us and moving forward.

And what better time to start than now.

twenty-three

• • •

Adelaide

DINNER WAS GOING BETTER than I'd ever imagined it would. I was shocked when Mama told me Jett was joining us. This was her version of an olive branch. She'd also had a heart to heart with me about why she'd hidden those college acceptance letters from me. Turns out part of her obsession with me and Alec being together, and attending the same college, with me living at home—it was all a way for her to keep me close. My mother was even more controlling than I'd ever realized. I guess the idea of me spreading my wings terrified the hell out of her. I didn't think what she did was right, but I understood her fear. And we were working on mending our relationship.

Mama T had even come over after school today and she'd asked me all about the colleges that I was considering. I knew my mother must have talked to her because she'd barely acknowledged me for months. And it felt good to put it all behind me and focus on the future. I loved Alec's family, and I didn't want to lose them just because we weren't together anymore. I'd known them my entire life. And I still held out hope that Alec and I would be friends again someday. But with him trying to hurt Jett right now, I didn't see a way for that to happen. Maybe time would heal all of these hurts.

Mama asked Jett dozens of questions about what he planned to major in and when he'd leave for school. She wanted to know what his long term-goals were and how long he planned to play football. I held his hand beneath the table as he fielded the grueling interrogation with ease and confidence.

Jett Stone had nothing to hide. He knew what he wanted, and he made no apologies for it. And I loved that about him. He never wavered when it came to his hopes and dreams, as he'd been planning them his entire life.

My sister made googly eyes at my boyfriend the entire dinner, and I couldn't help but laugh. And Dad and Jett had somehow formed a friendship and shared an easy comfort with one another now.

"Thanks for having me, Mrs. Edington." Jett helped clear the dessert plates and said he needed to get home.

Mama dropped the dish towel on the counter and my father, sister and I all followed her movements. We were on the mend, but we had a long way to go and I didn't totally trust her just yet. And I'd be dammed if I'd let her do anything to hurt Jett again.

"I'm going to say this in front of my family, as I think pulling you out on the front porch for another chat might put everyone on edge." She chuckled, and I could see how nervous she was. "I owe you an apology, Jett. I was wrong and I'm embarrassed about how I behaved. And the things I said about your mother were unfair and cruel."

He nodded. "I appreciate that."

"I know I can't fix things over the course of one dinner, but I'm hoping you'll give me a chance to earn your forgive-ness over time."

His hand tightened around mine, and I knew he was uncomfortable with the whole exchange. I'm sure he wondered how genuine she was. I wondered the same thing and I'd known her my entire life.

"I'm good with that."

"Good, because we sure enjoy having you around," Clem said wriggling her brows and breaking the ice the way only my sister could. We all broke out in a fit of laughter and I walked Jett outside and down the driveway to his bike.

"Thanks for doing this tonight," I said wrapping my arms around his middle and breathing in all his goodness.

"Of course. Your dad's a cool dude."

"No one has ever called him *cool*. He'd be so excited right now to hear you say that." I laughed, because my dad was the sweetest guy, but his cool factor was not high.

"And Clem's pretty awesome."

"You're only saying that because she has a mad crush on you."

"And I have a mad crush on you, Ace." He kissed me.

Soft.

Slow.

Perfect.

"Yeah? And my mom is at least trying, right?"

He nodded. He didn't trust her. I saw it in his eyes, but he wouldn't say it aloud. "She is. And I want you to get to a good place with her because I know it hurts you."

"We're getting there. And Mama T was actually friendly to me today for the first time in months. Maybe everyone is coming around."

"Maybe." He ran the pad of his thumb over my bottom lips, and chill bumps spread down my arms. I wanted to climb on his bike and kiss him. Touch him. All the things that had been consuming my every thought. But I knew there was a good chance my mother was watching us from inside. "So, tomorrow, I'm leaving school a few minutes early. Can you meet me out at our spot on the lake? I have something for you?"

"Oh, you do, do you? Does this have something to do with prom?" I teased. Everyone was starting to ask their dates to the dance. Each one more creative than the next. But I didn't care how he asked me. As long as I was going with Jett, I'd be happy. He wasn't a showy guy, but he was the most thoughtful boy I'd ever known. I knew he'd do something that actually meant something to *me.* Because that's who he was.

"All right. See you tomorrow. I love you."

"Love you more," I said. Because saying I love you, too, didn't feel right with this boy. I wasn't just copying the sentiment or going through the motions like I'd done for so long with Alec. I truly loved him in a way I'd never experienced. And there were no words to express how deep my feelings ran.

I watched his bike drive down the street and I walked back inside. I helped Mama clean up the kitchen and thanked her for inviting Jett and making the effort. Our home felt a little less fractured today and I was happy about it.

Clem came in my room and dropped to sit on my bed.

"Have you ever heard Mama apologize before? That was a first."

I laughed. "Definitely a first. But she owed him an apology."

"Absolutely. Damn, that boy is so fine." She fell back on the bed and giggled.

"You sure don't hide your crush on him."

She smiled. "I doubt any girl does. But he's crazy about you. Even a blind person could see that. Do you think you'll go to TU with him?"

"I'd like to go there. And not just because Jett is going there, but that's certainly icing on the cake. But they have such a good journalism program, and I wouldn't be too far from home, but far enough, you know?"

"So why not just hit accept and be done?" she asked,

pushing to sit up.

"Because I know Mama doesn't want me to go there, and even though I'm mad at her, I don't want to hurt her. I just need some time to figure it all out."

"You're a much more thoughtful person than me. Always have been." Clem pushed to her feet and hugged me before leaving my room.

I pulled up my account on the TU portal and stared at the box asking me for a decision. I had a little more time. And I hoped Mama would come around before then. It would sure be nice to have her blessing when I pressed that button. I declined the other schools aside from state and TU. I just wasn't ready to crush her just yet.

But at least I knew where I wanted to go. And that was progress.

I drove out to the lake to meet Jett after school and parked beside his motorcycle. I had the top to my car down as the weather was finally warming up and I loved the feel of the breeze blowing all around me. When I stepped out of my car, I saw pink flower petals on the path that led down to the water and I held my hand to my chest. I bent down to pick up one of the petals and recognized that it was a peony petal right away. My favorite. He knew it. He knew me. Better than anyone. I'd shared things with Jett that I'd never told anyone. Things about my family, my dreams for the future, my fears of not making everyone I loved happy. He listened. He held me. And we loved each other a little more each time we shared a different piece of our hearts with the other.

I followed the petals down to the hammock where he sat holding a bouquet of peonies. My short white eyelet dress was flowing in the breeze, and my favorite cowboy booties kicked up dirt as I made my way to him.

"You know those petals are from this bouquet and Violet would be none too happy that I ripped them off of three of her flowers to make that path."

I laughed. "It's perfect. I won't tell her, I promise."

He handed me the bouquet when I dropped down to sit beside him, and I held them up to my nose and breathed them in.

"So. How does one ask a writer to prom?" he asked, and his tongue swiped out to wet his bottom lip and it took all I had not to climb in his lap and kiss him. It was getting more challenging to not take things further. I wanted him in a way I'd never experienced. I'd never had physical needs before Jett. Sure, I'd felt like it was something I was supposed to eventually do in the past when I'd thought about taking things further with Alec. Like it was something I was supposed to do. But now…it was something I wanted to do. Something I dreamed about and thought about all the time. There was a fire burning so strong in me, that I'd never felt before. And I loved that he wanted to make sure I was ready. And I most definitely was ready.

"Hmmm…great question. What did you come up with?"

"Words. They're your thing." He laughed and handed me the Willow Springs newspaper. "Search the want ads."

I flipped through the paper frantically, my heart racing as I did so. Because I loved the newspaper. I read it every morning before school with my dad and he knew that, but I'd never paid much attention to the want ads. And there it was.

Ace, Will you go to prom with me? I love you, Jett

My breath caught in my throat, and a tear rolled down my cheek. This was quite possibly the most thoughtful thing anyone had ever done for me. From the flowers, to the newspaper—this boy just got me. He took the time to think about what I'd want, and that wasn't a common occurrence in my life before him.

"Oh my gosh. This is so sweet. Yes, of course I'll go with

you," I whispered because my emotions were making it difficult to speak.

"Eh, eh, eh…not so fast." He set the paper on the hammock and reached for my hand. I followed him down to the water pausing when I saw the rock display. The words YES and NO were spelled out in rocks right near the water. This took some time, and he'd done it for me. The water lapped against the shore, making one of my most favorite sounds in the world. Cypress trees surrounded us, and I took in the little white buds that had popped up all over the dark bark as the fresh scent of sage and lemon flooded my senses. I loved Texas in the spring.

I covered my mouth with my hands and shook my head. "I love this."

"So, I know you like rules. The rule is…you have to skip the rocks that hold your answer. And I sure as fuck hope it's yes because it took me forever to get the rocks straight." He laughed and my head fell back in a chuckle.

"Let's do this, Jett Stone." I leaned down and picked up the first rock at the top of the Y and skimmed it across the water with absolute precision. Just like he'd taught me.

He wrapped his arms around me and engulfed my small hand in his, skimming the next one together.

Because everything was better when I was with this boy.

We hung out at the lake until the sun disappeared behind the clouds and I kissed him goodbye. When I got home, dinner was ready, and I washed up before joining my family at the table.

We'd just finished eating and I'd shared how Jett had asked me to prom. Clem collapsed on the floor after falling from her seat in dramatic Clem fashion. We all laughed.

"That boy is something else. I need to get me my own Jett Stone someday," she said, returning to her seat.

"There's no rush," Mama said.

twenty-four

. . .

Jett

I'D BEEN WORKING for Wren for a few weeks and the pay was decent. But the perks were the best part. Wren loaned me his 1965 vintage mustang to drive Adelaide to prom. It was black and sleek, and I'd be lying if I didn't say I felt like a badass when I got behind the wheel. The dude had stepped up for me, offering me a job and insisting I take his car tonight.

Addy had told her mom that she was sleeping at Coco's with all the girls after prom, but she and I were going to camp out down by the water when we left the after party. The thought of spending the night with her had my adrenaline pumping, and my dick was on high alert. She was ready, and god knows I was ready. The timing felt right, but I wanted it to be special for her.

Shaw, Jax, Coco, Maura, Gigi and Ivy had all helped me set up a little camp site down by the water at our private spot that was not so private anymore. Hell, it was fine. They all wanted to help. Gigi had brought a tent that we'd set up and Coco contributed a bunch of battery-operated candles and lights for the tree beside the tent that she'd hooked up to a few remotes for me to use when we arrived. I hadn't seen it lit up at night yet, as we'd gotten things together this morning, but seeing as she'd brought around forty large candles, and several strings of lights, I imagined it would light the place up once it was dark. Maura brought a speaker for me to use to play some music and Ivy had gathered some blankets and pillows from home. Shaw and Jax stood there like the dumb asses they were most of the time, but when the girls walked away Shaw handed me a box of condoms and Jax pulled out a bottle of Axe cologne.

"Nobody likes a smelly lover, Jett," he'd said, and we'd had a good laugh.

It was a little odd that everyone seemed to know what we were planning to do, but to hell with it. They were just trying to make it special for us, and I didn't give a shit as long as Adelaide was happy.

I pulled up to her house and made my way to the front door anxious to see my girl all dressed up. I'd grown close to Clem and Mr. Edington as he'd come down to the motor shop a few times when I was working, claiming he needed a tune up on a brand-new car that clearly didn't need any work. But he'd chat with me about school and football, always making plans to come to TU to see me play at a few games.

Adelaide still hadn't decided where she was going to school, and she all but begged me to tell her what I thought she should do. To tell her it was okay to break her mother's heart and go to the school that she wanted to. And as much as I knew that's what she should do, I'd be damned if I'd be the one to say it. She had enough people in her life telling her what they wanted her to do. I wasn't about to be that guy. She needed to start making decisions for herself. Decisions that made her happy.

"Looking fine per usual Jett Stone," Clem said when the door flew open. Her auburn hair was piled on top of her head, and a few freckles peppered her cheeks making her look even younger than she was.

"Right back at you, Clem." I stepped inside, just as her father came down the stairs.

"You look very sharp, son," he said, and my chest squeezed. Something about a man I admired calling me son made me a little soft. And it didn't hurt that he was the father of the girl I loved more than life itself. I pushed away the thought that I'd be breaking his trust by spending the night out by the lake with her. But Adelaide had come up with this idea. I'd gone along with it happily of course, but I wanted the ball to be in her court. I'd quickly come to learn that the ball was rarely in Adelaide's court. It was time to rectify that.

"Thank you, Sir." I shook his hand and he pulled me in for a hug.

"You look very nice, Jett," Adelaide's mother said as she came down the stairs. "Addy will be right down."

Her gaze locked with mine, and I saw something there. Guilt? Empathy? I wasn't sure, but it was new. And it was different from the usual cold stare I'd always received from her.

"Thank you," I said, as I looked up to see my girl coming down the stairs. Her dark hair fell all around her shoulders in loose waves, and she wore a light pink fitted dress that hugged her curves in just the right places. Thin straps kept the dress in place on her shoulders, and it ran all the way down to the floor. Her tanned skin sparkled, and her dark eyes locked with mine.

I knew in that moment if I didn't spend the rest of my life with this girl, I'd never recover. She was everything that had been missing from my life, and now that I'd had a taste at happiness, I couldn't imagine living without it.

"Wow," I said under my breath, clearing my throat because I could feel her mother watching me. "You look gorgeous."

"You don't think the light pink is a little bland? It definitely wasn't my pick," her mother said, and everyone turned to look at her.

"I think it's perfect." Ellis shook his head and turned back to his daughter.

"I think it's elegant and beautiful." Clem's smile spread clear across her face.

I chuckled just slightly before my gaze locked with Adelaide's again. "The most beautiful girl I've ever seen."

She smiled and walked right into my arms when she got to the bottom of the stairs. I didn't care if her mom was standing right there, or that we had an audience. I just wanted to wrap my arms around her and keep her close.

"Thank you. Your mom and Gram are meeting us for picture's right?"

"Yep. They were already on their way when I left to come here." I laughed, and she interlaced her fingers with mine.

"You should drive with us to the photos, Addy. God knows you can't ride on a motorcycle in that dress. It'll be filthy," her mother said.

"I have a car," I said, trying to hide the irritation from my voice. Obviously, I wouldn't pick her up on my bike when she was wearing a formal gown.

"Darn. I like the back of your bike." Adelaide glared at her mother. She'd already known Wren had loaned me his car, but she was making a point to have my back just like she always did.

"All right, we'll meet you over there," her father said.

Adelaide bent down to grab her duffle bag for the sleepover she was supposed to be having at Coco's and I took it from her hand and slipped it over my shoulder. And I didn't miss the heat in her eyes when I did it.

"Oh my gosh. This is the car?" Clem shouted as they all followed us outside.

"Yep. It's a loaner."

"Very James Dean of you," her sister said, as she ran around the car to check it out.

"Why don't you ride with us," I said, winking at my girlfriend. I knew how important Clem was to her, and I didn't mind having her tag along at all.

"Are you serious? I don't have to ride over with the old folks." She clapped her hands together and Adelaide's head fell back in laughter.

"We heard that," her father said and I waved before opening the back door for their youngest daughter and the front passenger door for Adelaide.

"Thank you," my girl whispered in my ear and kissed my cheek.

The pictures seemed like they'd never end, but I didn't even care. Adelaide never let go of my hand as we smiled and laughed and posed for endless photographs. We took several pictures with all of our friends, some in large groups, some in small groups and some with just us. I was forced to let her go when she took a few photos with her best friends, and I smiled as I watched them hug and laugh and pose for different pictures. No wonder she loved this fucking town so much. She had so many good memories here. It surprised me when I realized that I did too. I looked around to see all the friendships I'd formed over the years. I caught my mom staring at me with watery eyes and I nodded. She'd sacrificed a lot to get me here, and I was damn well going to make her proud as I moved on to the next chapter.

"Hey Jett, do you mind if I get a photo with you and Addy? The Three Musketeers," Sherman asked, and my fucking chest squeezed. I loved the dude. Never in a million years thought that would happen.

"Of course," I said, pulling him in for a hug as his parents and his girlfriend, Sadie, laughed. We waited for Adelaide and the three of us posed for a few photos together.

"I'm happy for you two," he said. "You guys have become the best friends I've ever had. And Addy, I hope you go to TU. Don't sell yourself short. Get out of here for a little while and spread your wings."

Damn. Who knew Sherman Saxe had such a way with words?

They were equal parts nasally and brilliant.

"Thank you, Sherman. It's been an honor being pushed by you the last four years."

"Right back at you. I plan on coming to at least one game next year to see you play, Jett." He fist bumped me.

"I'd be honored. Text me and let me know when you're coming, and I'll do what I can to get you a good seat for the game."

"Sounds like a plan. See you guys at the dance. Will you be attending the after party?" he asked.

Adelaide's cheeks pinked, so she was obviously thinking about what we'd be doing after the party. "Yeah. We're going to go for a little bit," she said.

"Just for a little bit, Ace." I winked, and she squeezed my hand. I couldn't wait for her to see it all set up with the tent and the candles. And just to get to spend the whole night together. That's how it would be if we went to the same college and fuck if I didn't want that to happen, but I'd be dammed if I'd be just another person pushing my hopes on her. This was her choice, and I'd support her no matter what.

"I'll meet you there," Sherman said, pulling her in for a hug before turning to high five me.

"Jett, Addy," a voice called, and I turned to find Lenny Balsalcki standing there. At our senior prom photo's. What the hell?

"Lenny, hey. What are you doing here?" I asked, as Adelaide rushed toward the crazy old man and hugged him.

"I heard you were down here taking pictures, and I was in

the neighborhood. Thought I'd stop and get a photo of my two-favorite young people. Heck. You just might be my two-favorite people period, seeing you're the only ones I even like."

He was in the neighborhood? Willow Springs was fairly small, so I guess you could be in the neighborhood of anything you wanted to attend. The dude had become a permanent fixture in my life. He stopped by the auto shop often for bullshit reasons, and Adelaide and I went to his shop for hot chocolate at least once a week.

I laughed. "You like a lot more people than you let on. Nice of you to come here, though. Are you going soft on me, Len?"

He rolled his eyes. "Not a chance. Although if you ask Dr. Peabody he'll tell you a different story. That man finds every reason under the sun to run tests on me. Claiming my bones are brittle, my heart is weak, and my cholesterol's high. That bloodsucking scoundrel is robbing me blind with his nonsense. Just a way to charge up my bill."

Joseph Peabody was a doctor in town that I'd grown up with. Hell, the man was older than dirt and probably one of the nicest, most honest men in town.

Lenny held up a camera that looked like it was from another time period. "Okay, get together you two. God knows I won't be around forever. Hell, death's been knocking on my front door for years. I don't have all day."

We laughed and smiled as he took a few pictures.

"Wait. Mama, can you take a picture of me, Jett and Lenny?" Adelaide called out to her mother, who didn't look pleased with the request.

"What? No. I don't take pictures." Lenny shifted on his feet.

I raised a brow and tried to hide my smirk. "Get in the photo, Len. We're leaving for college soon, and we need a picture together."

The old grump moved to the other side of Adelaide, putting her in the center. "Fine. But I'm not smiling."

Adelaide's head fell back in laughter, and I'm sure I was looking at her instead of the camera, but it was a photo I'd be taking with me to college none the less. The man had grown on me. Hell, this whole damn town had grown on me more and more this last year.

The party was packed, and a group of us had settled in the large backyard at Ty's house. His parents had gone out of town, and their home was massive. The large yard had views of the lake, brick pavers covered an oversized patio with a U-shaped sofa and a firepit. Large cypress trees surrounded the patio, and white lights were strung over the sitting area. Music trickled through the speakers, and I sat with my arm around Adelaide, rubbing my hand up and down her arm. The temperature had dropped as the night sky blackened, and I hoped we wouldn't be too cold out in the tent. I leaned forward and pulled off my suit coat and wrapped it over her shoulders.

Shaw and Coco sat beside us, and Ivy, Maura and Gigi were sitting on the other side of the couch. Ty was in the house making sure things weren't getting out of control, and Jax walked outside and dropped to sit on the other side of me.

"Where's Lydia?" I asked.

"Her friend, Breanne just puked in a potted plant in the living room, so she's trying to get her to the bathroom. I don't think Ty is all too happy about it." Jax shook his head and chuckled.

"I knew this was a bad idea. Of course, Alec pressured him into having the after party because his parents were going out of town. I need to go help him." Ivy pushed to her feet.

"I'll help you," Maura and Gigi said at the same time and everyone laughed as the three girls made their way inside.

"Well, if it isn't the devil himself," Coco hissed, as Alec stepped outside.

"Hello to you too, Coco," Alec rolled his eyes and shot her a glare.

"You do know that your best friend's house is getting trashed. This was supposed to be a small party and somehow everyone and their fricking mother is here." Coco raised a brow at him in question.

Ty had told us that he was pissed because Alec took it upon himself to invite way more people than Ty had agreed to.

"It's a party. Aren't you the queen of a *good time*?" Alec said, his words slurring, and everyone stiffened at his comment. The dude was an asshole. He never wavered.

"Are you seriously slut shaming me, you piece of shit. You know nothing about me. And seeing as you only sleep with people that you aren't actually dating, doesn't seem like you're in a position to throw stones." Coco sat forward on the couch.

"Watch yourself, Taulson. You're out of line." Shaw pushed to his feet, squaring his shoulders as he moved in Alec's space.

"I've got no beef with you Coco. Just saying, lighten' up. I actually came out here to find you," Alec said, turning his attention to my girlfriend.

"Why?" she asked, irritation rolled off her as she moved her body closer to mine.

"Come on, Addy. I just wanted to talk to you about an issue with my parents. It's not something I can really talk to anyone else about. Unless you aren't allowed to be away from your boyfriend for two fucking seconds to have a conversation with a friend who you've known your entire life."

The piece of shit had no shame. He'd guilt her into doing

what he wanted because she'd finally seen through his bullshit and it was the only way he'd get her to agree.

Adelaide turned to face me. "Give me a minute."

I let out a long breath and every muscle in my body tensed. He was clearly drunk, and the dude just rubbed me wrong. Always had.

"You sure?" I leaned closer and whispered in her ear.

"Yeah. And then we can head out, okay?" Her little nose skimmed against mine before she pushed to her feet.

"You can't talk to Karina about your problems?" Coco asked, when Alec's fake ass smile spread across his face because Adelaide had agreed to speak to him.

"I haven't known Karina my whole life, Coco. But thanks for fucking asking." He shot her the bird.

"That fucking guy. I will not miss seeing that asshole every day," Shaw hissed, dropping back down to sit beside Coco.

I pushed to my feet and watched as Alec led Adelaide around the side of the house. What the fuck was he up to? I paced around the patio, trying to figure out how to handle the situation. I wasn't going to tell her who talk to. I wasn't an asshole. But I sure as fuck didn't like it. Alarm bells were going off in my head, and I fought with every instinct that I had not to react. Not to make a scene.

"I don't fucking like this. I don't trust him." I tugged at my hair and glanced back around beside the house, but I couldn't see them anymore.

"It'll be all right. He won't do anything." Coco pushed to her feet and moved beside me. "She loves you. You know that. But she has a lot of guilt about Alec and all he's going through, because that's Addy. And he knows how to prey on that. He's so manipulative. And he reeks of whiskey, so I'm guessing he broke into Ty's dad's liquor cabinet. He has zero respect for anyone but himself."

The sound of a muffled scream came from around the

corner, and I was moving before I could even process what it was. Coco and Shaw were on my heals and when I rounded the corner of the house, I saw red.

twenty-five

. . .

Adelaide

"STOP BEING SO DRAMATIC. I just want to talk to you." Alec's grip on my arm was so tight, I'd slapped it away. But he'd gripped harder, his hand came over my mouth and I'd startled. He'd never been physical with me. But he shoved me up against the brick siding of the house, and his eyes were wild. "You need to stop this game, Addy. You've made your point. It's enough. You know we're going to be together."

I bit down on his hand and stomped hard on his foot as I tried to catch my breath from him practically smothering my airways. He reeked of booze and his hair was disheveled. He was a mess in every sense of the word.

"Fuck. You bit me? What the hell," he said through his laughter. Obviously, it hadn't hurt him much, or the boy had just lost all ability to feel anything anymore.

"Let me go," I shoved at his chest and tried to get around him. Two tall evergreens were beside us, and it felt as if the walls were closing in around me. My breaths grew labored, and panic was setting in.

Was I afraid of Alec?

The boy I'd known my entire life?

We may not be together anymore, but we were family. He'd never hurt me, would he?

"Why? So you can be with that piece of shit? Enough is enough. I said I was sorry about Karina. Stop this shit. We're going to school together next year, and it's time to put this behind us." He pressed hard against my shoulders, trying to keep me in place. His face was so close to mine and I turned my head as fear engulfed me.

"You're hurting me," I shouted, hoping it would snap him out of it, or someone else would hear me. Alec was a lot bigger than me, and my first attempt at pushing him away had been an epic failure.

My mind raced with what to do.

I couldn't believe this was happening.

"Yeah? Well, you're hurting me, Addy. You're hurting me so fucking bad. My fucking family is falling apart, and you haven't been there for me. My dad is moving out. My mom is a mess." His words broke on a sob, but he pressed me harder against the wall, and shook me. My head fell back, slamming against the brick twice and I yelped.

Alec jerked back and tears that I hadn't even realized were falling made it difficult for me to make out what was happening. Jett was there. Everything blurred together as the movements were fast and jerky. Jett was on top of Alec, and he hit him hard in the face as fury spewed around him. Shaw and Jax were there, pulling Jett to his feet. Coco hurried toward me, and I shook my head with disbelief.

"Addy? Are you okay?" Coco reached for my arm and I jumped. I glanced down to see Jett's jacket had slipped from one shoulder and I pulled it into place quickly.

"Yes. I'm okay." My hand flew to my chest as I tried to get my breathing under control. My gaze locked with Jett's as he shrugged his two best friends off and moved toward me.

"What happened?" he asked, searching my face, and gently tucking my hair behind my ears.

"He, I don't know. He was angry, and…" I couldn't find the words for what had just happened, because I was still trying to process it.

"She's fine. Fuck you all. I thought I knew you, Addy. I was wrong," Alec shouted as he pushed to his feet, and spit on the ground before storming away.

"Did he touch you?" Jett asked, and the look of concern in his eyes nearly brought me to my knees.

I shook my head, but when I tried to speak, a sob escaped my throat. The tears came faster and more hurried now, and I covered my mouth to try to stop my emotions from overflowing.

Alec Taulson had just been aggressive with me. Physically aggressive. I was afraid of him. The boy I'd known my whole life.

Jett wrapped me in his arms, and I buried my face in his chest. "Come on. Let's get out of here."

We stepped out of the bushes and I looked up to see the faces of a very worried Coco, Shaw and Jax. "I'm okay. I think he's really drunk. He's never done anything like that before."

Coco wrapped her arms around both Jett and I, which made me laugh through my tears.

"Will you text me later and let me know you're okay?"

"Of course," I said.

Jett's fingers intertwined with mine, and he led me to the car. Neither of us had any alcohol. We wanted to be clear headed tonight. I was spending the night with him, and I wanted to remember every moment. But now, Alec had left a dark cloud over our heads, and I hated him for that.

Jett leaned over to buckle my seatbelt once I was in the car.

"Do you want me to take you home instead? You've had a rough night," he asked after he slipped in the driver's seat and turned to face me.

"No. I think he probably wanted to ruin my night, and we

aren't going to give him that. I want to be with you. Nothing's changed." I lowered the interior mirror and tried to clean up my face.

"You were just assaulted by that asshole. Everything has changed."

"Not between us. I love you. That hasn't changed. And honestly, that's all that matters right now. Please, please, don't let him ruin this for us."

His jaw clenched, but he nodded. "I'm sorry I didn't get there sooner. I was trying to be respectful. Can you tell me what happened?"

"Thanks for coming when you did. He was drunk and angry. Shouting at me that I haven't been there for him with all he's going through." A tear ran down my face and I swiped it away. I looked down to see my hands trembling in my lap and I squeezed them together to try to stop the shaking.

"That piece of shit. I love you so much, you know that, right?" he asked.

"I do."

"Did he put his hands on you?" His gaze studied mine, searching me for answers. I got the feeling that he was waiting for my answer before he'd pull away from the curb.

"He just shook me a bit. I'm fine. I really want to get out of here though, Jett." I wiped away the last of my tears and forced a smile. Alec wasn't going to ruin this night for us. He was drunk and lost and I'd tried to help him, but I was done. He'd crossed a line tonight that I didn't know if we would ever recover from.

And I was okay with that.

Sad? Sure.

But after what he'd just done, I was certain I didn't know him at all anymore.

Jett pulled away and reached for my hand. "Okay. It's

taking everything in me to drive away. I want to go beat his ass."

"Please don't. I just want to go. Just you and me."

He drove down the dirt road toward our favorite spot on the lake and told me to wait in the car for a minute before he stepped outside. I looked through the front window just as candles lit up the space around the hammock. Jett opened the passenger door, my overnight bag slung over his shoulder, and I took his hand.

"What is this?" I asked, my gaze moving around to see a tent surrounded by white candles. Even the large tree had twinkle lights.

"We were out here today setting it all up," he said, holding up two little remotes in his hand.

"I can't believe you did this" I said, as he led me over to the adorable little campsite. He dropped my bag at his feet.

"I had help. Your musketeers are quite the little worker bees when they're doing something for you." He wrapped his arms around my middle, my back to his chest, as I took it in.

"*Magic willows*." I laughed and turned in his arms. "Thank you for doing this."

"I'd do anything for you, Ace." His words were sweet, but I saw the struggle in his dark eyes. Anger. Sadness. Frustration.

"I'm fine. I promise. He was just drunk."

"I wanted to hurt him. If Shaw and Jax hadn't pulled me off, I don't know if I would have stopped," he said, his thumb grazing along my bottom lip. "You sure he didn't hurt you?"

"I'm sure. He just squeezed my shoulders." I said, not wanting to tell him that the back of my head had also taken a couple shots when he shook me.

He slipped his coat down my shoulders and pulled his phone from his back pocket. He turned the flashlight on and held it above my arms, scanning each one as he cursed under his breath. I looked from one shoulder to the next, taking in the bruising that had already turned a purplish-blue.

"I'll fucking kill him," Jett hissed.

I shifted my arms, slipping his coat back in place.

"He's miserable, trust me. You don't need to get in trouble over him. And we actually have tonight together. Just you and me. I don't want to waste another second on him."

"Okay." He nodded, and I didn't miss the stress that he tried to hide from his gaze. "What do you want to do?" He asked, as he pulled me back into his arms. My hands tangled in his hair and my breathing picked up at his nearness.

"I know it's cold, but I think we should night swim." I bit down on my bottom lip at the thought. Night swimming was on my bucket list, as was swimming in my birthday suit with my boyfriend.

He cocked his head to the side. "Did you bring your swimsuit?"

"Nope." I shook my head, feeling the heat spread up the back of my neck.

He quirked a brow. "Me either. Let's do it."

He carried my bag and we slipped inside the tent. There were several candles inside the cozy pavilion and even after all that had happened in the last hour, I was suddenly overcome with desire. I think having the warmth of someone I cared about was really important to me right now and to make us both forget what happened earlier in the evening. This was what I wanted to remember, the night I was finally going to get to spend the night with Jett. God knows I'd thought about it more times than I could count.

I pulled two towels out of my duffle bag and handed him one.

"You brought towels?" His head fell back in laughter. "No bathing suit, but a towel to dry off with. I like your style, Ace."

The way that he looked at me, left me weak in the knees

and he hadn't even touched me yet. He unbuttoned his dress shirt and shrugged it off his shoulders. My breath caught in my throat as I studied his chiseled abs and muscled chest. I moved closer, running my fingers over his tattoo, wanting to touch every inch of him. He undid the button on his dress pants, and they dropped in a puddle on the floor. His black briefs hugged his body like a second skin, drawing attention to the enormous elephant in the room.

And oh my god.

Calling it enormous was an understatement.

"Wow."

His head fell back in laughter, and his tongue darted out to wet his lips and I sucked in a long breath.

"You know we don't have to do anything tonight. There's no pressure. I'm just happy we get to spend the night together."

"I want to do things," I said, startled by the sound of my own voice. It was gruff and laced with need.

He chuckled. "Oh yeah? What things do you want to do?"

I leaned forward and reached for the hem of his briefs. "All the things."

I tugged his briefs down and stared in awe at the sight of him when they dropped to his ankles. He stood there totally confident, like this wasn't something we hadn't done hundreds of times before.

"When do I get to see you?" he rasped.

I turned around and waited for him to unzip my dress. I could feel his warm breath on my skin and goosebumps ran down my neck and back. He leaned forward and kissed my shoulder, unsnapping my strapless bra as his lips trailed back up my neck.

He turned me around to face him and I held my breath, unable to move.

"So beautiful, Ace," he whispered.

I stood there, completely bare aside from my lace panties.

"You still want to swim?" he whispered, and he leaned down and kissed my shoulders again where Alec had marked me.

"Yes. Let's go in the water first." I needed to calm down. My body was on fire. Desire all but engulfed me. I didn't know how to handle these feelings. I leaned down and slipped my underwear down my legs as he studied me as if he were memorizing every inch of me. Every curve. Every line. I shivered and he reached for a towel and wrapped it around me.

"Are you sure those bruises don't hurt?"

I tucked the top of the towel around my chest and watched as he wrapped the other towel around his waist. I reached in my bag for a hair tie and piled my hair in a bun on top of my head. There was a makeshift bed with lots of blankets and pillows on the tent floor and butterflies rushed my belly.

"I'm positive. Come on." I ducked through the small opening to get out the door and we walked down to the water where we'd stood hundreds of times before. But this time things were different.

"You sure you want to do this? The waters going to be cold," he quirked a brow.

I dropped my towel and ran into the dark, cold water. I didn't stop until I was neck deep and howling in laughter. Jett came up behind me and wrapped his arms around me.

"It's not as bad as I expected." I turned so I was facing him and reaching my hands around his neck. He hiked me up so he could hold me, and my legs came around his waist. My head fell back in laughter again as I felt his desire beneath me.

He smirked. "Are you seriously laughing because I have a boner? You do realize that you're naked in my arms."

"I thought cold water took care of that?"

"I don't think anything could take care of that when I'm with you," he said, his lips grazing mine.

His mouth covered mine, tasting and exploring, and my hands tangled in his hair. We were both breathless and I couldn't stop my hips from grinding up against him. It was clear that he wanted me as much as I wanted him. I was no longer cold, not even a little bit. In fact, I was burning up.

"Let's go back in the tent," I whispered against his mouth.

He continued to kiss me as he walked back toward the shore with me in his arms. Once we were out of the water and the light breeze hit my skin, he set me on my feet and wrapped the towel around me again before pulling the other around his waist.

We walked back in the tent and he zipped the door closed. I dropped on the floor to sit on the blankets. "This is really sweet. I love all the candles." I glanced over and beside the bed there was a small bouquet of pink peonies tied with twine. "My favorite flower."

"My favorite girl." He dropped to sit beside me.

I pulled him down and kissed him again. My towel coming undone as I did so. I tugged at his, wanting to press against his bare body.

"I love you."

"Love you, Ace." He stretched out beside me and we both rolled on our sides so we could face one another.

I gripped his erection in my hand. "Show me what to do."

His hand came over mine, and slowly guided me up and down his shaft.

"Jesus. Just like that," he whispered.

His hand let go of mine and moved down my back, and over my chest, stopping to cup my breast. His fingers teased my hard peaks and I arched into his touch. He rolled me on my back and my hand fell to the side as he kissed his way down my neck, pausing to kiss each breast, licking and sucking and driving me wild.

"Jett," I whispered, and I couldn't stop the little pants that followed. I writhed beneath him, desperate for more.

His hand moved between my legs as he'd done before but being naked and alone in the dark only intensified everything. He teased my most sensitive spot and I grinded up against his hand.

"I know, baby," he said, as one finger slipped inside, and I bucked against his touch frantic for relief. "Let yourself go."

I cried out his name and gasped as I continued to move against his hand.

"Oh my god." I rolled on my side to face him. "Did you bring a condom?"

"I did. But there's no rush."

"I want this to happen. Please don't make me wait."

"You sure?"

"Positive." I ran my fingers over his rope bracelet that matched my own, thinking about all the ways I'd frayed this year. All the ways I'd found myself, found what I wanted, who I was. All because I'd met this boy who believed in me.

I wanted this.

I wanted him.

He leaned forward, capturing my mouth as he settled above me.

"I swear you're the most beautiful fucking girl in the world Adelaide Edington. I don't know what I did to deserve you."

A tear ran down my cheek, and he caught it with his thumb.

"I don't know what I did to deserve you," I whispered.

"I guess we're just lucky we found our way, huh?"

"So lucky. I'm going to tell my parents that I'm going to TU tomorrow. I don't know what I'm waiting for. It's not like my mom is suddenly going to be okay with it. So, I just need to do it."

"Is that what you want?"

"Yes. Without a doubt. And it's not just because you're going there too. Sure, that's a massive bonus. But it's the best journalism school that I got into. One of the best in the country. They offered me a partial scholarship, and it's not too far from home. The only negative is that my mom won't be happy about it, and I know I shouldn't care, and I really wish I didn't." I was rambling, because all these emotions were overtaking me.

His gaze searched mine. "That's part of what I love about you. You care so fucking much. Don't ever apologize for that. But you should do what makes you happy and she'll have to get on board."

I nodded. Staring up into his dark eyes as he remained propped above me. "You're right. And I'm happy we're here tonight. Happiest with you."

"I'm happiest with you. Tell me what you want. What you need."

"You," I whispered, urging him closer.

He leaned over me and reached for his backpack, pulling out the foil packet. He pushed up on his knees and tore it open with his teeth before rolling the latex over his thick, hard erection. His eyes never left mine. I bit down hard on my bottom lip, praying it didn't bleed, but doing everything in my power to stay calm.

He kissed me so soft as he settled between my legs, teasing my entrance. I gasped and arched toward him, needing to get closer.

"Are you sure?" he asked, and I heard the struggle in his voice. The desire. The restraint.

"Please. No more waiting."

Those simple words were all he needed. He slowly moved, inch by inch as my body adjusted to the intrusion. The sensation was equal parts pleasure and pain. I gasped and closed my eyes as he pushed a little further.

"Are you okay? Does it hurt?"

"It hurts and it feels good. Is that normal?"

"Yes. But tell me to stop if it's too much," he said, before his mouth covered mine. His tongue exploring my mouth, as he tipped my head back to take the kiss deeper.

He pushed in the last bit and he groaned, waiting for me to show him I was okay. He remained perfectly still before I started to move, and we found our rhythm. The sensation so overwhelming, I never wanted him to stop. His hand moved between us and he rubbed little circles between my legs as we continued to move. He let me set the pace, and he followed my lead. Our labored breaths the only audible sound in the tent, as the water lapped against the shore in the distance.

My body tingled and my legs started to shake as I moved faster and faster, and he did the same. His fingers keeping the same pace, driving me wild with need, before the most overwhelming feeling in my life ripped through me. I shattered into a million little pieces and cried out a sound I'd never heard before. He continued to move his hand against me as I rode out every last wave of pleasure just as he went over the edge himself. Hearing him cry out my name while his face was buried in my neck was the best thing I'd ever heard. Seeing him come undone and lose control because of me was the most empowering feeling of my life. I held him close as he continued to rock against me.

"Holy shit, Ace. That was amazing." He brushed the hair that had broken free from my bun away from my face.

"Is this how it always is?" I asked because no one had ever told me how incredible it would be.

"Only with you."

I smiled up at him. Feeling connected to him in a way I'd never experienced.

It was more than love.

Jett Stone was…everything.

twenty-six

. . .

Adelaide

I FELL asleep in Jett's arms to the sound of crickets chirping and waves rolling against the shore. The temperature had dropped and we'd both bundled up in sweats at some point during the night. I couldn't remember a time in my life where I'd ever been so at peace. So content.

A loud honking woke me from my stupor. Jett jerked, shifting me to the side, and sitting up.

"Stay here," he said, pushing to his feet.

"What's going on?" I asked, rubbing my eyes, and reaching for my phone. It was just after three o'clock in the morning.

More honking.

He unzipped the tent and stepped outside, and I couldn't help but to follow him. I wasn't about to let him go out there on his own.

"Coco?" he called out, and I didn't miss the concern in his voice.

Coco emerged from her car sprinting toward us. It was dark, but the bright lights from her car lit up the space around us. My stomach flipped at the sight of her. Swollen eyes, and red cheeks. It was apparent she'd been crying.

"Oh my god. What's wrong?" I asked, running toward her.

"Alec was in an accident. He's hurt bad, Addy. Your parents called my parents, and they know you aren't at my house. I tried to cover for you, but I don't think it even matters at this point. I need to get you to the hospital right away."

"Jesus. What happened?" Jett asked, as I turned to run to the tent for my bag.

I heard Coco tell him that he and Karina had gotten into a fight at the party, and he'd left angry. She didn't know much more, but she didn't hide her concern when she told us she'd heard he left in his car, but she wasn't certain.

Alec was way past being in any condition to drive when I'd been there, and I took a minute to catch my breath. Had he driven drunk? Would he do that? Was he in an uber and they'd been an accident?

Oh my god.

I ran back toward them with my bag strung over my shoulder. "Can you drive me to the hospital?" I asked Coco.

Jett flinched at my words. I couldn't ask him to take me. And I didn't have time to argue about it. Coco's car was running, and I knew I needed to go there now.

"Of course," she said.

"I'm sorry. I have to go." I kissed his cheek and took off running to Coco's car.

The first few minutes we drove to the hospital were quiet. I shot Jett a text apologizing for running out and telling him how much I loved him.

I was processing what could have happened?

"Do we know for sure if he drove his car? Could he have called an uber?" I asked, swiping at the tears running down my face. I could only imagine how frantic Mama T and Boone Taulson would be. "Do we know how serious it is?"

"I don't know much, Addy. My mom said your mom was

crying and said it was really bad. Shaw said he saw Alec walking toward his car shortly before we left, and Ty was arguing with him to give him his keys and spend the night there. But I don't know what happened after that. I tried to call Ivy, but her phone must be off. I just drove straight to you because I knew you'd want to be there."

"Oh my gosh. Please say he didn't get behind the wheel, Co. He is acting so crazy lately. I don't know what is going on with him." My words broke on a sob as I thought about how bad this could be.

We pulled up to the hospital and I jumped out of the car before Coco even turned off the engine. She was on my heels as we both took off in a full sprint. When I reached the lobby, the scene before me made it clear that things were not okay.

I could not have prepared for the hysteria that followed.

My parents rushed toward me, tears streaming down their faces.

"Addy, my god, where were you," my mom shouted, before grabbing me and pulling me in for a hug. "Never mind. It's not important. What matters is that you're here now. Alec is in surgery. He was in an accident." She said through her sobs.

"What happened?" I croaked, looking to my father who appeared a bit more in control but clearly shaken.

"Alec hit a tree. He was pinned inside the car, and they had to cut him out. The paramedics placed him in a ridged collar to immobilize the head and neck to transport him here. They determined he has a herniated disc and, or possibly a fractured vertebrae that is compressing his spine. He was taken in for immediate surgery. That's all we know right now."

I covered my mouth with my hand and shook my head with disbelief. "What does that mean? Is he going to be okay?"

"He was conscious, yes. He spoke to his parents. But he couldn't feel his legs or feet."

Mama T stormed toward me with a look I'd never seen before on her face. Coco reached for my hand and squeezed my fingers so tight I thought they'd break off. "He told us, Adelaide. He told us that your low rent boyfriend hit him. And you did nothing. That's why he left the party upset." She spewed her ugliness at me, and I stood there speechless. Because she was hurting, and I understood it. But from what Coco had told me, he'd been at that party hours after Jett and I had left. "He needs you right now. More than ever. He may never walk again, Addy. Do not turn your back on him now. I swear to all that is holy I will report Jett for attacking him. Boone knows the dean at TU, and I'll make sure that boy loses that scholarship and winds up doing nothing with his life just like his mother."

"That's enough, Lila. You're upset," Boone said to his wife, and my father stepped beside me and wrapped an arm around my shoulder.

"You know I think of you as a second daughter, Addy. But if you turn your back on my son when he needs you most, I will never forgive you." She turned on her heels and walked back to the chairs to sit with her husband.

It was my mother's turn next. "I don't even want to know where you've been at this point, because you clearly lied to us. But I did not raise my daughter to turn her back on her family, and Alec Taulson is family, whether you like it or not. You've known him your whole life. You will step up. And if Jett had anything to do with this accident, he will be held accountable, Adelaide." My mother stormed off to sit with Mama T, and I stared with disbelief.

How did this become Jett's fault?

My father led Coco and me off to the corner across the lobby and bent down to meet my gaze. "Do you know what happened to Alec? Did he and Jett have a fight?"

I nodded and swiped at the tears streaming down my face. Coco squeezed my hand in support. "Alec was drunk and angry. He got, um, a little physical with me. Jett only stepped in to stop him from hurting me. You can't let Mama T make that call. This is not Jett's fault."

"What? He got physical with you? In what way? Did he hurt you?"

I looked over at the Taulson's as they sat in the chairs crying. "I'm fine. But Alec was pretty drunk."

"He was drinking?"

"Mr. Edington," Coco interrupted. "I was at that party. Alec stayed long after Jett and Addy left. He actually had a fight with Karina and stormed off toward his car. Shaw said that Ty was trying to take Alec's keys from him, and I don't know what happened after that. I didn't know he drove until I heard he was in an accident."

My father ran a hand down his face. "Jesus. This is not good. Let's just pray that he's okay first, and we'll deal with the rest as we go. Mama T is upset right now. This isn't your fault nor is it Jett's fault. But right now, we need to just support them and pray Alec will be okay."

"Of course," I said, swiping at my face for the millionth time since I'd heard about the accident. "Co, you should go home. Thanks for getting me. I need to be here. I'll call you when I hear anything, okay?"

She hugged me so tight I thought I'd stop breathing, and tears continued to fall down my cheeks.

"Do not let that woman manipulate you, Addy. You and Jett did nothing wrong. If Alec drove that car, that is on him. No one else," she whispered close to my ear.

I nodded and looked up at my father who clearly heard what Coco had said to me. He was deep in thought, and I was fairly certain that it was about the fact that Alec had been very intoxicated last night. My father loved the Taulson's, but he also respected the law and rules, and he would not be okay with Alec drinking and driving.

Coco left the hospital and Daddy and I went to sit in the chairs with my mother and the Taulson's.

"Where's Clem?" I asked my father, as he reached for my hand to comfort me.

"We woke her to tell her we were leaving. We didn't know how serious things were and wanted to come here first. I'll go pick her up in a few hours and bring her over."

We sat in silence as Mama T sobbed, and Alec's little sister, Maisie came to sit on the other side of me. She leaned her head against my shoulder and dozed off. I had a few texts from Jett and quickly responded to let him know that I didn't know much and would keep him posted. I did not want to get caught texting my boyfriend while my ex-boyfriend was currently in surgery.

I went to use the restroom as the sun shined through the lobby doors from outside letting us know morning had arrived. Hours had passed. When I returned, Dr. Toby was speaking to the Taulson's and my parents stood beside them. I walked over, as Mama T leaned against my mother and sobbed.

"So, you don't know if he'll walk again, John? We're just supposed to wait this out?" Boone said calling the doctor by his first name as they'd grown up together. Alec's father ran a hand through his hair yanking at the ends.

"Unfortunately, it's a waiting game now. We're optimistic that as he recovers the swelling and inflammation in his spine will decrease and we're hopeful that he will regain function. I've done everything I can on my end, and we'll have to see how he recovers and what kind of mobility he has. He'll need months of physical therapy to ensure his muscle tone returns. This is not a sprint, it's a marathon. Can I have a word with you, Boone."

My mother helped get Mama T to her seat and Dr. Toby

said the nurse would come and take us back to see Alec in a bit. I watched as Boone spoke to the doctor, his hands flying in the air, and then he pointed his finger in his face angrily. He squared his shoulders and Dr. Toby stared with disbelief. I'd never seen Boone Taulson quite so intimidating, and this was a side of him that was foreign to me. He was unraveling before our eyes.

Like father, like son. They were both full of surprises.

My father walked over and placed a hand on Boone's shoulder when Dr. Toby walked away. I tried to make out their words and I watched as Daddy startled a few times and shook his head. Boone stormed off and walked out the front door of the hospital.

"He just needs to walk it off," Daddy said to my mother and Mama T.

He came to sit beside me, as I'd purposely left some distance between myself and the angry mothers who'd been watching me with such disdain it made my skin crawl.

"What's going on?" I whispered. "Is it worse than we thought?"

My father nodded and my heart sank. What if Alec died? What if that was my last interaction with him, and we never saw one another again? The boy I'd learned to walk with. The boy I'd grown up with.

My father glanced over his shoulder to make sure no one was listening before facing me again. "Boone is using his legal expertise to make sure that Alec's blood alcohol report never sees the light of day. There's only one reason he'd be doing that."

"Can he do that?"

"If he has a legal reason for having it locked and sealed, I suppose he can. It sure as hell doesn't sound legal to me, nor is he doing his son any favors by not holding him accountable for his actions."

I shook my head and squeezed my eyes closed. How did

we get here? Alec had just come out of surgery after being in a terrible accident that he'd actually caused.

"They can't hurt Jett can they? What if they lie about what happened and he loses his scholarship?" I whispered.

I expected my father to say that it wasn't a possibility. That the Taulson's would never do such a thing. That doing something like that would never be okay.

But he didn't.

"They shouldn't be allowed to get away with doing that. But I don't know at the moment how far they would be willing to go to protect Alec."

I choked back the sob in my throat, as a nurse opened the double doors to take us back.

"Come on, Addy. He's going to want to know you're here for him. He's been a mess since you broke up with him," Mama T said.

I heard my father call out for my mother, and they said they'd meet us in back shortly.

When we stepped in the room, Alec was lying in a bed with both of his legs wrapped casts, his neck was strapped into some sort of contraption, and his face was cut and bruised.

I wondered if my tears would ever stop coming. I'd never cried this much in my life but seeing Alec so helpless and hurt was difficult. Worrying about how this happened and what the Taulson's would do made things even worse.

And worrying about Jett made me sick to my stomach.

Maisie sobbed and held on to her mother as Alec struggled to open his eyes. When they met mine, his lips turned up in the corners the slightest bit.

"Addy. You're here." His words were rough, as if someone had dragged sandpaper along his throat.

I moved toward him and gently placed my hand over his. "Of course, I am."

"They don't know if I'm going to walk again for sure," he

said, and I could still smell the booze on his breath. "But we'll get through this together, right?"

I nodded. "Yes. You've got this. I promise."

I didn't know what else to say.

"I love you. Thanks for being here," he said, and his eyes fell closed. Mama T grabbed a chair for me to sit in, and she wrapped her hand over mine and Alec's.

"I told you. You two can get through anything together," she said, as my parents entered the room.

"How is he?" Mama asked, and for the first time since I'd arrived at the hospital, she looked at me with a little bit of empathy.

"He was happy to see Addy here. She promised him they'd get through this together. Just like I knew she would," Mama T said, moving over to drop down in the chair on the other side of Alec. That wasn't exactly what I'd said, but I wasn't about to call her out.

My mom nodded, but she looked hesitant. Maybe dad had told her what really happened.

We spent the rest of the day listening to a few different doctors and specialists come in to give us their input. Mama T had called everyone she knew for guidance, and Boone Taulson had been on the phone with specialists all over the country over the last few hours. The bottom line was that Alec was going to have to work hard if he wanted to recover. There were a lot of unknowns right now, and it was a waiting game.

"Okay. Addy, I have you covered for school. Obviously, Boone knows Principal Horton, and we spoke to him an hour ago. Seeing as it's your senior year, and you only have three days of class left, they've excused both you and Alec under these circumstances. I knew you wouldn't want to leave him. He'll start physical therapy this week if he's up for it and he'll need you by his side."

Alec was awake but hadn't said much. But I'd sat there

beside him, just as I'd promised I'd do. My heart sank as I thought about Jett. The night we'd shared. This was my own private hell. I'd experienced the most amazing night of my life, only to be followed by absolute devastation. I didn't know how to feel. My phone was filled with texts from Jett and my best friends, and I hadn't responded to a single one in hours. I didn't even know what to say at this point and now I'd just learned that I wouldn't be finishing my school year. It was a lot to process.

"Thanks for being here, Addy," Alec whispered, catching me by surprise.

"Of course." I smiled, and my gaze searched his. The Alec I'd known my entire life had to be in there somewhere. And I owed him some loyalty, didn't I?

"Have you accepted yet to attend state? I know the deadline is coming up." he asked, and everyone in the room went silent putting their attention on me. Clem was there now, and her eyes danced between me and my parents as if she were hoping they'd rescue me. Alec was lying in a bed after drinking and driving and nearly killing himself, unsure if he'd walk again, and he wanted to know if I'd made my decision about college? Yet I felt as if my answer held as much importance as his recovery did.

I cleared my throat. "No. I hadn't made my decision yet. I was planning to talk to my parents about it this weekend."

"Well, you know where your Mama wants you to go. And now, with Alec's situation, he's got a long road to recovery, and he's going to need you if he hopes to get there," Mama T spoke, as she tucked the blanket in around his chest.

I nodded fighting back the tears that threatened to fall. I looked up to find both of my parents staring down at their feet. It was unbelievably awkward.

"Yep." It's all I could say. I was drowning in guilt and I didn't know what to do. I didn't know who to turn to or if anyone was actually looking out for me anymore aside from

Jett and my friends. And then I felt incredibly selfish for thinking of myself when he was lying there completely unsure of what his future held.

"We're going to take Addy and Clem and head home and give you all some time together. We could all use a shower and some dinner, and we'll check on you in a little bit," my father said, and I pushed to my feet, desperate for some space.

Some air.

Some room to think.

"You'll come back tonight, Addy, right?" Alec asked.

I nodded. "Yes. Of course."

"We'll be waiting for you, sweetheart." Mama T pulled me in for a hug. It didn't feel the way it used to. It didn't feel safe or genuine anymore. Maybe I was just tired. But when she pulled away, the way she looked at me felt more like a warning.

Her love came at a cost, and she'd just let me know what her price was. And I hadn't forgotten her threat against Jett. I didn't know if she'd just been emotional when she'd said it or if she meant it. But they were obviously willing to cover up the fact that Alec had been driving drunk and it made me wonder how far she'd go to get what she wanted.

My father stiffened as he placed a hand on the small of my back to lead me toward the door. Clem intertwined my fingers with hers and we all four walked out to the car in silence. The drive home was the same. Maybe we were all exhausted. Maybe we were just all at a loss for words. We pulled in the driveway and my father turned off the car, but no one got out. He turned in his seat to look at my mother and then glance at us in the back seat.

"It is not okay for anyone to ever put their hands on you. I don't care whose son he is. Nor is it okay to get behind the wheel of a car drunk," my father said, and Clem gasped.

"Who put their hands on you? Alec drove drunk?"

"I'm fine. Alec was drunk and acting erratic. But it doesn't matter now. He's sitting in a hospital bed and we need to focus on his recovery." I opened the back door and stepped out of the car. I was on overload. And now that it was actually out there, it felt like a betrayal to Alec with all he was going through. I went straight to my room and walked to the bathroom, turning on the water to run a hot bath.

I'd skinny dipped in the lake, lost my virginity to the boy I loved more than life itself, slept on the ground, and spent half the night sitting bedside my ex-boyfriend who didn't know if he'd walk again. A woman I considered a second mother had gone all gangster and was threatening to destroy Jett and disown me if I didn't do what she wanted. And Alec was desperate, and he needed me, and we didn't know what his future held.

I tore off my clothing when someone knocked on the door. I wrapped a towel around my body, just as I'd done less than twenty-four hours ago with Jett, and now I was here.

"Come in," I called out.

My mother stepped in and closed the door. "Daddy's right, you know."

"About?"

"About no one ever laying a hand on you." Her gaze moved to my shoulders and she gasped. "Oh my gosh. Did Alec do this?"

I looked down to see the bruising on my upper arms and silently cursed myself for letting her see this. Would it even matter? She'd always be loyal to Mama T and Alec, wouldn't she?

"Yes. He was drunk and stupid. It's fine. Jett pulled him off of me, and we left."

Her eyes welled with emotion as she rushed toward me and studied the bruises. "Mama T shouldn't talk to you the way she did. I know she's upset, but it's not her place to tell you what to do. She shouldn't have called the school on your behalf, that should have been your decision."

"Is anything my decision?" I walked in the bathroom and turned off the water, as it was dangerously high and threatening to overflow.

"It should be." She brushed the hair back from my face, and her fingers skimmed the bruising on shoulder. "And you obviously know more about Alec than I do. I never thought he would touch you or hurt you physically. I never thought he would get behind the wheel of a car drunk. My god, Addy, you could have been in that car with him. I've messed up so much, baby girl. I guess in a way I thought you and Alec being together made me a loyal friend to Mama T. I've just gotten so lost along the way."

Tears rolled down her face and she covered her mouth with her hand, shaking her head with disbelief.

"Yep. But it still doesn't mean that I don't want him to get better. Even after everything that happened, I still care about him. I care about their family," I said, as I fell into Mama's arms and sobbed. She wrapped her arms around me and hugged me so tight.

We sat there crying together for what seemed like forever.

Because we both knew nothing would ever be the same again.

twenty-seven

. . .

Jett

I HADN'T HEARD from Adelaide, but Shaw and Coco had spent the day at my house talking all this shit through. Coco informed me about Alec's mother's threats, and I needed to let Adelaide know that I didn't care what she tried to pull. I didn't buy into emotional blackmail. Coco said none of the girls had heard from their best friend, but they'd talked to Clem who'd said her sister had finally gone home to get some sleep and would return to the hospital in the morning. I knew I was taking a risk coming here, but I needed to talk to her.

I threw a rock at her window. Her room was dark. There was no response, so I chucked another rock up, just as a light turned on in her room. The window opened, and Adelaide looked down at me. She held up a finger to her lips and the light went out again. I stood beneath the oversized tree, wondering if she was coming down, or if she was just going to call me.

We'd had an amazing night together, if you ignored the fact that her ex-boyfriend had physically attacked her. We'd had mind blowing sex, and seeing as it was her first time, I knew that wasn't the norm, yet everything was different with this girl. We just fit. And now I didn't know what the fuck to think. Was it all going to be thrown away because of Alec fucking Taulson's accident?

Did I want him to spend his life in a wheel chair? Hell no. I didn't wish that upon anyone. But everyone in town was talking about the accident now, and everyone knew the asshole had gotten behind the wheel drunk. He'd made a choice, that once again his daddy would cover up and he'd get away with it. If this were me or Jax or Shaw, we'd be locked up right now. The selfish prick had put others' lives in danger, and he'd hurt himself. It was a tough lesson, but maybe it was time the dude started accepting some responsibility for his fucked-up choices.

Don't even get me started on the fact that I'd found him shaking Adelaide against a brick wall. He'd marked her arms and scared the shit out of her. All because she didn't want to be with him anymore. He'd had another damn temper tantrum, and now he was playing the victim as he lay in a hospital bed. He's lucky he didn't kill anyone.

Adelaide emerged from the window and made her way down the tree as I stood beneath it ready to catch her if she fell. Hell, I'd always catch this girl if she fell for as long as she'd allow me to.

When her feet hit the ground, she turned immediately into my chest and my arms wrapped around her, and she cried. We just stood there for a few minutes, so she could let it all out.

She pulled away and looked up at me. Her eyes were puffy and swollen as if she'd been crying since I'd last seen her nearly twenty-four hours ago. So much had changed in such a short time.

"Jett. I'm so sorry. My phone died. My life is a mess. Things are so bad." The tears started to fall again as she spoke. Her voice trembled, and I could hear all the sadness in her words.

"I've heard some. What's the prognosis?" I asked, knowing that she needed to talk about it.

"They're hopeful that he'll walk again. He had surgery and it's a waiting game now. It's going to be a long road. I mean, what if he can't leave for school in the fall? What if he's in a wheelchair forever?" she said, covering her mouth to muffle her sobs.

"Then he'll work hard to survive. He's alive. He's speaking. He'll get the best medical care out there. He's going to be okay either way." I reached for her hand, intertwining our fingers.

"He can't' do it on his own." She wiped her nose with the back of her hand.

"He has a family, Ace. And they have all the resources, so he'll get the best care out there."

"His mom is threatening to call the dean at TU and tell him that you punched Alec before the accident. She's going to try to blame you if I don't do what she wants me to do," the words came out like she'd been holding them in for far too long and she just needed to say them. The hurt in her eyes caused my breath to catch in my throat.

Jesus Christ. She wanted to protect me.

"Listen to me. Let her make the call. I will not be yet another person who lets you make a decision based on me. Let her give it her best shot. I don't give a shit. I pulled that son of a bitch off you, and unless he wants his family to know the truth, he won't let this go that far. Because I'll tell the fucking truth. He hurt *you*. I saw the bruises. And I didn't put him drunk behind the wheel. I'm sure his rich daddy is going to get away with covering up what he did, but Alec knows the truth. He made choices that he has to live with. And he can blame as many people as he wants, but it won't change what he did."

"They don't care, don't you get that? So, what, they just cause you to lose your scholarship and he wins? No. You've worked too hard for this. I won't let that happen. I don't care what I have to do." She looked up at me and I saw it all right there.

Her need to do what she thought was right. Her need to do for everyone else but herself.

But I also saw the fear. She was afraid of the Taulson's and fuck them for doing that to her.

"No, Ace. You don't get to use me to take the easy road. Fuck that." I crossed my arms over my chest and studied her.

"What do you mean?"

"It would be easy to just do what everyone wants you to do. To go to state. To help Alec. To make your mother happy and Alec's crazy ass mother happy. And for what? Life is short. Stop living for everyone else. What do you want?"

"You know what I want."

"I do. I think you're the only one who needs convincing. But don't leave here thinking you're doing me a favor. I don't need a favor, Ace. I only need you. I can handle whatever they want to throw at me. I have a good relationship with the coach at TU. There are several witnesses that saw Alec last night, and the state he was in. They may be able to bully the doctor, but everyone in this town knows what went down. I have the truth on my side."

She covered her face with her hands and sobbed. "I know, oh Jett — I'm scared, I don't know what to do."

"Yeah, you do. Trust yourself." I pulled her in for a hug when the sound of a door opening startled me from around the corner.

"Adelaide Charlotte, get inside," her mother said, standing there in a long dark robe looking at her daughter like she'd just committed the cardinal sin.

She pulled away, and her gaze locked with mine. No words were said. But we both knew how we felt without speaking a word.

I walked to my bike and fired up the engine, not knowing

where to go or what to do. There was a good fucking chance that she'd do what was expected of her. Hell, she'd been doing it her entire life. The thought of losing her left me feeling gutted. I pulled into the motor club and sat on my bike until a light came on upstairs. Wren lived in the apartment above the shop and he pulled the door open.

"Heard a lot of shit is going down with that asshole that used to date your girl. Come on up." He held the door open, and I made my way up the stairs and inside.

"I didn't know where to go," I said, over the lump lodged in my throat.

"You came to the right place. I know a little something about this shit."

"Well, looky here. Didn't expect to see you in here without your better half. You want one hot chocolate with extra sprinkles?" Lenny asked.

The fucker knew I didn't like sprinkles.

"One hot chocolate, no sprinkles."

"Coming right up."

I moved to a table in the back. No one else was in the shop, which was exactly why I came here. I'd just had my last day of high school, and I hadn't heard more than a text from Adelaide since I'd left her standing in her front yard after her mother found us outside three days ago. Coco, Ivy, Maura and Gigi were touching base with me every day, and none of them had spoken to her. They were receiving the same text I was.

I love you.

She texted it every morning, and that was the only contact we'd had. Apparently, she was spending her days at the hospital, being emotionally blackmailed by Alec and his family. I hadn't heard anything from Coach Devo at TU, so I doubted the Taulson's had made the call yet. Not that I gave a shit. I wasn't afraid to tell my story if push came to shove. I'd do the same thing all over again if I saw Alec hurting Adelaide. Even if it cost me everything. Because I loved her that much.

Lenny dropped my drink on the table, and I rolled my eyes when I saw the abundance of sprinkles on the whipped cream.

"It's a wonder I keep coming back here with you ignoring my requests." I grumped, taking a spoonful of whipped cream and sprinkles off the top and popping them in my mouth. They were fucking good, but I wouldn't tell him that.

"I see we're still in a mood. You haven't heard from our girl yet, I take it?" he asked.

Our girl? How was she his fucking girl? She was mine, or at least I thought she was. But I didn't know what the hell to think anymore.

"Just the one text every morning. She's still at the hospital helping that douchebag."

"Are you really surprised?" he asked.

"Uh, yeah. I am. We talked a hundred times a day, and now I barely hear from her in three days. She missed her last few days of senior year. Her best friends have barely heard from her. I'm fucking surprised."

"You shouldn't be. It's who she is. Who she's always been. Hell, the little angel has been coming to my shop for a decade now. Ever since she could ride her bike here on her own. She stayed loyal to me when everyone turned their backs on me for the donut king next door," he hissed. "My point is. She's a good girl and that's what you love about her."

I stayed quiet while I processed his words. "So where does that leave me ole wise one."

"Well, so far it leaves you here with an old man that no one else can stand. Sort of a shitty spot for you, kid," he said with a chuckle.

"Great," I hissed.

"The thing about Miss Adelaide is she's loyal to the core. That means, she's loyal to you too. You just don't need her right now. You've got to remember, she's grown up with that, what did you call him? A douchehat?"

"*Douchebag*, Lenny."

"Ah. Douchebag. That's my new word. Any-who, Violet was over at the hospital today and she said Alec's in physical therapy already, and things are looking a bit better for him. His daddy found a way to lock up that blood alcohol report, but everyone in town is talking about the fact that the kid was drunker than a skunk when he got in that accident. He's real lucky he didn't hurt someone else, because I don't think all his father's money would have saved his ass then. Never cared much for the kid. His only redeeming value was that Miss Addy liked him."

"Doesn't that rub you wrong? That he just fucks up and someone keeps covering for him?" I finished the whipped topping and started in on the chocolate.

"Nope. I'm glad I never had anyone doing that garbage for me. It hasn't helped Alec none, has it? Didn't make him a better football player or student or even human being. Those aren't the kind of favors I'd ever want. Just because he has money doesn't mean he has everything he needs, am I right? But you got everything you need, don't you, Jett?"

I thought about it. I loved Ma and Gram. I had good friends. Hell, Wren and Lenny had even become people that I depended on. And I had the world's best girl just a few days ago.

"I guess you're right. But it still doesn't make him less of a douchebag that he'd get behind the wheel drunk. That's his problem, he'll blame his father now for covering his ass. He always blames someone. I just hope Adelaide sees him for who he is." I wouldn't mention the fact that he'd put his hands on Adelaide. It wasn't my story to tell, and I respected her too much to say it just to hurt Taulson.

"Why wouldn't she? She's one of the smartest ladies I know. Don't you agree with me?"

I nodded. But she also had a way of seeing the good in people who didn't deserve it. A sick feeling settled in my stomach at the thought of it.

"Hey there, Jett," Ellis Edington stood in the motor shop looking down at me as I rolled myself out from under Wren's mustang.

I pushed to my feet. Surprised to see him with all that's going on. I wiped my hands on a towel and faced him. "Hey. What's up?"

"Not much. Just in the neighborhood and thought I'd stop by and see how you're doing. Are you getting ready for graduation next weekend?" he asked.

Did he really stop by to make small talk?

"Yeah, sure. Is Adelaide going to be attending graduation or will the Taulson's not allow that because Alec can't go." My words were seeped heavy in sarcasm and anger and I didn't give a shit.

I missed my girl. I missed everything about her.

And this shit wasn't right.

He scrubbed a hand down his face. "She'll be at that graduation if I have to drag her there myself. If it makes you feel better, she's just as miserable as you are."

"Oddly, that doesn't help." I rolled my eyes. "What is it with this shit? The kid is sitting in a hospital bed because he made a really dumb choice. Why is this her job to fix him?"

"It's not, and you're right. This whole thing with my wife and Alec's mom started out as just two best friends wanting to see their kids together, and I didn't have a problem with it until I realized my daughter wasn't happy. And do you know when I realized that?"

"When you realized she wasn't a robot and had a mind of her own?" I said, with one brow raised in question.

He nodded. "I understand your anger, Son. I do. I never realized that Ladybug was doing everything her Mama wanted just to please her, until I saw my girl with you. I saw her come alive. She started talking about her dreams and her future. I'd never realized how stifled she'd been until you came along. And I wanted to thank you for pulling Alec off her and making sure she was safe that night."

I studied him. Hadn't expected him to know about that. "She told you what he did?"

"She did. And my wife saw the bruising. We aren't okay with it."

"Yet Adelaide remains at his bedside." I shook my head with disgust.

"My daughter is at his bedside because she feels she needs to be there right now. It is not at the insistence of my wife or I at this point. Savannah is devastated hearing what Alec did to Addy, but she's also saddened to see her best friend in pain over her son's injury. We're all just doing the best we can right now, but I came here to tell you that I see you, Jett. I see a young man who protected my daughter. A young man who was raised right and has a good head on his shoulders. A young man who loves my daughter and has a bright future. A young man who my daughter happens to love. So, give her time to find her way. I believe she will, and I wanted you to know that I'm rooting for you."

I stared at him with surprise as I gathered my thoughts. "Thank you, Sir. That means a lot to me."

"It's the truth."

"So, your wife and Lila Taulson aren't forcing her to be in that hospital right now?" I asked. "Because even Coco and those crazy magic musketeers only get the one text from her each day, just like I do."

He chuckled. "We don't chain her up if that's what you're asking. But Adelaide is as loyal as they come and she sees a boy she's known her whole life in pain, and her instinct is to help him. It doesn't mean she's choosing him over you, I think everyone knows we're well beyond that."

"So, what does it mean? Why isn't she talking to anyone?"

"I'm guessing it's because for the first time in her life, she is tuning out all the noise and trying to find her way on her own. She told me that you're the one who encouraged her to do that. To find her voice and her way—figure out what she wants? Kind of hard to do that with everyone trying to tell you what to do. She goes to the hospital every day and supports a kid she's known her whole life because right now he's drowning, and that's who Ladybug is. Regardless of the mistakes he's made, she'll be there to help him find his way and encourage him to do better. And I believe that's what she's trying to do with her Mama. Because she cares so damn much, and isn't that what we both love about her?"

I leaned back against the wall and nodded, before crossing my arms over my chest. "And what if she gets lost there, and never comes back?"

"Then that will be her choice. But I'll make damn sure no one is making those choices for her. I give you my word on that."

"I appreciate it."

He offered me his hand and pulled me into a hard hug and held me there. "She'll come around. Just be patient with her."

That wasn't something I had to ponder.

Because I'd wait forever for Adelaide Edington.

twenty-eight

. . .

Adelaide

I GOT to the hospital and responded to the magic willow group text the same way I did each morning with just three simple words.

Me ~ I love you.

I sent the same text to Jett. I never responded with any more information than that, because right now I was drowning in life. I'd missed my last few days of senior year but I was due to speak at graduation. I had dreamed of giving my salutatorian speech for months, but I hadn't written a single word of it yet. I'd been coming to the hospital every day for a week now, and he was making progress.

Alec was hoping to attend graduation in his wheelchair, as they'd gotten him up and in his chair several times yesterday. Today I was going to be there when he did his upper body exercises with his physical therapist. His parents were driving him crazy wanting him to get up and walk, wanting him to be back to normal, and talk about housing for college next year —when he didn't know what tomorrow would hold. I understood it.

I paused outside his hospital room when I heard my mother's voice. She didn't sound happy, and I froze in place.

"It's enough. All of it," Mama said. "I'm ashamed of how we've behaved."

"So now that my son isn't walking and isn't a football star, you don't think he's good enough for Addy?" It was Lila Taulson's voice now.

"Oh please. If you believe that, then you don't know me at all. But we've taken this too far, Lila. And some things have come to light, and I need to protect my daughter. I've failed her miserably, and I have to live with that." Mama's voice broke on a sob, and my hand flew to my chest. Were they having this discussion in front of Alec? Maybe he'd gone to get some tests done.

"Failed her how?"

"Alec was drunk that night he left the party, I know Boone knows and I'm guessing you know it too. He was angry with Addy, and he pinned her to a wall leaving marks on her arms. I saw the bruises. Jett only hit him because he'd found him hurting her. And Alec got behind that wheel drunk. He needs to start taking accountability for his actions, Lila. You know I love him like he was my own son, but he has made some mistakes. And he'll have to work hard to fix them. But it is not Adelaide's job to fix Alec. It's his job."

My heart raced at her words. Never in a million years did I expect my mother to see the light. To defend me and to call Alec out for his choices.

"Boone told me he was drunk," Mama T said as she broke down in sobs. "Do you know why I always wanted Addy and Alec together? Because she's so good for him, Savannah. He's spiraled since she left him." The sadness in her voice caused a sharp pain to settle in my chest. I swiped at the tears that ran down my cheeks.

"She didn't leave him, Lila. He cheated on her. Repeatedly. And you know what? I'm proud of her for walking away. For demanding to be treated better. And I'm ashamed that I pressured her to stay with a boy who mistreated her just because

—because he's my best friend's son? How could I be so blind?"

"But he's young. Kids make mistakes," Lila said, and I didn't miss the desperation in her words.

"Yes. They do. And so do adults. You and I have made our fair share. And we'll support Alec as he fights to recover. But my daughter is not going to be the sacrificial lamb. She's not going to be his caretaker. She didn't do this. He did. And because she's got a good heart, I know she'll remain supportive of him when most would turn their backs after what he's done. And you need to be grateful for that. No more pushing. No more threats about calling TU on Jett. He's a good kid. A fine young man. And we've treated him and his family horribly. So, it looks like we all have work to do."

"Hey, what are you doing out here?" Alec asked, as a nurse pushed him in the wheelchair down the hall toward me and I startled and turned around.

"Hi. Just got here. Where were you?"

"More tests. But they think I might get out of here soon, and Dr. Toby gave me the go ahead to attend graduation."

"That's awesome, Alec." I followed him into the room, as my mother used a tissue to swipe at the moisture beneath her eyes.

Mama T had her back to us, and I heard her clear her throat before she turned around. Eyes wet with emotion and her face puffy.

"Thanks for being here, Addy."

"Of course," I said, and my gaze locked with my mothers. She looked at me with so much adoration my heart ached. I hurried toward her and wrapped my arms around her. "You okay, Mama?"

"No," she whispered in my ear. "But we're all going to be okay. I'm going to make things right."

I pulled away and nodded.

"We'll leave you two alone. We're going to go grab a

coffee," my mother said, grasping Lila's hand and leading her out of the room.

"What did I miss?" Alec said, and the nurse chuckled before pulling up his side table beside his chair and filling his water cup and excusing herself.

"I'm not sure. I think they are both just trying to figure things out."

"Yeah?" he asked. His gaze landed on my wrist as I fiddled with my charm bracelet from Jett. "Where'd you get that?"

My heart ached every time I thought of him. I missed his voice. His words. His touch. He'd become my best friend. Someone I depended on. But he was right, it was time for me to figure life out on my own. I didn't need anyone to tell me what to do anymore. I'd found my voice and I was happy to use it now.

"From Jett. Both of them, actually." I laughed. "The rope bracelet is a reminder, you know. That it's okay if the edges fray a bit. That's part of life."

He nodded. "I guess you could say my entire rope frayed, huh? God, Addy. I've really lost my way."

We hadn't had the deep talk yet. We'd skirted around all the issues. He was processing his recovery, and I'd given him the time he needed to accept his new normal. But there were things that needed to be said.

"You did. And that's part of life. But it's all about what you do after you fall down, right?"

"Did you just give me a football metaphor?" he teased.

I smiled and reached for his hand. "What happened that night isn't okay. Not any of it. You know that, right?"

He nodded. "I'm sorry." He pulled his hand away and covered his face. "I was horrible to you. Jesus. I lost my shit."

"I had bruises on my shoulders, Alec. A huge lump on the back of my head. And then you blamed Jett to your parents. Do you know your mom threatened to call the coach at TU and report him for hitting you? You could have cost him everything he's worked for."

He closed his eyes and let out a long-labored breath. "I already talked to her about it and cleared that up. She was appalled with me. I didn't tell her I left marks on your body, because I didn't know that at the time. I'm sorry Addy. It's inexcusable. My drinking somehow has gotten out of control. I've used it as an escape, and it has certainly not made things better."

"What are you escaping from?"

"My parents are definitely separating. I'm pretty sure my Mom's kept things hidden from your mom. She's embarrassed, I think. Wants everything to be perfect all the time. And it's not. It's so fucked up, Addy. *Karina's pregnant.* That's what we fought about that night. And I'm pretty fucking sure that it's mine. And I treated her horribly."

He shook his head and tears streamed down his face.

"You can't change the past, Alec. But you can change how you handle things moving forward. Stop drinking and clean up your life. Take ownership for your mistakes. *You drove drunk.* You're here because of that choice. My god, you could have killed someone. Killed yourself! And you have a child on the way. It's time to grow up," I said as I reached for both of his hands.

He nodded. "I want to be better, Addy. I just don't even know where to start."

"Start with owning your mistakes. Every one of them, Alec. Start by telling your parents the truth and asking for help. I'll support you. I'm not turning my back on you. But it will be as your friend. As someone who knows there's good in there and wants you to find your way out of this."

"You really love Stone, huh?" he asked, cocking his head to the side, and smiling like he already knew the answer.

"So much it actually hurts."

"I think that's why I acted like a little bitch. I saw it from the beginning."

"Saw what?" I asked.

"That it was different. What you had with him. What you and I had was convenient. More of a friendship. And I was jealous that you had something with him that we never shared."

That might be the first honest admission I'd heard from him ever.

I nodded. "Maybe you have that with Karina. At the very least you two share a child, and you need to get it together. You're going to be a father, Alec. That's big. That's worth fighting for, right?"

"Right. Tell me what to do. You're the best person I know. I'm asking you to tell me what to do."

"I think you start with an honest talk with your parents. And then you talk to Karina and you figure out how to move forward. And I think you might want to consider a program to support you to find other ways to cope with things. Alcohol is not the answer, Alec. Look where it's gotten you."

"Shit. How'd I get here?"

I shrugged. "Don't spend so much time whining about how you got here. Put your energy into changing course. You need to focus on your recovery and your future. There are tons of programs, and I'll help you find one. Heck, I'll even attend a meeting with you if that's what you need. But you've got to want to take this first step."

"I do. I'm sorry I fucked things up for us."

"You didn't. We weren't meant to be together. Not that way. We were both just playing roles that were assigned to us for a long time. But we have no one to blame moving forward. It's time to make choices for ourselves from here on out."

"Damn Addy, how'd you ever get to be this smart?" He

winked and continued, "And you know I'll support whatever you choose to do with college. I should never have pressed you to go where I was going. I think I was just afraid you know — to lose everything…you were my solid after I'd learned my parents were calling it quits. We've been friends, family, since we were kids and losing you was like the last straw."

Alec's opening up to me was shocking, but I really see what was going on in his life, not that he handled it well. "Alec, we'll always be friends, good friends — dating doesn't solidify friendship. Truthfulness and sharing does."

He winced and said, "I know. I just wasn't thinking straight. God, what I've put you through. I'm sorry."

"We'll survive." I smiled, because I really thought we'd get through this now.

"So, what school are you going to?" Alec asked. "I'm guessing you aren't going to state with me?"

"I'm not. But you've got a baby mama to think about, right? And I'll be there cheering you on just like I always have."

"Of course, you will."

There was a knock at the door, and a tall man stood there with a wide grin on his face. "Hey, Alec, are you ready for me to torture you? I'm Joey, your physical therapist. Today is the first day of your road back."

"Let's do this," Alec said.

"Who is this?" Joey asked, as he moved behind Alec's wheelchair. "Is this your girlfriend?"

"Nope. She's so much more. I guess we can call her my conscience. My guardian angel. And my best friend." His eyes were wet with emotion and I fought back the lump in my throat.

"Wow. I like a girl who wears a lot of hats. Are you coming with us?"

I nodded. "Yep. Let's kick his ass today."

Joey laughed. "I like this girl."

"Yeah. She's the best," Alec said smiling up at me.

I cheered Alec on through a couple hours of grueling physical therapy. I truly believed for the first time in a long time, that he was going to be okay and find his way.

I hurried home and opened my laptop before texting the girls.

Me ~ I'm sorry I've been MIA. So much to tell you. But I need to find Jett. He hasn't responded to my texts and I need to talk to him.

Coco ~ Girl! I missed you. He has a fight tonight. They reopened. Wren agreed to let him have a few fights before he leaves for school. Let's all meet at Addy's in ten minutes, and we can go to the warehouse together. Good to have you back, bitch.

Gigi ~ Thank god. Yes, I'm down to go. I missed my girl.

Maura ~ I'm in. Love you, Addy. See you soon.

Ivy ~ It's about damn time. We haven't put one thing in the book since you went radio silent. Magic Willow meeting tomorrow. But tonight, we have a fight to attend.

Ivy ~ That's going in the book by the way.

I laughed before staring at my laptop and hitting accept.

Me ~ See you soon. Love you.

I jogged downstairs and found my Clem and dad sitting in front of the TV. Mama walked in holding a laundry basket and set it on the ground.

"I made my decision about school. I'm going to attend TU. It's an amazing opportunity for me, and I hope you'll support me. As far as my personal life goes. I will support Alec as much as I can, because I really do want him to be okay. But I love Jett, and nothing is going to change that."

"Yes," Clem fist bumped the sky. "You make me proud, Sissy." She hurried to her feet and hugged me tight.

My dad stood and walked toward me. "Proud of you, Ladybug."

"Thanks, daddy." He wrapped his arms around me and kissed the top of my head.

When he pulled away, I looked up to meet my mother's gaze. Her eyes were wet with emotion, and she cocked her head to the side. "I've made a lot of mistakes." Her words broke on a sob, and I hurried toward her, but she put her hand up to stop me. "Let me say this."

I nodded.

"I'm proud of you, Adelaide Charlotte. I'm so sorry. I'm going to do better if you'll give me a chance," she said, tears streaming down her pretty face.

"Of course, I will. I love you, Mama."

I hugged her and we both cried as we stood there in the living room.

The doorbell rang and I pulled away. "Okay. The girls are here. I haven't spent any time with them, and we need to catch up. I won't be home late."

Dad chuckled. "Tell Jett we said hello too." He raised a brow as if he knew where I was going. He wasn't wrong.

"I will. Love you," I said, as I made my way to the front door.

I filled the girls in on all that had happened with Alec, and the conversation between Mama and Lila Taulson. They understood my need to support Alec, even though they were all struggling to forgive him at the moment. I hadn't forgiven him for getting behind the wheel drunk or for putting his hands on me. But I would support him and give him a chance to do better. Because I wanted that for him.

I'd seen the remorse in his eyes when we spoke. And maybe for the first time ever, Alec was taking accountability for his actions. I understood that his parents' divorce and learning that he was going to be a father had been a lot to process, and though there was no excuse for what he'd done, I could empathize with what he was going through. "Oh. And in other news. I'll be attending TU with you Gigi. I hit accept just a few minutes ago. You didn't find a new roommate over the last week, did you?" My chest filled with something I couldn't explain.

Joy.

Hope.

Excitement.

"Hells to the no. It's you and me, girl." Gigi leaned over and hugged me.

"There is so much to put in the book today," Ivy shouted.

"Proud of you, girl," Coco said. "And we'll only be a road trip away from one another."

"Oh my gosh. We all know where we're going now. And we'll be close enough that we can see one another on the weekends." Maura unbuckled her seatbelt when we pulled up to the warehouse.

"Yep. Here's to the next adventure," I said, putting my hand forward, as Coco and Ivy both turned around from the front seat and all five of us put our hands in. "Magic Willows for life."

"Magic Willows for life," they all said at the same time.

"Now let's go find your hot boy. He's been so tortured and sad lately. Shaw said he barely speaks to anyone and he keeps hanging out at that damn chocolate shop with crazy Lenny." Coco opened her door and stepped outside.

The warm breeze swirled around us, and I paused to hug each of my friends. "Thank you for always having my back. I love you."

"Love you," they each said one at a time.

"Let's do this," Ivy said, leading the charge toward the door.

When we stepped inside, I saw Jett in the cage. The fight had already started. And as always, there was a force that connected us. His head turned and his gaze locked with mine, ignoring the hundred some people that were scattered between us. He was all I could see.

The loud cheers knocked me from my dazed stupor, as Jett got taken down to the mat.

"Jesus," Wren shouted, as he moved beside me. "I've got her, you jackass. Focus on your fight."

A few people around us laughed, and Shaw and Jax waved us over.

"Good god, girl. You're going to get that boy killed." Wren laughed as he walked with us.

"Thanks for looking out for him," I said, looking up and smiling before training my eyes back on my boyfriend.

"Always. Looks like we both have his back."

I nodded and moved between Shaw and Jax as my best friends stood right there beside me.

Just as it should be.

twenty-nine

. . .

Jett

I WON the fight by the skin of my teeth because seeing Adelaide there had me all kinds of distracted. I just wanted to be done with it, so I could talk to her. I'd missed the hell out of her.

When I stepped outside to find our friends all huddled in the parking lot, I'd asked her if she wanted to go for a ride. Everyone laughed. Hadn't seen the girl in days, and all I wanted was to have her on the back of my bike and talk to her.

She'd nodded, and we said our goodbyes to everyone.

I buckled her helmet, her gaze locking with mine. Hadn't asked her a thing yet. No words needed to be spoken.

She was mine.

Always had been.

Always would be.

I jumped on my bike and her hands came around my waist, tucking beneath my T-shirt just like they always did.

When we pulled up to the lake, I took her hand and our fingers interlaced as we walked toward the hammock.

"Sorry about distracting you at the fight?" she said, and it was the first time I'd actually heard her voice in days. I wrapped an arm around her shoulders and pulled her close.

"I never mind being distracted by you, Ace."

She leaned her head on my chest. "I'm sorry I was MIA. I listened to what you said the last time we spoke, about me needing to figure out what I wanted."

"Yeah? Did you figure it out?"

"Yep." She fiddled with the rope bracelet on my wrist that matched hers.

"So, what do you want?"

"Well, obviously I want you," she said, turning to face me and meeting my gaze.

"Obviously," I chuckled. "I mean, we have the matching bracelets and all."

"Right. It would be silly to have to get rid of the twine."

"Definitely," I said, moving closer and grazing her lips with mine.

"What else did you decide? You going to stay here with Taulson?" I pulled back to look at her, because I needed to know.

"Nope. I'm going to be attending Texas University this fall. Hey, isn't that where you're going?"

I smiled. I was so fucking happy. "Yep. Looks like we'll be at the same school."

"I'm going to be there for Alec from a distance. It's obvious that he has a problem with alcohol. I researched a few programs for him, and I think he's going to do it and try to turn things around. Karina's pregnant. He's got something to work for."

I didn't hide my surprise. "Wow. That's—a lot. He's lucky to have you in his corner. But it's not your job to fix him, you know that right?"

"I don't want to fix him. But he needs a friend, and I can be that for him right now."

"Such a good person, Adelaide Edington. I knew it the day you gave me half of your PB & J."

"Oh yeah? What did you know?"

"I knew that if I ever had a chance to make you mine, I'd take it," I said, rubbing my nose against hers.

She laughed, and her breath tickled my cheek. "You did not. You were eight. You just wanted the sandwich."

I chuckled, and I nipped at her bottom lip. "Fine. I wanted the sandwich. But now, *now* I know that if I ever had the chance to make you mine, I'd take it."

"I'm all yours, Jett Stone."

"Thank god. I don't think I could function without you, Ace. I've missed you so fucking much."

"Me too. Especially after that night we had right over there," she said, wriggling her brows.

I laughed. "Oh yeah? You liked that, did you?"

"I really did." She nodded, and her smile caused my god damn stomach to flutter. I'd just fought a bad ass fighter and won, and here I was fighting off butterflies because the prettiest damn girl in the world loved me.

Weak.

And I wouldn't have it any other way.

"You know, we could do that again any time you want. And it doesn't even have to be in a tent."

"Oh really? You can make that kind of magic when we aren't in a tent?" she teased, and I tipped her back on the hammock. My hand slipped beneath her shirt, needing to feel her soft skin.

"Baby, it doesn't matter where we are. When I'm with you, it's all magic. Which reminds me. I got you a graduation gift." I pushed back and yanked my t-shirt over my head and reached for my phone to turn the flashlight on my arm.

Right below Ma and Grams birthdates, I'd inked my girls birth date in roman numerals.

Her finger ran over the ink and a tear ran down her cheek. "You put my birthday on your arm? Why?"

"Turns out the day you were born is best day of my life, Ace. I wanted to tattoo the date of the first time we had sex, but I thought that might embarrass you."

Her head fell back in laughter. "It's tattooed on my heart forever."

"Yeah? My girl is so poetic with her words. I love you," I said, tipping her back down again.

"I love you more."

"Not possible," I said, covering her mouth with mine.

Because the way I loved this girl was something I couldn't even put into words. And I knew I'd found my forever.

It didn't matter where we were.

She had my heart.

And I had hers.

Always and forever.

epilogue

. . .

Adelaide

I STOOD at the podium and stared out at all the faces of the students I'd attended school with since kindergarten. The families that had supported us and been there every step of the way. My hands shook as I settled the paper against the wood surface and my gaze locked with beautiful dark eyes that always grounded me. My nerves dissipated.

Jett.

I cleared my throat and adjusted the microphone, so it was sitting just beneath my chin.

"Good morning parents, friends, teachers, administrators, and graduates. As I look out at all of you now, I realize that I know every single student in our graduating class. I've spoken to each of you, laughed with you, and shared memories with you at one time or another over the past four years and beyond, as most of us have been together since kindergarten." I paused to look out at the audience, smiling as I scanned the room to find my sister Clem beaming up at me like I hung the moon. I fought back the emotion stirring within.

"Most of us have known one another our entire lives. Some people might find it odd to attend a school so small that you know everyone in your senior class. I don't. I'm grateful that I've been fortunate enough to experience this journey with people who feel more like family to me than strangers. To call East Texas High School and Willow Springs my home. *The heart of Texas rings true*. I believe we are the lucky ones." My gaze finds Mama, as tears stream down her pretty face and I take a minute to swallow the lump in my throat.

"Some people think of graduation as an ending or a finality, but I believe this is just the beginning. And we don't have to have everything all figured out. We don't have to know exactly who we are or what we're going to do with our lives after today. We just have to believe that whatever we set our minds to, whatever we dare to dream—that we have the capability to achieve it." I reach for my water bottle and take a sip and calm my racing heart as I screw the lid back into place. The auditorium is quieter than I've ever heard it before.

"When I was pondering my own future and apprehensive about which path to take, the words of Nelson Mandela helped me to find an inner strength that I'd been afraid to unleash for so long. He said, t*here is no passion to be found in playing small, in settling for a life that is less than the one you are capable of living."* My eyes find my father, and his smile is so wide that my chest squeezed with pride.

"I've learned that we don't have to live life perfectly. It's okay to unravel a bit. My greatest journey happened when I allowed myself to *fray*. And to grow. And to find my own way." I run my fingers over the rope bracelet on my wrist. "So, go out there and live your life to the fullest. Whether you choose to attend college, enlist in the military, go to trade school, become a homemaker or backpack through Europe in need of finding yourself," I paused as the audience laughed. "Do it with pride. Do it with purpose. And most importantly, do it because *you* want to do it." Cheers erupt in the crowded auditorium and it's difficult to see the words I have written in front of me through my teary eyes.

"We've been given the tools to achieve our greatest dreams. And as you look around this room today it is evident that we have the support of our friends and families as they've all gathered here to celebrate us. So, in finality, I'd like to close with the words that rang out at our kindergarten graduation ceremony when Principal Douglas sent us on to first grade." More laughter.

"In the words of Dr. Seuss, don't cry because it's over. Smile because it happened. Thank you."

Applause filled the space around me, and I made my way back to my seat for a few final words before we all moved our tassels at the same time. Everyone cheered and the room was chaotic. Jett found his way to me and tugged me against him.

"Damn good, Ace." His mouth covered mine and I tangled my fingers in his hair.

"You killed it, girl," Coco said, as she moved beside me, and I reluctantly pulled away from Jett.

"Thanks. I'm relieved it's over."

Maura, Gigi and Ivy hurried over, and we all hugged, as Jett talked with Shaw and Jax. Ty walked over and wrapped his arms around Ivy's middle with Alec right behind him in his wheelchair. Karina stood behind him pushing him toward me. Her gaze locked with mine and she smiled. It wasn't a full blown happy-to-see-you smile, but it was progress.

"Just wanted to tell you that your speech kicked ass, Addy," Alec said, and everyone remained quiet around us.

"Thank you. I'm glad you're here today." I nodded.

"Yep. I think it's the first step toward getting my shit together."

"Well, it's about time," Coco snarled, and everyone laughed, including Alec and Karina.

"All right, we'll talk soon. I need to go find my parents," he said.

I waved as Karina wheeled him away. Gigi's brother Cade and his best friend Gray walked over. "You did it, G-money,"

Gray shouted and picked her up off the ground and spun her around before putting her down. Everyone burst out in laughter.

Except for Gigi.

She scowled and adjusted her gown as her cheeks pinked. "Can I not have one day without the ridiculous name?"

"He just likes giving you shit," Cade said, pulling his sister in for a hug. "Proud of you."

"Thanks."

"I can't believe we're all going to be at the same school. Think of all the fun we'll have," Gray said, looking from Jett and me to Gigi. Cade turned to talk to Shaw and Jax about football but Gray never took his gaze from Gigi.

"Yeah. Lucky me," she said, trying to hide her smile. We all found her hatred for Gray hilarious.

"I think you picked TU because you knew I was there." He winked at her.

Jett and Coco were talking, but I kept glancing over at Gigi and her nemesis because they were very entertaining.

"Of course, you'd think that you pompous ass."

"You sure seem to bring my ass up a lot, G," he said, running a hand through his longer in the front shorter in the back hair.

"Bite me, Gray," she hissed. I'd never seen Gigi so tough with anyone but Gray. He brought something out in her that was definitely out of character.

"If only," he smirked before leaning over and rumpling the top of her head with his hand before walking away.

"I can't stand that guy sometimes," she huffed when her gaze locked with mine and I laughed even though I wasn't sure if what she said were true.

Coco turned to face us, as Maura and Ivy walked over. "We did it, girls."

"We sure did," I said, as Jett came up behind me and reached for my hand.

"Are you guys ready to head to my house?" I asked, as we all made our way out of the auditorium.

My parents were having a graduation party for all of us.

"Let's do it," Maura said. "I'm going to drive with my parents, I'll meet you there."

Gigi left with her brother and his best friend and I heard Gray teasing her as they walked away. Coco said she'd drive over with Shaw, and we told Jett's mom and Gram we'd meet them at my house.

We walked toward my family and they went on and on about my speech. Clem said I was paving the way for women everywhere.

"Really proud of you," Mama said before she pulled me in for a hug.

"Thank you. Are you ready to head home?" I asked, knowing we had people on their way.

"Are you going to ride with your family? Should I meet you over there?" Jett asked.

"Don't be silly. You know she wants to drive over with you." Mama smiled at him, before reaching for my cap and gown and slinging it over her arm.

My eyes bulged out because I was in a dress, and I figured she'd have a fit if I wanted to ride on the back of Jett's bike.

"She's right. Looks like I'm going with you," I said before hugging my parents and Clem good-bye.

"I was hoping you would. I've been dying to get you all to myself for hours." Jett led me to his bike and I hiked my dress up a bit and dropped down to sit.

"Oh yeah?" I asked with a chuckle. "Why's that?"

"I mean, we have the bracelets and all." He leaned down and his lips grazed mine.

"And don't forget I gave you half of my sandwich back in the day."

"Damn straight," he said, as he nipped at my bottom lip. "Love you, Ace."

"Love you the most," I said, wrapping my arms around his neck and urging him closer.

His mouth came over mine and I was lost in the moment.

Everything had come together.

And I couldn't wait to see where the future took us.

The End

Thank you so much for reading! I hope you loved Jett and Addy as much as I do!

Do you want to see Gigi start college with her brothers best friend, Gray, hovering around every chance he gets? This enemies to lovers, brothers best friend, forbidden romance is FREE IN KINDLE UNLIMITED AND AVAILABLE NOW! Click below to continue with the series!

https://geni.us/TANGLED

acknowledgments

Greg, Chase & Hannah, YOU are the reason that I work hard every day!! I love you more than I love winning Backy-G, Rocky, Unicorn Donuts and Bernedoodles!! Thank you for always being my biggest cheerleaders!

Pathi, Abi, Annette, Natalie, Doo, Lara and Caroline, thank you for being the BEST beta readers EVER! Your feedback means the world to me. I live for your comments and suggestions!! I would be lost without you!

Sarah, (Okay Creations), thank you for creating this gorgeous couple cover for Addy & Jett!

Emily (Emily Wittig Designs) thank you for creating stunning special edition covers for the Willow Springs Series!!

Sue Grimshaw (Edits by Sue), Thank you for your encouragement, your guidance and your support. I honestly don't know what I would do without you. Thank you for always going the extra mile for me. Your feedback is always spot-on, and I am so incredibly thankful for you! I appreciate you more than you know!!

Tamara Cribley (The Deliberate Page), so thankful to get to work with you again. I love all of the little details that you add to the formatting and appreciate your patience and support so much!! Thank you, my friend!

Sarah Ferguson (Social Butterfly PR), I appreciate you more than you know!! I am looking forward to many more releases together!! Thank you for all of your support and encouragement!!

Danah Logan, Thank you for the beautiful graphics and for bringing this story to life with the teasers!!!

Dad, you really are the reason that I keep chasing my dreams!! Thank you for teaching me to never give up. Love you!

Mom, thank you for your love and support. So excited that you loved Jett & Addy as much as I did!! Love you!

Sandy, thank you for reading and supporting me throughout this journey. Love you!

Lisa, Julie, Eric, Jen and Jim, I am very thankful to have such supportive and encouraging siblings in my life. Love you!

Pathi, I am so thankful for you! You are the reason I even started this journey. Thank you for believing in me!! Thank you for ALWAYS supporting me! Your friendship means the world to me! Love you!

Natalie (Head in the Clouds, Nose in a Book), Thank you for all that you do for me!! I cannot even put into words how much I love and appreciate you!!

Nicole, Our snaps give me life and keep me sane! I am so thankful that we get to talk in ridiculous filters every day! I love you!

Willow & Catherine, I would be lost without the LOVE-CHAIN! Thank you for giving me the push that I need every day and cheering me on. So thankful for you both!! Love you so much!

Sammi Sylvis, Thanks for making me laugh and helping me stay sane through these releases! Glad we have one another to lean on!!

Adriana Locke and Marni Mann, I cannot tell you what your support means to me!! Thank you so much for encouraging me and being huge inspirations at the same time!! I am so grateful to have found you both!! Very proud to call you my friends!!

Megan Stillwell, Thank you so much for working with me

to come up with adorable merchandise for this series!! So incredibly thankful for you!!

To all the bloggers and bookstagrammers who have posted, shared and supported me—I can't begin to tell you how much it means to me. I love seeing the graphics that you make, and the gorgeous posts that you share. I am forever grateful for your support!

A HUGE thank you to every reader who chose to read my words!! I am honored that you took a chance on my book, and I hope that you enjoyed your time with Addy and Jett and will come back for more!!

keep up on new releaes

Linktree Laurapavlovauthor
Newsletter laurapavlov.com

other books by laura pavlov

Magnolia Falls Series
Loving Romeo
Wild River
Forbidden King
Beating Heart
Finding Hayes

Cottonwood Cove Series
Into the Tide
Under the Stars
On the Shore
Before the Sunset
After the Storm

Honey Mountain Series
Always Mine
Ever Mine
Make You Mine
Simply Mine
Only Mine

The Willow Springs Series
Frayed
Tangled
Charmed
Sealed
Claimed

Montgomery Brothers Series

Legacy

Peacekeeper

Rebel

A Love You More Rock Star Romance

More Jade

More of You

More of Us

The Shine Design Series

Beautifully Damaged

Beautifully Flawed

The G.D. Taylors Series with Willow Aster

Wanted Wed or Alive

The Bold and the Bullheaded

Another Motherfaker

Don't Cry Spilled MILF

Friends with Benefactors

follow me

Website laurapavlov.com
Goodreads @laurapavlov
Instagram @laurapavlovauthor
Facebook @laurapavlovauthor
Pav-Love's Readers @pav-love's readers
Amazon @laurapavlov
BookBub @laurapavlov
TikTok @laurapavlovauthor

www.ingramcontent.com/pod-product-compliance
Lightning Source LLC
Chambersburg PA
CBHW021812210725
29891CB00012B/461

* 9 7 8 1 0 8 8 2 8 7 4 8 4 *